winter
passing

A NOVEL

winter
passing

Cindy McCormick Martinusen

TYNDALE HOUSE PUBLISHERS, INC. | WHEATON, ILLINOIS

Visit Tyndale's exciting Web site at www.tyndale.com

Designed by Justin Ahrens

Published in association with the literary agency of Janet Kobobel Grant, Books & Such, 3093 Maiden Lane, Altadena, CA 91001.

Scripture quotations are taken from the *Holy Bible*, King James Version.

This novel is a work of fiction. Names, characters, places, and incidents are either the product of the author's imagination or are used fictitiously. Any resemblance to actual events, locales, organizations, or persons living or dead is entirely coincidental and beyond the intent of either the author or publisher.

Library of Congress Cataloging-in-Publication Data

Martinusen, Cindy McCormick,
   Winter passing / Cindy McCormick Martinusen.
     p. cm.
   ISBN 0-8423-1906-9 (sc)
    1. Austria—History—1938-1945—Fiction. 2. Holocaust—Jewish (1939-1945)—Austria–
Fiction. 3. Jews—Austria—Fiction.   I. Title.
PS3563.A737 W56 2000
813′.6—dc21   00-036411

Printed in the United States of America

06   05   04   03   02   01   00
9   8   7   6   5   4   3   2   1

To David,
my beloved and kindred traveler

For, lo, the winter is past,
The rain is over and gone;
The flowers appear on the earth;
The time of the singing of birds is come.

Song of Solomon 2:11-12

AUSTRIA
August 11, 1941

Her eyes weighed heavy, but Tatianna could not sleep. Time ran too quickly against her life for one moment to be wasted in rest.

A movement disrupted the silence. She waited, but nothing. Someone in another cell must be stirring. But soon the footsteps would come. Then Tatianna would hear soldiers' boots beyond her door, the clang of a cell opening, and the scrape of shackles against the floor. A frantic plea for mercy would descend into the prison, or more often, an eerie stillness. Tatianna would sit unmoving, knowing unseen strangers in their cells listened with her. She imagined they held their breath as she did, until the sound of bullets erupted.

They would come again. Yet today would be different. It wouldn't be the cell down the hall or the cell beside her that would open. Today Tatianna's door had been chosen. No lamb's blood covered her doorpost. The death angel in SS uniform would find his way inside. Today her shackles would scrape the tile floor. Today the bullets would burst into her chest.

God, will you not send me a savior even now as I go to my death? I chose your way, but I'm afraid to die.

Tatianna folded her hands and winced in pain. That was good—to feel pain in her stiff and broken fingers. The throbbing up her arm reassured her that life survived within her. The gaunt and tattered body, though foreign to her eyes, continued to breathe and move. They'd tried everything to make her speak, but, thank God, she didn't have the information. Through their torture, Tatianna knew she would have cracked. But she didn't possess the answers they sought. And the one piece of the puzzle she did know, they'd never asked.

Tatianna sat on the floor and drew her legs to her chest. Fleas scampered away as she leaned back against the thin mattress. She smiled, feeling her lips crack. For Tatianna had one victory over them—one they would never know. They saw her as useless now, so she could take her secrets with her. But could there still be a way in her final hour? Miracles always happened in the books she read. At the last instant, the heroine was rescued. But there was no one to save her. No one near enough to help.

A stream of light shot through the high bars of the cell. The beacon of morning would have meant warmth and security if shining through the glass panes at her home, but today it signified her approaching death. Her time drew to the end as rapidly as light gathered and crept along the top of the cement wall.

Tatianna closed her eyes. Her mother would say, "Keep your jaw set and your way clear. Everything will work out." *Will it, Mother? Will everything work out today?* Her mother and thoughts of home brought doubts that clouded out hope once again. Hope, then fear; hope, then fear. Tatianna had made the right choice, hadn't she? Hope, fear.

A creaking noise rang down the hall. Tatianna jumped. The first gate opened and footsteps approached, then stopped at her cell. Keys jingled in the lock and the door opened.

Tatianna didn't look into the faces of the two soldiers as she walked between them. The thud of their boots and clang of her shackles echoed through the stone corridor. She knew the other prisoners sat and listened. Did they hold their breath?

A guard bent and removed her shackles. As they entered the open courtyard, a chill of morning cold grasped her body.

Next it was down stone steps and out of the execution area. She looked at the wall where she had expected to die. Should she feel hope? Were they releasing her instead?

They crossed the roll call area but did not turn toward the main gate. And then she heard the music: a Mozart tune, one she'd played on her own violin a hundred times. Tatianna knew what that music meant. And she knew where she was being taken. Today she would die, but not alone.

Bits of gravel cut her bare feet as they moved down the roadway between blocks D and E. What would it feel like? How much would it hurt?

Panic seized Tatianna with a frantic desire to escape. Could she somehow jump or fly beyond prison grayness into the colors of life: green trees, yellow flowers, purple mountain peaks? Today couldn't be her day to die. Not today. The sun shone too brightly. She knew people strolled the streets beyond the cinder-block walls. In the village below, they shopped, laughed, and picked flowers in their gardens. Surely a family packed for an afternoon picnic. A mother held her child in her arms. A girl read a book on a park bench, perhaps nearing the end when the heroine against all odds and challenges would finally get away.

They made their way between barracks. Tatianna saw eyes stare from behind warped glass. She'd escaped what the other prisoners were granted with intense work and starvation: a slower pace toward death. Instead, she'd been the honored guest of the camp's prison where torture, a quick bullet to the neck, and a mass execution were the gifts of hospitality.

Tatianna looked again toward the faces behind barrack windows. She recognized fear in their open stares. *Please, let that girl's death not be mine,* they thought.

She turned away, and with each step toward the open gate, the "I'll nevers" came flooding back. *I'll never wear a bridal* veil. *I'll never experience a man's love. I'll never hold my child in my arms. I'll never hug my kindred friend again.*

She must stop. These thoughts had tormented her for days. Tatianna must fold the remnants of "I'll nevers" and banish them to some darkened crevice in her heart. *Remember you promised to be strong. Go to your death with dignity. Keep your jaw set and your way clear.*

She saw her place in line. The open gate revealed a row of several dozen breathing skeletons. There had to be many thousands more in the barracks and jailhouse behind them. A few skeletons dared to peer her way as a soldier pushed her against the wall. Hollow and haunted, their eyes reflected fear—an old man in tears, another with prideful defiance, a father and son clinging as one being.

Her fingers trailed a crack in the wall, touching the granite, feeling its coldness in the shadows. She filled her lungs with the cool freshness, savoring its flavor in her mind. She glanced again at the strangers who were now her family as they stepped into eternity together.

Tatianna turned her eyes to the stiff column of marchers lined up before her. Here were the witnesses, and the executioners. She searched the eyes of every face. Ten soldiers, twenty frozen eyes. Wait—she knew that face. The last soldier in the line. His blank expression mirrored the others. She had known that boy at one time, but she did not know him now.

She forced herself not to look below the men's shoulders to the guns they held. She waited, jaw set. Something caught her eye. Above the wall, a bird glided on the morning breeze. It rose and danced above the prison wall, above the distant treetops. The sunlight caught the sheen of black wings before it dropped from view.

A soldier shouted. Guns raised. Tatianna's eyes jerked toward ten barrels.

Someone cried out; a child screamed. Where was her savior? Today the heroine would not get away.

Her body jumped as ten rifles cocked. The sound resonated through the courtyard, echoing within her body. Suddenly the winged creature rose again to soar high above the walls. Tatianna's eyes lifted to the bird as her body exploded in shaking. Her Savior had come, and he brought freedom on his wings.

Tatianna had chosen well.

CHAPTER ONE

SEBASTOPOL, CALIFORNIA
Autumn, Present Day

Tatianna! Tatianna!"

"It's okay, Grandma. Calm down."

"Tatianna!" Grandma Celia's frail cry rose to a shriek.

"Grandma, wake up!" Darby Evans tried to hold thrashing arms and shoulders. Her grandmother was slow to calm and return to her pillow. The woman's eyes did not open, but her mumbling quieted.

"*Hilfe,*" she whispered, and Darby remembered it was German for "help." But her grandmother never spoke her native tongue. Why now?

Darby put her hand on Grandma Celia's warm forehead.

"*Machen Sie schnell!*" The older woman's expression turned fearful again. "Tatianna!"

Darby held her grandmother's shoulders. "It's okay, Grandma." Her grandmother's hands grasped and fought unseen devils; her features contorted with inward struggles.

"I'm here, Grandma. It's Darby. There's nothing to worry about." The old woman calmed once again. Darby opened the fingers clutching her arm and held them within her own. She brought the bony hands to her lips. They felt like tissue paper drawn over bone and blue veins.

Darby moved a chair close and rested her arms around the old woman. She hummed a Mozart tune, one her grandmother had hummed to her in the late-night hours of her childhood, and watched Grandma Celia slowly slip into a peaceful sleep. After a while, Darby tenderly pulled the covers up and smoothed strands of gray hair from her grandmother's face.

The dim lamp cast shadows along the top of the bedroom walls, creating dark eyes that followed every movement, listened to every word. This house of her youth had never held the presence of shadows, at least none Darby had known. But tonight it seemed that a secret had slipped from the lips of her dying grandmother. It was the name of a stranger. Tatianna. The callings in German had quickly turned to frantic cries that sent a shiver down Darby's spine. It frightened her to think that, although flowery body powder—a familiar childhood aroma—scented the room, and her grandmother's personal items appeared in proper order, there were secrets in this house. And now the shadows, like a pack of jackals, circled their prey. She could almost hear their high-pitched laughter and leering words: "There are secrets here. We know them, but we won't tell."

Her grandmother stirred, and Darby could see the name on her lips before breath brought it to life. "Tatianna."

She waited for another rise of panic, but Grandma Celia slid more deeply into sleep. Darby stood and walked toward the window. The moonlight brought an ethereal glow to the back-yard. Even the rosebushes around the gazebo looked ghostly, with silhouetted fingers pointing skyward. The dim light exposed stray weeds twisted along the stone pathway. She shook her head to cast away the fears. This was home. Even though she now lived a few hundred miles north in Redding,

California, Grandma's home in Sebastopol always welcomed her back. How could her grandmother's cries for a stranger bring such darkness here?

Darby could see herself from the age of five until she left for college, growing, changing, all here in this house. Had hidden secrets stalked and crept while she, in childhood oblivion, laughed and played unaware?

Perhaps she was making too much of this, and there was a simple explanation. Maybe her grandmother was reliving wartime memories. Or could the elderly woman be hallucinating from the myriad of painkillers and medicines? Yet Grandma Celia's anguish appeared real, not imagined.

Darby extracted a letter from her jeans pocket and smoothed the envelope. Another secret, but this one Darby would keep. She probably should have followed her first reaction to burn the letter. How dare this man, Brant Collins, write such words to her grandmother? The stamp and return address were evidence of its European origin. Her grandmother would have eagerly checked the mail each day in hopes of receiving this letter if her illness hadn't progressed so rapidly.

Darby reached to touch the top of her grandmother's head. She held her hand an inch above her skin, not wanting to disturb her, but wishing to hold the woman against all pain. *I don't care about some inheritance. I only want you,* Darby thought, tracing her grandmother's face without touching her cheek. Her grandmother had begun searching for the family inheritance, hoping the recovered treasure could be a gift for her grandchildren. "I want to pass on what belongs to our family," she'd stated firmly. Grandma Celia had written Holocaust organizations and even learned to use e-mail and the Internet.

"Can you believe your old grandmother is surfing the Web?" she'd asked Darby on the phone. It hadn't really surprised Darby. Grandma Celia was always involved in something—country and western dancing at the senior center, volunteering in the local kindergarten class, sending letters to congressmen. The notion that Nazis had confiscated her family inheritance wasn't new—only Grandma's sudden search. Why now? Perhaps terminal illness and the reluctant opening of Swiss banks? Darby usually tried to encourage or help her grandmother, but this time she was involved in the remodeling of her photography studio and she thought the pursuit of fortune a bit far-fetched.

Darby examined the soft lines in her grandmother's face. Her cheeks revealed sharp bones beneath; her eyes had sunk deeper into their sockets. It had only been a few months since Darby's summer visit. The cancer had progressed more rapidly in the last months than anyone had expected—except, perhaps, Grandma Celia. Darby had found a paper on the table when she'd arrived that evening from the local hospice care. The information gave signs for patients who had one to two weeks left of life: "Agitation, talking with the unseen, confusion, pale and bluish, sleeping, but not responding." Many were the signs she'd seen in Grandma Celia. The list moved down to the signs for patients with only days and hours left: "Surge of energy, irregular breathing, glassy eyes . . ." The list went on and on, but the last sign, "fish-out-of-water breathing," terrified Darby.

Darby's anger rose as she thought again of Brant Collins and his letter. The most endearing, honest woman rested before her, and that man had actually accused her of illegal activities. He wrote that he knew the truth about the Lange family, and if Celia continued her pursuit, impersonators would be prosecuted. Darby would keep that secret from her mother and grandmother—she'd deal with it herself.

"Where are you, Grandma?" Darby whispered. "I want my fireball grandmother who'd call this Collins character and give him a piece of her mind."

She could picture it now. Grandma got stirred up when she

believed in something. It had only been a month ago that Grandma had declared to Darby over the phone, "Those Nazi pirates aren't keeping what belongs to my family!"

Darby had laughed. She'd enjoyed the story about one of her grandparents being an archaeologist and finding two rare Celtic coins. Her favorite part of the inheritance story was the relative who had helped an Austrian empress, receiving the empress's personal brooch as a gift. Yes, she'd enjoyed the story, especially as a child, but that was as far as Darby had taken it. It was simply another story. The family inheritance, if it had ever existed at all, was certainly long lost or forgotten in some museum or personal collection. Darby had been surprised by Grandma's fierce determination. The dear woman certainly would have been upset by Mr. Collins's words.

Darby blinked as she sat in the recliner beside her grand-mother's hospital-style bed. Her eyes wouldn't stay closed. Sleep wouldn't come. Were there many things she didn't know?

Footsteps sounded down the hall. Darby's mother peered in from the darkened doorway. "How is she?" she called softly.

"She's fine—now," Darby answered as she tiptoed into the hall. "You're supposed to be sleeping. Tonight's my watch."

"I know. But I heard her call out and couldn't go back to sleep," Carole Evans said. "I'm so glad you came."

Darby rested her head against the doorjamb, the collection of family photos catching her eye on the opposite wall. Though the dim light hid the faces, she knew each picture by heart. The top three portraits displayed her all-female family: Mother, Grandma Celia, her younger sister, Maureen, and herself. Uncle Marc and Aunt Helen's photos were below. Beside those was Darby's favorite. The framed photograph captured her mother sitting beside a window with Grandma Celia brushing her hair. The lighting had been perfect, and the expressions on their faces depicted an older version of mother and child. Darby had won an award in college for that photograph.

As Carole peered into Grandma Celia's room, Darby noticed how the late-night shadows heightened the circles under her mother's eyes.

"You should have called me sooner. I would have come, you know."

"I know, but you have a life too, and I didn't want you to cancel that photo trip."

"Grandma's more important. Have the doctors said anything more?"

"Well," her mother admitted, "they say she's at the two-week stage. I try to prepare, but even though I see her decline, I'm not ready. There are so many things I still want to do with her. Things I want to know about her. I'm not ready to lose my mother."

Darby looked over her mother's shoulder toward her grandmother. *I'm not ready to lose her either.*

She wanted to pull her mother into her arms. Instead she placed a hand on her shoulder. Even that slight touch seemed to break something within the older woman as a quiet sob erupted. Darby patted her awkwardly, as if her hand was out of rhythm to the beat of a song. This was not her mother's way. While love had always been given freely in this house, sorrow and tears were kept to the privacy of their hearts. Darby fought her own grief and fear, remembering the only other time, outside of a romantic movie or a memorable event, that she'd seen her mother in tears. While playing hide-and-seek with her younger sister, seven-year-old Darby was under her mother's bed when she heard sobbing. Her father had left that morning, but Darby expected him to return. He always had before.

"Mommy, why are you crying?" she asked as she slid from under the bed. "Is it 'cause of Daddy leaving?"

"Yes, honey." Her mother had turned away.

"I'm sad too. But Daddy said he'd write lots and lots of letters while he's working in Texas."

Her mother wiped her eyes. "I just wanted you raised with a daddy. Not without one like I was. . . ." She'd wrapped her arms around Darby, and the tears broke out again.

Darby hadn't known her father was more than just working in that place three states from their Californian home. He'd found a new woman to build a family with. Darby received a few letters, but eventually they stopped. Soon after, Darby, her mother, and sister had moved into her grandmother's home in Sebastopol, a stone's toss north of San Francisco.

Somewhere over the years and conversations with her mother, Darby surmised that much of her mother's sorrow wasn't from the loss of her husband, but from the loss of a father for her children. Her many comments about never knowing her own father emphasized that point.

Now Darby's mother cried again. Darby's father had disappeared almost as if he'd only existed in a dream. But this time it was Grandma, the solid rock of the family. The anchor that kept everyone grounded. Darby had never lost a loved one to death, especially someone so close to her heart.

"Oh, for pity's sake," her mother said as she cleared her throat. "I'm sorry, Darby."

"This is Grandma we're losing. That's reason for tears."

Her mother breathed a long sigh and smiled. "Grandma would say, 'Look, you've gone and watered the carpet.' "

"She's right. And tomorrow we may find a bean stalk here. I never did find those magic seeds of mine."

Carole chuckled. "I'm so glad you're here. You could always handle hardships better than your sister. Maureen tried to help, but she was so emotional and with the kids running around, well, I'm afraid she was more of a burden than a blessing."

"I'm here for as long as it takes." Darby nodded toward her grandmother. "Clarise can handle everything at the studio, and I'm caught up on my deadlines for a while. I'll take night watch. After all, you never were a night owl. I don't know how you've handled it these last months."

"I'm simply thankful for some help now." Her mother patted Darby's hand, then took a step down the hall.

"Mom?" Darby hesitated. "Grandma keeps calling for someone. Who is Tatianna?"

The hallway had little light, but Darby could see the weariness in her mother's expression. "Honey, I don't know. Grandma has called that name during her bad spells for weeks. She also says words in German. I've started to ask a dozen times, but I haven't. She has so few good moments."

"Grandma's never mentioned her before?"

"I've never heard the name *Tatianna* until last month. And Grandma has never mentioned her except in her sleep."

"Okay. Now *you* need to sleep."

"Good night, honey."

When her mother disappeared into the darkness, Darby turned back to Grandma's bedroom. She stared at the shadows that now hid her grandmother's face. After a lifetime of family and love, why were Grandma Celia's last thoughts possessed by a stranger?

Darby leaned over the edge of the bed and touched her grandmother's skin-and-bone arm. She remembered how Grandma Celia would pat the mattress and gather Darby into her bed whenever Darby had a bad dream. It was Grandma who always soothed away her troubles with a story during a tea party or while brushing Darby's long, brown hair.

"Princesses didn't have dirt-colored hair and eyes," Darby had whined at age five.

"No, but our princess has dark gold strands that look like sunshine on the mountain. Our princess has eyes like a tender doe in the meadow and a pretty heart-shaped face."

Tonight it was Darby who lowered the bed rail and gathered her grandmother in her arms. "I love you, Grandma." She closed her eyes to the shadows surrounding them while one question returned to her mind: *Who was Tatianna?*

⋆═◉═⋆

HALLSTATT, AUSTRIA

His wooden cane slipped in the loose rocks and the flashlight's beam made a wild dance as the man caught his balance and limped onward. The shuffle of his footsteps along the road harmonized with the mournful song of a cricket. One sang and another more distant joined the tune.

He tried to keep his steps quiet as he trudged along the narrow lakeside road. At the end of a cement wall, he found familiar steps leading up the darkened mountain. Higher, through blind turns and covered walkways, he headed toward the church spire that was silhouetted against the moonless night sky. He was almost there. His chest grew tight with the raspy breaths that fought the frozen air. The last turns up the mountain, the steps he once could run up with stealth, now stole his strength. He rested at the wooden gate, leaning heavily against his cane. When he pushed the gate open, its familiar creak welcomed him to the sentry of headstones and soft red candles that lit his way.

He moved forward, past names he didn't need to read. He knew them all by heart. With great care, he climbed the steps to the upper level of the cemetery and plodded toward a large, white structure. The graveyard and church were cut into the mountainside just like the village below. When autumn leaves crunched beneath his boots, he stopped abruptly and bent before the grave, looking for any weeds. None. He'd made sure the rectangular patch would be well cared for in his absence. He sat on the edge of the concrete border and laid his cane on the ground.

"I—" His voice caught, and he cleared his throat. "I've come again."

He examined his work and smiled. Such passion of youth had stirred him to spend hours on the wrought-iron headstone. Other headstones were iron or wood, but he could not purchase her marker. He had to do it himself, to feel the metal turn in his hands, to sweat, to cut his hands and bleed as she had—though so much less than she had. He'd needed to carry the finished work on his back—his cross to bear forever. Though friends believed the war had turned him crazy, he'd needed the work to survive the day and the day after that, until he stood here now all these years later. For his work was more than a headstone; it was his memorial to his young wife. It was the closest thing he could have of her. For no, she wasn't here. Her body didn't rest beneath the earth. That had tormented him in the beginning. For there was nowhere he could go to find it, except to take a bit of ground from the place where she'd died. That was all he had left of her and so he brought only dirt to where he could visit and feel close to her again.

The old man removed his tweed hat and set it on the edge of the cement. He strained to rise and limped toward a stone faucet capped into a mountain spring. He turned the handle, and water gushed loudly into the tin watering can. He closed the valve and carried the can to the grave.

"Let's give those flowers some water," he said to himself, glad that the pansies and fall daffodils appeared healthy. The man reached to yank some dead petals from the rosebush that grew around the base of her headstone, and a thorn pricked his gnarled finger. He opened the iron cover plate to see her name. His fingers traced the neat letters on the metal, leaving a smear of blood around the curve of the C.

"I feel this could be my last visit," he told her tenderly. "No, it's not our anniversary already. I just needed to come tonight. You've been in my thoughts so often lately. But it won't be much longer until I can't hike this trail. I won't have to wonder and fear. I'll know everything for certain. And we'll be together—at last. And, my dearest, I'm very ready to be with you again."

In the red candlelit night, the man studied the last blooming rose on the bush. Its petals were perfect. The pale yellow roses continued to blossom well in the early autumn days. It seemed they knew this would be the last chance for him to see them grace her grave. So for one last time, he'd see his final offering of love.

The man bent to place his lips upon the cold metal nameplate. Just one more look at her name before he closed the cover. That name he loved so well, even after all these years. If he suspected correctly, soon he'd speak her name, and they'd be together again. Forever.

CHAPTER TWO

The window shade jolted upward and morning pierced the room.

"Wake up, honey."

Darby groaned and squinted in the brightness. "Mom, I just closed my eyes. Do I *have* to go to school today?" She grinned with her hands shielding her eyes.

"You probably did just go to sleep. I didn't want to wake you. . . ." Her mother's features came into focus. "But Grandma's having an exceptional morning, and I knew you'd want to talk to her."

Darby kicked off the quilt. "Can I see her now?"

"She's waiting."

Darby hurried from her old bedroom back into Grandma's down the hall.

"My Darby. Finally, you are here." Grandma Celia sat up slowly. Daylight heightened the sallow coloring of her skin. "You've kept an old woman from her grave so you could traipse the mountains for weeks at a time."

Darby smiled. This was the Grandma Celia she knew,
though the name Tatianna still echoed in her mind. Grandma's
lively expression kept away her questions. At least for now.

Darby moved to the chair beside the bed. "Who hooked me
on the mountains with years and years of her Austrian Alp
tales?"

"Not me." Celia looked at her innocently. Darby always
loved the woman's soft German accent, though Grandma Celia
denied she even had one, saying, "I w-worked too hard to
sound American." Darby would try not to laugh. Grandma
sometimes tried so hard to sound American with her proper
English, emphasizing slangs and especially accentuating the
ws in an effort not to pronounce a v sound, that she actually
sounded more foreign in her efforts.

"You're just jealous that I found a way to make money
hiking among the pine-scented forests." Darby reached for her
grandmother's hand. "And what's this about keeping you from
the grave? It looks like you have enough spunk to chase the
Grim Reaper away for the rest of eternity!"

"W-well, let me tell you." Grandma pointed a trembling
finger at Darby. "Mr. Reaper and I have developed a nice relationship. You know, he's been misunderstood over the years.
I've found him a pleasant fella once you get to know him."

"Are you giving my daughter a hard time this morning?"
Carole entered the room with a bottle of pills and a glass of
water.

"I wouldn't want to disappoint *my* granddaughter."
Grandma winked. Darby, who was watching her carefully,
perceived an underlying weakness in her tone.

"It's time for your medicine!" Carole said loudly, putting
two pills in her hand.

"I've told you before, Daughter, I may be dying, but my
hearing is just fine!"

"Oh, hush, and open your mouth."

Darby watched her mother hold two tablets and a glass of water before Grandma's mouth.

"I'm not a child either. I can take medicine all by myself, thank you." Grandma Celia grabbed the pills and swished them down with the water.

"Grandma, you're as feisty as ever."

"What did you expect? That I would get docile in my last days? Goodness, no! I'm ready to march up to those pearly gates and give Jesus the biggest w-whomping kiss he's had in the last millennium."

"You mean *whopping*. Here, give me the glass." Carole took the cup and walked out.

"No, a w-whomping kiss," Grandma Celia called after her, then turned back toward Darby. "I like the sound of that better—no matter what it means."

"Well, Jesus can wait awhile longer for whatever kind of kiss you give him," Darby said, crossing her arms. "You aren't leaving us yet."

"Quit that nonsense talk, my dear. Look at me. I'm as thin as a pencil."

Darby didn't want to look at the arms she had stared at the night before.

"You young whippersnappers believe you must pretend life on earth does not end. But it does, and that's certainly the way it is. A time to be born and a time to die." Grandma Celia patted Darby's hand and sighed. "But I must say it's an odd place to be, on the threshold of death's door. You look back and see it all, your whole life. The mistakes, sorrow, joys, triumphs. Then you look ahead and wonder what's really on the other side."

Darby leaned closer in surprise. "Grandma, are you doubting?"

"Mercy, no! God has w-worked enough in my life for me to know that he is real. But I think it'll be more, so much more—

w-what's the w-word?—immense or spectacular, than I ever imagined. It's very exciting, with maybe a hint of scariness mixed in."

Darby wished she could argue with her grandmother. She wished she could promise a longer life, but Grandma Celia spoke the truth. Celia *was* dying. But how could her grandmother speak so casually about death and seem almost excited about the prospect? Even with Grandma's body waning before her eyes, Darby could not imagine life without her.

Grandma fumbled with the pillow, and Darby noted how even such small movements caused her breathing to labor. Grandma Celia squirmed into a comfortable position, took another long breath, and addressed Darby again.

"Tell me all about your latest work. Not the boring stuff you do in town, pictures of weddings and snooty-nosed children. I want to hear the mountain adventures! Did the group go to the Trinity Alps like you suggested?"

"Yes, and it was wonderful!" Darby exclaimed.

Grandma Celia reached over to move a few brown tendrils of hair behind Darby's ears, just as she'd done for years. That touch and the excited light in her grandmother's eyes caressed Darby's entire being.

"You remember it was that same hiking club from San Francisco? They told me the photographs have been all the rage in the office of the hiking club's president. He's the CEO of a San Francisco insurance company and a hiker in his spare time."

"Is he married?"

"Yes, Grandma. His wife came along and is a wonderful lady. I've told you, the good ones are taken."

"Oh no. Your man's out there waiting. He's a nice fellow, too. I pray for him all the time. He's sick of you hiding beneath your work and ready for you to meet him."

"And who is this man?" Darby tapped her finger against her cheek.

CINDY McCORMICK MARTINUSEN

"I'm not certain. But I know he's out there."

"Anyway, let's stick with my story. The club wanted more photos this year and chose a more adventurous expedition with eight days and a forty-mile trip with some face climbing. It's a good thing I joined the gym over the summer. The elevation is over eleven thousand feet." Seeing her grandmother's smile, Darby tried to conjure up the storytelling vividness that her grandmother always used. "The best part of this trip was this one total city boy."

"This isn't the CEO guy?"

"No. This guy is in insurance also, but you could tell he only did the trip to get some photos in his office. He wanted me to take his picture like he was hanging from a rock when really his feet were on the ground!"

Grandma's laughter brought a smile to Darby's own face. She felt like a little girl, telling her grandmother about her day's woes or adventures. After she told her story, Grandma always had a similar tale or story of encouragement. Darby remembered being more enthralled with these stories than with her favorite television shows like *Scooby-Doo* or *The Bloodhound Gang*. Nothing compared to Grandma's vivid tales of the Austrian Alps. Those mountain tellings had bred Darby's own love for the wilderness and a desire to see the towering peaks of her grandmother's childhood. Darby had never made it to Europe, probably never would, but the scent of pines and the crisp mountain air tugged at something within her. It was a feeling she could never quite explain— because of the stories. Grandma's stories lived within Darby now. Yet in all those countless tales, Grandma Celia had never mentioned the name Tatianna.

"Oh, I wish I could have been there!" Grandma's laughter broke into a low, rasping cough. "I'd—have pulled a few pranks on that city fella!"

"Well, just wait till you hear the rest!" Darby continued

with a chuckle. She ignored her grandmother's condition and pretended she was telling just another story on just another day. "We reached the crest of Siligo Peak, overlooking Deer Creek Canyon hundreds of feet below, when something catches my eye."

"City Boy?"

"Yes! He's clinging to this rock, scared to death, with his eyes shut! So, since I was assigned to take pictures . . ."

"Oh, you naughty, naughty girl! Did he even know you took pictures of him?"

"Oh, yes! He heard the camera clicking and opened one eye. Then he starts yelling at me to stop. Of course, I didn't. For the rest of the trip, this guy was begging to buy that roll of film from me."

"I've never been so proud of you!" Although Grandma's tone was light, her eyes appeared glassy, and Darby wondered if it was from the laughter or the coughing.

She continued to describe her trip but noticed her grand-mother's eyes blinking heavily. Grandma sagged back against her pillow and squirmed deeper under the covers.

"Well, I can see my stories just don't hold your interest anymore."

"It's this horrible medication. I can't stay awake for long with it, but it pains me too much to live without it. We have a real love—" Grandma burst into another coughing fit—"hate rela-tionship." Darby propped her forward as her body was racked with uncontrollable spasms. "W-wa-ter," she sputtered. Darby grabbed the glass and placed it to her grandmother's lips. Drop-lets flew across the quilt as Grandma Celia struggled to drink. Finally the cough subsided, and Grandma leaned back. She closed her eyes, then her smile came in slow motion. "I've got to hear the rest of your story, my dear. You know it's not fair I got stuck in this hilly country. You're lucky to be in the real north of Northern California near all those mountains."

Darby stared at her grandmother for a minute. How she loved this woman. She didn't want to be part of this game of telling stories, joking while disease consumed her grandmother before her eyes. But she swallowed the tears that threatened—there would be plenty of time for crying later. These last moments needed smiles, stories, and joy. And below it all remained the unanswered questions.

"I guess you'll have to wait to hear about the cricket in City Boy's sleeping bag. I'll let you rest." Darby forced a smile and rose to leave.

"Wait." Grandma Celia grasped Darby's hand. "I need to talk to you about something."

"Okay. How about as soon as you wake up?"

Grandma Celia's grip tightened around Darby's hand. The intensity in the older woman's gaze startled her.

"Yes, it'll have to wait. But it's very important."

Darby could feel her heart beat faster. Maybe she'd discover the secret the shadows held. She had fought the desire to ask, fearing, like her mother, what the mention of that name would do to her grandmother. Darby wanted the real Grandma Celia this morning.

"What's it about?"

"I couldn't explain it to your mother. She w-worries, and she couldn't do anything. Besides, it's something you should do. I've known that for a long time."

"What do you want me to do?"

Grandma Celia's eyes were shut for so long that Darby thought the older woman had fallen asleep. But when Darby drew closer, a second later, Grandma's eyes fluttered half open.

"I need you to do what I can't do."

"Anything. What is it?"

"I need you to make things right with Tatianna."

"Who is Tatianna?"

As Grandma Celia gazed toward the ceiling, an age-old weariness poured into her features. "Tatianna was my best friend."

Sensing their time together was short, Darby wanted to hurry her, to ask question after question, but she held her tongue to give her grandmother space to open at will.

"I have a small safe that Fred is keeping for me."

"Fred Bishop, your lawyer?"

"Yes . . . you'll find some answers in there. I'll tell you more when I wake up. But Darby—" Celia held her granddaughter's arm with two hands. "You must make things right. Make them right for me, please."

"Make what right?"

"You'll know when you get there."

"Where?"

Grandma's eyes flickered shut, then opened slightly. "Tatianna needs her name. I'll tell you later. I need some rest first."

"Her name? What do you mean?" Darby asked, startled.

Grandma's hand motioned *not now, not now,* then she fell asleep.

SALZBURG, AUSTRIA

The rain slapping Brant Collins's face was neither felt nor acknowledged. The drops streamed like tears from his jaw, nose, and chin. His legs walked without direction across wet streets. He even crossed a busy intersection without looking. A loud horn and the *whoosh* of a bus focused his thoughts. He stepped onto the bridge and finally stopped at the crest.

Resting against the railing, Brant glared into the gray fingers of the Salzach River below. He noticed the newspaper clenched in his hand. It had long ago turned limp and now dripped like a leaky faucet. He wiped rain from his face and unrolled the paper where much of the black ink had worn off against his wet hand. The faces in the photo were now contorted images, quite suitable for the people they represented. The man had been captured with his eyes toward the ground, but the woman stared straight from the page into Brant's eyes. Her smile was a twisted sneer—the person she really was. Her eyes still met his defiantly beneath the headline: COUPLE ACCUSED IN HOLOCAUST SURVIVOR FRAUD.

Brant had given much of the past year to the Aldrichs. The woman had begged his help to find her family's lost paintings. They were the last link to her father, who had not escaped the Nazis. More than oil and canvas, they were the only portraits of her childhood. "Please help," she'd pleaded. "I want to die with those paintings on my wall." So, of course Brant had helped—that was what his work was all about. More than papers and research and digging into the past, his work at the Austrian Holocaust Survivors' Organization was for people— for making a difference in the individual lives that had been tormented by war, incarcerated in camps, and tortured. He longed to see Frau Aldrich's expression when he told her they'd recovered her dream.

And Brant had done just that. He did find the art in a small collection in the United States. He did see the joy in Frau Aldrich's face. But he also saw the torment of the rightful owners.

It had all been an act. The Aldrichs—brother and sister, they said—had come to his office door after another newspaper account reported a victory for one of Brant's clients, a French woman survivor. They'd told their sad story and walked from his office surely laughing at his concern and commitment to help. Not only were the Aldrichs not Jewish, nor brother and sister, Greta was actually an ex-Nazi camp guard. Her information about the art had come from one of the inmates under her guard. It was suspected that Frau Aldrich had even selected her victim for the gas chamber because of the information she'd obtained. Greta Aldrich had been unable to find the art after the war, but with Brant's help she'd almost gotten what she wanted.

He couldn't believe he'd been duped. Brant tore the soggy paper into several pieces and released them over the railing. The river's ripples gathered the pieces and carried them away.

This had not been the first attempt at a fraudulent claim, especially since the opening of Swiss banks. Brant had immediately identified a recent claim as false—an American claiming to be Celia Müller. He had prided himself on the fact that he could not be deceived, and now the Aldrich story had shattered that illusion.

Angry, Brant turned away from the river. He moved quickly, suddenly aware of the cold that clutched him. When his pager sounded, he paused beneath the eaves of a weathered white-stucco building. Brant was about to turn it off when he noticed the number. Why would she be calling? There could be only one reason. He found his phone in his coat pocket and punched in the number.

"This is Brant. What happened?"

"We think he had a stroke," the woman said.

"No."

"You better come."

Brant was already running.

CHAPTER THREE

Darby saw death in Grandma Celia's face. It wouldn't be long. As Grandma's breath grew more labored, Darby's day was consumed with watching that breathing. Her mother seemed to accept that this was the end, though her expression shifted from the weariness of waiting to the clinging hope that Grandma's life wouldn't slip away quite yet. But Darby couldn't accept it. She even prayed for the first time in years. *God, don't take her, please, don't take her.*

Darby's childhood in an all-female home had been with an example of strength in both her grandmother and mother. She tried to maintain that strength on the outside but felt herself weaken as her grandmother walked closer to death's door.

Death is part of life, she reminded herself throughout the week. *Everyone loses loved ones. Everyone dies. I need to be ready. But how can I prepare?*

Grandma had been her cheerful self only a few short and treasured minutes. Although she continued to call Tatianna's name in the late-night hours, there was less urgency in her voice. Yet no opportunity had arisen for Darby to ask about her grandmother's mysterious friend.

Darby waited until her mother went grocery shopping, then found the number for her grandmother's lawyer.

"Is she gone?" Fred asked before saying hello.

"No, not yet."

"Oh, thank goodness. I see my share of lousy people in this profession. It's an honor to know someone like your grandmother."

"I agree. But I'll get to the reason for my call." Darby propped her elbow on the counter beside the telephone. "Grandma told me about a personal safe she has left with you."

"Ah, yes. She brought it to me about a year ago. I don't normally keep such things and encouraged her to get a safety deposit box, but you know her thoughts about financial institutions."

"Yes. In high school, she'd let me leave an IOU note for every ten-dollar bill I borrowed from her mattress. Does she have her savings in the safe, or should we check under her bed?"

"Actually, I'm not at liberty to tell quite yet. Besides, I don't know the complete contents. My instructions are to wait for her passing, then we'll move to those details."

"Grandma didn't tell me anything except that you had a safe, and I'd find some information she wanted me to have inside."

"I understand, but those were the instructions."

"That's all I needed to know. Take care, Fred."

"You too, Darby. And take care of our lady."

"I promise." She hung up the phone and sat back in her chair. Whatever was in the safe, it wouldn't help her at present. Soon, too soon, the safe would be opened, for her grandmother would be gone.

⋆═◉═⋆

Darby spent the nights in Grandma's room, in case anything happened.

The days and nights blurred until their borders appeared as one continuous fog, only distinguished by the house lights being turned on or off. In the middle of a night, a voice stirred Darby. Fatigue held her as she struggled toward the surface of consciousness. Suddenly, she sat upright, seized awake.

The voice traveled its own journey, moving backwards along a near-forgotten path as Darby's eyes sought through the dim light to where her grandmother sat up in bed.

"Perhaps in another time or place it would not have felt so intense—but we were there, in that troublesome time. People fear hard times, but challenges usually make strong bonds stronger. We found great love in the midst of turmoil."

Darby strained forward, mesmerized by Grandma's voice. Its rhythm was like a midnight hymn rocking her back and forth.

"Would our love have changed if given the chance to be together all these years? I've wondered, can't imagine it, but we only had six months as husband and wife." A chuckle escaped. "We cherished every moment of that time." Her voice seemed to drift away to memory.

How welcome this dreamlike spell was compared to the coughing fits or troubled callings. Grandma Celia reached for Darby's hand. Darby moved forward and grasped the outstretched fingers, surprised to see her grandmother's eyes shining lucid and full of comprehension in the reflected light. "Darby, will you open the window for me?"

"Of course." Darby leaned awkwardly over the bed to pull the window up an inch. Cool air swam into the room, and moonlight filtered through the parted curtains.

"That box on my dresser, the one Uncle Marc made me. Bring it to me, please."

Darby moved toward the lamp switch.

"My dear, please don't turn on the light. The moon is bright enough. I don't want to lose this—this magical night. I have found your grandfather in my memories here."

"Yes, Grandma."

Darby retrieved the miniature carved box. She turned and stopped, seeing Grandma Celia with streams of moonlight flooding the bed. She was beautiful. Her rumpled gray hair glowed like an angel's cloak down to her shoulders.

Celia's hand trembled as she reached for the wooden box. For a moment, Darby wondered if this was real, or if perhaps she was still asleep. Even the questions she'd been holding all week vanished while she watched her grandmother search inside the carved box.

Grandma Celia's voice again broke the aura of silence in the room. "I haven't spoken about him in a long time. It was easier for me, and for your mother. She wanted to know him so badly. Even when my hope had died, your mom's continued. I had told too many stories about her daddy, though eventually her hope was crushed by reality. That's why I quit speaking of him, since we had to leave him behind. But he's been locked inside all these years, always near." Grandma patted her heart.

A sharp cough interrupted the stillness. Grandma Celia placed a tissue over her mouth, then crumpled it in her bony fist. Her weak smile reappeared. "Perhaps it would have changed if your grandfather and I had been given a life together. We might have become like some couples who have grown old together. But in my mind, he's still that wonderful man who swept me off my feet. You would have loved him, Darby. You've reminded me of him. You both were full of life, laughter, and adventure. Ready to tackle anything that comes along."

Darby had never heard her grandmother talk this much about her grandfather, and for some reason, she'd never asked many questions about him. He was long dead sometime during the war, and there was little else she knew. The way her grandmother spoke of him brought such curiosity, and Grandma Celia's voice had never sounded the way it did now. She seemed to spin memory on her lips, like she tasted each thought, kissed each moment.

The moonlight touched a tiny object Grandma withdrew from the box. "And here it is."

Darby looked closer.

"It's too late for the two of us in this life, but there is something that must still be done—" Another cough seized Celia. Darby leaned Celia forward, groping for the water behind her. Grandma's thin frame jolted into slower coughs until they died away. Darby reached for the tissue over her grandmother's mouth and offered the glass. Even in what Celia called the magical moonlight, Darby saw bright red splotches on the tissue she tossed into the trash.

"I want you to have this." Grandma's voice was hoarse, her hands shaking.

"A ring?"

"Only half a ring. This is the engagement part. The wedding half is gone. Do you see the diamonds on top?"

Darby saw where, in place of the usual setting, there was another ring of gold with diamonds attached around the rim.

"Your grandfather designed this ring." Grandma cleared her throat and sat up a little more. "When joined with the w-wedding half, that circle becomes two small rings locked together, surrounded by lasting treasure."

"It's beautiful," Darby whispered, looking at her grandmother's face. *She should rest now.* But the expression on Grandma's face, tired and weary though it appeared, held a sense of purpose. "What happened to the other half?"

Grandma Celia smiled. "So many stories I have told you, my Darby." Her fingers caressed Darby's cheek. "Since you were a

child, so full of wonder, I have told you my tales. But I kept
hidden the real stories because I didn't want to steal the joy I
saw in your eyes. When your mother was a child, I stole many
moments from her because I was consumed with my own
sorrow. I tried to protect you, but other forces have taken the
wonder from your eyes. I see an empty place in you—one I
recognize from experience. And you run from it, afraid to face
your own heart."

Darby stared at her grandmother for a long time. How had
the past so quickly turned to focus on Darby's life? "Grandma,
don't worry about me. I'm happy, very happy."

"But you've lost your joy. It's taken years for me to see it. I
saw your spirit wounded as a little one when you finally
understood that your father was not returning. I also don't
think you've ever gotten over you and Derek breaking up. I see
it most clearly through your work. You hide behind the
camera, where once you danced with it. Yes, I see the change
most in your work."

Darby sat back in the chair. What could she say to these
words that cut so deep, even as she denied them?

Grandma squeezed her hand and breathed deeply. "Don't be
afraid. Don't hold me so tightly. You must know that you can't
put your faith in people—they fail you, break your heart, die on
you. You can love them and receive love, but don't put all of
yourself in another human—we are too imperfect of creatures."

"So what can I do?" Darby asked. "How can I let you go?"

"I will be with you always—don't let me go. But you need
more than me inside that heart of yours. I couldn't really find
God until I lost my husband. Not that I think God wanted me
to lose Gunther—I still don't understand all the workings of
God. Of course, I couldn't. Though soon, I will know him,
even as I am known." Grandma smiled, though her voice grew
raspy. "I do know that when I was weak, the Lord made me
strong. People are for loving and for loving you back. But God

is the place to put your heart, soul, and mind. He'll never let you down, I promise."

Grandma closed her eyes for a long time. Her hand weakened its hold on Darby's. Her voice was low and labored, barely above a whisper. "This ring is part of my last story for you. And my story now becomes yours. But, my little one, I'm not going to finish it. You must."

"Do you need your oxygen?" Darby asked while reaching for the mask on the nightstand and turning the valve on the tank. Grandma accepted the mask and took two or three breaths before setting it on her chest.

"Can't explain now. Trust me. You'll know when you get there." Her eyes opened as she took several more breaths, and she smiled weakly. "You'll discover more than I can imagine. And it becomes your life after mine—new journey, unraveling past secrets, and making injustices right." Grandma inhaled a long, full breath. "Your future will change. I pray you will choose the right path when the time comes. I'll go soon. I'm ready. Then you'll find your start in the safety deposit box. Your mother has the key."

"Grandma, I don't understand any of this." Darby's body trembled.

"I know. I know, my dear."

Darby could see her grandmother desperately needed rest. Yet there was so much she needed to know. What did her grandmother want from her? How could she finish a story she knew nothing about? And what had her grandmother meant about Tatianna needing her name?

Darby grasped her grandmother's hand. She opened her mouth to allow the flood of questions, but Grandma Celia held up a hand to stop her.

"Not now, little one. In time. It will all be revealed in time. For now, this is all."

"But, Grandma . . ."

"Trust me?"

"Yes."

"Then, trust me. You will know. Step-by-step. Very soon."

Darby wanted to argue and to stop the motion of time for just a little while—to pause this moment.

She knew they would not speak like this again.

⊷⇒◜⇐⊷

Sometime in the morning, voices reached her. Darby awoke in her own room and tried to remember when she'd moved there. Her feet shuffled along the carpet in weary motion, stopping at her grandmother's doorway. Her mother was holding Grandma Celia's hands. A tear dropped from Carole's face. Again, her mother was in tears. Darby's legs felt like cement blocks of fear. But then she heard her grandmother's voice—so slow and labored between breaths. Darby remembered the hospice list and "fish-out-of-water" breathing.

"I must say sorry," Grandma Celia was saying, then a breath and a slower breath. "No matter w-what you say."

"I love you, Mother."

"I wish. I wish I had done better by you." Grandma's eyes were closed and only lifted now and then. Darby knew she should leave them alone in their moment. But her feet wouldn't move, her hand wouldn't release the doorway. She knew little of her mother's childhood. What had it been like in a postwar world with an immigrant mother and a father lost across the sea? And what had later led her mother to drop college for a man who ended up dropping them?

"It took long—too long—for me to be strong," Grandma said in a whisper. "I leaned too much on you."

"Mother, you had to reinvent yourself. Even your language wasn't the same." Carole drew closer. "I wondered what you lost by giving up your native tongue. Words in English that took too long to think up. Stories that could never be translated correctly. I saw you make your change and grow into something new."

"At your expense."

"No, I admired you—even if it took awhile to realize it."

"You wanted a father. And I made you hate Austria, our home."

"You didn't make me. I hated it because it took everything. I didn't want to hear about Alpine sunsets when all I could see was the missing face of my father and the grandparents I'd never have. It wasn't you. It was reality that makes me still turn cold at the thought."

"But God gave more—more than I had. Though I was very slow to find it. But you—my daughter. You don't need to live your life that way. Embrace God, and he will help you find healing, so you may be spared some of the hardness I faced. I don't want Darby to go through life that way, either. That's why I've made the special request of her that I talked with you about. . . ." Saying the words seemed to drain all of Grandma's energy. Darby stepped forward, but her mother saw it too. She shushed her gently.

"Rest now. Just rest. If it helps, know that I forgive anything you feel you're sorry for. But I think you are a wonderful woman, and a wonderful mother."

⊷═◉═⊷

For the next few days, Grandma Celia remained more unconscious than awake. The hospice nurse stopped by daily, and Darby and her mother kept watch—every missed breath brought fear. But her grandmother rested soundly, her medications helping with the pain and coughing fits. Several times she wrestled, fitfully mumbling words in German—the language she'd forbidden from her life long ago.

One morning as the light began to touch the darkness, Darby wearily glanced toward the bed. She bolted upright and looked at Grandma's chest. Her grandmother's eyes were closed; the painful sound of struggling breath was silent. Grandma Celia was gone.

CHAPTER FOUR

Darby produced a smile at the appropriate
times. Words of comfort to family and friends somehow came
to her lips. The checklist she'd prepared with her mother had
lines drawn through it—words like *Lincoln Funeral Chapel,
visitation times, Deb's Florist, burial clothes.*

Conversations with relatives she hadn't seen in years,
arrangements with the funeral parlor, even the stories she told
her two nieces, all seemed to take place somewhere outside
her being. She could hear herself speak and her mind regis-
tered, but everything seemed distanced and misplaced. Inside,
Darby kept a surreal hardness to bring herself through that
first week after Grandma's death.

Tatianna, what about Tatianna? The question weighed on
Darby's mind, while the greater sense of loss made her withdraw
into a shell. She wanted to question her mother about Grandma
Celia. She wanted to discover the contents of the safe. But the
mysteries would have to wait, at least until the details of the
funeral were completed and the visiting family departed.

During the funeral dinner, Grandma Celia's closest friend, Maisie Hansen, pulled Darby aside. Darby looked across the room at the empty punch bowl, wanting to fill it, but she knew she should take a moment with Maisie. The elderly woman had been a friend of the family for years and would soon be returning home. Darby pried her eyes from the drink table in an attempt to give Maisie her full attention. There was just so much to do.

"Darby, I'm so sorry about Celia. A blessed many years she lived, though." Maisie placed her hand on Darby's arm. "She was the sister I never had."

"I know, Maisie."

"Life passes you by. Take my word, your days of youth should be cherished."

"Yes, I know." Darby thought about the two casseroles she had left in the oven. Hopefully Mother had gotten them out.

"This may sound petty, but . . ."

"What, Maisie?"

"There was a mistake in the pastor's eulogy and in the obituary. I wanted you to know."

"A mistake?" Darby heard the words while looking at her two nieces trying to scrape a last scoopful of punch from the bowl. "I checked everything myself."

"It's Celia's place of birth. She wasn't born in Vienna, Austria, but in Hallstatt."

Darby's eyes flickered back to Maisie. "That's not what her papers said."

"Well, I'm certain she was born in Hallstatt. She told me herself. All of her mother's family was born in Hallstatt. Your great-aunt even traveled in her last month of pregnancy from Salzburg to deliver your cousin Henri in the family birthplace. It was tradition, well, at least until the war changed everything."

Darby's mind spun with Maisie's words. Grandma Celia had

told her many stories about Hallstatt, the village she had grown up in. But when she read in Grandma's personal papers that her birthplace was Vienna, she assumed they had moved to Hallstatt when Celia was young.

"Thank you, Maisie, for bringing this to my attention." The older woman appeared relieved. "I'll check into it, okay?"

"Good. I was hoping maybe the newspaper could print the correction or something."

"Yes, maybe." Darby moved away, back to the busyness of the funeral plans. But her mind kept returning to Maisie's words.

⋅⇒◉⇐⋅

Eventually the phone calls slowed, and the relatives said their good-byes. Darby's sister, Maureen Lamont, and her twins left for Sacramento. The refrigerator still overflowed with the food prepared by friends. Darby had been surprised by the people Grandma Celia had influenced over the years as they came to bring food comfort—though Darby hoped never to eat another casserole again. With the funeral over, the silence in the house seemed to shout, *What now?*

Darby observed her mother and realized they were alike in one way. Both tried to keep busy when tragedy came. But what would her mother do now?

"You know you can move up to Redding with me." Darby brought up the subject as she helped her mother unload the dishwasher. "I'll have that extra room in my apartment when the school semester is over and Clarise's niece moves out."

"Thanks, honey. Maureen offered for me to move to Sacramento. And Aunt Helen and Uncle Marc invited me to Southern California for as long as I like. To tell you the truth, I don't know yet."

Darby glanced at her mother, who'd never looked so vulnerable and frail. Darby felt a sudden urge to wrap her arms around her but continued, instead, to put the plastic bowls away.

"It's not like this was unexpected," Darby's mother said, staring outside past the tree-lined street to the sloping vineyards beyond. "I've thought about this. But now that Grandma is really gone, I don't know what direction I should take. It's a strange feeling having your mother die. No one loves you like a parent. Well, except for the Lord. I guess it's time for me to ask God about my future."

Startled by her mother's words, Darby almost dropped the bowl she was holding. Though they all attended church fairly regularly, only Grandma spoke about her faith. To the rest of them, it was just another part of their lives, like grocery shopping or going to the movies. Well, maybe more, but then maybe less too. Darby remembered the words she had spoken so long ago. *Forgiveness. Surrender. Come into my heart.* But somewhere along the way, the words merged into her being and became a hidden part of her life. Hearing her mother talk about God left a strange sensation within her. How many times had she heard Grandma speak in such a way? *My prayers are surrounding you, Darby. God's not finished with you yet.* Darby had heard her mother say religious words a few times prior to Grandma's death, but not like God was part of her daily life.

The dishes were finished without further talk. Mother stacked the clean cake pans and casserole dishes, then set them in a box to return to friends and family. Darby decided now was the time to ask. The questions had waited long enough.

"Mom, Grandma Celia told me some things before she died. She wanted me to do something." Darby watched her mother stop and turn toward her.

"I know. Grandma and I discussed it before you came down. I guess today is the day. I'll call Fred to see if he's available. He said he'd like to make a house call to go over the will since Grandma was such a good friend. And I have the key."

"To the safe?"

"Yes." Carole patted Darby's hand. "I wish Maureen could have come back for the reading, but this will have to do. Could I have until this afternoon?"

"Okay, this afternoon."

⊹≡◎⊜≡⊹

Darby paced the house. She wanted answers, and she wanted them now.

She wandered the rooms of the home she'd spent much of her life in. Little had changed on the surface—Grandma and Mother's Victorian décor remained the same, and Maureen's room still had a Bryan Adams poster on the wall, though it was currently the sewing room. Darby's room had been converted into neat guest quarters with her same violet-and-white comforter. Everything looked normal, like any other house on rural Poplar Way. But now it felt different. How could such a normal appearance hold so many hidden secrets? Darby knew that, like specters, the ghostly questions had been lurking, waiting to be answered.

Unable to stand the thoughts any longer, Darby knew where to go. Through all the busyness of the funeral and company, she had veered away from saying good-bye to Grandma. Now it was time.

In the back shed she found the clippers and walked straight to the neglected flower garden. Grandma had designed the garden in a circular path with her favorite bush in the very center. Darby stood before the rosebush and cut the best flower the autumn bloom had given. She stripped away the lower leaves and left their remnants on the ground as she walked toward her car.

The gate to the cemetery driveway was closed when Darby arrived. She parked and went through the walk-in entrance.

Grandma's grave was easy to find. The plot she had chosen years ago rested beneath one of the few great oak trees.

Darby stared at the mound of green sod with fresh, black dirt along the edges. It seemed unreal that her grandmother rested somewhere beneath that plot of earth. The fingers that had caressed her cheek since childhood now were cold and dead. How long until flesh returned to the earth? That thought pricked a chill from her scalp down her back. Not Grandma, not my Grandma Celia. But death was as natural as birth, right? The body was just a shell for a spirit that would live on. Next came heaven, angels, God. For Grandma's sake, Darby willed it to be true, truer than life. But heaven was so distant and far away as she stood there, staring at the place where soon only a headstone would mark an entire life.

Celia Rachel Müller. Beloved Grandmother and Mother.

The woman she loved so deeply would be another name among the long rows of granite stones, in just another cemetery, in just another place.

I hope there's more after this life.

Darby knelt in the grass to feel closer. The cold dampness pressed round, wet circles through her pants and around her knees. She scooted forward to run her finger along the dirt edging. Grandma Celia's ring tumbled forward, suspended in the air by the gold chain around her neck. As Darby held the ring, tracing the circle of warm metal with one finger, a few oak leaves drifted down.

Is my life drifting apart and away like those leaves? she wondered. She'd built a wall that was nicely kept around her life. Now that wall was crumbling. What had Grandma said the last night they talked? Something about this last story becoming part of her future too—about Darby needing to make certain decisions—hopefully the right ones? It shook her to the core, touching inward places she'd never dared to think about because if she did, she didn't know what she'd find.

Maybe she didn't want to move into this place of mystery and the unknown. Darby had always planned her own course, and as a result, things worked out perfectly. At least that's what she continued to tell herself whenever the doubts arose. And now this. Tatianna. Secrets. Shadows. Perhaps the truth would destroy everything she knew, everything she was. But there was no turning back. The first step would be the safe. From there, she didn't know.

Darby placed the single flower on the new sod.

"I came to say good-bye. Yet even now, I can't stand the thought that you are gone from me. But I know and vow, whatever you want of me, Grandma, I'll do my best. I promise you that."

She stood and began to walk away. With one last backward look, Darby thought how pleased Grandma would be with the flower on her grave. Her favorite, a pale yellow rose, shone in the late-morning light.

CHAPTER FIVE

Brant stared at the black-and-white photograph. In the many years he'd known Gunther, his mentor had
never shared this picture with him.

He settled back in the leather wingback. Gunther's chair.
Just sitting here made Brant feel closer to him. The light scent
of apple pipe-smoke lingered in the soft leather and further
reminded Brant how much he missed spending time with the
old man. He knew this would be one of the last times he
would sit in Gunther's study. After today, the room would
never be the same without his dear friend's presence. And once
it changed, Brant would not often travel from Salzburg to his
old summer home next door to Gunther's. With Gunther gone
from this place, there was nothing but memories to bring him
back to Gosau. How he hated changes—especially ones this
severe and permanent.

Brant's gaze returned to the aged photo. "So this is your
long-lost love," he muttered, looking at the two faces.

"Yes, and his only love too."

Startled, Brant turned to see Ingrid, Gunther's wife, in the doorway. He started to speak to somehow take away his words. He wouldn't have spoken had he known she watched him.

"Don't look so surprised." Ingrid moved into the room. She walked up beside Brant and gazed at the beaming smiles worn by the young man and woman in the picture. "Gunther only married me because I needed his help. Postwar Europe wasn't exactly a safe place for an unwed mother of two. Gunther took pity on me, which was enough at the time."

"I'm sure he grew to love you," Brant said quickly. When he slid the photo back into the manila envelope, he felt something at the bottom. But with the ever-watchful and acidic Ingrid in the room, he ignored it.

She laughed. "You never were a good liar, Brant. Even as a little boy, I could always tell. You look away and start doing something when you lie."

Brant gazed at the sharp contours on her wrinkled face as she propped a hip against the chair across from him. Was that pain in her smile?

"Gunther didn't love me like a wife. For a long time I thought it was because of my past. It's hard to respect an ex-breeding cow for Nazi officers."

Brant clenched his jaw. These were things he had no desire to hear. He sought words but was left empty.

"I should have known the reason. It was her." Ingrid pointed at the envelope beside Brant's chair. "He never got over her. I knew them both when we were younger. I'll always remember how they looked at each other. I wanted him to look at me that way. But she had his heart, even in her death. He made his trek up that mountain to her grave at least once a year for their anniversary. We never once celebrated ours."

Brant watched Ingrid. What could he say to her? In all the years he'd known Gunther and Ingrid, she'd never spoken so openly to Brant. He was the little brat who she was glad only came to the neighboring cottage in the summer. She had called him that when her kitchen window had been shattered by a rock. Little did she know it had been her grandson, Richter, who had thrown the rock.

"We lived under the same roof all of these years, but we never shared each other's lives. So Gunther told you about her?"

"A little."

"What did he say? He never spoke of her after our marriage."

Brant hesitated. He didn't want to reveal too much, even such long-dead secrets. "Only that the Nazis got her. They were trying to escape Europe and had to separate. She got caught, went to Mauthausen, and was executed. I'm sure you know that."

"Yes. She came from a well-known family and was half Jewish. That's why the Nazis took her."

"He didn't tell me much." Brant averted his eyes and picked up Gunther's pipe from the desk beside him.

Ingrid didn't speak for several minutes. Her eyes pierced Brant with such intensity that he shifted self-consciously in the chair. Ingrid had always frightened him when he was a child, and some of that fear remained. While Gunther exuded warmth with his many rough hugs and slaps on the back, even in Ingrid's smiles there was a coldness. Though she had probably been a beautiful woman in her youth, there was a look in her eyes he'd never liked. Gunther had once told him that Ingrid had, like everyone else, been through hell during the war. But Ingrid hadn't been freed from the demons that trailed her path.

"If you knew more, you wouldn't tell me anyway. I know that." Ingrid rose. "If you could move everything into the attic, I'm going to store it all there until I decide whether to sell the cottage or keep it for summer use. With Gunther's health, he won't be back."

"Don't get rid of Gunther's things."

"I won't, Brant." Her voice sounded condescending. "But I'm going to get my use from this room. I've always loved the deck and French doors and thought it a waste to be a smoke-filled study. I may make it a knitting or tea room. I'm staying in Munich over the winter, then I'll decide. How long until you'll have his things boxed up?"

Brant stood. It took everything in him to bite his tongue. And Ingrid wondered why Gunther could never love her? "I'll have everything moved this weekend."

Brant didn't enjoy the idea of packing up this room. But, after all, he was closest to Gunther. Ingrid had called him in Salzburg every week for the past month to remind him that the job was his. Brant didn't want anyone else going through Gunther's books and papers, yet he still avoided the duty until Ingrid threatened to call the movers and ship everything away. He wished the room could remain forever. The idea of Ingrid turning it into some flowery tea room churned his stomach. No, he wouldn't return to this house of so many boyhood memories. He'd probably even sell or rent out his cottage next door.

"I have dinner waiting for you. It's probably cold now."

"You didn't have to. I brought some food to my house." Brant didn't relish the thought of spending dinner alone with Ingrid.

"No, you can eat here. I'm making you do this work. Richter should arrive soon. I asked him to come for the weekend."

Brant kept his expression the same, for he could see Ingrid was looking for a reaction. He wondered why she'd invited her grandson to Gosau. Richter and Brant had always disliked one another. Ingrid's grandson stayed with Gunther and Ingrid many of the same summers Brant and his mother stayed in the house next door. Brant knew Richter resented the close relationship between Gunther and himself. Ingrid had to know the boys, now men, had never gotten along.

She was up to something. He sensed it. Did she suspect he

knew more about Gunther's secrets? Brant knew only a little information. Gunther kept the most important details to himself. But Ingrid didn't know how much he knew. If Ingrid suspected anything, perhaps she'd invited Richter to keep an eye on him. Yet why not go through Gunther's things herself instead of insisting he do it? There were too many questions and too many suspicions.

"I made that recipe your mother gave me." Ingrid's eyes searched his thoughts. "Fried chicken, isn't it? An American dish for you."

Brant wondered about her thoughtfulness in fixing a meal from his birthplace. Was this Ingrid's peace offering?

"Thank you, I'll be right there," Brant called as Ingrid headed toward the kitchen. He picked up the manila envelope, walked to the bookcase, and placed the books back on the bottom shelf. It had been a surprise to find the envelope hidden behind this tall set of books. He decided to return it to its hiding place until he had more time to look through it. But when he felt the object at the bottom again, he couldn't resist a peek.

Just as he opened the top to look inside, Ingrid's voice sounded down the hall. "Are you coming?"

Brant shoved the envelope back into its hideaway. As he flipped off the light, he wondered if Ingrid already knew about the object and the envelope. The lovely features on the face of the woman in the picture returned to his thoughts. He hoped he was making the right decisions. He was determined to protect Gunther's secrets, even if he didn't fully know what those secrets were.

He'd have to be careful.

⊷≡◉⊂⊶

That is the mysterious safe? Darby thought as Fred Bishop, the family lawyer, set it on their dining room table. Any Wal-Mart or hardware store carried a similar kind of steel "fireproof home safe." Darby hadn't expected a wooden treasure chest with a rusty lock, but this seemed a bit too commercial for the secrets inside.

"Let's open it," she said, rubbing her hands together.

Fred Bishop and her mother looked at each other, then back to Darby.

"First, I'd like to go over a few things." Fred extracted a folder from his briefcase.

"Am I the only one in the dark about the contents?"

"Neither of us knows," her mother said. She carried three cups of coffee to the table.

"What do you know?"

"Patience, honey," Carole said with a laugh. "You act like it's Christmas Eve."

"No, this is worse." Darby sat at the table. *Why the wait?*

"First we'll talk about monetary assets." Fred shuffled through the papers. "We'll look at her life insurance policy and investments."

"Grandma had investments? She was afraid of banking systems."

"Yes, for what she considered her base money—money she wanted to hold on to, whether inside the house or in the safe. But she enjoyed a bit of investing with her 'extra money,' as she called it. It wasn't much. But in fact, she made some good choices in her finances. For one, she invested in Microsoft. Always said she had a good feeling about that Bill Gates."

"What?" Darby and her mother said in unison.

"As in computers?" Carole asked.

"You have to be joking." Darby stared incredulously at the papers.

"Yes, computers, and no, I'm not joking. In fact, she sold those stocks several months ago and made a fifty-thousand-dollar profit even with the drop in stocks."

"What?" Carole and Darby said again in unison.

"She was one sharp cookie, ladies."

"You didn't know this?" Darby asked her mother.

"I knew she played around with stocks and invested a bit. When she bought her computer, I never even learned how to turn it on. But she was on it all the time. Well, you knew that—she e-mailed you constantly. But I never expected this."

"She never mentioned a word of it to me, either."

"I think she wanted to surprise you both." Fred took a sip of his coffee.

"She succeeded." Darby shook her head. Grandma Celia investing in Microsoft? The woman never ceased to amaze her.

"Now, her life insurance was not particularly high. She always did fear the companies would fail, especially in the new millennium, so she had a medium coverage, also of fifty thousand. But since she paid for her own funeral expenses, this is a nice sum also."

"Grandma knew how to prepare," Darby said. She imagined her grandmother making all these plans and provisions for her family, knowing they'd be sitting here with Fred someday soon.

"Now, your mother gets the house, of course, and twenty-five thousand cash. Darby, you and Maureen were given several heirlooms that are detailed on page 18. And Maureen will also receive twenty-five thousand. But the rest of the money, as your mother already knows, goes to you, Darby."

"To me? Why?"

"That's what Celia wanted."

"But that's, what, fifty thousand?"

"Yes, it is."

"I don't understand. Why didn't she give me the same as Maureen?"

"I think there are several reasons," Fred replied. "First, your grandmother told me she was asking you to accomplish a task she was unable to complete. Perhaps because of that, she felt she owed you some help. Those are my words; Celia really didn't specify why. But she also knew that both your mother and Maureen are already taken care of."

"Did Grandma tell you what she asked of me?"

"No." The lawyer settled back in the chair and adjusted his tie. Fred seemed ageless to Darby. The patch of gray in his sideburns had grown larger and his stomach now filled out his dark suit jacket more fully, but other than that, he was the same Fred she'd always known. "Your grandmother wanted the details of her request kept private until she could speak to you. However, she was concerned about any hard feelings arising with the money. I wanted some precautions against family lawsuits—I've seen that happen quite often. So your grandmother and mother discussed this, and your sister has a letter of explanation."

"Honey, I also don't know what Grandma asked of you," Carole said. "But whatever it is, you don't have to do it. I respect your grandmother's wishes, but she's gone now. I don't like the idea of you digging up the past when you have your own life to lead. Don't feel pressured to put your life on hold to figure out what happened a long time ago, especially now with this financial backing. You can go back to Redding, put the extra money into your studio, and there'll be nothing tying you down. Grandma would understand if that's what you choose."

Darby nodded. She couldn't help but consider what that kind of money could do for the studio. She could pay her half of the business off and buy new equipment. But she'd made a promise to her grandmother.

"I agree with Carole." Fred closed his folder. "There are no stipulations with this money. Your grandmother knew your mother has sufficient retirement and her real-estate investments. Maureen, John, and the twins will receive some stock she still has invested. So accept this as a gift, free and clear."

"I'll think it over."

"Can you tell us what Grandma asked of you?" Carole queried.

"To be honest, I'm not exactly sure. I hope there's something inside the safe to tell me. She told me about Tatianna, her best friend, and that Tatianna needed her name. She asked me to give Tatianna her name—but I have no idea what that means."

Fred looked at her strangely. "Really? That's not at all what I suspected. I assumed your grandmother wanted you to take up the search for the Lange family inheritance."

"Tatianna?" Carole queried. "That's the person Mother's been calling for during her bad spells. I too thought she wanted you to search for the lost heirlooms."

"The Lange heirlooms were real?" Darby asked.

Fred shrugged. "I have no idea. Celia's been on a crusade to find them, especially in the last year. I think she's written to every organization on the planet."

Darby remembered the letter from Brant Collins of the Austrian Holocaust Survivors' Organization that she'd kept from everyone. "I know, but she didn't ask me to continue that search. We had little time to talk before she passed away. Perhaps that was part of what she wanted and never asked."

"Did Grandma tell you who Tatianna was?"

"No. She gave me no last name or any information—only that she was Grandma's best friend. I hope the safe will have more information."

"Whatever we find inside," Carole said, putting a hand on Darby's, "as I said earlier, you need to live for today, honey. Don't get too wrapped up in yesterday that you miss out on that."

"Can we please open the safe? The suspense is killing me."

"Certainly." Fred closed the folder.

"I have the keys." Carole went to a desk drawer and took out two keys on a wire ring. "Here you go."

Darby moved the safe over in front of her. It was heavier than it appeared. The key turned, and the lid opened easily. She peered inside and carefully removed papers and folders, lining them up on the table. Fred and Carole drew their chairs closer.

Darby took a rubber band from a pack of envelopes. The postmarks were from the late forties and early fifties—addressed to different people. One was addressed to Tatianna Hoffman.

"Now we know her last name." Darby opened it. "Anyone know German?"

"Your Uncle Marc does, but he won't be here until Christmas." Carole reached for the letter. "I'm shocked Grandma would write something in her forbidden native tongue."

"It's written November 1945, perhaps before her vow?" Darby pointed to the date at the top. She examined the words that might hold all the answers she sought. "I think we need to find someone who can translate for us."

"What else is there?" Fred asked. "Oh, I guess this isn't any of my business and I should be going."

"You can stay—please do." Carole lifted his coffee cup. "I'll fill you back up."

"I have been staring at that safe with curiosity about killing me. If you both don't mind?"

"Not at all," Darby said. She handed him a pile of papers wrapped in a plastic bag. "We'll put you to work."

"Thanks. This does feel like Christmas Eve." And Celia was Santa Claus.

Darby flipped through several photographs. She didn't recognize the faces, and nothing was written on their backs. The documents she found also were written in German.

"What is this?" Darby moved around the table beside Fred.

Carole returned with a coffee filter in hand and looked over their shoulders.

"It looks like travel documents—a passport would be my guess."

"Look at the name." Darby pointed to a line on top. "These are Tatianna Hoffman's documents."

"The issuing date says 1939."

"So this is Tatianna." Darby studied the black-and-white passport photo of the young woman. By her birthdate and the 1939 stamp, Darby knew the girl was about nineteen at the time. She was pretty with dark eyes and hair. There was no smile on her face, but humor glinted on the edges of her lips and within her eyes. Darby had seen that expression a dozen times when she'd taken a serious photo of a client and someone beyond the camera was trying to make the person laugh.

Carole bent in close. "Why would my mother have this person's passport?"

"I don't know." Fred stroked his chin in thought. "Unless they came to the United States together. Perhaps some of these other papers will tell us that. Darby, here's a letter addressed to you."

Darby set down the passport of Tatianna Hoffman.

The letter wasn't weathered by time like the other papers. Darby carefully opened the envelope, read it to herself, then aloud.

> *My dearest Darby,*
> *I have given you a lifetime of stories and words I'm tempted to repeat, for I know these are my last words to you. The rest are already in your memory. But you don't need a Sunday school lesson, and I'm far from perfect enough to give you a life map to follow. God has his own course for you. But my many prayers for my Darby-girl have helped with the boldness I'm about to express. I know I'm asking a lot of you. But sometimes the past cannot be buried. Sometimes the past must be put to rest for the future to be clear. I*

cannot tell you for certain what you must do; you must decide. There is so much right beyond my vision that I do not know. But I feel one thing so strongly, and so this I ask. Go to Austria.

I can see your shocked expression. I can really see your mother's. Yes, Darby, go to Austria. I send you on a mission. What I hope I was able to ask before I died was that you give my closest friend, Tatianna Hoffman, her name back. That will make no sense until you get there. Then you will know. Also, if in your search you discover our family heirlooms, guard them well. Many have died because of them. I hoped to retrieve them myself, but I cannot ask you to take up that search, for I do not know the danger behind such an endeavor. But Tatianna deserves what I ask you to return to her—her name. Yet in all of this, I know you are going for more than the quest I send you on. I feel so deeply that God has something for you there. He wants you to find him again.

Take your time. Discover who you are. My heart goes on this journey. A journey we should all make.

Forever,
Celia Rachel Lange Müller

Darby set the letter on the table.

"Whew." Fred was the first to speak. "Celia is full of surprises today."

Carole sat at the table with the coffee filter still in her hand.

"It looks like I'm going to Austria," Darby said. Her mother didn't look her way.

CHAPTER SIX

We have a problem." Richter stretched back against the chair and put his feet on the table. He exhaled a stream of cigarette smoke into the night sky.

Ingrid wrapped her sweater tighter and half sat on the porch railing.

"We waited too long with the old man," Richter said.

"There's still Brant." She turned toward him. "I know Gunther told him something. We need to find out exactly what that is."

"And how do you suppose we'll find anything out?"

"We'll watch for an opportunity."

"Waiting gets us nowhere, and I'm not a man of patience. We need action."

"No, we must wait. Then we act."

"What if Brant doesn't know anything?"

"Brant may not be our last chance."

Richter's feet hit the ground as he faced Ingrid. "Another person who knows something?"

"Perhaps. Be patient. We'll know what to do soon enough."

⊹⇒◎⊂⇒⊹

"I'm leaving, on a jet plane."

The tune hummed from Darby's lips as she rolled her clothing into neat stacks and put them into her suitcase. As a child, she'd mapped her path through the Alps from Vienna to Switzerland. As an adult, she'd long since put the map away and left the dreams behind. Reality didn't leave room for fairy tales. But the plane tickets, round-trip with three weeks between arrival and departure dates, were proof that Darby was at last going to Austria.

She carried her luggage toward the front door, pausing by Grandma's room. Neither she nor her mother was ready to start boxing things up—it could wait. They had made the bed with Grandma's white embroidered bedspread and dusted the dresser with its perfume bottles and jewelry boxes. Everything appeared normal, as if Grandma Celia had simply gone to the store or was in the backyard with her flowers. Darby hated the images that told her differently—the headstone that had arrived and the newspaper obituary on the refrigerator, the one with its possibly wrong birthplace.

When Carole had set the safe key on the kitchen table a few weeks before, Darby had been sure the shadows she felt every night would finally be vanquished by truth. But that didn't happen. The documents, papers, and photographs only resurrected greater secrets. And with them came two paths—bury the past and concentrate on the present, or seek the answers from yesterday.

When faced with this decision at different stages of her childhood, Darby had turned away from the past. She had her own life of volleyball tryouts, new makeup, hairstyles, "What are we doing this weekend?," and "What do you want to do when you grow up?" Only once did Darby look toward the questions that sometimes arose.

She'd watched the TV mini-series, *War and Remembrance*, on her bedroom television. Before Darby's eyes, the beautiful character Natalie, played by Jane Seymour, was reduced to a starving animal with fear alive in her eyes. Natalie endured a concentration camp. Darby knew that word. Part of her family had died in places like the one shown on the screen. Finally she asked her mother about it. But Carole was angry she'd stayed up late for the entire week, even grounding Darby from her bedroom television—that act alone showed something more in her mother's anger. Darby was rarely grounded and never from the TV. Grandma Celia took her aside and told her it was good she now understood what family members had endured, but they would not speak of it again. Only the Austria of Grandma Celia's childhood was told. The good, adventurous stories, not the terrifying ones that marched in time with Nazi boots. And so Darby discarded her questions, her curiosity abated. Something terrible had happened, but she didn't want to know, didn't need to know. She wasn't any different than her friends. Tammy Dodd's dad had fought in Vietnam. Michelle Ingalls had a grandpa who died in Korea.

In high school, Darby had received a *C-* on the Holocaust unit of history, though she usually received *A*s and *B*s. She'd forged her mother's name on the report card and also performed her one and only act of skipping school the day her class watched a documentary with real footage of a concentration camp. Years later, when a friend invited her to watch *Schindler's List*, Darby had other plans. It wasn't exactly that she was avoiding the subject. But after the intense reaction from her mother and the silence of her grandmother over a television mini-series and simple questions, Darby had received the unconscious message that looking back was not good—until Grandma Celia's letter.

So she picked up her luggage and said good-bye to

Grandma's empty room. She was leaving on a jet plane. And though Darby knew she'd be back in three weeks, the next line in the song kept echoing through her thoughts: "Don't know when I'll be back again."

⋅⇒◯⇐⋅

San Francisco International Airport was like a city in itself. She had to carefully follow the right exits and get in the correct lanes without being run over by a shuttle bus or taxi. Her mother gave advice as they looked for a parking place close to the international terminal and Lufthansa Airlines.

Darby had been there a few times to pick up friends, but she preferred the smaller airports in Redding and Sacramento for any trips that required air travel. The farthest she'd gone was New Mexico for a photography conference and Montana to visit a friend. Darby suddenly wondered about her old friend Tristie Grant in Columbia Falls, Montana. She'd received a nice sympathy card from the Grant family, and though distance in both miles and lifestyles had pulled their friendship apart, Darby knew she could always call her college friend and have a ready ear to listen. If only someone like Tristie was traveling with her, then perhaps the knot in her stomach wouldn't be growing so quickly.

Darby's mother listed everything to beware of as they entered the airport. Darby tried not to laugh as her mother handed her a list of "be carefuls."

"Mom, did you write my name on my socks and underwear too?"

"I should have," Carole said as they stopped at the baggage check-in.

"I can handle it from here. Thanks for coming down with me, Mom."

Carole hugged Darby. "Okay, this is it, then."

"I'll be fine. It's not like I've never traveled. I'll call when I get there."

Darby wanted to make a quick escape. Good-byes were hard enough without long hugs and her mother dabbing her eyes on a tissue.

"I'm praying for you and still trying to believe this is somehow the right thing. But I'm just going to leave now. Call me."

Darby hugged her mother one more time. "See you later, Mom."

As she left Carole behind, Darby began to feel the doubts growing. The last time she'd allowed any of her old Europe dreams was with her ex-boyfriend Derek Hunt. He was an avid cyclist and wanted them to ride across the countryside. They'd made plans, checked airfares, and studied maps, but it never happened. None of the dreams she'd had with him ever happened. Life became cameras, good lights and flashes, appointments, and faces on 8 x 10s. Now she'd volunteered to rip herself away from what had become familiar—even safe. Why was she doing this again?

The doubts turned to pricks of fear after she boarded the plane and stowed her luggage in the overhead bin. She was really doing this, really going to Austria. But it didn't feel like a magical and grand adventure. Suddenly Darby felt like she was clinging to the side of the swimming pool, and her fingers were being pried away. Would she sink or would she swim?

As the plane taxied away from familiar land, Darby wasn't quite sure.

CHAPTER SEVEN

I'm alone. *Alone, alone,* Darby's mind whispered as she followed a crowd of people toward the baggage area in Salzburg, Austria. For the first time, she understood being a stranger in a strange land. Sure, she took wealthy executives on backpacking expeditions, but that somehow seemed safer— back in the good old United States.

She paused in the smoky terminal, which bustled with noise and movement. She felt trapped, surrounded by people speaking different languages, and uncertain in a country she knew little about, beyond Grandma's alpine trails and the smell of the trees. Would she get lost in the airport or once she stepped outside? Where exactly was customs, and would they rifle through her belongings like in the movies? Had she forgotten anything?

Darby touched her passport in the front zipper pocket of her purse for the third time since they landed. The line around the luggage wheel was packed. Finally, her two black suitcases arrived, and she squeezed in to grab them. Along with her camera case, carry-on duffel, and purse, it was a job organizing and carting everything toward the next checkpoint. Darby's eyes burned, and suddenly she was thankful for California's strict no-smoking laws. The customs sign was the next stop, and she moved to the Non-EU line for non-European citizens. She slid her passport to the young man behind a glass window.

"I'm sorry. Your passport is not valid," the customs officer stated.

"What?"

"You have not signed your name," he said with a large smile. He set a pen in front of her.

"Oh, sorry," she said, not finding his humor funny. She quickly signed her name and watched him stamp a blank page. Darby continued through, realizing she'd just survived her first customs.

People hurried around her, some toward families for excited reunions. Other people waited near walls, eyes searching the crowd, with names written on papers. She thought of the six thousand miles separating her from anyone who would race to enter her arms.

The Austria of Grandma Celia's romantic and adventurous stories was not the Austria she entered. Though she allowed little time to give it a fair chance, Darby felt a foreboding, down to her bones. *Get on the next flight to the United States, back to English and baseball and apple pie—back to home,* her mind said frantically. Why had she come in the first place? All her reasons were instantly blurred by the desire to go home.

Darby continued to follow lines of people and signs toward the airport exit. Rain poured upon the historic city of Salzburg. Taxis waited outside the airport doors, so Darby hopped into one and gave the driver the name of her hotel. Angry clouds and an annoying drizzle made it hard to see beyond the windows as the car shot from the parking space. But once she was in the taxi, she had no interest in the city except for surviving the ride. The cab lurched forward, then slammed on its brakes behind a truck, narrowly missing it, then jerked forward again. It reminded her of the New York cab stories, something she'd never cared to experience. The driver was friendly enough, greeting her with a hearty "*Grüß Gott.*" She wasn't sure what that meant but said it back anyway.

"Zee," he said, pointing to a tall church.

Darby barely glanced away from the road. The cabbie spoke what she thought was a history of the city, but his broken English was beyond her distinguishing except for a Mozart reference. She remembered that this cold, wet city had birthed the talent of the great musician, and probably every corner shop would have Mozart memorabilia as a marketing scheme to prove it.

"Here, your hotel." The cab came to a hard stop. He hopped outside and opened her door. "Eighty schilling, *bitte,* uh, please."

"Schillings?" How could she have been so stupid? Of course, she couldn't pay in United States dollars. She'd meant to change some currency at the airport, but with the bustle of customs and getting her luggage and finding the exit, she'd forgotten. "I'm so sorry, I don't have—"

The cabbie's expression changed, becoming thunderous.

"I have money, but it's American dollars."

"No, no American dollars," he said, his face stern. "Eighty schilling, or you has euros?"

"No, I don't have euros or schillings. Is there a bank or exchange or something?"

"There, you get schilling or euro." He pointed to what appeared to be an ATM machine at the end of the block. Darby hurried toward it, checking behind her to make sure her luggage didn't disappear from where the cabbie was stacking it at the doorway of the Salzburg Cozy Hotels International. The

green-and-yellow cubby was an ATM. An English version
helped, but how much should she get out? She punched in
three thousand schillings since cab fare was eighty. With a few
pushes of the button, Darby had Österreich schillings from her
United States bank, hoping she hadn't just drained her
account.

"*Danke,*" the cabbie said before hopping into the car and
speeding off.

Darby wiped a wet strand of hair from her eyes as she
picked up her bags on the hotel doorstep and walked inside. A
young woman dressed in the traditional Austrian *dirndl*
greeted her at the front desk. "*Grüß Gott.*"

"*Grüß Gott,*" Darby replied. "I have a reservation. My name
is Darby Evans."

"Yes, here you are. Breakfast is included, you know. Your
room is number 14." The woman smiled and handed Darby
the room key and some papers. "Payment is when you check
out, and please let us know if you need anything or if your
room is not to your approval."

"Thank you," Darby said, relieved that the woman's voice
reminded her of the soft German accent Grandma Celia had
tried to hide. It calmed her frazzled emotions—a little.

She balanced her luggage and peered around for a hallway
to the first-floor rooms. The simple yet elegant lobby was
connected to a restaurant and sitting room.

"You can take the lift to your room, if you like," the woman
continued.

Darby noticed the elevator, or "lift," the woman pointed
toward. Aware of the woman watching her, she thanked her
again and entered the elevator. The doors closed, and Darby
examined the buttons. When she pushed the 1 button, the
door opened without the lift moving. She was still in the
lobby. The woman saw her and smiled.

The doors closed again. Rechecking the room number on

the card, Darby guessed that the first floor must actually be what was considered second floor in the United States. As the elevator rose, Darby realized how much she'd been assuming during what should have been a simple journey from airport to hotel. Europe was much different from what she'd expected, in the littlest ways that made her feel uncomfortable and shaken. *If today has been a challenge, how will I ever get any information from this trip?*

Darby hauled her luggage up several marble stairs, its weight seeming to increase with every step. She found room 14, yes, on the second floor. The room in the old building was neat and simple. There was no flowery wallpaper or brass fixtures like the Cozy Hotels she had stayed at in the United States. It was low on fluff, but high on efficiency. A white down comforter lay folded sideways at the bottom of the bed atop crisp, white sheets. A small mint sat in the crease of an extremely fluffy-looking pillow. She dropped her belongings in the entry, locked the door, and flopped across the inviting bed. "Safe at last."

Streaks of dull sunshine filtered through the blinds as Darby's head sank into the down pillow. She hadn't slept on the plane. Too many thoughts had swirled inside her head. Every time her eyes closed, she'd thought of the enormous gravitational force pulling hard on the jumbo plane with the cold Atlantic waters waiting to swallow them up. She'd listened to every word of the flight attendant's instructions—even checking for that life preserver under her seat. The person next to her mocked her inexperience with his smile. But Darby figured she'd be the one laughing when he sank to the bottom of the Atlantic while she floated.

The ten-hour flight from San Francisco had felt longer than she had anticipated. The book of essays a friend gave her, *A Dose of Medicine for Travelers,* had quickly bored her. She had already received *A Dose of Medicine for Single Women* and *A*

Dose of Medicine for Photographers. There was only so much medicine a reader could take. Darby planned to read *The Lonely Planet Austria* guidebook she'd bought to be prepared for her arrival in Salzburg. But the international flight allowed only one carry-on bag, and she had accidentally checked in the bag with her in-case-your-luggage-gets-lost outfit and her travel guide.

Darby's next airplane mistake was the two cups of coffee she'd drunk, then regretted when four times she had to hobble over three people to go to the bathroom. Later, she'd attempted to sleep right when turbulence began to jar the plane nearly into pieces—though more experienced travelers continued to sip drinks and tap on laptops. Right then Darby connected with the ominous feeling that had lingered the entire day. She made a plane switch in London and finally arrived in Austria. The flights distanced both time and miles. She had flown into the next day. While home prepared for bed, Austria was grumbling for lunch.

"If you want to beat jet lag, you have to stay awake, stay awake!" Clarise, her business partner, had instructed. "Get on your current time schedule, no matter how tired you become. Get on their schedule, get your work done, and get back to the studio."

Clarise's reminder opened her eyes. She dragged herself from the embrace of the down pillow and comforter. Her shirt stuck to her back and felt like she'd worn it for a month. Her hands cried out against the millions of germs they carried— airport germs, taxi germs, doorknob germs.

She went to the blue-and-white-tiled bathroom and washed her hands. What had happened to her childhood hours dreaming of Europe—hours that took more time than adult hours, for they held her hopes along with her dreams? That little girl had planned to explore every nook and cranny. She'd rent a moped and putt around, because at ten years of age, the idea of a driver's license was more frightening than traveling to Europe. Grandma Celia's Austrian stories had coincided with Darby's first viewing of her favorite movie, *The Wizard of Oz*. Darby would change the few letters in her name to spell "Dorothy" as she imagined herself flying away to the magical land of Oz, the place somewhere over the rainbow where all her dreams would come true. Europe became that magical place with castles beside every alpine lake and kings and queens who would bow to her highness.

"You aren't in Kansas anymore, Dorothy," she told herself. With all the hubbub at the airport, the fright of getting to the hotel, and not being able to speak the language, Darby could almost believe this Oz was the habitation of the wicked witch—not of the west, but of the east.

She walked to the window and opened the shade. Beneath her, a muddy river flowed under a bridge and past tall church spires. The water's surface was pecked with raindrops. Up the mountain, the Hohensalzburg fortress stared at her as if she were an intruder invading the land. When would she be brave enough to venture beyond the hotel window? Not today. Weariness sank into her bones. Her shoulders ached from hauling her luggage from airport to hotel. A headache formed on the rim of her temples and moved outward. No matter what Clarise said about the jet-lag cure, she needed rest. After all, there were lions, tigers, bears, and witches to face in this land far from home.

⊷═◦═⊶

Brant unlocked his door and met the familiar musty scent of his third-story apartment. Late October brought a deeper cold to the corners of every room, forecasting the coming winter even earlier than the leaves on the surrounding mountains donned their autumn coats. Brant awoke each morning to stale

air and came home to it every night, even though he'd bought
plants that were now dead and several room deodorizers.
These mixed scents only made the smell worse. He promised
himself a year ago he'd look for a new place. But with most of
his life spent at the office, he hadn't taken the time.

Brant tossed his briefcase onto the leather couch and scoped
out the refrigerator. Nearly empty racks reminded him, as they
had every day that week, that he needed to go grocery shopping. He picked up the end of a salami stick and a lone apple,
smelled the cheese in deli wrap, left it there, and headed back
for the couch.

After a day of noise, the stillness of the apartment echoed in
his ears. Every other sound—the rumple of leather as he rested
his head, the hum of the furnace, the evening sounds of the
city behind the single-paned windows—intensified the
vacancy of the room. Usually Brant felt unnerved by silence.
He'd turn on the TV or some music. But tonight he needed the
quiet to think.

For three years now, he'd juggled double careers. His technology advisory company had helped at least thirty Austrian
companies make advancements into the age of technology,
enabling them to compete with dominant European markets.
And his work with the Austrian Holocaust Survivors' network
had helped numerous families, in many ways—except for the
Aldrich fiasco. His work was important, essential—wasn't it?
At the end of the October evening, nothing of his work felt
important, let alone essential. The financial world dipped up
and down, often crumbling even strong businesses. And the
Holocaust survivors—they were at the eve of an ending era. In
the near future, not one would remain alive to tell the story.
And Brant grieved that his work moved too slowly to help the
majority of them.

But tonight something else added to his musing. Richter and
Ingrid. Since Brant had spent the weekend boxing up Gunther's

things a month earlier, Richter had decided they were now friends. He came down from Munich to Salzburg nearly every week and invited Brant to lunch or a soccer game. It felt obvious to Brant that nothing had changed between them, no sudden bonding had occurred. He didn't feel Richter liked him any more than before, so why the continued charade? Brant suspected the two were up to something—yet since the Aldrich fraud perhaps he'd become too suspicious. He'd keep his eyes open until this all blew over. Then maybe he'd get back to normal life—whatever that was or whatever that needed to become.

Brant tossed the heel of the salami onto the coffee table. What kind of a dinner was that? He rarely had a home-cooked meal or much social contact. Perhaps that was it. When he had first arrived in Salzburg, he'd dated, attended social events, and been considered one of the most sought-after bachelors in the area. But then he'd dived into work, way too deep.

"You need to find yourself a good wife," Gunther had told him on his last visit to Brant's apartment. His old friend had looked into the refrigerator, shaking his head. "Yes, a good wife will keep your belly filled with warm food and your nights with warm love." The older man had winked slyly.

Brant would have loved to hear Gunther say those words tonight. He'd love to have an ear to help him wade through all the things bothering him. But the night Gunther had told him to "find yourself a good wife," Brant hadn't been amused. It had been an especially stressful day with the death of Avia Gerstein weighing heavily upon him. Her only wish, to receive her father's Swiss bank funds, would never be granted. They had worked hard, but time had worked harder against them.

"You say I should marry and what, then be as happy as you?" Brant had immediately regretted his harsh words. Gunther didn't respond; he simply closed the refrigerator and turned toward him.

"Gunther, I didn't mean to make such a judgment. I'm sorry."

"Oh, but you speak what you perceive to be truth. That can be a good quality at times, but honesty tempered with grace is a greater quality."

"I know."

"Do you? And yet, you speak of my marriage to Ingrid. But after all these years, Ingrid isn't my true wife. I was married once and will be married to her until I die. I did Ingrid a favor because we were friends at one time. And in grief and for her, I spoke vows I have done my best to follow. But she has never been my true wife."

Brant stood, speechless.

"I am not sorry. I was granted more love in a short time than many people have in a lifetime—and that is a gift."

Brant shook his head. Gunther held no anger or bitterness, even though all he had left of his wife was a grave on a mountainside.

Gunther always seemed to read his mind. "Listen to me. You fill your life with work—worthy work, don't get me wrong. Much has been accomplished for survivors due to your dedication. And Austria will be a stronger nation as it enters a new age. You are taking our country there. But though this work is worthy, don't forget to live. Cherish each day as a blessing, no matter what God opens or closes in your life. People want to thank God for the good days, then accuse him for the bad. Everything in life is for a reason, to fulfill a purpose, even when it's beyond what our mortal eyes can see. But you need to live, to breathe, to love, even when it hurts and causes pain. But to have love for a moment is greater than never to have it at all. So don't forget to live, to breathe, to love."

Those words haunted him tonight. He was supposed to be figuring out what Richter was up to, or at least consider what to do with his careers. Perhaps he needed to choose between his dual roles. Either he could keep the lower paying and highly stressful job of helping Holocaust survivors reclaim their heritage and record their stories, stories that would soon be lost as the survivor list dwindled. Or he could resign from his CEO position at the Austrian firm that helped the emerging country compete in the age of computer chips and megahertz.

Tonight Brant wished more than anything to have his old friend sitting beside him. He missed the man who'd helped with every major decision since his mother's death when he was in high school. He missed the one person he loved the most, the person who loved him the most. Instead, Brant heard Gunther's words again: "Don't forget to live, to breathe, to love."

The problem was, Brant had forgotten. And he couldn't remember how to get another chance.

CHAPTER EIGHT

Darby awoke to darkness and reached to turn the clock face toward her. It took until her hand grasped for the lamp to remember she wasn't in her Redding apartment or in her grandmother's home, but in a Cozy Hotel International in Salzburg, Austria.

It was midnight, and her body was refreshed and ready to go. The streetlight outside shone foggily through the closed blinds, and Darby heard the occasional slush and fade of a car on wet roads. She dug into her purse for the pack of airline pretzels. The salty snack did little to placate her stomach.

After a hot shower, she sat on the bed in an oversized T-shirt and flipped through the TV channels. At last something resembled home, a *Magnum, P.I.* rerun. But then handsome Tom Selleck was oddly matched with a German-speaking voice. She continued through the round of channels, then returned to the German *Magnum, P.I.*

She still wasn't sleepy and finally picked up the telephone. It took several tries to use her calling card with the international access code before she finally got her mother.

"I'm here!" Darby said in a cheerful voice that sounded strange in the quiet of the night.

"Darby! I was just thinking about you. It must be late over there."

"Actually, it's early. 12:30 A.M. I wanted you to know I arrived safely." She noticed a slight delay between their voices.

"I've watched for airline crashes or terrorist activity. So what do you think?"

"About airline crashes and terrorists? I don't like them at all."

"All right, smarty-pants." Carole chuckled. "I meant, what do you think of our family's homeland?"

"It was raining when I arrived and I haven't ventured out, so not much to tell. I'll have many stories soon enough and a ton of postcards."

"I'll look for them. But don't talk too long—I'm sure these are expensive calls. Just please be careful. There are men who prey on young women, you know."

"How was today—or the last few days? With the time change I'm confused as to how long ago I left you." Darby tried to sidetrack her mom from her fears.

"It was just yesterday, though it seems longer. But I'm fine, thank you. Maureen checked on me and the pastor called too. I somehow volunteered to get more involved at the church, which actually sounds nice. I may even start working on Grandma's room this week. But with you so far away, that's keeping my mind busy enough."

"It's only a place, Mom, like L.A. or New York. Well, those are bad examples because Salzburg is small for a city—only 144,000 people. It's not all that far from home, really, just a hop in the plane. And I read tonight that the greeting here, 'Grüß Gott,' means 'Greet God.' So I'm safe in a country like that."

The line was silent for a moment. "I just don't like my girl there all alone. If you weren't an adult, I would have grounded you home."

"I'll be back, I promise. Clarise only gave me three weeks to return to the studio or she'll be completely bald from pulling her hair out."

"That Clarise needs to take a chill pill."

"Agreed." Darby paused, feeling so very, very far from her mother. "I wanted to say, I'm sorry, Mom."

"For what?"

"I never asked about your father and never even thought to wonder about him. Grandma told me a little before she died, but I'm sure it was hard having a hero father you never met."

"He was always a legend." Then, after a slight hesitation, Carole continued, "Now your bill is really getting high. Be sure to check in every four or five days, so I know you're okay. And call collect next time."

"I'll call."

"Take extra precautions. I heard that train stations can be dangerous if you act like an inexperienced traveler."

"Me, an inexperienced traveler?" Darby bit her lip to keep from laughing. She sat on the bed and bunched up a pillow behind her neck. "Any other travel tips?"

"Keep your wallet deep inside your purse or in the inside pocket of your jacket. Don't walk alone after dark—"

"I was kidding, Mom."

"I know I'm overreacting, but you feel so far from me. I look at the globe and can't believe my daughter is way over there. And I'm reading too much of the newspaper with all the terrible things that are happening—terrorists, kidnappings, disappearances. I miss you already and wish Grandma would have left this alone and not involved you."

Darby smiled. How often had she heard her mother say this in hints or nuances since the day Carole gave her the key to the safe and Darby had decided to come here? Perhaps she should have backed out after all. Her mom wanted to leave the past buried probably because of her own years of relentlessly pursuing her father, finding only disappointment time and time again. But it was different for Darby. She was seeking answers for her grandmother, not trying to fill in the pieces of her own life.

"Here are my suggestions. Put the globe away and quit watching the news. I miss you too, and it won't be long until I'm home. Clarise will hunt me down if I don't return in a few weeks. And Mom, if you aren't ready to go through Grandma's things, wait till I get back."

"Thank you, honey. Remember I'm praying for you."

"Okay." There it was again—newly religious Mom.

They said their good-byes, and Darby hung up the phone. She snuggled down against the pillows, her eyes watching a fistfight between Magnum and the "bad guy." No matter how much she told her body to sleep, she was wide awake.

If she wasn't going to sleep, she could refine her strategy. Once Darby had decided to come to Austria, she'd been so busy preparing for the trip that she'd had little time to figure out what she'd do when she actually arrived. Clarise was her toughest obstacle. Her partner in the photography studio did not encourage her decision.

"You've missed three weeks because of your grandmother's illness. I understood that, of course, but why do you have to go to Austria now?"

"I'm trying to get there before winter settles in and I have to worry about storms and driving in the snow. Or I could wait till spring when we have our wedding assignments."

Clarise finally agreed, though not happily. Darby ignored her comments in the following weeks. After all, she never took vacations, while Clarise took time off every month to do things with her family. It seemed the unspoken rule that since Darby wasn't married and didn't have children, she naturally should work more than Clarise. She thought of mentioning this, but at the time she hadn't minded the extra hours. Darby dated sporadically, hadn't had a boyfriend in years since she and Derek had broken up, and she worked most weekends. So why not make the studio her life? But since Grandma Celia's death, Darby had been seeing things differently—and Clarise wasn't looking for change.

The weeks before the trip evaporated quickly with long hours at the studio and driving the four hours down to her mother's on her Monday and Tuesday days off. Now here she was in Austria with hardly a plan. Well, there was no time like the present, she decided.

She'd made copies of the documents from Grandma Celia's safe. She'd put one copy back in the safe at home, and another set was safely tucked into the inside pocket of her suitcase. The originals were carried at her side in a long, black purse. She'd almost left the originals at home, but many of the letters were still unopened, and she hoped to find an expert who could examine and translate them.

Grandma had said the safe would give her information. Instead, the contents brought more questions. Darby now knew what the coins and brooch looked like by documents she'd found. She had the engagement half of a ring, enough money to live abroad for a long time if necessary, and other documents that didn't make a lot of sense.

She parted the window shade and looked at the dark, deserted street below. Over the bridge, spotlights shone on the church spires and toward the white monster fortress on the mountain. How could she open and run a business and backpack into the wilderness, but feel so intimidated by foreign travel? People did it all the time. Grandma had escaped this country during the Nazi occupation, and she was alone, pregnant, and facing real danger. If Grandma could do that, then Darby could play tourist and ask a few questions in the process. But perhaps that was part of it. Sure, it was the Nazis who had sent her grandmother fleeing for her life to the States. But this was still the same country.

I came here to seek answers for Grandma Celia. I'm not giving up. This isn't some Third World country. Austria is developed and cultured with many English-speaking people.

She sighed and turned from the window. *Even if I don't know a soul for thousands of miles, I can do this.*

Darby spotted the letter she disliked the most—the letter from Brant Collins. He worked here in Salzburg, perhaps even slept somewhere nearby. He had accused her grandmother of being an imposter when the elderly woman lived thousands of miles away. It would be different now that Darby was here. Corporations easily shrugged off individuals as if they were wiping mud from their shoes. But she wasn't so quickly scraped away, not when it came to defending Grandma Celia. Yes, she could face Brant Collins. Darby awaited the chance. And in the process, perhaps, she'd find out why her grandmother had contacted him in the first place.

"Well, Mr. Brant Collins, you may write your letters to old women, but I'm not letting you get away with it."

CHAPTER NINE

Brant turned away from the computer screen. He'd spent the morning staring into the humming business world via e-mail and videophone that lived and breathed within the computer. After weeks of working with Österreich Forest Products, the company had entered the technological age with full capacity to compete with other European lumber companies. One more down, and only a few thousand Austrian companies to join the new millennium.

Brant stretched in front of the window. His shoulders felt tight though it was still morning. Sleep came hard for him these days. He looked toward Hohensalzburg, resting confidently above the city in a mass of gray clouds. The fortress had spent seven hundred years staring from the mountain. It reminded him that some things endured long past today. Such success gave him a slight hope for his own work.

"Herr Collins?" a voice crackled from the small speaker on his desk.

Brant turned in his leather chair toward his desk. "Yes, Frau Halder."

"You have a call from a woman named Darby Evans. And she speaks only English."

"What company does she work for?"

"No company—she says it's a personal matter."

"A personal matter?" Brant was stumped. He didn't know anyone by that name.

"She said it concerns a woman named Celia Müller."

Brant paused. "I'll take the call." Frowning, he waited a second before picking up the line. "This is Brant Collins. What's this about?"

"My name is Darby Evans."

"I know that already."

"Okay. Well, I'm calling because I received the letter you sent my grandmother, Celia Müller—"

"Celia Müller died over sixty years ago. I don't know what you want, but like I wrote to whoever that was—"

"What are you talking about? She didn't die sixty years ago!"

"Listen, I'm not playing games."

"Perhaps *you* could listen for a moment, Mr. Collins, without interrupting me."

"All right," Brant said, clearing his throat.

"Thank you. First of all, my grandmother never received the letter you wrote. I picked up the mail and never showed her because she was very ill at the time. But I have some things we need to discuss, and since I'm here in Salzburg—"

"You're in Salzburg?" Brant stood and turned again toward the window.

"May I finish, or are you going to interrupt every time I open my mouth?"

Brant didn't respond.

"I'd like to discuss this with you. In person."

His eyes felt drawn again to Hohensalzburg. The fortress had watched the comings and goings for hundreds of genera-tions—protecting, eyeing, always knowing. Brant remembered that the woman who claimed to be Celia Müller was trying to locate information on the Lange family inheritance. Gunther had told Brant little about it, but he knew the inheritance was worth millions—if someone found and claimed it. If he met with Darby Evans, perhaps he could find out what the two women wanted.

It was better to have an enemy below your gaze than out of view.

"When would you like to meet?"

⋆═◉═⋆

Darby pushed back from the small desk in her hotel room. Their appointment set and her notes in order, she was ready to face Brant Collins.

A gurgle rumbled through her stomach. At least one part of her was on schedule. Darby's eyes were bloodshot and finally she was tired, but at nine o'clock in the morning. The day had just begun, and she was ready for food and a long night's rest.

After a quick shower that helped wake her up, Darby hooked the electrical converter and blow dryer to the bath-room outlet in the slight fear she'd fry the hotel fuses or blow herself up. She sighed with relief when the dryer hummed alive. As she dressed in jeans and a long-sleeved shirt with the black scarf and boots Maureen had sent her, she remem-bered the note from her sister: *You'll look like a beautiful European in these. Remember, no tennis shoes or sweat suits—that's a dead giveaway you're an American tourist. Dress nicely.* Maureen and John had spent three weeks in France and Swit-zerland on their honeymoon. Her younger sister was the trendsetter of every new fashion so Darby listened to Maureen's advice, except for the faded jeans she couldn't live without. With hair semi-dry and makeup mostly on, she grabbed her purse and headed downstairs before breakfast was over.

She followed her nose to a cozy sitting room with a dining area at one end. It looked tidy in soft burgundy and white with perfect table settings, as if she were the only person who'd come to eat, ever. The food was just like home—pancakes and bacon, muffins, and whole-grain breads.

A woman entered wearing a neat Austrian *dirndl*. "*Guten Morgen. Wie geht's?*"

"Uh."

The woman waited.

"English?"

"Ah yes." She smiled. "I say good morning. How are you?"

"Oh. I am very good, and good morning to you."

She nodded. "Vould you like coffee or tea?"

"Coffee would be very nice. Thank you, or *danke*."

The woman nodded graciously and left the room. Darby picked up one of several different-sized plates from her table. She was probably doing everything wrong but was too hungry to care. The woman returned to set a cup of coffee on the small table, arrange some food on the buffet, then left once again.

Darby sat in the quiet of the white-plastered room and took a couple of bites of the whole-grain pancake. Then a thought struck her—*my curling iron*. Had she left it plugged in? She often did at home and would call her neighbor to check. In fact, the woman had her own key to Darby's apartment, it happened so often. The hotel brochure said the building was over five hundred years old, and it would be just her luck to burn the entire thing down.

Darby left her food, hoping it wouldn't disappear into perfect cleanliness before she returned, and hurried up the stairs. She put her hand on the door to unlock it. Instead, it pushed open.

Hadn't she locked her door? Yes, she was sure of it. She peered inside, but no one was there. She was tired—perhaps she hadn't locked it. Or perhaps the maid? Darby spotted her suitcase on the bed and knew something was wrong. She clearly remembered returning it to the wood cupboard.

The squeak of wheels made her pivot toward the hallway. A maid came from another room.

"Excuse me."

The woman looked up.

"Have you or anyone else been in my room?"

"*Nein. Kein Englisch.*"

"You don't speak English? No English?"

"*Nein.*"

Darby motioned to her room. "My door was open." She pointed to the door and opened and closed it. "Was someone in here? A person?" She tried to think of any German words or something from her high school French classes that might help. "A woman or man?"

"Ah. You *Mann*."

"My man? Oh, *Mann* means husband, right?"

"*Ja. Mann.* Husband." The woman grinned and nodded. "*Ja, you husband.*"

Darby stared at the woman. "But I don't have a husband."

The woman continued to grin. "You husband," she said and made a movement like she opened the door for someone, obviously Darby's husband.

"No. I don't have a husband. Me, no *Mann*."

The maid's smile disappeared.

"We need the manager. Your boss. Manager." Darby pointed toward the stairs until the short woman hurried away. She touched her purse, to reassure herself that the packet of original documents was present, then stepped toward her room. A shiver raced down her back. Perhaps the man was still there.

⋆⟶⟩⟨⟵⋆

Brant checked his watch. He'd kept his eyes down the approaching street for over twenty minutes now. Every time a woman walking alone approached, he expected it to be her. He could see her hotel down the street. Brant had chosen this café in the Old City as the meeting place. She couldn't get lost with only a block to walk. So why hadn't she arrived?

A woman stepped quickly along the narrow sidewalk toward the café. Brant stood up, but she didn't hesitate as she continued past. That was it. He wouldn't play these games. The woman had called him. His work at the office was piling higher every minute he sat here. Brant paid his bill, then decided he'd drop by her hotel to see if there had been a mistake or if, perhaps, there was no Darby Evans.

Brant pushed the lobby door open and headed to the front desk.

"Darby Evans's room, *bitte*."

The woman looked at him with a strange expression. "Are you the man who was here? Are you her husband?"

"No, I'm not her husband."

The woman stared over his shoulder. "Please wait here a moment."

"Is something wrong?"

"*Nein, nein.* Just wait here, please." The woman hurried around the desk and through the entry to the sitting room where Brant could see a group of people and one police officer standing together. The desk clerk approached and spoke to a dignified, older man from the group. Brant wondered what would call a police officer to the five-star hotel. A short, older woman was speaking to the officer in rapid German, but Brant was just out of range to understand exactly what was said. Another woman, probably in her late twenties or early thirties, stood with her arms crossed. Probably a maid caught snooping or stealing a patron's jewelry. Then the younger woman spoke to the officer, and Brant caught a few words in English. He took a curious step forward. The young woman had long, dark hair and appeared, from his profile view of her, to be unhappy about something. She wore jeans and a shirt that was a bit rumpled in the back.

Brant saw the desk clerk and the older man look his way. The man spoke to the policeman and the three of them walked toward him, leaving the young woman and maid behind.

"Is there a problem?" Brant said as they approached.

"You asked to see Fräulein Evans?"

"Yes. That must be her."

The young woman, obviously Darby Evans, came up behind them.

"It seems she's had some trouble today."

"Could you please speak English? Is this the man?" Darby asked the officer.

"I'm Brant Collins. You know, the guy you had an appointment with this morning."

She looked surprised. "I didn't forget. Someone broke into my room."

"That is not exactly certain," the man in the suit said quickly. Brant knew he must be the manager of the hotel.

"I think it's pretty certain. After I came down to breakfast, I returned to my room for a moment and found my door open. This woman said a man asked her to open the door—he'd lost his key. At least, that's what I think. He told her he was my husband, or he acted like my husband. I'm still unsure what she said about that either."

The hotel manager motioned for the maid and pointed to Brant. "Is this the man who was in the room?" he asked in German.

"What?" Brant said.

"*Nein, nein.*"

"Okay. You may go back to your work," the manager said to the maid.

"*Danke, danke.*"

"Yes, *danke*," Brant said and glared at Darby. "I get stood up for a business appointment and suddenly am a suspect in some woman's break-in."

"I apologize but must check all options," the manager said. "This does not happen at Salzburg Cozy Hotel."

"Well, it did," Darby said. "And where is that woman going? You aren't going to do anything?"

"Fräulein." The policeman spoke in slow, broken English. "Nothing missing from your room. We keep contact with you and hotel and see what happen."

Within a minute, the hotel manager said a quick apology and hurried to the front desk, where concerned patrons watched and questioned the desk clerk. The officer also left after giving Darby Evans a business card, an apology for her difficulties, and a promise to find out what had happened. She stared at the card after he left. A long strand of hair fell across her cheek. Darby pushed it behind her ear and looked up at Brant just as he wondered why he was still there.

"This wasn't exactly the meeting I had in mind," Darby said. "I'm sorry for making you wait."

Brant didn't like this either. He'd been prepared to find out what this woman wanted and who she really was. The woman in front of him was nothing like he had expected. Her soft brown eyes with the dark circles beneath them appeared tired from deep within. She bit the side of her thumbnail, then seemed to realize it and dropped her hands to her side. The woman took a breath and attempted a brave look, but she appeared near tears—God forbid that. How could he be shrewd and hard against her?

Brant had to look away from her eyes. "Why don't you call my office tomorrow and we'll reschedule?"

"Sure."

"Fine." He began to walk away, then turned back. Her gaze hadn't moved. Was she wondering what to do? Or was this all a ploy to get information from him? Brant hated that he was so suspicious, but lately it seemed he had to watch every strange occurrence. And Darby Evans was one of them. But the maid did say she had seen someone in the woman's room. "So what are you going to do now?"

She shook her head slightly. "I'm not sure."

"Perhaps you should go lie down or something." He knew as soon as he spoke that his words sounded uncaring, even condescending—more so than he had intended.

"Thanks. That should make everything better."

"What do you want me to say?"

"Nothing. This has nothing to do with you. I apologize for missing our appointment. I'll call your secretary tomorrow. I don't need or expect anything else, is that what you want me to say?"

"I just asked."

"Don't you understand, Mr. Collins? Someone broke into my room whether you, the police, or that manager believe so or not. And what a charming pleasure it's been meeting you. Everyone in this horrible country treats me like an idiot or a criminal. I know I closed my door. I'd know if I had a husband or boyfriend. I don't have one friend or acquaintance for six thousand miles—and I know it's that far because I checked my map last night! I keep asking myself what I'm doing here."

"That's what I'm wondering."

Darby stared at him, anger burning in her eyes. The rims turned red as tears gathered.

"Oh no. Don't you dare cry."

She turned away. "Will you just leave? Forget I contacted

you. I'll find out what I'm looking for on my own." He heard a sniffle.

"You better not cry. I can't have a discussion with you if—"

"I am not crying." He caught the strain in her voice. She was crying, though fighting hard not to. "Just leave me alone, okay?"

"Listen. Just stop that. Why don't we go get something to eat and talk? I'll quit being a jerk, you can quit crying, and this will all work out fine."

"No thanks."

Just then the hotel manager stepped forward. "Fräulein Evans?"

Darby quickly wiped away her tears. The man glanced at Brant with an accusing expression.

"Yes?" she asked.

"I want to apologize. Our hotel has never experienced something like this before, and I promise you are safe here. I sincerely hope the person who entered your room did so mistakenly. We have many guests this week, so we are checking to see if we can find any additional information. We gave strict instructions to our housekeeping staff so this incident will not occur again. I sincerely hope you will continue your stay with us?"

Darby seemed to consider for a moment. "Yes, I suppose I will for now. Thank you, Herr . . ." She looked on his bronze nameplate. "Herr Braucher."

"*Danke*," the man said, relief spreading across his face. The onlookers were dispersing, and the manager was obviously happy to have his hotel back to working order.

Darby still looked uncertain as to what to do. On impulse, Brant took her arm and said, "Come on, let's get you out of here for a while. We'll get coffee or, or something."

Nearly before he realized it, they were walking out of the building.

CHAPTER TEN

Why had she agreed to come with Brant Collins? A stranger had entered her room and what had she done? Left the hotel with another stranger to go for coffee.

They walked without speaking, though Darby's thoughts wandered loudly through her mind. Had someone intentionally entered her room, or could it have been an accident like the hotel manager indicated? Nothing was missing. Her suitcase was open, but nothing had been moved. Darby had run straight for her camera case in the wardrobe, but not even a roll of film had been taken. Then she thought of the spare copies in the suitcase pocket—but they were there. The originals hadn't left her side. Perhaps the man believed her room was his, then realized his mistake when he opened Darby's suitcase and left. Yet despite her attempts to calm her thoughts with logic, she felt as unsettled as when she first felt the door open at her touch. The only person in Austria who knew she was here was Brant, and he had been at his office. Or had he? The maid had not recognized him. Was she now walking into a dangerous situation by leaving the hotel with him, or was this an opportunity to find some information for her grandmother's quest? As long as they stayed among other people, Darby would continue with him. If he led her away, she'd run and cry one of the few German words she knew: *Hilfe!* meaning "help."

"Your first time in Salzburg?"

Darby jumped at the sound of his voice. He was making small talk, she knew. And something in his voice betrayed that perhaps he was regretting his decision to invite her out of the hotel.

"Yes."

"So how much are you paying to stay there?"

"Excuse me?"

"No, let me guess, about eighteen hundred Austrian schillings, or did you use euros?"

"I figured it out to be about one hundred and fifty United States dollars."

"Yeah, that's close to what I said. Figures."

"What do you mean by that?"

"Inexperienced travelers can be so gullible."

"I'm not gullible." She didn't mention the inexperienced part, but her unmistakable blush told all. "I paid exactly what it says in my travel brochure—they didn't raise the prices for me."

"Don't you realize this is off-season, between summer and winter peak? And now after the break-in, I bet I could get them to drop forty dollars a night."

"No, thank you. After today, I'd rather leave well enough alone." Darby glanced at Brant from the corner of her eye. Who did this guy think he was?

"If you want the Austrian experience, stay in an Austrian hotel, *Gasthaus,* or *Pension.* You'll pay maybe three times less a night. Or look for a sign that says *Zimmer frei.*"

"A what?"

"There are many varieties. Most often the owner of a private home rents out a room or two for a little extra cash. Almost all include breakfast, an Austrian breakfast. Some include dinner. What did you have this morning—American pancakes?"

Darby didn't answer.

"Why travelers stay in a clone of the country they came from I'll never understand."

Darby wanted to hit him. And this man had actually made her cry, something she very rarely did, and never in public.

A drop of rain hit her on the head. Darby had left her umbrella in her room. More drops began to fall on the newly dried sidewalks.

"Take my umbrella."

Up to then, she hadn't noticed he carried an umbrella and satchel. He extended the umbrella.

"I'm fine." A drop hit her in the eye, and she blinked it away without looking at him.

They continued to walk another half block as the drops increased.

"Just take the umbrella." He opened it. "I insist."

"No, thank you."

Brant stopped. "Look, I'm sorry about the hotel thing. I've been rude since I met you. But take the umbrella, will you? Please?"

Darby sized him up. His dark eyes did look apologetic. And she'd either accept his offering or soon be drenched. "Okay." She took the open umbrella and began walking.

"Thank you," they said in unison. Darby didn't look his way.

Pit, pat. As the rain increased against the umbrella roof, Darby noticed Brant's dark hair was getting wet.

"We could share it." She lifted one side as an invitation.

"I'm fine."

Stubborn man. He wiped a streak of rain from his cheek. The street was now slick with wetness as the rain pelted the ground.

Darby stopped. "Just get under the umbrella, okay? Please."

Brant's jaw clenched, then relaxed. "All right."

A couple passed, snuggled together under a shared umbrella. It made Darby feel all the more awkward as they both tried not to touch or get too close under one umbrella top.

"Where are we going?" she asked to break the silence.

"There's a restaurant I like another few blocks away. Very authentic Austrian."

"Sounds good," she said, trying to think of what else to ask or say. She'd forgotten the list of questions and comments she'd outlined in her room and nothing came to mind, or at least nothing that seemed appropriate beneath a shared umbrella.

After several blocks along the narrow cobblestone street, Darby realized she'd undertaken her first trip out of the hotel. Their footsteps echoed up the walls of the tall, straight buildings.

"Is this your first time in Austria or just Salzburg?"

"My first time in Europe, actually." *My first time outside the United States.*

"Well, this is Kaigasse. Several streets over you'll find Getreidegasse, a famous shopping street for many centuries. When you see *straße* at the end, like Franz-Josef-straße, that means Franz-Josef-Street. If the name ends with *gasse*, like this one, it means small street, often one-way since they're so narrow."

"Okay."

"I'm sounding like a tour guide." Brant shook his head and smiled slightly. The rain bounced harder on the black cloth above their heads.

The buildings opened to a square with cobblestone streets leading out from its corners. A large fountain bubbled at one end, and arched walkways led to another square on the other end. Darby tilted the umbrella to see the top of the church with its green domes. Raindrops hit their faces, and the points of the umbrella poked Brant's head.

"Oh, sorry. Maybe you should hold it since you're taller." She knew he didn't want to be under it with her, but it was raining harder.

"We're almost there," Brant said, taking the umbrella from her. "I've taken the roundabout direction so you can see the city."

A sign on a building read *Residenzplatz*. The fountain gushed water from horses' mouths and nostrils like bubbles of froth after a long, hard ride. Darby wondered about its history but didn't ask. She suddenly saw beyond her fears of being in a foreign country and her hotel troubles to the wonder of Old Salzburg. The clouds hung low against the towering Mönchsberg mountain, where the Old City nestled beneath the fortress's gaze.

"That's St. Peter's Church," Brant said. "It has a beautiful dome ceiling you'll have to see from the inside."

"I will." Darby felt drawn back in time. Salzburg certainly had charm with this old section ancient compared to her Californian heritage. It smelled of wet stone and breathed of age chiseled from hundreds of years of dreams, work, and sweat.

They had found a comfortable pace beneath the umbrella, and though she disliked this man for his hard letter to her grandmother, it felt good to have someone with her, to not be alone for an hour or so. She just wanted to walk in the rain with him, even if she struggled with the thought that she might be betraying Grandma Celia. But her grandmother always gave people the benefit of the doubt.

Brant had a look that told of his love for the city. Darby observed that he was good-looking in a quiet, withdrawn sort of way. Probably the kind to be careful of because you never really knew what he thought. She glanced down and didn't see a ring on his finger, which figured. He was probably controlling and domineering. She already knew he was stubborn. Soon she'd strike hard and get the answers she sought, but for now the rain on an umbrella and a little companionship lured her questions away.

They passed stone archways, a line of horses and carriages, and artists sitting with their Salzburg watercolors under the eaves of buildings. They arrived at a two-story restaurant that had white tables and chairs on the second-story balcony.

"We'll have to eat inside with this weather," Brant said. "This is Café Tomaselli, probably Salzburg's most famous restaurant."

Darby noticed the specials menu as they passed but didn't recognize anything. Her stomach reminded her that she'd missed her breakfast, and it wasn't happy at all.

"Have you eaten?"

"Almost, until the guy-in-my-room incident." The cheery dining room was warm, and inviting smells surrounded them.

"Hopefully it was a mistake." Brant walked to a corner table for two and pulled out her chair.

"I hope," she said, grateful that he was a gentleman.

"*Guten Morgen.*" The waitress handed them menus and spoke in rapid German.

"Would you like coffee and some breakfast?" Brant asked.

Darby suddenly wondered if this was supposed to be the meeting they'd missed. She had planned that encounter to be formal as she addressed his response to her questions. But right now, she was hungry and not prepared to interrogate her tour guide.

Her eyes scanned the menu on the table and recognized only one thing. "I'll take ham and eggs. And some hot chocolate sounds really good. Do they have that?"

Brant asked the waitress, who nodded and smiled. They

CINDY McCORMICK MARTINUSEN

spoke a little back and forth, and then the young waitress smiled only for Brant, glancing back at him as she walked away.

"What did you say to her?"

"Nothing. She made a reference to you as my breakfast date, and I told her it was business."

"Ah, I understand." Darby chuckled.

"What?"

"Nothing. I just wondered about her smile toward you, and that explains it."

"I missed something here."

"You say I'm a gullible traveler. You're a bit naïve, I'd say."

"I'm not naïve."

"She was flirting with you. Couldn't you see it?"

"No."

"Oh, here she comes."

The waitress set the cups of hot chocolate on the table. As she stepped back a handful of napkins fell at Brant's feet.

He picked them up for her, and the woman smiled widely. "*Danke.*"

"And so early in the morning," Darby said as the girl walked away with a blush on her face.

"What are you talking about? She dropped . . ."

"Exactly. Oh, so gullible."

"She needed assistance."

"Gullible."

"Okay, okay. You got me back. Can we call a truce now?"

Darby shook his outstretched hand and settled back in her chair. The bright room was cozy. Her eyes focused on Brant. He was handsome enough for a waitress to make an immediate pass at him, but Darby also measured him up as a rigid neat freak by the perfect crease in the collar, smooth wrinkle-free slacks, clean shave, and dark hair with only one place a bit messed up where she'd almost stabbed his head with the umbrella spike. His closets at home were probably as perfectly composed as he looked.

But who was she to judge on appearance when she must look a fright? Her hair had been only half dry and uncurled when they left the hotel and now felt limp and flat from the weather. Her eyes were likely bloodshot from so little sleep. What would Brant think he knew about her by today's appearance?

Darby knew she should be more concerned that she was facing Brant Collins—the man she'd planned to interrogate, stand strong against, press for answers. But the room was warm, food was on the way, and two hot cocoas in short, wide cups were on the table. Now the idea of her great concern over the stranger in her room seemed a bit foolish. Her paranoia over being in a foreign country had gotten the best of her. But at present she was away and able to look at it objectively.

Darby watched Brant take his first sip of the steaming cocoa. "I haven't had this in years," he said, wiping a drop of whipped cream from his upper lip. "Austria is a coffee country."

"You speak perfect English."

"I should. I was born in the States and have dual citizenship. My mother and I spent summers in Austria so it was my second home. Now it's my home."

"You're an American?"

"Yes. I was born in Portland, Oregon. My father was American, my mother Austrian. They compromised by living in the States except during summer."

"Portland is a beautiful city. I was there a few months ago at a photography conference."

"My father still lives there. We don't see each other as often as we'd like."

Darby thought of her own father, the man without a face. In the sparse memories she had of him, his face was never there.

"When did you settle in Europe?"

"I attended two years of university here in Salzburg, then decided to stay."

"And what about your mother—still in Portland with your father?"

"She died." Brant took a quick sip of cocoa.

"I'm sorry."

He met her eyes and for the slightest second Darby saw her own reflection.

"Ham and eggs for you." The waitress stood in front of them. They leaned back as she set the steaming platters in front of them. The eggs sizzled above a layer of ham on the hot plates.

"*Danke*," they replied in unison.

"Enjoy," the waitress said, looking only at Brant.

The eggs weren't completely done, but as Darby moved them around the sizzling platter they quickly cooked through. As they ate, she searched words for more small talk. She could mention the weather or ask about the sights in the area. Brant certainly liked the tour guide role. Then Darby recalled the last image of Grandma Celia, eyes closed, hands stilled in her coffin. Sure, Grandma gave people the benefit of the doubt, but could she so easily ignore the fact that this man she chatted so amiably with was the same person who had accused her grandmother of being an imposter? That was a pretty strong charge. Yet here she was chatting and eating ham and eggs with him. Darby couldn't eat the last bites.

"We were meeting to talk about my grandmother."

Something changed in Brant's expression as if he too suddenly realized their roles and the fact that they had crossed an invisible line. He crumpled the napkin in his hand.

"That's right. We've wandered from the intended topic." He glanced at his watch. "The lure of a Salzburger morning . . ."

"We can reschedule."

Brant seemed to reconsider. "No, this is fine. Let me just check my phone for a second." He reached into his black satchel beneath the table. Darby noticed his frown as he stood up. "My secretary called three times. Please excuse me for a minute."

"Of course." Darby watched him walk out of the restaurant. At least Brant wasn't the type to chat in a restaurant on his cell phone—that always annoyed her. She drank the last chocolate-rich sip in her coffee cup, then looked toward the doorway, wishing she'd insisted they reschedule. Darby could barely remember the questions she'd prepared and all at once felt like crawling back beneath the down comforter in her hotel. The cozy ambiance of the restaurant didn't blend well with the type of meeting she'd envisioned. Perhaps she'd meet him at his office the next day.

Brant returned moments later and sat back down.

"Is something wrong? If you need to go, I'd rather . . ."

"No. I have someone at my office waiting for me, but—well, it's someone I'd rather avoid. Let's talk about your grand-mother." He rubbed his chin, waiting.

Darby realized she needed to collect her thoughts, and quickly.

Brant leaned back in his chair. "We've taken a bizarre trip around our meeting. But let's get back to the subject. I assume you are here because your grandmother continues to claim to be Celia Müller."

Something in the way he said her grandmother's name and "continues to claim to be" stirred her anger.

"My grandmother *is* Celia Müller, or rather, she was."

"Was?"

"She passed away last month."

An expression flickered across Brant's face. His tense jaw relaxed as he stared down at his plate. Both were silent for a minute.

"What I'm wondering is why you don't believe my grandmother is Celia Müller, and why she wrote to you in the first place."

"She didn't write to me, in particular. She wrote to the Holocaust Survivors' Organization I work for. Our Salzburg office is not large. In fact, I run two businesses from the same office. Your grandmother wrote us last summer. I brought the letter with me for our meeting."

"You did?"

"I keep records of all correspondence, whether we believe the claim or not." He reached into the black satchel and pulled out an envelope. He looked at it once, then handed it to Darby.

The letter was basic and formal, and thankfully in English.

> *My name is Celia Rachel Lange Müller. My father and brother, Simon Lange and Warner Lange, and aunt, Milda Lange Bergmann, were taken by the Nazis and all sent to KZ Dachau and/or later KZ Mauthausen and Mauthausen/ Gusen, where they perished. I alone escaped Austria. I am writing in regard to a family inheritance that was lost during the Nazi occupation. It consists of two coins and a priceless sapphire brooch. I hoped that you could have possible information on how I can seek these items or what would be the next step in my search. I believe that the Nazis stole these items from my family after I escaped the country. Please call, fax, write, or e-mail me with any information you need or how I should proceed next.*
>
> *Thank you for your time and work. I eagerly look forward to your response.*
>
> *Sincerely,*
> *Celia Müller*

Darby read the "eagerly look forward to your response" twice. "That's a pretty basic letter. Your response was pretty harsh."

"I'm sorry, I don't recall."

"I have the letter with me." Darby opened her pack and handed Brant the letter. He read it, then handed it back with a frown on his face. "I imagine if this was to my grandmother, I would think the letter harsh. But you have to take it from our viewpoint. My organization helps Holocaust survivors. If you knew these people, saw their faces—you can only imagine the horror these people endured. It's a miracle anyone survived. But then after liberation, when they should have had freedom and time to rebuild their lives, they received instead another slap in the face. Their homes, property, assets were unavailable for redemption. For example, a bank account in Switzerland or a life insurance policy—the recipients were turned down because there were no death certificates for family members, no proof of their death. How do you prove or disprove that a relative died at a particular camp? We may have a record of them being sent, but did they arrive? Did they really die there? That's what makes our job difficult. So our organization and other groups try to help, but only in the last ten to twenty years. These people have been brutalized again and again and have come to the end of their lives. Groups such as ours try to offer them and their families hope—or at least a bit of closure before their deaths. So when someone attempts to cash in on that suffering, it provokes some anger. I did respond to your grandmother in this manner."

"I can understand your strong emotion toward fraudulent claims."

"And unfortunately, there are many."

"But what I don't understand is *why* you believe my grandmother is not Celia Müller."

"I look into each claim. And I know the town of Hallstatt quite well. That's where Celia Lange Müller was born."

Darby's thoughts went back to the day of the funeral and Maisie's insistence that Celia was born in Hallstatt, not Vienna as her papers said.

"My mother's summer home was in Gosau, just over the mountain from Hallstatt. I learned to scuba dive in Hallstattersee—Hallstatt Lake. It's not that big of a town. I check out all claims such as the one your grandmother sent. And the papers were very clear, unlike others I've dealt with. I had the birth record and found the death records at the camp she was sent to. Now I don't know you, Ms. Evans. You seem to genuinely believe your grandmother. But understand my position. I have a hard time believing anyone when I have hard facts stating otherwise."

"So what you're implying is that perhaps I'm an imposter also?"

"I didn't say that. But really, I'm not sure what to think about this. What I do know is, Celia Lange Müller died in 1941. She was born in Hallstatt and died at Mauthausen Concentration Camp."

"Mauthausen? You have information that Celia Müller died at Mauthausen? My grandmother told me we had family members who died there, like the letter said. It's a camp here in Austria, right?"

"Yes, it's near Linz. Mauthausen was the largest Austrian camp and ran the many satellite camps here."

"Maybe the records show another Lange, but not Celia. Or perhaps a relative with that same first name?"

"No. I'm certain."

"You can't be. I know who my grandmother was. I know she lived many years in Hallstatt, where her father was an archaeologist in the Celtic diggings there. She met and married a man named Gunther Müller."

Brant jerked his head up and stared hard at her.

"She escaped from Austria in late 1939."

"No," Brant said firmly. "Celia Müller died in 1941 at Mauthausen. I'm not saying that your grandmother was a bad person. Perhaps she really believed she was Celia Müller. The war did strange and horrible things to people's minds. In that era people didn't seek psychological help like practically half the world does now. I don't know about your grandmother, but I know for certain that Celia Müller died a long time ago."

Darby shook her head. Brant thought Grandma Celia was insane or mentally warped? But then, if she saw the facts on paper and didn't know her grandmother personally, perhaps she'd feel differently too. "Can I see these records?"

"My records are confidential. But you could try Hallstatt or Mauthausen. Many camps are establishing on-site records with victim lists."

Darby wondered how she could convince this man, and if she really needed to at all. She had her answers and understood his letter to her grandmother—she didn't need him to believe Grandma Celia. But she wanted him to, and she wanted him to believe her.

"You've come a long way for me to tell you that."

"It's not like that at all. I knew my grandmother. I know what she believed in and who she was. She wasn't a liar."

"So then, you'll take up your grandmother's cause to find the Lange family inheritance?"

"What do you know about the inheritance?"

"Nothing." Brant took a bite of his ham. "It was in your grandmother's letter. I know it adds to the motive of your grandmother seeking a claim that wasn't hers."

"Well, the Lange inheritance is the least of my concerns. I'm not here to get rich or find some items I'm not even sure existed. My grandmother had some last wishes. . . ." Darby wondered if she should mention Tatianna. Brant seemed to have his mind made up, but she decided to risk it, in case he'd know how to get information. "My grandmother had a friend. Her name was Tatianna Hoffman. I'm actually here searching for what happened to her—that was one of my grandmother's final requests. Grandma asked that I give Tatianna her name back."

Brant's eyebrows lowered as he leaned forward across the table. "What does that mean?"

She wished she hadn't said it, for the words sounded strange. Even she didn't understand. "It doesn't matter. I don't quite know yet. You are the first person I've sought because of the letter you sent her. But I didn't contact you to pursue the Lange inheritance."

"Tatianna Hoffman? Your grandmother sent you here, searching for this other woman, but she was also interested in the Lange inheritance?"

"And you find that suspicious."

"I find most everything suspicious. Unfortunately, in my profession I've become low on trust."

"That's too bad." Darby looked at his hands on the table. "I don't understand you. In all your work, you know how rumors and mistakes abounded during the war. Why is it completely out of the question that my grandmother could be Celia Müller? People thought to have escaped were killed and people believed to be killed actually escaped. I remember hearing that about the Anne Frank story. Neighbors and friends believed the Franks had escaped from the Nazis years before, while all the time they were hiding in their attic. How can you be so sure this didn't happen to my grandmother?"

"I'm well aware of the Anne Frank story. I know hundreds of stories as tragic as that one. But I have documents that prove Celia Müller died at Mauthausen Concentration Camp. I'm sure this isn't easy for you to accept. I can understand that. But, if you need proof . . ." Brant rested his head on his hand as if considering something. "Go to Hallstatt and look in the cemetery. Go to Mauthausen and see the ovens. Then you'll have your answers."

"You certainly think you know a lot about Celia Müller," Darby mumbled, more to herself than to him.

"It's my job. It's what I do." He crinkled the napkin into a smaller ball. "I looked up Celia Müller's information when your grandmother wrote." He paused for a long time, and Darby could see his mind working. "This friend of your grandmother's. Did you say Tatianna Hoffman? Have you ever considered that perhaps your grandmother is Tatianna?"

She stared at Brant. The idea should have angered her. But Brant's words were the spoken fear Darby had tried to reject every night since she'd found Tatianna's documents in the safe—while the records of her grandmother's immigration to the United States were not found.

Could Grandma Celia actually be Tatianna Hoffman?

CHAPTER ELEVEN

Where would you get the ridiculous idea that my grandmother could be Tatianna Hoffman?"

"For many reasons. It seems strange your grandmother, who has searched for the Lange inheritance, abandoned her search before she died, and instead asked you to give Tatianna her name back. Perhaps your grandmother spoke of herself."

"My grandmother was Celia Lange Müller."

"Darby, she wasn't. If you need further proof, go to Hallstatt. Go to the cemetery and see if that doesn't change your mind."

"What do you mean?"

"Just go see for yourself."

Darby was ready to leave. "I guess that's all I wanted to know. Perhaps, if you have time, you could look up Tatianna Hoffman's name in your accurate files and see if any information appears on her also."

"I'll do that—"

A man stopped in front of their table.

"Richter." Brant's voice didn't seem happy to see this man.
Richter raised one eyebrow. "*Guten Morgen.*"

"Speak English, Richter."

"Do we have an Englishwoman among us?"

"No, an American. I told Frau Halder I was in a meeting and
I'd catch up with you later."

Richter portrayed a mock expression of hurt. "Is this the
welcome I receive? You are a difficult man to track down, and
this doesn't exactly look like a meeting. More like pleasure."
He smiled at Darby, then spoke to Brant without taking his
gaze off her. "I get no introduction to your beautiful friend,
only accusations. I came into Salzburg to see you, have been
waiting for hours for this meeting to adjourn—but I now see
why it takes so long."

"What did you need?"

"It's not what I need, but what I give. I have two extra tickets to a ballet at the Landestheater and wanted to give them to
you. You work too hard and date too little. This is my gift to
give you a life back. Perhaps you and your American friend . . .
I still have yet to be introduced."

"Darby Evans, Richter Hauer."

She reached for Richter's extended hand. Both men were
handsome in completely different ways. Brant might not turn
heads at first glance, but Richter exuded a savvy charm that
was noticeable at once. He seemed confident, even extremely
conceited. He reminded her of a college classmate who liked to
use Rhett Butler lines while seeking the affections of Darby
and her friends, all at the same time.

"Nice to meet you." Darby noticed how Richter held her
hand longer than necessary, while evaluating her with hard,
gray eyes.

"So, an American." He added another chair to the table.
"The two of you are then perfect for a night together—two

Americans in Salzburg. What songs are written about. Or if Brant will not take you, perhaps I'll take you myself."

"I have not come to Salzburg to have songs written about me," Darby said insistently.

Seeming surprised, Richter replied, "Brant, this woman is not easily charmed. Good for you, but good luck also." He winked at Darby.

"Here are the tickets." He set them on the table. "I will leave the two of you alone. Brant, I'll catch up with you later. And Ms. Darby Evans, it has been a pleasure."

Both Brant and Darby watched Richter's departure.

"You don't like him, do you?" Darby said.

"I don't trust him." He studied Darby.

"You don't trust many people, do you, Mr. Collins?"

"A habit learned through experience, unfortunately. But I do apologize for Richter. He—there's no one quite like him." Brant looked at the tickets. "We don't have to go."

"Of course we wouldn't."

Darby insisted on paying the bill since she had the right currency and had originally initiated the appointment. But Brant paid the tip. Darby noted that he gave the extra money to the waitress instead of leaving it on the table like at home. That detail would come in handy for future dining.

The rain had stopped, though dark clouds continued to hang low over the city. Darby drew her coat tightly around her and tasted snow in the air as they stepped from the restaurant. She turned to say good-bye, hoping she could find her way back through the labyrinth of streets.

"I'll walk you back."

"It's not necessary."

"I don't mind. I won't allow a fellow American to get lost."

"It's not far."

"Really, allow me."

"If you insist."

Again silence walked with them. Darby didn't feel compelled to think of small talk. Instead, she listened to the sound of their footsteps on the pavement. Cyclists on old bikes with wire baskets jingled past. It was a favorite mode of transportation, she noticed. They passed a vendor selling something that tantalized the air with a warm, nutty smell.

"Have you tried *Maroni*?" Brant asked, stopping at the end of the line behind the vendor.

"No, what is it?"

"Roasted chestnuts."

"I've heard the Christmas song—'chestnuts roasting on an open fire.' " She chuckled, then felt foolish. "But no, I've never had them."

"You can't experience autumn in Salzburg without *Maroni*." He waited in line and bought a paper bag of the round, dark nuts. He offered Darby one, then showed her how to open the shell.

The meaty texture reminded Darby of the acorns she'd peeled and mashed as a child with the neighbor kids. She hesitated before taking a bite, remembering how she'd accepted the dare to try an acorn and immediately spit out the bitter nut to the laughter of her friends. She took a breath and popped the white meat into her mouth, determined not to spit it out, whatever it tasted like. To her surprise, the warm nut wasn't bitter, but had a subtle taste that somehow reminded her of autumn woods. "Wonderful."

"My favorite this time of year."

They walked, sharing the bag of chestnuts until they reached the Cozy Hotel. Darby noticed as they passed other hotels how Americanized this one appeared.

She stopped in front of the door. "Here we are. You didn't lose a fellow American."

"Good thing. I don't need anything more on my conscience." He smiled, a nice smile, but Darby wondered about the words. She almost asked what things bothered him—perhaps writing angry letters to old people?—but she held her tongue.

"I do know someone who may help you. A professor at the university, a short distance away. He may be a good source if you need more research."

"That would be great." Darby wrestled a pen and paper from her purse and handed them to Brant.

"His name is Professor Peter Voss, and here's his phone number." Brant handed her the paper. "And I'll check for a Tatianna Hoffman."

"Suddenly so helpful?" Darby grinned.

Brant examined her thoughtfully. "I do hope you find what you're searching for, and that the truth doesn't hurt too much."

Darby shook her head. He didn't understand and couldn't believe. If their roles were reversed, what would she believe? What did she believe now?

"We better just leave it at that so we don't start arguing." Brant smiled. "Good idea."

Darby extended her hand. "Good-bye, Mr. Collins."

"Can we forget the proper names?"

"Sure. Good-bye, Brant."

"Good-bye, Darby."

He held open the door as she walked in. At the stairwell, Darby looked back. He waved, then disappeared. She watched for a minute, then looked at the phone number and hurried upstairs. Brant could not be right. She hoped.

⋅→═◦═←⋅

Frau Halder had a stack of messages when Brant finally returned to the office. He had returned slowly, taking back streets and strolling along the river before arriving at the second-story office.

"You missed your friend," Frau Halder said as Brant arrived.

"What friend?" Brant picked up his messages. "Do you mean Richter?"

"Yes. He waited and waited. Such a nice young man he is."

Brant glanced at his secretary as he flipped through the messages. "Actually, I did see him."

"Really? I'm glad." She smiled. "You know, he thinks of you like a brother. The two of you should do more things together."

"Is that what he said?"

"Oh yes. We talked for quite a while. He worries about you, just like I do. We think you need to work less and have more fun." Frau Halder gave him her classic mother-hen look.

"When did Richter get here?" Brant asked.

"Right after you left. I told him you had an appointment, so he just sat down and chatted with me for a while. Then he got hungry and went to breakfast, even brought me back a pastry. Such a nice young man."

Brant wondered why Richter had come and gone and come again. Frau Halder was a kind woman, though not always the most astute. But she'd always been caring and concerned toward Brant. On his walk to the office, he had planned to make sure Frau Halder never revealed the location of another meeting to Richter again. But as he stood before her, Brant knew she had no idea she'd done that. He sighed and glanced through the mail basket.

"Thank you for covering while I was gone so long," Brant said.

"I'm going to lunch now, if you don't mind. I'm meeting my grandchildren at the park if the rain holds off."

"Tell the boys to call me, and we'll play soccer again."

"They've been practicing the moves you taught them. I'll tell them you're ready to play." Frau Halder went into the back room and returned with a lunch basket.

Brant watched her leave. How good it must feel to have

lunch with children. To not wonder about every person's motives. How freeing to simply live life. To meet a pretty woman and actually have romantic thoughts about her, instead of questioning who she was.

He closed the door of his office and thought about Darby. He found her interesting, intelligent, beautiful—especially when she tried her stubborn act. He almost laughed, remembering the expression on her face when she refused to use the umbrella of the enemy. She was too stubborn to even wipe the raindrop that hit her forehead. But she also could make him laugh, something Brant rarely did anymore. It felt good to be with Darby Evans, perhaps because she reminded him of the States—his other home. A few years ago, perhaps even six months ago, Brant might have pursued her. But now he felt rusty, not knowing what to say or how to act. And still, he battled the motives of every person around him—especially of someone who claimed to be the granddaughter of Celia Müller.

Brant set the messages on his desk. It would take the afternoon and evening to get back on schedule, but first he wrote down the name of Tatianna Hoffman. He promised he'd check. What Brant did know beyond a doubt was that Celia Lange Müller died long ago in Mauthausen Concentration Camp. Gunther hadn't spent sixty years mourning his wife for nothing.

Brant wondered how Darby would handle the truth about her grandmother. It had hurt him to discover the Aldrich deception, but the betrayal of a loved one would be even worse. He couldn't imagine the pain he was forcing Darby to face.

⋅⟶═◉═⟵⋅

Darby shut her door, locked it, and rested her head against the wall. She closed her eyes, then turned to look around the room, remembering that a stranger had been here. The stranger's fingerprints seemed to glow around the room.

She considered changing rooms, but would that help? Darby
went through her luggage and investigated her belongings
closely. Her hands felt dirty after touching her suitcase. Someone had picked up her black suitcase and unzipped it. How long
had he looked inside? What clothing had he touched? She organized her clothes and hygiene supplies and slowly began to
reclaim the room and her things as her own. The man had made
a mistake—there was absolutely no other explanation.

The white curtains swayed slightly from the window she'd
cracked open, and the cloudy sky outside brought a soft light
that drew her weariness deeper. Tired through every part of
her body, Darby wished to roll up in a ball beneath the down
comforter for a year or two until her strength returned. There
inside her feather womb she wouldn't feel the presence of a
stranger or hear the words that had haunted her since her
meeting with Brant: *Could Grandma Celia actually be Tatianna
Hoffman?*

Instead of the escape into sleep she desired, Darby forced
herself to focus on her strategy. Rest would not come with the
upset of her questions. She organized her information into
neat stacks on the desk: letters in one pile, information on the
Lange inheritance in another, photographs and miscellaneous
papers in another. Brant, her first contact, had yielded three
more leads: Professor Voss, Hallstatt, and Mauthausen. Darby
found Hallstatt on her Austria map and marked the highway
route, then continued it on to the Linz region in Upper Austria
near the Czech border. She'd rent a car and go there in a few
days, but first attempt a meeting with Professor Peter Voss.

As Darby made her list and plans, she noticed the Austrian
passport. The yellowed pages worked to form doubts in her
mind. Inside, the name said *Tatianna Hoffman*. Place of birth:
Vienna, Austria—the same city Grandma Celia's records indicated, though Maisie insisted all family members were born in
the village of Hallstatt. Though Darby had defended her grand-

mother to Brant, now her inklings of doubt turned to fear. A scenario grew. Tatianna Hoffman and Celia Müller were best friends when Tatianna escaped from Austria. She came to America, changed her name to Celia Müller since she knew her friend had been sent to a camp, then moved in with Uncle Marc and Aunt Helen, who'd never seen her or the real Celia before. Uncle Marc was Grandma Celia's brother, Darby's great-uncle, though only a few years older than Celia. He had moved to the United States when they were children, and though they wrote for years, the two never met until Celia's immigration. When her grandmother said Tatianna needed her name, perhaps she *was* speaking of herself as Brant suggested. Perhaps Darby's grandma couldn't admit the truth in life and wanted Darby to discover it. Maybe that was why Celia wrote in her letter how Darby's own future would change as she found the truth.

The more Darby thought of it, the more she believed in the possibility. Didn't everyone know how a small lie could wrap itself around an entire life? Could this have happened to Grandma Celia—or was it Grandma Tatianna?

Darby remembered decades of little moments with the woman she knew as Grandma Celia: Band-Aids, gardening lessons, bicycle races, marshmallow roastings, and late-night stories. Darby shook her head. If her grandmother's name wasn't Celia Müller, but Tatianna Hoffman, she was still the woman who loved Darby, and whom Darby loved back.

She put the passport in one of the piles and found a picture of her grandmother in the photograph pile. It had been taken when Maureen had the twins. Darby gazed at the face she knew so well. This woman was the truest, kindest, most sincere person Darby had ever met. This woman could not be a fraud or an imposter. That would shatter everything Darby believed in.

"I believe her. I believe she was Celia Rachel Lange Müller, just like she signed her name in her letter. She didn't sign simply 'Grandma.' Wouldn't she do that if she weren't really Celia?"

If her grandmother was Tatianna, Darby would confront it when she had solid proof. But no matter what name her grandmother went by, Darby knew who the woman had been.

CHAPTER TWELVE

T he streets of Salzburg drew Darby from her hotel that evening. After an afternoon nap, she'd made a quick call to Professor Peter Voss. He'd agreed to meet her at his university office the next day.

Hunger and curiosity alike escorted Darby along the city streets. The main roads bustled with taxis, electric buses, and cars as she made her way back into the heart of the Old City. Here only a few cars wound their way around pedestrians and cyclists with baskets on the front or back of creaky bikes. Darby noticed that both residents and tourists were drawn outside while the rain was held within the dark clouds above. Though most of the shops were closed, people were everywhere. They walked at leisurely paces—elderly couples, a group of teens, people of all ages and races. The outdoor cafés brimmed with lively customers who laughed, smoked, and ate platefuls of food that made Darby's mouth water. She walked past a musician playing his saxophone beneath a stone arch-way and an artist drawing a beautiful chalk mural on the sidewalk. She wound down cobblestone streets that opened into different squares, finding Getreidegasse, the famous shopping street Brant had told her about. There she looked up at one of the tall, flat-fronted buildings to see Mozart's birthplace. Her hands reached for her camera—her faithful manual Nikon— that usually hung around her neck. "Old Nikki" had gone on every trip Darby had taken since Grandma Celia and her mother had presented her with the gift for high school gradua- tion. Though she'd bought new equipment, her Nikki camera forever stayed her favorite. But so far on this trip, her camera had been safe in the tan case, well hidden in her room. For the first time in her adulthood, she was completely without it. So as she walked, Darby simply enjoyed what she saw instead of clicking away at it with her camera covering her eyes.

Darby continued down the skinny street, peering in the windows of perfume, shoe, and specialty shops. The buildings towered above and were connected in rows a block long. Ahead she could see the end where sheer rock rose above a church steeple. Darby bet she could have walked here hundreds of years ago and found the place exactly the same— until she spotted the golden arches of McDonald's. Her hunger drew her toward the quaint building that suddenly trans- formed into an American fast-food restaurant as she opened the door. Though it was fun paying sixty-three schillings for a meal, Darby felt a little guilty buying a Big Mac when she should instead try Austrian cuisine.

The street was still lined by late-night strollers when Darby found her way back to her hotel. The palm of the bed cradled her into a long, deep sleep without dreams or interruptions.

⊸⇒◯⇐⊷

Morning shone above the buildings and through the window coverings that Darby had forgotten to close. She awoke refreshed but wary about the day ahead—the day she'd meet another man who would most likely not believe her story. But Saturday lifted sunshine above the mountains onto a freshly cleaned city, a sign of better things, she hoped.

She pulled on a cream-colored wool sweater before leaving the hotel. Once outside, she discovered that Salzburg awakened early on the weekend. A family in traditional Austrian attire pedaled past on squeaky bikes as she wandered the damp streets. An intense blue sky grew brighter as the sun awakened behind the mountain fortress. The sunrise brought contrasts of light that caught her photographic eye. Darby saw a picture in a woman carrying a bundle that smelled of warm rolls into a hotel, and another in a man reclining on a bench with a plume of cigarette smoke rising in the morning air. But her Nikki had been left in the room once again.

She continued to explore Salzburg's streets with her cheeks stinging in the morning chill and hands rubbed together from time to time. Around a corner, Darby was certain she'd stepped back in time. An open market stretched through a narrow *platz* beyond the stone archway of a building. People carried baskets and bags while waiting in lines before vendors who sold baguettes and rolls, meats and cheeses, arts and crafts, and giant pretzels in barrels. The only evidence of the twenty-first century, besides a few people in modern clothing, was a soda vendor selling Coca-Cola— America comes to Austria.

Instead of returning to the hotel for breakfast, Darby waited in a line and bought a warm, round roll from a vendor. She walked away feeling proud of herself. She'd said the greeting, "*Grüß Gott,*" bought the food, and left with a "*Danke*" and "*Auf Wiedersehen*" like any resident of the city.

After checking her watch, she followed the signs toward the university building. A whistling song nearly slipped to her lips, but she caught it with a smile. Pigeons flew from the shoulders of Mozart's violin, fluttering into the friendly sky, as she walked past.

The lights were out when Darby pushed open the door to the university building. Her walking boots echoed loudly on the marble floor as she tried to walk lightly up to the second story. The entire building seemed deserted as she squinted at room numbers. She turned a corner and noticed a doorway with light shining from within. Darby hesitated. Was she prepared for another rejection? If Brant did not believe her, why would this man?

She slowed her steps and heard the scrape of chair wheels on the tile floor.

"Is that Darby Evans?" A head poked from the doorway.

"Yes."

"Oh, so sorry I forgot to turn lights on for you. We are the only ones here. Come on in."

Professor Peter Voss met her with hand outstretched. He was younger than she had expected. A man in his early fifties, he was handsome and smiled easily. Darby instantly felt at ease in his presence—not at all like some of the professors she remembered from college who seemed to enjoy a self-proclaimed sense of power.

"Welcome. I am happy to meet you. This is my humble and not always so organized office."

Initially, the room appeared like any history professor's office at any university: stacks of papers around the desk, a couch, and bookshelves bursting from two walls. But small objects gave remarkable uniqueness—an odd sculpture that resembled hands reaching upward sat on the corner of his desk, a bright finger painting on a bulletin board, and a framed yellowing newspaper on the only bare wall with a headline reading: GERMANY QUITS. Darby walked closer to see the American paper announcing the end of the war. The professor chuckled as she noticed a box of toys and a child's easel behind the door.

"They are my daughter's, I promise. Sara enjoys coming to the university when my wife has to work weekends. But I will admit, I sometimes find myself playing with the Slinky—what a great invention. Please do not run from the office, thinking I am a crazy professor."

Darby laughed. "I've been known to enjoy a Slinky myself."

"Then we will get along just fine. Here, have a seat." His smile invited while his eyes sought hers curiously. Darby instantly perceived something about Professor Voss. He was one of those people who found everything fascinating because everything had something to teach. While Darby's mind looked for photographs, this man's sought knowledge.

The professor motioned toward a vinyl chair. She sat down, noticing how the window framed the fortress on Mönchsberg. "Great view you have."

"Ah, yes. Between the Slinky and my wonderful window view, I should be inspired toward great things—at least that is what you would think." Professor Voss chuckled, showing laugh lines around his hazel eyes.

"Sometimes great things can distract instead of inspire."

Now he grinned. "Yes, we will get along just fine. Now, tell me a little about yourself before we get started."

"Well, there isn't a lot to tell."

"Oh, come now. Do not be humble."

Darby laughed. "Believe me, I'm not. But let's see . . . I'm a photographer, and I live in California. I don't have a cat, dog, or children—not that I include children in with the others."

"Oh, but at times you can," the professor said with the grin that came easily to his lips. He sat in the chair behind the desk. "Go on."

"I'm pretty much a typical person—nothing extraordinary.

No Pulitzers for photography, but I take pictures at the studio I co-own."

"That sounds interesting."

"It can be. I much prefer my occasional work outdoors. I go on expeditions with groups—hiking clubs, mountaineers, things like that, to get in-action photos. But I'm just establishing myself in that area. Now tell me about yourself."

"Nothing as exciting as that, I must say. I am an indoor man most of the time. I teach several history courses here at the university and sometimes teach at conferences in other countries. I am married and have an eight-year-old daughter, so my traveling is not as exciting as it once was. I miss home when I am gone." Professor Voss rubbed his chin. "Now on the telephone, you said your grandmother was from Austria and you were searching for information about her."

Darby took in a breath. *Here we go.* "Actually, my main focus is for information about my grandmother's best friend."

"If you are searching for people, Brant could give you the names and telephone numbers of several organizations, or he could possibly help you himself. Why did he direct you toward me?"

"Brant is looking for information about my grandmother's best friend, Tatianna Hoffman. But . . ." Darby hesitated. "But Brant isn't giving me help in the area of my grandmother because he doesn't believe she was the person she claimed to be."

"What do you mean?"

Darby focused her eyes downward, toward the desk. "Brant believes my grandmother was attempting to impersonate someone else to claim a family inheritance."

"Really?" Darby saw immediate suspicion in the professor's eyes. "And how does this connect with your search for . . . did you say, your grandmother's best friend?" The professor extracted a pen and pad of paper from inside the desk. "Let us have some names also."

"My grandmother, Celia Lange Müller, wrote to Brant before she died, asking for information about her family inheritance. He wrote back claiming she was an imposter—I have that letter if you want to see it."

"Perhaps. First continue."

"I'll start from the beginning."

"That is always the best place." His open expression encouraged her to continue.

"My grandmother began searching for her family inheritance in the last few years, after she saw the Swiss banks opening and artwork being returned to the original owners. I never believed in the existence of a family inheritance in the first place, though I wondered about it when I saw my grandmother's determination. But I lived several hours away and my photography kept me busy, so I never helped or found any real facts. Those are lousy excuses, I know, especially when she found out she had cancer and . . . well, I'm getting off the subject."

"That is fine."

"My grandmother was diagnosed with cancer, and it had progressed too far to save her. For a long time, it seemed she didn't have it because her energy didn't lag. During that time, she wrote to many organizations looking for information. Last summer, she wrote to Brant, and that's when he answered the letter."

"Why did Brant not believe her claim?"

"He says he researched and found the real Celia Lange Müller with records of her death at Mauthausen Concentration Camp."

"But you do not believe him."

"I don't believe the records."

"So you are searching for the inheritance and the best friend?"

"I'm searching for the best friend. Confusing, I know. I only contacted Brant because of his letter to my grandmother. I hoped he'd perhaps give me some lead into finding Tatianna, the best friend. As of now, I'm not interested in the family inheritance like my grandmother was. Perhaps I will be later— but at this point, my main objective is to find Tatianna."

"Why?"

"Before my grandmother's death, she asked that I give Tatianna her name."

"You give Tatianna her name?" The professor set his pen down. "What does that mean?"

"I'm not sure, but that was my grandmother's dying request. She didn't mention that I pursue the inheritance, simply that I give Tatianna her name. Since I don't know how to do that, or what that entails, I'm first attempting to find Tatianna or some evidence of her. Then I'll go from there."

"So Tatianna is the key to everything."

"Yes. If I can trace her, then perhaps I can figure out what my grandmother meant. But I've wondered if Tatianna may actually be in the United States."

"Why would you think that?"

Darby opened her black bag and brought out her folders. She set one folder on the desk. "I hesitate to show you this, for it's actually evidence against my grandmother. After seeing this, my only true defense is that I have faith in her. She was a woman of her word and believed strongly in God, truth, honesty, and morality."

The professor didn't respond, but opened the folder and riffled through the documents. "These are United States immigration papers and an Austrian passport from 1939. Where did you get these items?"

"I found them in my grandmother's safe."

"Did you find your grandmother's immigration papers and passport?"

"No."

"These are Tatianna Hoffman's."

"Yes, I know."

"Yet you do not believe your grandmother was Tatianna Hoffman?"

"No."

"Why?"

"Because I believed her. She told me who she was. Her last letter to me was signed with her full name. I know it sounds unbelievable, but there has to be another explanation. Why would Celia ask me to give Tatianna her name, if she was Tatianna?"

"Did you show these papers to Brant?"

"No, because they would only confirm his belief. And he was very unwilling to discuss any possibility that Celia Müller was alive—he was very adamant."

Professor Voss strummed his pen on the paper. "Brant's response is not surprising. He encounters many attempts at fraud. We have been friends for many years, though we see each other only a few times a year. But only a month or so ago, some clients he had invested a lot of time and faith in were discovered to be frauds. Brant believed the story and risked his reputation by pushing the claim. Then the entire case fell apart. I have not spoken with Brant since it occurred, but I am sure it has been devastating. Brant is a fine man who gives himself completely to his work. So do not take his suspicions personally. You learn to be careful once you have been burned."

"That better explains his attitude, but . . . ."

"But it does not help you much." The professor nodded.

"That sounds selfish, I know."

"It is natural. But perhaps I can help."

"You're still willing to help even after what I told you?"

"If she was Tatianna Hoffman and not Celia Müller, we will find that out. I have nothing to lose here. An historical mystery is always of interest to me, and this one is intriguing."

Darby smiled and sighed in one breath. "Thank you."

"First, tell me what you know about your family. Then let us try to re-create it all."

Professor Voss wrote as she spoke, sometimes looking at papers she handed him. He'd circle one note, then cross out another. After an hour, he sighed and looked at the mess of notes on several pieces of paper.

"Let us go over what we do know." He turned the papers around. The scribbles made little sense until he spoke and pointed to diagrams and connecting lines. "Here is Gunther and Celia who are married, and Celia is expecting a child. Celia and Tatianna are friends. Do you know if Tatianna was married?"

"I don't know anything except her last name and that she was my grandmother's friend."

"Then we will keep Tatianna alone here." He pointed with the pen.

"Most of your grandmother's family were sent to the camps?"

"Her mother died when she was young, and one brother left for America before my grandmother was born. Her father, aunt, and younger brother were sent to concentration camps."

The professor drew another circle, connecting a dotted line to Celia. "Why has the escaped uncle not tried to locate the family inheritance?"

"I don't know. My Uncle Marc has never mentioned it in my presence. I'll ask when I see him over the holidays."

"Your great-uncle cannot help us prove your grandmother's identity if he left the country before she was born."

"Right."

"Why did he leave Austria?"

"I don't know that either. He must have left when he was very young, because he doesn't seem much older than my grandmother was. I don't even know if he went with family members or not, but it must have been twenty years before the war."

"I am assuming the family was Jewish."

"My grandmother's mother was an Austrian Jew."

"That was a difficult time for mixed marriages." The professor scratched his chin in thought. "Here is what I imagine. The Langes have this valuable inheritance." He picked up the information on the coins. "Two Celtic coins from Hallstatt. I wonder why they were not put in the Celtic museum in Hallstatt instead of made to be part of a family heirloom?"

"I didn't even know the Celts had coins, Professor."

"That is not my area of study either. But Lange. That sounds familiar. I will do some checking." He scribbled on the paper and picked up the other papers. "Then, this other item. A brooch—wait a minute, what is this? Could this be possible? The brooch was a gift from Sissi?"

"Who?"

"Empress Elizabeth, called *Sissi*, is probably the best-known Austrian empress, or Austrian woman, in our history. You must have seen pictures of her in the storefronts."

"I think I did see some candy with a princess or queen on it."

"Probably Sissi. She was an amazing woman, deserving of the popularity she continues to have over a hundred years after her death. There have been several movies and plays about her. She would be like . . . whom could I compare her to? Most often Sissi and Princess Diana of Wales have been compared because both were great beauties, lived healthy and active lifestyles, were strong and determined women, though rebellious and uncomfortable with royal traditions, and both experienced unfortunate deaths. It is quite astounding to consider that this heirloom could have been hers. But you know, I believe I heard a rumor of such a story—that must be why Lange sounds familiar to me."

"How did Elizabeth die?"

"She was stabbed in 1898 by a young anarchist beside a Swiss lake, though the man actually planned to kill another dignitary."

"I don't remember much about the story my grandmother told me. She said a great queen gave it to her grandfather when he helped her after a riding accident."

"Yes, let me translate this paper for you. It was written by Herbert Lange in 1887 and must have been handed down by family members since that time. Herbert was visiting Bad Ischl and, while on a walk, he claims to have seen Empress Sissi fall from her horse. He helped her up and caught the horse for her. He says she asked him to promise not to tell anyone about the fall."

Professor Voss stood up with the paper in hand. "This is plausible, for Sissi was an avid rider even as she aged. She was an excellent athlete in a time when women rarely did such things. This paper says that Sissi asked Herbert not to tell anyone she had fallen, because Emperor Franz Joseph did not want her riding if she continued to fall. A few months later, Sissi invited Herbert and his wife to the Kaiservilla in Bad Ischl, where she presented them with her personal emerald brooch for keeping her secret and for his chivalrous help. Herbert and his wife never told anyone until after Sissi was murdered eleven years later."

The professor whistled in awe. "You know, I am certain I have heard something of this story, which I assumed was only a legend. If I remember correctly, Herbert Lange claimed the heirloom after Sissi's death, but most people did not believe the authenticity. Supposedly, and this paper concurs with what I have heard, Emperor Franz Joseph himself gave a written document confirming to the family that the brooch did belong to his wife. He gave authenticity to the story that the brooch was given to the family, evidently the Lange family, as a gift. He wrote this paper after Sissi's death when Herbert

Lange claimed the story. But I do not see a copy of the letter from the emperor here."

"I haven't found it."

"Then the entire story and Franz Joseph's letter could all be legend, perhaps the existence of the brooch also."

"My grandmother said she saw it when she was a child."

"Interesting. And why would your grandmother try to search for the brooch if she did not believe it existed? I believe it could all be true. This record, written in 1887 and amended in 1900 after Sissi's death, appears accurate. And I am certain I have heard the same story, though I must go back and discover from where."

Darby sighed and rubbed her eyes. "We're getting more rabbit trails than facts."

"Rabbit trails?"

"More questions."

"Yes. But, Darby, you do not realize the magnitude of this story. The story is only a hundred years old, which is fairly young for European history. We do not know whether the legend really involves your family or if the brooch actually was a gift from Empress Sissi. If it is true, this piece would be extremely valuable. Anything associated with Sissi is worth a lot, but especially jewelry from her collection and given as a gift. Something like this, even as a rumor, would have been fascinating to the Nazis, or to anyone seeking wealth. And there was probably a lot more information sixty years ago. We now have a war to lose any evidence, including your family. But this is amazing—you could be the rightful heir. Or perhaps your uncle would be. My advice, either way, is not to spread this information around. Even today, the story could spawn a media frenzy or treasure hunt crusade, or even worse, possible danger. These coins and especially the brooch could be priceless if found today. It is possible that your family was sent to their death because of it, and we know there are greedy men and women in every generation."

Darby hadn't considered any danger besides her mother's list of warnings, such as "watch out in train stations." She had considered the story as long ago, and her focus had been on finding Tatianna, not the Lange heirlooms. It also shocked Darby that the story involving an Austrian empress, ancient coins, and a mysterious brooch could actually be factual. When Grandma Celia would tell the story, Darby always said the appropriate *oohs* and *aahs*, but that was all.

"We are finding pieces of the puzzle. Let us return to your grandmother."

"My weak link."

"Possibly, but there may be other options. If Brant investigated, then we know there was most likely an actual Celia Lange Müller. It would be quite a convenient fact for a Nazi interested in the Lange heirlooms to know that Celia's father married a Jewish woman. After the Anschluß, German law became Austrian law. It was illegal to have biracial marriages. Now his wife was dead, but still this man's children were half Jew. If someone wanted the Lange treasures, here could be a perfect opportunity. So perhaps they take Celia's father into custody. Perhaps Celia and her husband, Gunther Müller, realize that, for her own safety, Celia must leave the country. And here, yes, this could be the answer." Professor Voss looked up from the papers and smiled. "Perhaps Celia uses her friend's papers and escapes the country as Tatianna Hoffman."

Darby stared at the Professor and spoke slowly, "That could be it. That would explain her coming to the United States and having Tatianna's papers. Though it still doesn't explain the birthplace mix-up. Remember that all my grandmother's papers say she was born in Vienna."

"That is to be expected."

"Why?"

"If Tatianna were born in Vienna, and your grandmother came to the United States using those papers, she would be able to change her name, but not her birthplace, right?"

"Probably not. So she always held to the record on any paperwork."

"Also, let us think about this. Countries were very tough on immigrants at that time. Many, many people were trying to flee from Nazi Germany and Austria with the flood increasing as the Nazis conquered most of Europe. It would be difficult enough for a young, pregnant woman to come to America. Even harder if she admitted the papers she held were not her own, and that she was half Jewish. If Celia had said, 'Please let me come to your country, but I am not who my papers say I am,' she most likely would have been denied."

"So she kept the false name of Tatianna until her immigration. Then once in the United States, she changed her name back to Celia Lange Müller, but—"

"She could not change her birthplace," they said together.

"But wouldn't Tatianna need her papers if she remained?"

"Yes, she would need them, but if she was not Jewish, then it would not be too serious. Tatianna could apply for new copies, saying her old ones were lost or stolen. And we know she was not Jewish or it would say so on these papers." The professor held up the worn passport and looked through it again.

Darby sat up in the chair. "If Tatianna is alive, we can discover the truth."

"And that is a possibility and where we need to look next."

"Grandma's comments about Tatianna needing her name—she may have meant returning these papers to her. Grandma told me that I'd find the information in the safe and that's where I found these items."

"That seems to be stretching it a bit, but then your grandmother was dying. She might have wanted you to find Tati-

anna if they lost contact over the years. Giving the papers back
may have been Celia's way of saying thank you for saving her
life. That might have been her desire."

"Yes, that would be like Grandma. She'd want to thank
Tatianna and show her what her gift produced—another
generation of people."

Professor Voss touched his fingertips together, deep in
thought. "One life for a new generation of lives. Quite amazing."

"How do we find Tatianna? Do we check phone directories?
If she married, her last name would be changed."

"There are several routes available. If Tatianna had been
Jewish, we could have looked through the World Jewish
Congress—they have done amazing work locating people and
connecting families. But there are other organizations, including the International Red Cross, that have lists of displaced
persons and refugees."

"And we have Tatianna's birthplace and can contact Vienna
for records, perhaps a marriage or death certificate."

"It looks like we have our work cut out for us." The professor glanced at the clock on his desk. "The morning has
escaped us, and my wife and daughter will be arriving home
from visiting family."

"I didn't realize I'd kept you so long. I'm very sorry." Darby
stood up.

"Please, do not apologize. I am enthralled by this story."

Darby began to put the papers in their rightful folders. She
placed one into her satchel and noticed the bundle at the
bottom.

"The letters."

"Excuse me?"

Darby extracted the yellowed envelopes, wrapped in plastic—
treasures she couldn't read. "They were with my grandmother's things, and I noticed one addressed to Tatianna.
They're in German, and I didn't have time to find someone

who could read them. Perhaps there's information that will help us find Tatianna."

She held them for a moment. They were a part of her grand-mother's heart—the part Darby knew nothing about. Slowly she handed them to the professor. He accepted them reverently.

"If you don't mind, you could take them with you and read them."

"You would allow me to take them?"

"Yes."

"Thank you. I will take excellent care." The exchange of letters was a pact of trust. Darby knew Peter Voss understood that also.

"I will make copies of the letters and translate them. My wife would be interested. Do you mind if I share them with her?"

"Not at all. I could use all the help I can get." Darby put her purse on her shoulder. The professor shook her hand.

"Then we will meet again. How about Monday evening?"

"Monday evening would be great."

"Perhaps you can come to dinner. I will discuss it with my wife and call you at your hotel. I have the number."

"Great—I'd love to meet her, and the daughter who draws such beautiful pictures."

Darby's eyes caressed the letters once again. She was putting her complete trust in this man she had just met. Yet she knew he understood and wanted to find the truth. Finally, there was someone on her side.

That night she couldn't sleep. The letters were being read, maybe at that very moment. Darby flipped through the TV channels, looking for a diversion. She found it in a Brad Pitt movie, *Legends of the Fall*, though it was so odd seeing native Americans and rugged Pitt speaking German that the drama turned comical.

The late-night insomnia caught up with her in the morning

as she slept in. Darby hurried down the marble stairs the next morning, sure that breakfast was over. As she hopped to the bottom, she heard her name spoken at the front desk. A man and woman stood at the counter, talking to the clerk.

"Professor Voss?" Darby asked.

The couple turned toward her, and she noticed their worried expressions.

"We almost came last night, but it was late." The professor took a step toward her. "We have translated the letters."

"What's wrong?"

CHAPTER THIRTEEN

L et us go somewhere," Professor Voss suggested, with a nod at the desk clerk who kept looking in their direction.

"We could go into the sitting room or somewhere else?"

"The sitting room will be fine."

Darby led the way into the small, private lounge. She sat on the plaid couch, and Peter Voss and his wife sat across from her.

"Hello." Darby extended her hand to the woman. "I'm Darby Evans, and I assume you are Frau Voss?"

"Forgive me—I behave rudely," Professor Voss said.

"When Peter gets something inside his mind, manners and etiquette go away." The woman was younger than the professor, not much older than Darby, with beautiful olive skin and dark hair. She smiled warmly, then she seemed to remember why they were there. "I am very pleased to meet you, Ms. Evans."

"I am pleased to meet you, though call me Darby, please."

"I am Katrine."

Darby studied Professor Voss, whose restless hands moved as if they balanced an invisible Slinky. "You have me worried. What did you discover? Is it something terrible? Do I need to prepare myself?"

"It is good you are sitting down, as they say." Peter Voss looked at his wife and back to Darby.

"Is it my grandmother? Is Grandma Celia really Tatianna Hoffman?"

"No, I believe in your grandmother."

Darby felt a load lift from her shoulders.

The professor set a folder of papers on the coffee table between them. "The letters confirmed to both of us that your grandmother was Celia Müller. I have written the translations so you can see for yourself. I am going to give them to you in the order we read them."

"Just tell her." Katrine nudged him.

"No, let her read first." Professor Voss handed Darby an envelope and a sheet of paper. The envelope was the letter addressed to Tatianna Hoffman. The paper was the translation. Confused, Darby looked at the Vosses, then read.

22 November 1939

My dearest Tatianna,

I write to a blank page and hope my words and heart will reach you. I know many others will read these words before you, but hope it will eventually find you, my dearest friend. I pray for you with my every breath. You gave me so much, but I hope not too much. The baby kicks furiously, especially at night, and often gets the hiccups. If not for this coming child, I would not want to go on. I fear for you all. How can one be separated from her best friend and her husband? I owe my life and my child's life to you. I believe in my heart that we will all be together again.

There is a beautiful park here in New York and I imagine us here, pushing the baby carriage, and dreaming of all that the world has to offer us. I hope we will grow old together, still reading our books and telling our stories. I pray God will let it be so.

With all my heart,
C. Rachel

Darby didn't speak as she set the paper down. She thought of her grandmother as a young girl with an aching heart, yet clinging to a hope that would never bring happiness. For Darby knew the rest of the story. Grandma was never reunited with her husband or best friend. She never shared her child with either.

"You gave me permission to share the story with Katrine," Professor Voss said. "And we have spent most of the night translating and making our own hypothesis."

"And what do you think of this?" Darby asked, bringing her mind back to the facts within the letter that would help find Tatianna.

"We discovered several things from this letter." Peter Voss bent forward eagerly. "This line here, 'You gave me so much, but I hope not too much.' That indicates what we considered— that perhaps Tatianna gave her passport so Celia could escape, but Celia fears this could cause trouble for her friend. See, 'I hope not too much.' "

"So this evidence gives us hope of finding Tatianna."

"Read the next one and we will discuss that." Professor Voss shifted in his seat.

Katrine put her hand on his arm. "Should she skip to the last? It has the real information."

"No, she should read them as we did. This one your grandmother wrote to her husband, Gunther Müller."

Darby took the paper.

3 April 1940

My Gunther,

    I've waited for months and months now, but you have not come. We have a daughter. I named her Carole Marlene Müller.

    I try not to believe the worst or let myself get down. I had such faith for the longest time, but now my faith wavers. You have not come. I've waited and waited. I see you on the street and call out, but it is not you. I know somewhere on this earth you are moving and breathing, or maybe you aren't and your spirit longs to tell me. Have I not really listened?

    Where do I send this letter? Who is still there? What has happened to our home in Salzburg and my childhood home in Hallstatt? I will write this letter a hundred times, but know I will never send it. It is for your eyes alone. But I will send letters to others, and I will search until I know for certain. I will seek every address I can remember, for I must find you. I do not believe I can endure this life without your love. I do not want to try.

    We need you, Gunther. Carole and I need you. Find us, please, my love.

                      Forever I give my heart to you,
                      Celia

Darby stared at the letter and read it again. This was Grandma Celia—separated from her closest friend and husband and in a new, unfamiliar country, sending letters with hopes of finding answers and a link to her life. The girl who wrote these letters had died before Darby was even born. Darby had never had the chance to know her.

She glanced up to concerned expressions. Tears pooled around her eyes as the professor stood and walked to the window. Katrine patted her knee.

"It's like I'm reading the words of a stranger. I had no idea what she felt or how badly she hurt."

"Children never do," Katrine said softly. "I never knew my parents' love until we had our own daughter."

Darby nodded and looked at the last letter. She could see the anticipation in Katrine's eyes but almost didn't want to read it. Darby was surprised to see the letter was written not *by* Grandma Celia, but *to* her instead.

> *6 January 1942*
>
> *Celia,*
>
> *By miracle, I am able to send this letter. I have terrible news. Tatianna is dead. She died at a labor camp near Linz. Also, I am deeply sorry to tell you, Gunther is also killed. He did not make it across the Sudetenland border in time, though I do not have all the details. I am so sorry to give you this news. But please, you must not send any more letters. Others have said you have written them also. Are you so foolish not to know there are eyes everywhere? A letter from America will obviously be read. I have been questioned twice and have only escaped suspicion because of my friendship with a Nazi officer.*
>
> *I understand your desire to find Tatianna and Gunther, but you put us in danger by such foolishness. I ask you not to write me again unless this war someday ends. I have created safety for myself. I may even marry my Nazi friend. I know that must disgust you, but you escaped from this place, and I must look out for myself. If I hear any more actual information about Gunther, I will attempt to write the details. Know that I am sorry to give you such terrible news.*
>
> *—I*

"Who wrote this one?" Darby asked.

"We do not know. There was no signature or name on the envelope, just that 'I'."

Darby set the letter in her lap. "Tatianna is dead."

"Yes." Professor Voss returned to sit across from her.

Sickness rose in Darby's stomach. "I guess that ends our search."

"We will not find answers from Tatianna, yet, in a way, we can," Katrine said, trying to sound hopeful.

"What do you mean?"

"These letters give us good information. We can seek Tatianna's family and look for records of her death. What do you know about Gunther and his family?"

"Very little. Rarely did I hear any information about my grandfather. My mother had searched for him when she was a young woman. She hoped he'd somehow escaped the war, and I think Grandma Celia even had hidden hopes for the search. It was painful for both of them to find nothing. I know his name, and that they met in Hallstatt one summer and fell quickly in love. I believe he was an orphan or adopted. My grandmother once told me her aunt wasn't happy to have someone without a family past."

Professor Voss folded his arms. "That does not provide much information. What kind of a search did your mother conduct for her father?"

"I'm not sure, but I can find out. It looks like I need a list to remember all the questions for my mother."

"Your mother will answer them?"

"I hope."

"There is something else that Katrine noticed and we found very interesting." Professor Voss pointed to a sentence in the last letter. "The writer in this letter says Tatianna was killed in a labor camp. Brant told you that Celia Müller died at Mauthausen Concentration Camp. The camp is located near Linz. During the war, the public was told that people were sent to labor camps, which were often labor death camps. If we know

Celia Müller escaped to America, but Tatianna Hoffman died in a labor camp, then . . ."

"Tatianna Hoffman died with the name Celia Müller." Darby said the words, but it took a moment for them to fully reach her mind. Could it be? "The letter said that Tatianna died in a camp near Linz. That must be it! That must be what my grandmother meant. She knew from this letter that Tatianna had died and perhaps she knew Tatianna was thought to be her. So that's what she meant about giving Tatianna her name back."

"Yes, yes," Professor Voss said, sitting beside his wife again. "Either Tatianna gave Celia the papers and then, because she had none to prove who she was, she was arrested as Celia, or perhaps they switched papers."

"It makes perfect sense." Darby stared upward, her eyes trailing the coffered ceiling. Relief pulsed through her—finally she knew what her grandmother's allusive words meant. Yet at the same time Darby felt sorrow for a woman she didn't know, a woman who had not only saved her grandmother, but provided Darby's life as well. And still there was the question: how could she give Tatianna her name back if the woman was dead?

"Thank you for coming so quickly," Darby said.

"We knew you would want to know. I am curious about the writer of the last letter."

Darby picked up the paper. "Yes, it would help to know who it was. Obviously, a woman."

"Your grandmother was never reunited with anyone from Austria?"

"Not that I'm aware of. I'll check with my Uncle Marc about that one." Darby looked at the three letters. "I wish there was more actual information in the letters. Names, places, exact events."

"Understand that your grandmother knew every word

would be looked at and could possibly be endangering someone's life. She had to write with very limited information."

"There are still many unanswered questions, but we know so much more now." Darby's mind was racing over the information.

"We will do a bit of investigating of our own, right, Katrine? Perhaps we can find some information about the Lange inheritance, if you would like, of course."

"Yes, we want to help very much," Katrine said. "I can do some Internet research while Peter looks through the university library. Are you staying in Salzburg?"

"Actually, I plan to go to Hallstatt in the morning. Will I be able to look at birth certificates and things like that?"

"Try the administration office in Hallstatt," Peter said. "I wonder how accessible the information will be since you are an American with no proof yet about your grandmother. And then there is the language barrier. I have classes tomorrow and a conference to prepare for, but—"

"Professor Voss—"

"You must call me Peter, please."

"Peter, then. I can take this trip myself. I brought along a handy German phrase book that I need to try out anyway. You have helped so much and I know you both have your own work. Thank you, both of you. I feel much stronger simply knowing the two of you believe my story."

"We are on your side, yes," Katrine said. "I feel we are already friends."

Darby looked at her beaming brown eyes and shy smile and knew she did have a friend, not thousands of miles away, but sitting a few feet from her.

"Call if you need help, with anything." They shook hands.

"Thank you, both."

Darby held the letters and translations to her chest as she watched the couple leave the hotel. The answers were close;

she could feel it. She'd leave in the morning for Hallstatt, then Mauthausen Concentration Camp. Were the answers simply waiting to be found?

CHAPTER FOURTEEN

The highway was a ribbon twisting gently through sharp peaked mountains that sprouted straight from the valley floor. Darby had never seen such a beautiful place. It reminded her of northwestern Montana, where her close friend had moved after college. Darby had flown up to Columbia Falls for Tristie's wedding and found herself struggling to attend the indoor wedding obligations of bridal showers and rehearsals while feeling the lure of green, rolling valleys beneath the jagged mountain tops of Glacier National Park. The Salzkammergut Lake District of Austria looked similar, but as if the single Flathead Valley had magnified and multiplied into many mountains and valleys in every direction, growing quaint European villages on their edges. What her eyes discovered seemed unreal, like a fairy-tale world come alive. The ranges of mountains looked like blue giants sleeping in haphazard mounds on carpets of green.

The rent-a-car topped a hill to the sight of a sprawling lake with a tall church tower silhouetted against the deep blue

waters. Darby instantly pulled off the road and hopped out of
the car. Perhaps it was simply a Hollywood painted backdrop,
not really an Austrian village with a lake reflecting sky, clouds,
and mountains. Her camera waited inside her car, but Darby
again didn't retrieve it. Her breath frosty in the cold air, she
clicked shot after shot into heart and soul instead. Bare trees
with a handful of clinging autumn foliage framed crystal waters
with jagged, whitecapped mountains rising above. The mountainside burned with sienna reds and yellows. Darby knew she
could never gather the images into a two-dimensional photograph. Usually, that would pose a challenge and she'd search
filters and angles to get the best shot. But as on the rest of this
trip thus far, she kept the moment for herself and felt no desire
to capture and share it with others. Grandma Celia had been
right. Darby did hide behind the lens she manipulated to
shape her world. Only in the last month had Darby been
unable to keep her life in a tidy framed photograph. Suddenly,
all her images were shattered.

Standing before an Austrian lake with nothing left to blind
her vision, Darby could almost see God and not fear a world
beyond her making. In college, the religion du jour was her
belief. She'd moved from Christian to atheist her first year. But
out in the wilds of the mountains, she'd found belief in a God
again. The wonders and amazing design of the natural world,
how every part fit together, were proof of a greater hand. Just
as the winds and rain could not carve a da Vinci sculpture,
despite a million years trying, so Darby knew the intricate
weaving of life and land did not happen by accident. The sight
before her was like an outdoor cathedral inhabited by the God
of creation. But was it all made by the God of her youth? Was
the same God who designed the land she loved available to her
as an individual?

A gentle breeze stirred her hair. Days earlier Darby had
never seen this land; now it was hers. With an immediate

sense of belonging, she knew this. From Salzburg to the
Salzkammergut Lake District of mountains, lakes, and villages,
Darby had found a home.

⊶≡◉═⊷

The drive from Salzburg to Hallstatt didn't take much over an
hour, but at every turn a new lake and fairy-tale village
appeared. At the Bad Ischl exit, she glanced ahead to see a
town along a crystal river with a backdrop of another range of
white-capped mountains. The "Bad" meant "bath," meaning
that this was a spa town. This village held the famous summer
villa of Emperor Franz Joseph and Empress Elizabeth. Darby
determined to return and explore the city where Herbert
Lange might have helped the Empress Sissi after her riding
fall. The Kaiservilla where Herbert had supposedly received
the emerald brooch was the same palace from which Franz
Joseph had declared war on Serbia in 1914, commencing
World War I. Although Darby was drawn to these facts, today
she was going to Hallstatt.

She passed the town of Au, wondering how to pronounce
such a name. She tried to practice a few variations aloud until
the car rounded a bend and rose to a view of another lake
ahead. Hallstattersee—Hallstatt Lake—mirrored in its calm
waters the tall peaks that surrounded its shores. A sharp turn
pointed one way to Hallstatt, the other to Gosau. As she
followed left to Hallstatt, she remembered Brant telling her
how he'd spent his summers in Gosau and Hallstatt Lake.

Darby caught sight of a church steeple on the edge of the
lake before it disappeared as the road hugged the mountainside and entered a long tunnel. A sign announced *Hallstatt* as
the car exited the tunnel, but the town didn't look the same as
her first glimpse before the tunnel. Darby slowed and peered
back to see little Hallstatt clinging between the mountain she'd

driven through and the lake that stretched toward another range of mountains.

She whipped the car around, pausing on the shoulder. If any of the sights of the day appeared unreal, Hallstatt appeared much more so. Wisps of smoke rose from lines of houses and buildings dressed with thick autumn trees and bushes. A light fog danced inches above the black lake, though everything else was crystal clear. A narrow steeple pointed heavenward from the lakeshore and another rounded steeple jutted upward higher on the mountain. Hallstatt, a modest storybook village that could be missed in a blink, had a history dating back to ancient times. Grandma Celia had told Darby how this tiny village that clutched the side of a mountain for centuries had been a mecca of trade during the Celtic age.

Darby opened the door, stepped out, and rested an elbow on top of the car. She stared, finding every detail her grandmother had described in the stories of her childhood. Upward, she could see a tram to the salt mine where Celia's brother had worked. The tram now took tourists straight up a thousand feet to the oldest salt mine in the world, which continued to produce forty-five hundred years later.

She was there, at the setting of evening stories. The place that was interchanged with Snow White's woods and Hansel and Gretel's adventures. Darby had entered imagination and found it as magical as her mind could envision.

Darby finally returned inside the car to search for a place to park. A gate barred the street that took her toward the towering steeple and city center. She turned the car around several times before finding a place, then finally parked, grabbed her brown leather jacket, and left the car.

Seestraße was a paved road that wandered along the lakeside. Darby walked along, feeling the ground was almost holy, not only because of the tiny village's alluring beauty, but at the thought that this was the place where Grandma's stories

had been created. Right on these very sidewalks, her grandmother's feet had trod. She'd spent her summers swimming
and boating on that lake, climbing the surrounding mountains
in all seasons, skiing to the south in the winter, weaving her
hopes and dreams, and falling in love with her future husband.

Darby zipped her coat and put her hands in her pockets.
The air felt colder beside the deep lake than it had in Salzburg.
A man walking his dog nodded as he passed. A gathering of
black waterfowl dove near the shore. She looked up the mountain and remembered her grandmother telling her about the
houses built on different levels up the steep mountainside.
Somewhere, hidden in the trees, were the connecting walkways where Grandma Celia and her friends once played hide-
and-seek.

Darby passed a restaurant and several wooden docks, then
approached the heart of the town. She wondered about this
place that had lived a thousand generations. Darby had always
associated the Celts with Ireland. In her guidebook, she'd been
surprised to discover the Celts had settled throughout Europe.
She was further surprised to discover that this tiny village had
a large place in history. An entire epoch of the history of mankind had been named after it during the Iron Age. The British
Museum had a wing dedicated to the Hallstatt Age. Though
the Celts were the first to find precious salt there and establish
a community, they were by far not the last. Salt, the gold of a
past era, was later discovered by the conquering Romans.

Darby had read in her brochures how Hallstatt was thronged
in its summer warmth by herds of tourists. Thankfully, today
she found the streets empty.

She propped her elbows on a cold railing and watched a
white ferryboat move slowly across the lake. It had to be the
ferry that picked up train passengers from the station on the
other side. Darby watched the white *Stefanie* with its bubbling

wake, wondering how often her grandmother had done the same.

"Your grandfather drove the ferryboat one summer," Grandma Celia had told her in one of the rare moments she'd mentioned him. "He wanted to be an archaeologist like my father and had come to work a summer in Hallstatt to pay for university and to see the work in the village. I think he also hoped to meet my father, which he did, of course." Her grandmother had smiled like a schoolgirl.

Back and forth, back and forth across the lake—they'd discovered one another. What a wonderful companion her grandmother must have made during those trips.

"My father knew we couldn't get into trouble with me riding the ferry with Gunther. What he didn't know was that it provided the opportunity for us to know each other well in a very short time. All we could do was talk. But when the last ferry took people across, we always managed a little time alone."

Darby perused the waters of her heritage. But, she reminded herself, this journey had not been simply to see Grandmother's hometown. She was seeking answers here. She allowed herself some chilly time on the lakeside road, imagining Grandma Celia taking her hand and showing her sights. Then Darby returned to her mission. She followed the narrow straße as it turned away from the lake and into a gathering of straight-fronted houses and shops, then through a dark roadway between towering buildings and into the village center. The pale buildings of pink, yellow, and blue surrounded the cobblestone square with a tall statue of the Crucifixion in the center. Red and pink geraniums billowed from window boxes and green vines climbed several storefronts, despite the coming winter. Above the buildings a waterfall rumbled down the mountain and disappeared from view.

Darby spotted the Gasthaus Gerringer sign on the corner. She opened the door of the plain stucco building to find the rustic room greeting her with the snap of a warm, crackling fire. The neat breakfast area had fresh flowers on each table, and she noticed a long wooden desk with keys hanging on the wall behind it. Darby felt like she'd intruded into someone's private home without knocking, even though she'd called for reservations. She jingled the bell on the counter and heard footsteps from above. A moment later, a woman appeared on the staircase in front of her.

"Hello! You must be Ms. Evans—the American." Darby was taken aback by the bubbly woman in her late thirties, who shook Darby's hand with enthusiasm.

"Very nice to have you. My name is Sophie Gerringer— please call me Sophie. You are our only guest so far today. Would you like to see your room?"

"I left my car and luggage down the road. I didn't know how to get through the gate."

"I should have told you on telephone. You need resident card, and I give you one. You may park just few buildings down."

"Good. And you live here also?"

"*Ja*—yes. My mother, grandmother, and I live on the first floor and we have our guestrooms upstairs. Of course, break- fast provided for you. Please, let me show your room and make sure it acceptable."

"I'm sure it will be."

"Come," Sophie said, smiling. "Let me show you."

Darby walked beside the woman up the wide, wooden stair- case. She noticed a tangle of fishing poles in a corner and snow skis in another as they stepped into a hall. Sophie chattered about the weather all the way up in good English.

"And here we are. Your room."

Darby stopped before entering. It was exactly what she'd envisioned. The hardwood floor creaked beneath her feet as she entered. Red-and-white checkered curtains covered the doorway and windows that looked out toward the lake. The antique bed, soft and inviting, had a fluffy pillow and down comforter folded Austrian style, sideways at the bottom. The hand-carved headboard matched an antique vanity and armoire arranged in the corners. Sophie opened the curtains, then the French door. The balcony hung over a garden area and gave a magnificent view of the lake and mountain on the opposite shore.

"It's perfect. Absolutely perfect." She walked onto the balcony.

Sophie spoke softly. "Come down when you are ready, and I will give you key and parking pass."

"Thank you." Darby listened as Sophie's footsteps echoed away. Again she was alone with the stories of the past, stories linked closely with the answers she sought.

"Well, Grandma, I'm really here," she whispered, looking toward the black lake. But would this place of ancient lives and histories hold the answers she needed?

CHAPTER FIFTEEN

The morning grew warmer as the sun opened its eye over the crest of the mountain. Darby parked the car near the guesthouse but felt too eager for exploration to unload her luggage. She discovered quickly that Hallstatt took Mondays off. Many offices, shops, and restaurants were closed for the day. But those places could wait until tomorrow. Darby wanted to discover the streets and houses. She wondered which house her grandmother had been raised in. Why hadn't she paid better attention to the details when given the chance?

She assumed Brant wanted her to see a grave when he sent her there—a grave that matched the name of her grandmother's grave in California. Darby had discovered that most cemeteries were found beside churches. So toward the church towers she went. The lower church with the tallest spire, the Evangelical church, had no cemetery. She found a road up the mountain and hoped it led to the other church she could see above the lake-level village.

More people were on the streets now, walking dogs, carrying baskets. Darby found a stairway leading from the road. She began to ascend the steep stairs between tiny houses with miniature landscaped yards.

She climbed until her legs ached. Suddenly she wondered why there would be a grave for Tatianna or Celia here. If Tatianna had died at Mauthausen, her body would not be buried here. Darby thought of her grandmother's still and lifeless form. Even though the essence of Grandma Celia no longer remained, that body was still part of her grandmother and not easy to let go of, not easy to put into the ground. But bodies were not items of value for the Nazis—only waste to be disposed of.

She continued up the switchbacked and winding passageways until she reached the Catholic church with its open gate to a cemetery. She'd never seen headstones like the ones in Europe. They were wood or black wrought iron with tall stands holding the nameplates and topped with small, arrow-shaped roofs. While grass covered the cemetery grounds at home, here gravel provided a walkway to the cement-bordered graves. Within the cement rectangles was dark soil with a profusion of colorful flowers planted inside. Darby wandered back and forth, looking at names and dates. Close to a concrete retaining wall, she peered out across the great expanse of sky overlooking the lake. Far below were the parking lot and market square.

Which one would be her grandmother's? Darby wondered. Few of the graves were older than ten or fifteen years. Perhaps she was in the wrong area. The cemetery was in two tiers up the mountain. On the upper tier, Darby heard a noise behind her and saw she was not alone. A woman sat in a small covered area beside a cylinder-shaped building only steps from the graves. Darby walked past, but the woman didn't look up. Was that a cash register on the table beside her?

"Excuse me, *sprechen Sie Englisch?*" Darby asked.

"*Nein.*" The woman shrugged.

"Uh, what—*vas est*—this?" She didn't know if she had French or German in her mixed-up sentence. Darby pointed to the building.

"Twenty schilling."

The woman shrugged again. Darby dug for the coins in her pocket and was handed a brochure. She hesitated as she looked at the photo on the paper and approached the door. Down the thick double doors were squared pictures of leering skulls with crossbones below. She recognized the symbol for Alpha and Omega above the door as she opened it. Darby peered inside and jumped in surprise. Hundreds of hollow eyes stared back. The heavy door closed her inside a window-less crypt. If she ever wanted to avoid shadows, this was not the place to be. The floodlights shining in the cold, dank room made shadows on the walls and especially within the eyes and open jaws of hundreds of human skulls. Three walls had long wooden tables packed with skulls, while beneath were the stacked and organized remains of the skeletons.

Darby read the history with her back close to the exit. She remembered her grandmother telling of the Bein Haus but had forgotten it was in Hallstatt. She'd experienced many nightmares of this place, but the reality felt even more frightening than a nine-year-old child's imagination. This was a place of the dead.

The brochure told how residents had been exhumed from their tiny graveyard after ten to twelve years of peaceful rest. The remains were then bleached in the sun, painted, and placed for the rest of eternity inside the white *karner* bone house.

Darby took a step forward to see the paintings across the skulls. They had each person's name and date painted on the forehead along with vines, flowers, and other adornments. Some even had a snake weaving through an eye socket.

A short gate kept her a few feet away, but Darby leaned close to look at one delicate painting of flowers and vines. The gaping eyes and jagged teeth looked back at her. This had actually been someone, just like herself. Breathing, thinking, with dreams for tomorrow. Now that person, an empty skull, stared at nothing.

Darby felt a mixture of reverence and fear for these people whose once vibrant bodies slowly decayed into dust before the eyes of all who would come and see.

There was laughter outside. The door opened with fresh light and air spilling inside as a chattering German-speaking family pointed and exclaimed before even making it into the crypt. Already the camera was out, with its flash warming. Darby walked out, relieved to be free from the hollow stares as the door closed behind her. It seemed a strange tourist site.

She walked away from the woman with her cash register and the tourists enjoying their show. The gravel crunched beneath her feet as she trailed around the upper cemetery. She didn't find the name of Celia Müller. So why else would Brant tell her to come to the cemetery?

A wooden stairway inclined above the last village house. Darby pulled out the town map and found that the stairway led in a series of switchbacks to the waterfall and onward high above to the salt-mine entrance. Partway up the stairs, she found a wooden bench. Darby gasped at the view. The village, churches, and cemetery were below and she could see for miles across the lake to different mountain peaks, another village to the south, and a small castle on the opposite shore. Darby sat on the bench and gathered the view inside. As yet, Hallstatt hadn't offered any clues, but she felt a change within her, a touch of a deeper peace that she hadn't known in a long time. Her life had once been characterized by horizons, exploration, and tomorrows. Somehow along the way, it was consumed into work. But she'd seen a gentleness in certain people that didn't disappear with busyness—Grandma Celia, for one. And suddenly, Darby knew that was what she wanted most. Instead of her imagined life, she wanted the real thing.

She watched wood smoke rise from chimneys and wisps of fog lift from the silent water like morning spirits greeting the afternoon. Perhaps there was nothing about Tatianna in this place. Perhaps she had come here instead to find some of what her grandmother had possessed. Wasn't this where it must have been born and grown in her? But how could Darby bottle it up and take these feelings with her?

There was a noise she'd heard for some time but only now wondered about. Rhythmic movement—the *scrape, scrape* of rake against a concrete sidewalk—brought her eyes toward an old man raking leaves in his miniature yard at the bottom of the stairs below her. He didn't see her above. His back was hunched with the burden of years, but he pressed on against the wet, autumn scatterings of the night before.

Darby guessed he was older than her grandmother, due to his worn body. She wondered about his life. Had he lived in Hallstatt through the war? Suddenly she saw a story in every person older than seventy. *What were you doing during the war? Were you victim or predator or bystander? Did you save someone? Did you kill someone? What story can you tell?*

How she wished she could ask. Yet how could she approach someone and pose such questions out of the blue? Most likely, the old man didn't even speak English. Head of white, hands beaten by time, eyes turned downward toward his task, he was a mystery to her. He had a story. In ten to fifteen years at the very most, he'd be gone and his story with him. In that time or less, all their stories would be gone. Someone else would rake the leaves.

The sleepy town yawned and stretched below her. Then the sound of a distant chain saw interrupted the silence. No other noise reminded Darby of autumn more than that high-pitched sputter. Lawn mowers were spring, and chain saws were autumn.

Finally she stood and brushed off the back of her pants. Her cheeks stung in the cold air. She had come for a purpose—one other than to find an elusive peace. She might not find any answers here, but she at least had to try.

Darby returned to the village center and found the "I" sign that meant information office.

"*Guten Morgen*," she said to the woman behind the counter. "I need some information. You speak English?"

"*Ja.* How may I serve you?" The short, full-figured woman examined Darby from behind spectacles. "Do you have a map of the town?"

"Yes, I got one in Salzburg."

"There many tourist sites in the town and in the area. What you looking to do?"

"My grandmother lived here as a child and young woman. I was hoping to find records. Birth and death certificates? Is there an administration office?

"*Ja.* The municipal offices would be helpful for you. They located here." She pointed on the map with a plump, manicured finger. "Just across from here."

"They are closed today, correct?"

"*Ja.* Tomorrow, they open."

"Do you have any information about Hallstatt during or before World War II?"

"Uh. No, I do not. Perhaps municipal offices help, or museum."

"What about the cemetery? There isn't one for Protestants, only Catholics?"

"Hallstatt has one cemetery for all people. The first level you enter is Catholics' area; the upper level is Protestant."

"What about someone who was Jewish or with Jewish heritage, but she was perhaps Protestant?"

"I do not know. Maybe buried somewhere else or else in Protestant section. I help with tours, not much of history."

"Okay," Darby said. At least she knew there wasn't a cemetery she'd missed.

"There many activities available still in October in Hallstatt. I can arrange reservations for hotels and boating. Or you may go to salt mine."

"Thank you very much. I'll come back if I need anything. *Danke.*"

She turned back to Gasthaus Gerringer to unload her luggage and settle in.

For a second, she heard the *scrape, scrape* of the rake that had followed her down the mountain. It reminded her to stay focused. Some stories would fade away if not captured in time.

⌁

Darby carried her luggage into the dark dining area. The walls were cozy with cedar siding, and antlers hung above the fireplace. Sophie Gerringer appeared from a hallway around a corner.

"Are you enjoying our village? This first time, *ja?*" Sophie smiled as she stepped behind the front desk. Darby liked the sparkle of blue in the woman's eyes. Her dark hair was in a wild, full style that framed her clear skin.

"Yes, this is my first time, but my family is from here."

"Your family from Hallstatt?" Sophie Gerringer looked at her in surprise. "This like a pilgrimage for you to learn more about them?"

"Yes," Darby said in thought. "In a way it is."

"I live here only for last three year. My grandmother live in Hallstatt since she was a child. She maybe knew your family."

"And your grandmother lives here, right now?"

"*Ja.*"

"Could I ask her about my family?"

"Oh." Sophie stopped. "I not know. She is my grandmother but do not like foreigners much, especially not like Americans. This was American Occupation after war, you know? Maybe my mother could help instead?"

"I'd like to talk to either of them. Do you know why your grandmother doesn't like Americans?"

"She not tell us. I do not ask. But we take her to city for summers when many tourist here. She not nice to American or British tourist."

"My grandmother was eighty when she died, just last month."

"My grandmother age eighty-four. *Ja*, she must have known your grandmother and family."

Darby heard footsteps from a room down the hall. A woman walked out, but she wasn't old enough to be the grandmother.

"This my mother," Sophie said, introducing Darby. The woman gave a smile that matched her daughter's. She wore an Austrian-style apron, and her hair was neatly pulled into a bun. "Darby's grandmother lived in Hallstatt same time as Grandmother."

"Really?" the woman said with interest.

"She want to meet her."

The smile disappeared. As the two talked in German, Darby's heart raced. This woman would know Grandma Celia, even Tatianna and Gunther perhaps.

"You know about Hallstatt during the war?" Sophie asked after the volley of chatter.

"No, nothing."

"Hallstatt was about 90 percent Nazi. You see, it was a polit- ical party and gave good economics here. People had jobs. That what people in small village most concerned about—they must feed their families. They not know of Auschwitz and other camps. They have work after hard times. So they be

Nazis. My grandfather was Nazi—my mother not know if we should say that to you."

"My grandmother was half Jew."

Both women stared at her, their eyes large.

"My grandmother had family die in camps, but she escaped to America."

The two Austrians seemed embarrassed by their family past. But Darby at once felt old judgments vanish by an internal mirror that reflected her own life. Her political concerns in democratic America were over the economic growth in her own country. She didn't care what happened in Washington unless it involved taxes, small business interests, or the national, state, and local economy. "I can understand people joining a political party for economics. And I'd still like to talk to your grandmother if I could. She may know what happened to my grandmother's friend, whom I'm searching for."

The mother and daughter again conversed in German.

"I will ask her, but must translate if she say yes. She refuse to learn English. But remember I tell you about her and that she not like outsiders."

Darby listened to every creak in the wooden floor after Sophie and her mother left, expecting them to return from somewhere down the hall. After fifteen minutes, she heard a door open and footsteps. If she claimed to be Celia's granddaughter, would she receive a similar response to Brant's? Would this woman also believe Celia had died in the war? If she did, she'd probably not believe Darby or give any information.

"She will see you," Sophie said as they returned. "But she not happy. Are you certain?"

"Yes."

Darby followed Sophie down the hall. How could this old woman be that bad? As soon as she walked into the room, Darby knew. Grandmother Gerringer sat in a chair by the window with a scowl carved like marble into her face. Darby wondered if a smile had ever broken through the frown lines. The older woman sized her up in a glance and *hmmped* with disdainful satisfaction. *Yes, my perception of an American woman is correct,* she seemed to say. For the first time in her life, Darby faced a tiny glimpse of what a minority felt against the eyes of a racist. But her race wasn't in question—only her homeland.

"*Guten Morgen,*" Darby said softly, as if she were a schoolgirl sent to the principal's office. "*Danke* for speaking to me."

Sophie translated as they spoke.

"My family is from Hallstatt. The Lange family?"

The old woman *hmmped* again, shaking her head.

"Did you know them?"

Sophie translated Grandmother's answer. "She said, yes, she knew them, but they are all gone now. Said they were part Jewish family."

"Yes. Did she also know a young woman named Tatianna Hoffman?"

"She did," Sophie said.

"Could you tell me about them?"

The woman burst out in a torrent of harsh words.

"She wonder why she tell you anything." Sophie looked at Darby apologetically.

Darby swallowed and continued. "Before my grandmother died, she asked me to seek our family past."

Frau Gerringer responded angrily. Sophie tried to slow her down, speaking with her rapidly. "She is not happy with questions from yesterday. She say that everyone want to know what happened with their family after the war. Too much time passed for it now."

"Tell her that I have been raised as an American, but now I want to learn more about being Austrian."

"She say you still American, not Austrian."

"I am American and Austrian and others."

The old woman spoke only to Sophie, then turned her face away.

"I am sorry. She will not talk any longer to you." Sophie shook her head. "Please wait for me outside, and I will speak with her alone."

Darby told the grandmother thank you and left. She wandered the hallway that connected bedrooms and a private kitchen and living room, eventually making her way to the garden in the backyard. Wet leaves stuck to the walkway as she found a bench in the sun. It felt like the longest time before Sophie found her.

"She is sleeping now. I again must apologize for her. My grandmother is a very good woman, but the past is not good for her. She not want to talk to you, but this she told me. The Lange father, your great-grandfather, digged for ruins here."

"Yes, he was an archaeologist."

"And then, the girl, Celia, your grandmother, she was age of my grandmother, but a little younger. They went to the school here and at Bad Goisern—you go to grades one to eight here, then to the larger school in Bad Goisern or Bad Ischl. Our grandmothers were not good friends, but she say your grandmother was younger and had friend for many years."

"Tatianna Hoffman."

"*Ja,* that her. Grandma Gerringer say that Celia married a young Austrian boy, not Jewish. She say the girl and young man married and moved away—she thought Salzburg or Vienna. The friend, too, go away to school for her violin in Salzburg at the Mozarteum."

"Tatianna was a violinist?"

"That what my grandmother say."

"And what about the family?"

"Gone—before the war. She say all family left before Anschluß—when Hitler came to Austria."

"And does she know what happened to Tatianna Hoffman and her family?"

"All gone, she say. Tatianna have only mother; her father die long before in salt mine. That all she told me."

"I wish she would talk to me, but I don't want to upset her. Thank you for your help, Sophie."

"I hope you find what you seek," Sophie said earnestly.

Darby looked at the woman who seemed to understand her struggle. "I hope so too."

⋄≡◯═⋄

The next morning, Darby watched the figure skim across Hallstattersee in his black boat. It looked like the head of the Loch Ness monster with its smooth wake trailing behind. She rested against the balcony railing, fascinated, as if this same man had been there for a thousand years, pushing gently through the water, dropping his net in search of his morning meal.

Darby found herself ready for breakfast and decided on the way down the wooden stairway that she could live in this village for the rest of her life. But first, she must answer the questions that would not let her make serious plans for a future.

She carried down a thick paperback, *Hitler's Austria,* that she'd brought from home, though she had yet to crack its cover. Sophie brought coffee and a morning greeting as Darby set the book down along with a plate of food. She was about to bite into a warm roll when a voice interrupted. Grandmother Gerringer sat in a dark corner. Her German was decidedly unfriendly.

"I'm sorry, I don't speak German. No *sprechen Deutsche*."

The woman continued in a low voice, shaking her head with contempt.

Sophie reentered the room with a plate of sliced tomatoes and almost dropped it when she heard Grandma Gerringer. She turned quickly and spoke to her in German. But the old woman wouldn't be quieted.

"What is she saying?" Darby asked Sophie.

"Forgive us. I will take her to her room."

"No, I want to know what she's saying." Darby stood and entered the dark corner, sitting across from Grandma Gerringer. "Tell me."

"No, she offends you."

"I want to know, Sophie."

"She is an old woman and does not mean her words." Sophie set the plate down and hurried to the table.

"I think by her tone she does. Please."

Sophie sat at the table and covered her grandmother's hand with her own. She spoke to the older woman, whose words quickly flowed back. Sophie hesitated; Darby waited. "She say you are like all other Americans."

"Why?"

"She say Americans are arrogant. They come to foreign soil and demand answers when they not understand what they asking. She say, 'What would you do?'"

"What would I do?"

"Yes." Sophie translated as the old woman spoke. "She say you live in your home with only few Jews here. One is your neighbor, someone you know your whole life. We say we are Nazi for work and better Austria, then someone write and ask about Jews in village. We write and say yes, a few, but this is a good friend in Linz, and we think nothing of it. Later, another letter come and say all Jews must go to Linz. My husband know what happened and Jewish neighbor is his friend. He want to help, but I do not. We have own family to protect. Own family is first responsibility. It is not your own life you risk—it is your children. It is your elderly grandparents who live with you. Would you put them in danger, place them in death's grasp to save your neighbor?"

By the way Sophie was responding to her grandmother, Darby knew Sophie was hearing this for the first time.

"She say that none of us can understand. We only hear stories in books today. But she lived that time. One friend in Linz she knew hid Jewish children. Her old grandfather and grandmother were beaten with a club until dead. The rest of the family sent away and never return. She say there was no choice. It was suicide."

The old woman continued. "She ask you what you would do. What you do now? Do you have beliefs and not follow them? Do you see wrong in your government and say nothing? She say then you too guilty. As guilty as us who sat and did nothing. Do not judge me. I did not kill your family. They were gone by that time. Her neighbor she could not help when they came for him. She had to turn away or kill her family. Would you have done anything different?"

Frau Gerringer glared, and Sophie looked away. Darby needed an answer but didn't have one. She could see into the old woman's narrowed eyes. For her entire life Darby had had a set idea of what a Nazi was or had been. She'd see skinhead rallies on the nightly news, with their messages of hatred. Grandma Celia's family was murdered by the evil Nazis. Darby didn't want to sympathize or understand or even consider anything different than the image she had. The SS and Gestapo were men of evil and hatred. The Germans and many Austrians were pathetic in their attempts to protect themselves and not help the innocents. Right?

"She's right. I *am* an arrogant American. I have not understood." Darby stopped to face Frau Gerringer, then hurried toward the stairs as Sophie's soft voice told the old woman her words.

Darby rushed to her room and locked the door behind her.

She didn't want to know these things, to feel sympathy or understanding for those who allowed the terrors of the Nazis. Grandmother Gerringer taught her what she didn't expect. In a flash she also realized there were probably many Nazi sympathizers, Nazis themselves, still alive and well in this beautiful land. Of course, how could she be so naïve not to know? Many would not like the sins of the past resurrected—even and especially for the sake of truth. And here Darby had come with her swastika-covered *Hitler's Austria* book under her arm, practically proclaiming an attitude against these people.

I have judged people like that all my life without even knowing it until now. Yet, how different are we today?

The old woman's words frightened her. Darby had opinions and beliefs, but yes, she only did what was convenient for her own life. And did she do anything to help anyone else? She'd barely kept her trust in Grandma Celia when faced with the idea that the woman could be someone else.

Darby fell into bed, dragging a pillow over her head. This was a search for the past, not a digging into her own life. The shadows were stronger in this place, even stronger than the ones who had laughed from her grandmother's deathbed. And they wouldn't be satisfied until they took all of Darby with them.

CHAPTER SIXTEEN

Brant rested his head against his hands. He rubbed his eyes and looked at the door, wishing he could leave his office and never, ever return. Why had his work affected him so profoundly lately? He'd seen a hundred taped interviews of survivors. Yet now they came upon him like demons possessing his soul. He had several reviews to complete for the computerized Holocaust Survivor Library. But after today, Brant considered cutting reviews from his job description. It was taking too much from him, and he had plenty of other work he could do. He'd never enjoyed watching the tapes, though the work was preserving something essential for the future. But now it was all he could do to let the survivors' words enter his mind. He felt like an old, old man who had too much knowledge of the world's terrors.

Or perhaps it was because of Gunther. Because of Gunther's waning health, Brant couldn't simply run to his mentor at every turn or theological challenge. It wasn't that easy anymore.

Brant tried to focus on the computer screen. The man on the

frozen frame had an almost apologetic smile on his face. Brant clicked off the Pause button, determined not to let himself get too wrapped up in this.

David Weisman spoke, looking from the screen right into Brant's eyes.

"My brother, Henri, and I were liberated from Buchenwald. We were the only survivors in our family of eight children. I was sixteen and my brother fourteen. We were still very thin, under one hundred pounds, when we decided to make our way from the refugee camp toward our home. Our hope was to find any relatives or friends in our hometown. We were at a railway station in Poland waiting for our train when two Polish officers approached us. They began to ask us many questions. 'Who are you? Show us your papers.' We were surprised and showed our ID cards. My brother, though younger than me, had more bravery—I had lost mine long before. He said, 'We are Polish and survivors from the camps. We are going to our home.' This did not change their attitude toward us. We were ordered to go with them. My brother said, 'We will miss our train.' The officers did not care. We were naïve, believing there was nothing to fear because Hitler and his evil men had been destroyed. We were only upset to miss our train. But we believed that the world was better and would take care of us after we had endured so much.

"The officers led us away from the crowds and down streets that were dark and deserted. Our suitcases and belongings from the Red Cross quickly tired us, for we were still very weak. My brother asked how long it would take. 'Our train,' he said. 'It won't take long,' one replied.

"We turned a corner and it was a dead-end alley. I heard the sound of a trigger being cocked. We turned

and faced the cold eyes of the officers, the same look I
had seen so often at the camps. They both had guns
pointed at us. One hit my brother on the side of the head,
and the blow knocked him to the ground. 'You stupid
Jews. Why couldn't you die in the camps? Now we have
this job of killing when the job should have been done by
the Germans. I am tired of this work.'

"My brother and I were stunned. After all we'd endured,
how could we not have seen this? I could not move, I
could not cry or run or yell out. It seemed inconceivable
that we'd survived the most horrid of conditions and
endured the worst of man's evils to die in this empty alley.

" 'Please, please, why would you do this to us?' my
brother asked. I noticed the blood running down his face
after he spoke. 'We are Polish like you and have suffered
so much as we know you have. The Nazis were both of
our enemies, not one another. See my blood—it is red
like your own.'

"As they moved us against the wall, my brother continued to plead. I believe he wanted them to feel some human
touch, to see us as people. I could not speak, only accepted
that I was now dead. I was resigned to it. The SS and
Gestapo I escaped, but my own people I would not. But
somehow my brother's pleas made the officers waver. He
spoke about being my younger brother and how we
helped one another live through the war. Perhaps these
officers were brothers, for this seemed to have the greatest effect. I know Henri sensed this, for he continued to
speak about the two of us. He put his arm around me and
pleaded, 'My brother is the only person I have left. We
want to go home, to the place we grew up.'

"At last the officers looked at each other. 'They are
only boys. Not worth our time,' one said. They put their
guns away. Before they left us alone in the darkness, one

turned back and said, 'You better get to your home. There are many like us, and we don't let people like you live. You are the first of many.'

"We were saved by my brother. But the hit to his head had been harder than I thought. We were so weak that we had great difficulty returning to the train station and abandoned our belongings. Our train had left, but we crept onto another. It was very cold that night, and Henri and I warmed each other. But in the morning, Henri was dead.

"This was our welcome home."

Brant clicked off the video. He sat back in his chair with a sigh and noticed evening shadows had moved into the room. He'd been reviewing the stories for hours without thought of time or reality.

A quick knock rapped against his door. "Come in," he said, clearing his throat. The sound of his voice was amplified in the room.

"Mr. Collins, I'm leaving for the night." His secretary peered into the room. "Would you like me to order you something to eat?"

"No, I'm not hungry."

"Are you sure? You didn't have lunch either." Frau Halder looked concerned.

"I'm sure, but thank you. Have a good evening."

"You too," Frau Halder called as she exited.

When Brant's stomach rumbled, he realized he was hungry. But the thought of eating sickened him. He imagined what it would feel like to be actually starving. The faces he'd seen today knew that feeling. They knew true coldness, survival, and death.

Brant heard Frau Halder's laughter outside his closed door. Someone knocked twice, and the door opened before he responded.

"Hey, there's the man. Working late, as usual." Richter glanced over his shoulder. "I'll catch you later, Frau Halder." He walked into Brant's office and shut the door.

"What brings you to Salzburg again?" Brant asked, peeved at the interruption.

"Some business for Grandma. And what are you up to?" Richter rounded his desk and stared at the frozen image of David Weisman on the computer screen. "A survivor, I assume."

"That's right."

"What stories those people have to tell us." Richter shook his head as he sat on the edge of the desk.

Brant didn't respond but resented Richter's flippant attitude.

"I'm finding how important it is to discover the stories from our past. I've had Grandma Ingrid tell me quite a bit—what a time that woman had. It kind of explains why she's the way she is now, don't you think?"

"What do you mean?"

"I always thought of her as a cold, grouchy person. My parents hate her, and if I didn't hate them, perhaps I'd be more on their side. But in the last few years since my parents and I have been noncommunicating and I've gotten to know Ingrid, I've found out she's not so bad. Been through hell, that woman has. Used by the Nazis, doing whatever it took to survive and build a decent home for her boys, then they grow up and don't have any gratitude at all. I feel sorry for the old bat."

Brant thought of Ingrid. She didn't have it as difficult as Richter said. The Nazis took good care of her with parties, nice clothes, and jewelry—until the Allies shoved them out and Ingrid had to revise her story. She certainly hadn't experienced even a taste of what people like David Weisman had endured.

"It's a good thing Ingrid found Gunther," Brant said, closing the files on his computer.

"I don't know. That wasn't exactly a marriage full of love."

"Well, at least she was safe and had security. She never wanted for anything."

"But imagine not feeling love from your own husband. I've seen photos of Ingrid, and she was a good-looking lady. Wonder why Gunther never fell for her . . . what's his story behind it all?"

Although Richter sat relaxed in his chair, behaving as if this were a light conversation, Brant saw red lights flashing.

"You never asked Gunther about his past?" Brant asked.

"Not really. I knew he was married before Ingrid and that he was involved in the underground. But I don't know much more. I'm sure you asked. You always loved to hear those old stories, while I thought they were boring. Until now. Age is taking the playboy out of me, and I'm seeing a wider view of life."

Brant wondered about the validity of that—Richter no longer a playboy? Richter interested in history? The history of Gunther and his first wife in particular? "I don't mean to be rude, but I've got several more hours of work tonight. Did you need something?"

"Not in particular. Thought I'd stop by and see what you were doing—knew you'd be working late, as usual. Hey, we could catch a bite to eat. You could invite that good-looking American to come along." Richter adopted his most charming smile.

"Losing the playboy for history, I see."

Richter laughed. "No, I wouldn't move in on your prospect."

"She's not my prospect. I haven't seen her since the day you met her." Brant thought Darby probably now knew the truth about her grandmother—that she could not be Celia Lange Müller. She would have found the evidence at the cemetery and know. He wondered how she had taken the news, and whether he'd ever see her again.

"What? I expected great reports after I gave you the tickets. Saw a blooming relationship there."

"Not even close. I gave the tickets to Frau Halder."

"Ah, Brant, Brant. You have some lessons to learn. So you missed out on a great opportunity—you haven't even spoken to her since?"

"I don't even know if she's still in Salzburg. I believe she was going down to Hallstatt."

"Too bad. But I'll have to set you up with some women who won't let you go so easily. You need a social life. What's that old American movie say? 'All work and no play makes Johnny, or Brant, a dull boy.' Come on, take a break, live a little. Let's get something to eat. Frau Halder told me you haven't eaten all day."

Brant opened his mouth to decline.

"I insist." Richter picked up Brant's coat from the coat tree and handed it to him. Brant was hungry but wary. Richter liked to portray the best pals image, but Brant still wasn't buying it.

⊷≡◉≡⊶

"You are doing a great job, Darby," Professor Peter Voss said over the telephone.

"It doesn't feel like it." She closed the phone booth door behind her. Darby had stayed in her room most of the day after her encounter with Frau Gerringer that morning, finally venturing out in the evening to call the professor at the phone booth. Her room at the old house didn't have a phone, so she found one along Seestraße. Only locals and a few cars moved along the cold street after the sun dropped behind the Alps. "From the information I gained from Frau Gerringer, I wondered if perhaps my grandparents moved to Salzburg after they married so my grandfather could attend the university there. Do they have an archaeology department?"

"Actually, the university was not open then. The school closed down for a period of time."

"During the war?"

"Actually, for one hundred and fifty years."

"What?"

"Amazing, yes. We have an interesting history starting in 1617, but then it disbanded in the early 1800s until 1964. So your grandfather would not have attended here."

"Then that's a dead end."

"I will check and see if a Tatianna Hoffman was enrolled at the Mozarteum."

"Yes, I forgot about that. I'm glad you're listening."

"I think you have done excellent work. I am amazed the old woman would confess so much to you. Most people are very closemouthed, even with their own families. There are many adults who would be surprised at the Nazi past they have in their family. After the war, it was not often information passed to the children."

"I haven't talked to any of the Gerringer family since the grandmother gave me a good chewing out about being American and stupid. She probably would never have spoken if I didn't insult her with my swastika-covered book."

"You have a difficult job. You see, the people you wish to speak with lived in a time when America did not abide so abundantly here."

"What do you mean?"

"A colleague of mine has done intensive studies on the Americanization of Europe, particularly Austria, since World War II. You can not imagine how much World War II was a catalyst toward changing Old European culture—much of that due to Coca-Cola, rock and roll, and Hollywood. As you have seen, English is becoming the neutral language in most of Europe. But prior to wars, especially the first World War, Europe was the greatest influence on the world. And the

Austro-Hungarian empire was one of the greatest in Europe. So the elderly were raised with their parents' pride and patriotism for their great nation. The young people today live very much like Americans. Yet it is the elderly who will help you in your quest. Few will know the language. Few will trust you."

"I'm seeing that."

"The older generations feel their traditions are attacked by conquering Americans—no longer with troops, but with music and culture. And it is true. Imagine a foreign culture surrounding your children and grandchildren as you cling to the old ways."

"I can understand a little. In California, people protest schools that fly both the United States and Mexican flags. Others complain about the foreign cars on the highways and the influx of Asian and Hispanic people with Spanish often spoken more than English in certain counties."

"Imagine turning on the radio and having 80 to 90 percent of your popular music be German songs, sung in German. Also the majority of your movies and television shows are produced by Germans with dubbed-in English. Then two-thirds of computer software is in German, not English."

"I'm getting the picture. So what do I do?"

"Be sensitive. Respect their beliefs."

Darby thought of how she'd read the Nazi book at the breakfast table. That wasn't exactly respectful of Austrian feelings.

"It can be difficult for Americans to understand. Austria is an old place. Your America is a new land. Our heritage has been war and changing hands. In my parents' generation, this nation had been taken over, torn apart by differing beliefs, taken over again by the Allies, who were Soviets, British, and Americans, and divided among them, then given our freedom again. America is a land of discovery and settlement that has never been occupied by anyone other than itself. Unless you are Native American, you can find it hard to understand."

"I've been quite in the dark about all of this," Darby said regretfully.

"You are learning quickly. Are you returning to Salzburg soon?"

"Not for a few days or even a week, though I'm running out of time. There's much to look for—time has become my enemy."

"The secrets are not going anywhere, unless they are in human form. And then, yes, time is our enemy. What is your next move?"

"I may drive to Linz and maybe the concentration camp at Mauthausen. It wouldn't hurt to check records in these places after I look here in Hallstatt."

"Did you remember that I leave for a conference in Dublin in several days?"

"I didn't. How long will you be gone?"

"Until 17 November."

"I return to the States on the sixteenth. Unless I stay longer."

"That is unfortunate. But if you return to your home, I will not stop looking. You have e-mail?"

"Yes, at my office. I'll call or write you."

"Katrine will be coming with me to this conference. I am sorry, but you are back on your own for a while."

"And just when I was getting used to you two."

"I know. I want to tell you—to find the answers you seek, think with an Austrian mind, not an American. You must discover what we are like, what we have endured. War had split our country. Evil triumphed, not for a short time but seemingly for an eternity. We have been hurt because of that, scarred forever."

Darby paused, feeling the impact of his words. "I think that's exactly what my grandmother would have wanted."

⇥🕮⇤

Her luggage waited by the door. Darby stood on the balcony and said good-bye to Hallstattersee. As she turned away, she spotted something white upon the dark waters. A large swan floated along the edge with curved neck and pure white feathers glowing in the morning light. She hoped it was a message from above, telling her that everything would work out. The administration office had been helpful, proving that Celia Lange *had* been born in Hallstatt. There were other records that could be found at the church about family members who were either buried there or now the residents of the bone house. But Darby didn't want to know that information. It was time to leave, to seek the next piece in the fragmented puzzle. She was hopeful, for she was finding some pieces, though the puzzle grew larger with every discovery.

Darby hauled her luggage down the stairs and rang the desk bell to check out. Sophie hurried toward her with a large smile on her face.

"I am so happy to see you. My grandmother told me something for you today."

"She did?"

"Yes, she very thoughtful all yesterday and this morning she ask if you here still. When I say yes, she tell me some things."

"What?" Darby didn't know if she wanted to hear any more from the old woman.

"My grandmother saw your grandmother one more time after Anschluß, after the other Jews were gone from village. Your grandmother and Tatianna Hoffman came to Hallstatt. My grandmother not know why she come. Her family was gone and house occupied by different family. My grandmother was married and had a child already, and she did not talk to Celia. But they stay only one night in the village and came by train. But when they leave, a young woman pick them up in her car and they go with her."

"Did your grandmother know the woman?"

"No. This last time she see your grandmother, but she hear that all family went to Mauthausen and not returned."

"That gives me more to wonder about, but tell her I said thank you very much."

"One more thing. She say one man might have information, but not know if he still alive."

"Who is he?"

"He was a boy lived here in Hallstatt. He joined Nazis and was guard at Mauthausen."

Darby grabbed a pen and paper from her purse.

"My grandmother say this man maybe know about Lange people who died there."

"A man who knew Celia and Tatianna and was a guard at Mauthausen."

"His name is Bruno Weiler."

Darby drove from the village south around the lake. Had her grandmother taken the same route so many years ago? While Darby turned back toward Linz in Upper Austria, Celia had turned the opposite way, deeper into the Alps and Tirol region toward Switzerland. But in fleeing her homeland with Tatianna beside her, Celia had made a quick stop at her childhood village. Perhaps she had said good-bye to the place of her innocence, the place of first love.

Darby envisioned the girls fleeing the sleepy village with eyes turned in fear that someone followed. The sound of Nazi boots hid behind every crevice, in every corner. Would they make it out alive? Would they see one another again? Did they have any idea that these were their last moments together?

And who was the other woman? Perhaps the one who had written and told Grandma Celia of Tatianna and Gunther's deaths. Darby also wondered why Gunther had chosen another route to escape—through the Sudetenland, which was now the Czech Republic. A completely different route.

Darby spent the morning driving winding roads through mountains and hidden lakeside villages. Ebensee was a lakeside village that had been a subcamp of Mauthausen. Traunkirchen. Gunskirchen. Traunsee. Darby had heard these names from her grandmother and tried to recall the stories.

By early afternoon, she entered the *Autobahn* highway, expecting masses of cars driving over a hundred miles per hour. Yet, though cars sped along, it felt like a comfortable rate. She was never quite sure how many miles per hour she drove on her way toward the industrial city of Linz with the speedometer in kilometers per hour, not miles. Sophie Gerringer had helped her find a place to stay in Linz and had told her a brief history of Austria's second-largest city. Hitler had spent his childhood in Linz—a fact that surprised her. She hadn't realized the German Führer was a native Austrian. Unlike Mozart mania, however, Hitler was not a claim to fame for the country. Perhaps if he had won the war there would be Adolf candies and delicacies. When Hitler returned to his hometown with his German storm troopers, he already had great visions for Linz: to recreate it as the Jewel of the Danube. He'd hoped to retire here, if permanent retirement hadn't been forced upon him.

Darby followed the directions to the hotel and drove into the parking lot. The rural hotel sat on a green hillside with a view of the famous blue Danube River.

Only a few miles of bends downriver was Mauthausen Concentration Camp and its subcamps Gusen I, II, and III.

Suddenly, as if struck in the face, Darby realized where she was going. Her carefully planned list with its connections and leads included the name of Mauthausen. And not just any concentration camp, but the one that had held and stolen the lives of members of her family, and most likely Tatianna's life also. Number eight on her to-do list had once been a place of hell beyond hell, and for people with her same blood.

KZ Mauthausen. A place that stole tomorrows. Darby would be there tomorrow.

CHAPTER SEVENTEEN

Brant jumped awake. His chest and back were beaded with sweat, and the sheets were damp and twisted beneath him. The screams from the nightmare continued to echo in his ears. He saw the images that tormented his sleep—black figures with children and babies clutched within their grasp. A monotone voice spoke above the carnage.

"My baby had dark hair and brilliant green eyes. He would smile and laugh when he looked at me. As I patted his back and rocked him at bedtime, he patted mine and snuggled close to my chest until sleep overtook him. My baby was torn from my chest by a soldier. They threw him into the air and used him like a clay pigeon. I embraced death to escape insanity. But by another evil, I lived. After the war, I married again and had two more children. But never do I stop hearing my first baby's cry."

Brant tried to shake the story from his mind. But unlike a nightmare his own mind concocted, this was a true story. One of the many he'd witnessed on tape. Brant had always been haunted by the stories, but evermore he was becoming consumed. It seemed his future was to be forever crippled with the sufferings of others. No one understood, except those who survived. Yet Brant did not belong with them either, for he had not lived through it—only witnessed their stories.

How Brant wished to talk to Gunther. How Brant wished things hadn't changed. In other downtimes, the old man had words to help Brant through, allow him to see the value of life and living once again. He tried to resurrect the words, but the sound of Gunther's voice eluded him. He could only hear the cry of children.

Brant kicked the sheets and blankets from his ankles and sat on the floor, the metal sideboard cold against his bare back. The room was more than silent. It was empty—just like his life. Suddenly he couldn't take another day of it.

He turned onto his knees as he'd done when he was a child. "God, help me."

At that instant, Gunther's voice returned from a fold of memory. "Everyone asks how God could allow such a terrible thing." Gunther's voice resounded with spirit in each word. And tonight Brant listened again. "Why does man blame God? For I want to know how *man* could allow such a terrible thing. God gave man dominion over the earth. If we simply can't care for one another or stop evil from breeding and growing—"

"But Gunther, I hear their voices," Brant had said. "I dream about them."

"I've struggled as you are."

"I'm sorry, Gunther. Of course you have. I lost my mother to a disease, not by man. Why should I complain about hearing the sufferings of others? It should make me appreciate my life, not come to you complaining."

"You struggle because you truly care. You don't merely listen; you feel the words and hurts of others. That's a good thing, though more painful for you. It's easier to close your heart to others. But keep it open, Brant, despite how you bleed."

"So where is God in all this—if we can't blame him? You tell me he's active in individual lives. Where was he?"

Gunther had faced him then, kindness in his eyes. "And you want to ask, where is he now?"

"Yes."

"I do not know all the answers. But I know some things from my own life. I know God is quiet at times, but not absent. He hears our cries but allows man's business. He allows man his own course."

"And evil takes over."

"Only the evil that man warrants. That goes for yesterday and today. But still in individual lives and as a collective world, God allows choices. He doesn't want puppets to seek him. He wants man with a free will. Perhaps he is silent so that man's work without his involvement can be seen. I do not know. But because of the choice God allows in man, innocents do become victims. While I don't believe God wants this, he does heal all things and punishes all wrongs."

"I doubt everything. I don't know if I believe God exists."

"I must believe in God because I've known both evil and love. I've tasted evil within myself and by what's been done to me. This evil is alive, breathing, destroying. Yet I also have known the opposite of evil. I lived with an incredible, enduring love and found truth and hope in ashes. The good is often harder to find. Evil is easy. Love is hard. But one leads to death. The other to life."

"How have you survived it all?"

"My faith in Christ. I see what is not in our vision. I hear what few are willing to listen for. I feel what most would say is not there."

"I could never have such a faith."

"Do you believe?"

"I think I do, but my doubt is as great. Sometimes it's too much for me. How can I live with these stories in my head? How do they live?"

"I do not understand how the telephone works."

"What? What are you talking about?"

"I do not understand how the telephone works. A few days ago, I made a call and really took a look at the telephone. I've been told about a huge wire under the ocean or satellites that transmit sound, but still, I cannot fathom how my voice can be spoken and delivered across the world in one moment. Yet I use the telephone regardless. I cannot understand the telephone, or the computer, or a thousand things that are made by man. How can I claim to understand everything about God? Yet can I give up on God because of my ignorance?"

Gunther had put a hand on Brant's shoulder then. "One thing I must say to you. I think of you as my son and implore you. You must live, Brant. Live because you can. Live because others cannot. And in that, live for God."

The words faded away, and Brant was alone again with only past moments. He wanted the old times he'd had with his mentor, when they'd meet for coffee and sit for hours talking. "Who will help me, Gunther?"

A breath of answer entered his thoughts. *Come to me, for I know all the answers.*

Brant felt like Jacob in the Bible wrestling with God. But he finally had reached the end. He could not live as he was, and so he put his trust in the one he did not understand.

As Brant bowed his head, he still heard the stories. But a new strength arose in him that told him to live, to love, to breathe.

⊷⊜⊷

The day dawned with glorious greeting. Life breathed in hillsides of green, in clusters of trees adorned with their leaves of many colors, in a windless day of warmth. And Darby was driving to a concentration camp.

She wanted to tell the day to be ugly and sad, that an eternal cloud of stark weather should cover the land south of Linz. The sun should no longer warm the earth; geraniums should no longer bloom in window boxes. But the design of nature with its tearing and healing of seasons didn't mind her desire or her destination.

Darby followed the signs, exited the Autobahn, continued through towns, passing a McDonald's and a gas station. A wide, clean bridge crossed the Danube, reminding Darby of her grandmother singing the words to "The Blue Danube," Austria's unofficial national anthem.

When Darby turned the car toward Mauthausen, a hillside community, a sudden chill prickled down her back. The sign for the village shared the name of its concentration camp.

The KZ Mauthausen sign pointed the way. The road wound upward past houses, a beautiful tree-lined curve, open fields, up and up. The road was a perfect place for a Sunday drive until she reached the top. There it stood—a walled fortress stretching across the horizon. Guard towers with pointed tops, a straight concrete wall surrounding it, and a red chimney silhouetted against a brilliant blue sky.

She maneuvered the vehicle between the white straight lines of a parking space. A few other cars inhabited the paved lot along with a tour bus with advertisements for its other excursions—Danube Tours. Darby shook her head at the irony: *One of its stops took camera-happy tourists to a concentration camp.*

With her arms still on the steering wheel, Darby leaned forward, letting her eyes trace the length of the massive blocked wall with five rows of barbed wire on the top.

It's big. As big as I should expect, but bigger than I actually imagined. Tatianna, are you here? My family, are you waiting?

It was time to go in.

Darby carried her camera bag without the intention of taking photos, but for companionship. She stopped at the iron doorway. The structure towered above with a walled courtyard ahead. She felt small in the shadow of the massive stone walls.

No signs led her now, only blind direction.

I feel alone, Darby thought, though she imagined the cries of thousands who hadn't been alone, only dreamt to someday be.

She paused in the center of the courtyard, surrounded by the barbed wire–topped walls. Her entire life she'd denied that this place was part of her family heritage. She denied it from entering her life or thoughts. Now she was here. An instant thought told her to run, run, run.

"I feel a part of me has died too," she whispered to the shadows watching from every crack and crevasse. "Perhaps that's why I can't find love or peace. Part of me died here also—is that it? Not body or soul, but heritage and past."

Darby stood a moment longer. She heard voices from the parking lot, and a couple entered the silent courtyard. Holding hands and a tour book, they'd come to learn and remember. Wasn't that what this place was for—to help people never forget? The interruption brought her back to the place and her mission.

I'm here for a purpose, she reminded herself. *I've come to search for information, facts, answers. I'm looking for Tatianna, maybe my family too. Information is all I seek; nothing else.*

Darby moved toward the end of the courtyard, where wide concrete stairs led upward. Beside them was a plaque in both German and English. She paused to read while the couple passed.

> In remembrance of the members of the Second
> Armoured Division of the US Army who liberated the
> camps of Mauthausen, Gusen, Ebensee, and others

nearby in Upper Austria in May 1945. Their deeds will never be forgotten.

She climbed the steps and stopped at the top. To her left, monuments stretched away toward what appeared to be a massive gorge, which broke off as if the hillside had been eaten away. Darby assumed it must be the granite quarry with its "Death Walk" stairway. She wondered if any of her family members had died on that stairway. Had they stumbled under the weight of granite slabs as Nazis bashed clubs against their bodies? Had Celia's father, brother, or aunt died this way? Anyone against Nazi policy could have been sent here. What did those faces look like? She didn't know and wasn't sure if she wanted that knowledge even now.

Darby turned away from the memorials and quarry and walked beneath another set of stone archways with buildings beyond. A man in a booth sold tickets, tickets to a concentration camp. She understood the need for payment, since the place needed upkeep and financing. But still it made her shiver—she was paying to see where her family was murdered.

Darby handed the man the schillings and asked for a guide or map.

"Bookstore," came his simple reply. She considered asking for more information, if only she knew German.

Darby entered the main area of the camp, which stretched across the top of the hill. She spotted a bookstore sign beside the structure. When she stepped inside the small room, she saw that several other people were there, perusing books and videos. Darby glanced through the resources, too, picked out a few in hopes of finding more information, and bought a guide. On her exit back into the sunshine, Darby held the door for an elderly woman in a wheelchair. Their eyes locked for a moment. Was that sorrow she saw?

"*Merci*," the woman said as she passed. A French woman.

What's your story? Darby wondered as she watched the frail woman gaze around the little store. Darby wished she could have Grandma Celia with her, or someone to hold her hand and share this experience.

Guidebook in hand, Darby tried to refocus on facts. First, get a general overview of the camp, then look for the information needed.

She glanced from map to buildings and walls. The barbed wire atop the granite wall stretched around the camp on three sides. Another barbed-wire fence, once electrically charged, marked the back. Behind her was the entrance gate, while in front was the camp's main roadway with the roll-call area—where she now stood. Housing or "blocks" lined the left side of the road. At one time these buildings had been the first in several rows of blocks that housed prisoners. Upraised foundations marked where the now-missing blocks had stood. A kitchen unit, laundry building, sick quarters, and brothel—everything the Nazis needed—were in the front. Behind were the inmates from all over Europe—political prisoners, gypsies, criminals, "anti-socials"—with the farthest from the front being the Jewish block. Darby plodded down the long row to the last foundation. A headstone stood in the center with the Star of David and individual rocks covering the top. Darby reached for a stone on the ground and put it on top of the headstone with the others. She paused, feeling the heaviness of the moment, then moved back to the roll-call area.

On a granite wall near the bookstore entrance several plaques caught her eye. This was called "The Wailing Wall." Darby found the irony in the name. The famous "Wailing Wall" in Jerusalem, built next to the last-standing remnant of Solomon's temple, was a place of prayer for Jews. This wailing wall was for tears and death during long hours of torture.

Darby breathed in slowly. What did she feel? Was this even real? She moved on, walking in and out of buildings, looking at photographs and reading the guide. For minutes, she forgot where she was, as if she'd entered a library or museum. The next minute she again heard the deafening silence of a death camp—a scream that yelled, "I was murdered here, right where you stand and hold your guidebook. They murdered us all, and here the world ended."

Darby entered a grassy area surrounded by shorter granite walls. The manicured lawn was covered with stone crosses and headstones with the Star of David. No markings rested above individual bodies, since the entire site was a mass grave. Did Tatianna rest here, her body twisted together with Darby's other family members? Or was she in the ash pile behind the camp, dumped down the hillside slope where grass and flowers and trees now grew?

An aunt who'd rocked Grandma Celia, her daddy who'd wiped tears from her cheeks—somewhere like this they died. People, real people—parents, teachers, lovers, woodworkers, travelers, photographers.

Why had Darby never thought of them? In school, her class had done family trees and reports. Several of her friends were fascinated with their pasts and studied at great length. Darby hadn't had the interest. She did the work required, learned the basics of what had happened, but that was all. History was history and not a place for her to look. You couldn't take a picture of yesterday, only of today.

One of her worst school experiences was when her teacher learned she had family who perished in the Holocaust. He was fascinated and wanted her to do a family study for her final report. "You're a child of Holocaust survivors and victims. Which camps? Were they Jewish?"

She'd never been embarrassed about her Jewish blood until she met a friend's surprised questions.

"You're Jewish?"

"A little, just like I'm Austrian, Danish, Cherokee, and a bunch of other things."

Darby hadn't noticed many racial tensions or prejudice in her small town. She'd never quite understood it and became even more confused when she was the victim.

"Well, I'm glad I don't have Jew in me," the girl said.

"When did I become a Jew?"

But that was only a passing scene in the myriad of high school and college events. Darby buried it and hoped her classmates did also. She had many friends and was involved in student government, French club, the yearbook—as photographer, of course. Yet as she stood in the place where her own flesh and blood had died, she finally wondered and wanted answers. Was it simply self-absorption, or a partial reaction to the unspoken silence within her home about past events? Or had Darby herself somehow resisted, knowing the steps she now took were the requirement for such interest?

She wished she could travel back in time and help the ten thousand individuals in each mass grave. That she could tell them, "Stay alive, stay alive. In sixty more years, you'll see that Mauthausen and all the other camps are only museums. Tours will walk through and point to your grave unless you can keep living." And then make it happen.

After walking the length and width of the camp, Darby entered the museum. Two exhibitions were displayed in the long, narrow building. She sat with several others, watching the Mauthausen film that played every hour with different languages in different rooms. The images and information numbed her as she wondered if one set of those hollow eyes that stared from the black-and-white screen would recognize her as their descendant. Did they point and say, "There's my great-granddaughter. She's come to save us a few decades too late"?

Darby left the dark viewing room for the exhibit "Austrians in the Nazi Concentration Camps of Auschwitz, Buchenwald,

Dachau, Ravensbrück, Sachsenhausen, and the Theresienstadt Ghetto." After that, it was the exhibition on "The Mauthausen Concentration Camp and its Sub-Camps."

All of a sudden Darby wondered not about the victims, but about the men in SS and Gestapo uniforms. Germans, Austrians, farmers, banker's sons, poets, and woodworkers—they were men just like their victims and yet not like them at all. Darby stared at the photographs. Frozen eyes stared back.

Where are you now? Are you burning in some kind of hell? Did you finally see yourself before you died? Or are you still living, still hating, or still hiding? Maybe you there are the old man in Hallstatt raking his leaves. Or maybe instead he's the one you didn't get to kill.

Desperate to find something in their eyes—an evil or darkness, or even a glimpse of shadow—Darby moved closer. But the photographs—what she trusted to capture the moment— failed her. For there was nothing to be found. Nothing to distinguish an SS from Gestapo from soldier from civilian. Nothing to show a higher or lower degree of guilt or hatred. One man waved at her from the back of a truck; a mischievous grin sparkled from his face. In life he could be someone who'd flirt and ask her for a date or throw a football with the neighborhood children. In the photo he sat in the back of a truck brimming with human corpses.

Numbers, statistics, and maps depicted the facts, but the faces in the photographs argued it couldn't be true. They were just men and boys. They couldn't have experimented with that man's life or tortured that poor woman's body. Darby read a quote by a United States colonel, Seibel, about the camp's liberation: "Mauthausen was a reality . . . as was the brutal and inhumane treatment of human beings by human beings."

Examining each photo, she read in her book the English version. When she saw a display titled "Guard file cards," she stopped, remembering the information Sophie Gerringer had given her. She took the paper from her purse and searched the chart.

There. Darby couldn't believe it. There was the name. Bruno Weiler. It was difficult to understand what must have been guard information, and she could not find an English version. But she did find his name and "Hallstatt, OS," meaning he must have been from Hallstatt. There were several dates on the file, including 1940 and 1943. Did that mean he'd been a guard here during that time?

Darby left the museum, wondering what to do next. Should she seek to discover what happened to this man after the war? Bruno Weiler could have seen Tatianna before she died. He may also have seen her other family members. But would he still be alive today?

Once outside, Darby noticed a stairway leading downward. A group moved down it, speaking in hushed tones. If it was an English-speaking group, perhaps the guide could help her. Darby took the steps to the bottom, into an unlit room. The group had moved into the next room, but her feet stood still. There was no need for a guide or tour book to know where she stood. The tiled walls were clean, though the grout had been scrubbed till crumbly. Above her head piping crisscrossed the ceiling and faucets hung, faucets which had never felt water push through the spouts. Darby noticed the thick doors, one behind her, one at the other end. She stood in a gas chamber.

At this realization, her heart began to pound. The doors felt like they were closing. She had to force herself to breathe slowly and deeply. She saw hands clawing the tile walls, children crying, and men and women screaming. Her head said to run, but her feet wouldn't move. Darby wanted to vomit, but not even tears would come. Finally, her feet did move. She went numbly toward the opposite door, only to find a labyrinth of other shower rooms and then the ovens.

She stared into the open mouths of two black ovens. A

bouquet of silk flowers rested on a long, iron basket that pushed corpses into the ovens to turn flesh into ashes. Darby imagined the systematic machine, cooking, removing, cleaning, devouring. One human had lovingly buttoned a young man's sweater and brushed his hair—and someone else had put his body into that oven.

I feel you are still here.

Memorial plaques and photographs covered the oven room's walls. One had several toy cars and a plastic doll on the floor in front of it. Darby read the French words *Enfants morts*. A French community's plaque for their children who died at Mauthausen.

The horror was so intense that she had to look away from the plaques, but she was drawn to the wall of photographs. The smiles and faces of men and women, young and old. It seemed she could take an SS guard's photo upstairs and easily replace it here, for they were all flesh and blood, men and women. Only one had chosen to mutilate his brother, and the other was mutilated.

I have to get myself together. I need to focus on my purpose for coming here.

But Darby couldn't shake the sense of blood beneath her feet. And not just blood from veins alone. But the blood of hope, love, dreams, tomorrow—the blood of life poured into this ground. And that blood was her blood also.

She turned back toward the plaques on the walls and read each memorial in search of names. And there she found it, written in English: *Remembrance of the Lange family. Loved for all eternity.* Darby touched the engraved writing and hurried out.

The roadway moved too slowly beneath her feet. Through the stone archway, an echo chased her quick passage down the wide stairway to the last courtyard on the lower deck, then across the high-walled courtyard and out the iron door. She breathed more deeply but didn't halt her pace. She was free to leave—a simple act not granted to thousands of others.

Darby knew from the horror of this place she would never be the same. She also knew that SS guard Bruno Weiler, who had known her family and been their captor, must be found. Whether he was dead or alive.

CHAPTER EIGHTEEN

Mauthausen stayed with Darby. It followed her like a cloud around a mountain, covering, blocking, shielding rays of light. What she'd left with was an increased determination to find answers, and to find Bruno Weiler. But as days turned into more than a week of searching in Linz and back in Salzburg, Darby's determination wavered. Her newfound love for Austria grew weary as her eyes turned toward documents, museum information, book research. She returned to Salzburg with more untied ends than when she'd left. She didn't return to the Salzburg Cozy Hotel, but instead found a quiet place on a back street in the Old City. Time clicked toward her departure home and she found little success, some due to her language inability, some to lack of knowledge in seeking her answers. How could she find a man sixty years after he was last seen? Her biggest help had been Professor Voss, but he was in Dublin and wouldn't return until after she was due to leave for home.

Darby considered staying longer. She felt so close, but so

close to what? What she'd come for now seemed unclear. Her focus had been to find Tatianna or a way to fulfill her promise to Grandma Celia, but now she wanted more answers than that one.

She wondered about Celia's family, her family, and what their exact fate had been at Mauthausen. Darby also wondered about her grandfather, Gunther Müller. Where had he died in Austria? Was there a grave for him?

Inquiries into the Mauthausen Camp did yield some information. She learned that a woman named Celia Lange Müller, along with a group of other prisoners, had been killed by firing squad on the date of August 11, 1941. Then she'd been put into the ovens.

A few days before going home, Darby called her mother to pose the idea of remaining in Austria. Instead, she found the old life drawing her back. Her business partner, Clarise, had called in hopes that Darby had returned early. Her mother was marking the days on the calendar until her return. It looked as if her time was up. Darby consoled herself that in a way she'd done as her grandmother wished. She was certain Tatianna had died at Mauthausen. She had taken Celia's name and her place. Sure, there wasn't any hard evidence. But without solid proof, she couldn't get any records changed to Tatianna's name. And was that what mattered? She knew the truth and so did Grandma Celia and Tatianna. And Grandma's God knew. Did the actual names really need changing? Suddenly, Darby felt tired throughout her body, mind, and spirit. Home sounded even better than when she'd gone to youth camp and cried every day until they let her go home early.

With her heart turned toward home, Darby made a final phone call in Salzburg—one she'd avoided for weeks.

"Hello, Darby," Brant said when he picked up the line. "I've wondered how you are doing."

She didn't like the jumble of emotions she felt when hearing his voice. "I'm doing well, how about you?"

"Very well." He was quiet for a moment. "Would you like to meet?"

"No, but thank you. I'm leaving in the morning, but I have a question for you."

"You're going home?"

"Yes. I went to Hallstatt but didn't find whatever it was you wanted me to see. Will you now tell me what it was?"

"You didn't go to the cemetery?" He sounded surprised.

"Yes, but you didn't give me any more information than that."

"You didn't find her headstone?"

"Are you saying there is a headstone for Celia Müller?"

"Yes."

"But she was killed at Mauthausen. There would be no body to bury."

Brant hesitated. "I know that. But there is a headstone, for the memory, I suppose."

"Was this information in your confidential files? I didn't see one with her name on it."

"Perhaps my files were wrong. I must apologize."

"Well, it was a good trip anyway."

"So have you discovered anything?"

Darby paused. "Yes, but nothing that can prove or disprove who my grandmother was. And now it's time for me to return home."

"I wish you the best, Darby."

She caught sincerity in his tone. "I wish you the best also, Brant."

⊷⊜⊶

On the morning Darby left Austria, she felt no better than the day she'd arrived. As the plane lifted from Austrian soil, she watched the mountains rush away below her. Since no one was there to tell her good-bye, Darby left as she'd arrived— alone. Her heart turned toward home, to her grandmother's place and her own apartment in Redding. The things so familiar made her homesick and ready to be there. Once back, she'd discover if the shadows could be buried.

"Good-bye, Salzburg," she whispered. "I'm going home."

CHAPTER NINETEEN

When Darby's feet touched United States soil, relief washed throughout her entire body. America— home of the free and the brave. America—the Statue of Liberty, television in English, and no-smoking airports. Darby wasn't a foreigner here. She didn't have to ask anyone to "*Sprechen Sie Englisch.*" The feeling of home beamed strong and good, for the first few hours.

Her mother hugged Darby tightly as they met in the airport and said, "I'm so happy you're home safe," about ten times before they'd even left the San Francisco city limits. Not that they moved very quickly. The throngs of cars moved like a continuous line of ants; the traffic hadn't changed while she was gone.

They drove Highway 101 north with the world unchanged except for the vineyards and trees turning toward winter barrenness. It surprised Darby to realize how easily life contin- ued on with little change, even though she was completely changed. The grasp on life she'd hoped to reclaim by returning home was quickly running like water through her fingers.

Every mile closer to Grandma Celia's, Darby felt more like a
stranger, even in her hometown. It must be fatigue, jet lag, she
told herself, and the overwhelming relief from the last month
of stress. Surely she'd awaken the next morning renewed and
happy to leave Austria and its mysteries behind. She couldn't
live forever as a displaced person wherever she went. Perhaps
some buried secrets were right where they belonged.

"I'm so glad you're home safe," her mother said again as she
unlocked the front door.

Darby smiled wearily.

"I have dinner in the Crock-Pot, some new Mr. Bubble, and
the heating blanket will be warmed up in no time."

"That sounds wonderful. Mom, why don't you come to
Austria and take care of me like this?"

Her mom stopped in the kitchen. "You're going back to Austria?"

"Did I say that?" Darby rubbed her eyes and sat on a bar
stool. "No, I'm not going back. At least, I'm probably not."

"How could you consider it? I thought you'd gone, done
your work, and now you're home."

"I didn't finish anything, only found more trails. But you'd
know that if you'd asked. I noticed you had a dozen questions
about my flight, but not one about what I found there."

"You're tired," her mother said as she turned away, "so I
didn't want to grill you. I figured you'd tell me if there was
really important news."

"It's all important news, I think. But there's so much I don't
know and have no idea if I'll ever know. Aren't you curious?
This is your family and heritage, even more than mine. Both
your parents were there. One never made it out."

"I'm well aware of that. Why do you think I don't like my
daughter going?" She yanked two bowls from the cupboard
and closed the door loudly. "Can we argue on a different day,
Darby?"

She watched her mother shield herself in activity, putting

Darby's luggage near the hallway, getting a tray and spoon from the cabinets. "I'm sorry. We'll talk later. What's in the Crock-Pot?"

Her mother lifted the lid. "Ragout stew, of course."

"And my favorite baking-soda biscuits?"

"Yes." Carole smiled.

"Thanks, Mom." Darby wrapped her arms around her mother from behind. "I'm happy to be home safe."

"Go wash up, young lady," Carole said, laughing. She grabbed a dish towel and flicked it at her. "I'm glad you're home too."

Darby carried her luggage down the hall toward her old bedroom. She paused at Grandma's doorway. Everything looked the same as when she'd left, except for a few boxes in the corner. She walked to the dresser and touched the carved wood box. The lid to the Pond's cold cream bottle was askew, so she unscrewed the top and smelled the white lotion inside. One bottle of moisturizer was turned upside down to retrieve every last drop. "Every seed of waste can grow a tree of poverty," Grandma would say, her voice almost real inside the room. If her grandmother had been there, she'd have ushered Darby inside and demanded every detail of the trip. As tired as Darby felt, she'd share all the discoveries and new questions she had and sort it out with someone who cared and wanted to know. But Grandma Celia wasn't waiting anxiously to hear her stories today, or any day. Darby hadn't quite understood that until now. Throughout Darby's travels, Grandma's presence had been with her. Now Darby had returned to the fact that her grandmother was gone, forever gone.

◈══◈══◈

Darby was jarred back to reality by an early-morning call from her business partner. She was still in bed when her mother brought the phone.

"Welcome home, and now get back here! We're flooded, and we also got contracts on the Christmas Show at the Civic Auditorium and on Hartley's Thankgiving Party. It's time to come home, girl—mentally and physically."

"I'll be there later today."

"Thank God you didn't get stranded in an airport somewhere. I've been so stressed. We'd have had to cancel on the Hartley's Thanksgiving Party or something and that would never have been forgiven and I've been so worried, and . . . well, I'll whine and moan about all our woes when you get here."

"Good-bye, Clarise," Darby said with her eyes closed.

"Hurry! We're desperate up here."

⋆⇒◦⇐⋆

The four-hour drive to the north end of the long Sacramento Valley gave Darby time to remind herself of who she had been before flying off to Austria. Her life in Redding revolved around the photography studio, and not much more. And this was one of the busiest times of year, time for her to put her shoulder to the wheel despite the dust of her journey still surrounding her. Jet lag clung hard with nothing sounding better than cozy sheets and her mother's stew, but she was a co-owner of the business and needed to fulfill that obligation. She'd left her responsibilities for her grandmother's quest, and home had called her back.

Darby topped a rise on I-5 north to see two familiar volcanic mountains surrounding the Redding Valley. Mount Shasta resembled an ice cream cone on the northern horizon, while smaller Mount Lassen sparkled with white snowcaps in the east. As she turned into her apartment complex overlooking the wide Sacramento River, it felt like years had passed since she'd been home. Then the inside of her apartment appeared so changed, Darby wondered if she were in the right place. Her furniture looked familiar but the décor was far from her own with a fuzzy sheepskin rug, East Indian blankets, and carved wooden sculptures dressing the room. Darby had been thankful for a temporary roommate to water her plants while she was gone, but she hadn't expected Julie to become permanent. Her home was her solitude, and Darby shared that sparingly. However, since she was single, everyone thought Darby the perfect target for any college-aged girl in need of a place to stay. Julie, Clarise's niece, was finishing her semester at the local college before transferring to a university. Her roommate had moved out, and Julie couldn't afford the place on her own. Clarise had said the usual line: "Only for a short time, and then you won't be so alone."

Darby walked inside, stepping over a shoe and some laundry in the hall, and opened her bedroom door. She peered inside, glad to see her Ansel Adams black-and-white photos still on the wall along with her flannel comforter atop the pine four-poster bed. Darby only had time to dump her luggage on the floor and walk out.

Five minutes later, she pulled her tan Jeep into the parking lot of the small shopping center. It seemed a hundred years had passed since she'd last stood in front of "Hanrey and Evans Photography," but she didn't feel the rush of excitement she once had upon seeing her name on the window. This was her world, her big dream. Yet suddenly it appeared insignificant in the wake of losing her grandmother, walking the grounds of Mauthausen, and peering into the past. Coming back to normal life might take some time.

Darby stepped into the cozy showroom and paused. No one waited on the sage green chairs or paged through their portfolio binders. Today must be one of the scheduled workdays Darby had implemented the previous year during their busy seasons. It worked better to schedule shoots three days a week and leave the rest for full work days; their production increased this way. Darby took a breath in the calm of the showroom, then walked toward the back work areas.

Clarise popped up. "Oh, I thought I heard the bell. Thank goodness you're back. Come on, come on, let's get you in here."

Darby was surprised to see her partner with auburn, curly hair. When she'd last seen Clarise, her hair was straight and blonde. The auburn appeared more natural with Clarise's olive skin, but the puffed-up hair would take some getting used to. Darby barely had time to look at her partner before Clarise began updating her and delegating their commitments. The holiday crunch had descended. Clarise chose the Hartley's Thanksgiving Party because, after all, she could take her husband and they needed a date night. Darby got the Christmas Arts and Craft Fair—sticky kids, noise, and probably the same grouchy elf as every year—for after all, she *had* been on vacation for two months.

⋇⊙⊂⋇

Thanksgiving came and went with Darby's mother volunteering at a shelter, dishing up mashed potatoes and gravy, while Darby worked all day except for an evening stop at a friend's house. At least she didn't have to worry about her mother or feel guilty that she hadn't spent their first holiday without Grandma Celia together.

"Say Santa Claus," she found herself repeating behind her camera lens days later. "Don't cry, honey. What do you want for Christmas?"

While Darby usually loved kids and Christmas and capturing the perfect shot on Santa's lap, this year she felt near tears, along with the children. The same grouchy elf had arrived like the ghost of Christmas past and herded children on his assembly line. Santa was more interested in Darby than the children, even asking her for a date on his break. It was the first time she'd been asked on a date in months—and by a Santa who smelled like cigarettes.

The days and evenings flew by and Darby didn't feel any happier. She had arrived back in the States like Dorothy, clicking her heels together saying, "There's no place like home, there's no place like home." But Darby wondered about the rest of the story. Was little Dorothy content to be back in Kansas? Did she grow up, marry a farmer, and age against the rolling plains? Or did she remember that once she wore red, magic shoes—shoes that could kill a witch and possess more magic than all of Oz? Could she return home and exist with Oz in her mind? Or would dreams of yellow brick roads and an emerald city call her to return?

Darby didn't know about Dorothy, but she knew that the feeling of missing something grew with every moment.

Perhaps she'd changed too much to stay home.

⋅⋅⊰≡◎≡⊱⋅⋅

"I've waited long enough," Richter said. He paced the park walkway while Ingrid sat on a bench, feeding pigeons. "How can you be so calm about this? The woman went back to the States. Brant and Darby did not connect their information as you thought they would. How will we find the heirlooms now?"

Ingrid continued to drop crumbs of bread. "I said I hoped the two would connect their information. We simply don't know what exact pieces Brant knows and what this woman knows. We do know she's Celia Müller's granddaughter."

"That's another thing I want to know. How did you know she was Celia Müller's granddaughter? And how did you know for me to look for her to come to Austria?"

"There are some things I'll keep to myself, for now. I will say that I didn't know for certain she'd come. At least, not for sure. But the pull of riches lures everyone."

"Then why did she return to the States?"

"I don't know. I thought Darby Evans and Brant would discover the truth, but he is far more suspicious than I thought. Yet I know we are closer than before."

"How can you say that?" Richter wanted to take her bread crumbs and toss them away. "We have nothing, and I don't see how this plan is ever going to work. If we wait too long, the treasures will be found and claimed."

"Yes, but there's no other way."

"I can think of other ways."

"Patience, my grandson."

"I have debts that aren't waiting patiently. Perhaps you can wait a lifetime, but I can't. And I won't." A flurry of pigeons scattered to flight as Richter stalked away.

CHAPTER TWENTY

In her little free time, Darby took to driving country roads along cold irrigated pasturelands, through the rocky, oak-covered foothills and into the snowy mountains that surrounded the long valley floor. But for all her wandering, Darby was unsure what bothered her. The work she'd once tackled as a challenge now drowned her. Yet it was more than just her work. It seemed she'd become misplaced somehow, and if she didn't find out what to do, soon only a shell of herself would be left.

Every night she stayed at the studio late and began to find her way through the mess Clarise had made. Darby decided she'd never leave Clarise in full charge for that long again. She could shine in public relations, advertising, and photo shoots, but her organizational skills were lost behind the bubbly smiles she gave their clients. The office was a mess. Orders lost in stacks. Phone calls left unanswered. Darby's well-oiled machine had quickly turned to rust. As she sat in the late-night shadows, she thumbed through a stack of photos from the Redding holiday parade. She looked out the window and wondered

how the streets of Salzburg appeared dressed for Christmas.
What did tiny Hallstatt look like with snow covering the
village and surrounding Alps? The night sky was her connec-
tion as she imagined snowflakes falling beneath those same
stars, somewhere far away.

Back to work, she told herself. *You're home now. Leave it
behind.*

Darby ordered Chinese food and forced herself back to the
reprint orders. Yet every photo brought thoughts of her trip,
along with the questions she'd never found answers to. Finally
she gave up for a while and carried the white carton of sweet-
and-sour chicken to her computer. While in Austria, she'd
often wished for the use of the Internet in her research. Now
she tried to remember what she'd wanted to find.

Their studio office had connected to cyberspace when they'd
opened two years earlier, and both Darby and Clarise had been
hooked on the world inside the monitor. They chatted with
pen pals and other photographers and surfed for quality equipment at good prices. Clarise even found a guy for Darby on-
line, certain he was her perfect match like in the movie *You've
Got Mail.* He turned out to be sixty years old. The fun of
cyberspace slowly faded.

Darby logged on and tried to remember how many weeks or
months had passed since she'd last checked her e-mail. She
scanned the advertisements and photography E-news, surprised
to see her grandmother's pen name, "GramC," in the in-box.
Darby hesitated before clicking the button. The date on the
e-mail was near the time of Darby's trip to shoot the climbing
club in the Trinity Alps. Seeing the words on the screen was
like receiving words from beyond the grave.

> *Darby-girl,*
> *Old granny is feeling better today so I made it to check*
> *e-mail, of course. Can't wait to hear about your mountain*

adventure. I'm jealous, in a purely loving way. Be ready to tell me stories.

> *Love you with all my heart.*
> *Gram C.*

P.S. Need to talk to you about some things. Remember the Scripture I cross-stitched and have in my room? We'll talk about it when you come down.

Darby peered at the screen. What Scripture? She remembered a cross-stitched picture in the room but not what it said. Most likely her grandmother believed Darby had read the note and the Scripture when she came down to visit her. Could this Scripture be a key to Grandma's mystery—words that would have helped on her trip? Darby also hadn't thought to examine her grandmother's computer files. Grandma Celia had only purchased her computer six months before her death, but she'd worked on them at the library and taken courses for several years. Certainly she must have kept files on her search for the Lange inheritance.

Checking her watch, Darby decided not to scare her mother with a midnight phone call. But her mind tried and tried to recall the words of the picture. Darby rested her chin on her hand and read the words again. How strange to see Grandma's note so alive, like any normal day.

After several minutes, she clicked the print button, then began to use search engines for information she'd wanted in Austria. The Web site "Find-A-People" allowed specific or general searches on names. Darby typed in a variety—Bruno Weiler, Hoffman for Tatianna's family, Müller for her grandfather's, and Lange for her grandmother's family. Names appeared in discovery columns. No Bruno Weiler appeared, but many Müllers and Hoffmans. Not one looked like a good lead. She found Professor Peter Voss in Salzburg. The screen gave his address and phone number. Darby looked for her own name and found her address and phone number listed also. It was an eerie feeling to discover herself on the screen. Anyone could procure her address.

Darby joined a cyberlibrary and continued a search that would trace books, newspapers, magazine articles, and other documents. She typed and sifted through information, printing anything that could be good information. Her growing pile was transferred into a three-ring binder under different divisions—People, General Information, Mauthausen. . . . Suddenly an old newspaper from the 1950s revealed the name Bruno Weiler.

"I found you."

She printed the article as she read it. It reported a trial in the early fifties where five guards were indicted on charges of war crimes during the time they worked at Mauthausen and other camps. Bruno Weiler was one of them. They were all found guilty and sentenced to five years in a German prison. They would have been released in 1957.

Continuing to search, she found nothing more on Bruno Weiler but located a site named "Desperate Search." It recorded people looking for missing family members, friends, or wartime buddies. It shocked Darby to see so many people looking for displaced and missing people as far back as World War II. She opened one of the files: "Where is my father?" It had facts and locations of a soldier in the United States Army who had married an Italian woman, then disappeared after the war, abandoning his wife and two children. One of the children had entered "desperately seeking." She was in her fifties, but she still sought her father. Darby was tempted to return to "Find-A-People" and seek her own father, but knew she was far from ready to pursue those feelings.

Instead she added her own entry to the list: "Seeking Bruno Weiler. I am seeking information on a man named Bruno

Weiler. He was an Austrian Nazi prison guard at Mauthausen
Concentration Camp. Please send any information."

Darby added searches for the Lange and Hoffman families.
On impulse, she surfed to sites about coins and Empress Sissi.
After an hour of looking, she began to get a picture of the
value of her family inheritance and why it was so sought after
by the Nazis. Anything belonging to Sissi became instantly
valuable. The entire country of Austria had celebrated the one-
hundredth anniversary of her death in 1998. Darby started
searching for Celtic coins found in Hallstatt, but her eyes
began to feel heavy. Finally she turned off the world within
her computer and ate cold Chinese food alone.

Then she headed toward her car and home. At a stoplight,
she remembered a dark street—an escape from peopled
routes—that she'd found in Salzburg, right in the middle of
town. It was quiet and ancient, opening into a peaceful plaza
surrounded by buildings. Until now she'd forgotten about that
place. As she got ready for bed, more memories and questions
sifted through her mind. Even as she slept, she dreamed of
Austria.

As Darby blow-dried her hair the next morning, she still
couldn't shake her questions. She thought of Tatianna, then
Bruno Weiler, then the Lange inheritance, wondering about
her, what happened to him, and where the treasure was. As
she later parked in the lot, late for work, another question
arose. Was she just convincing herself that she needed to put
Austria behind her? Yet she felt it inside—not the dying slowly,
but a hopeful excitement. Maybe she needed that to get her
through this late-twenties crisis or whatever she was dealing
with. Her logical side reminded her that her future was in the
States, right at this studio.

Clarise met her at the studio door.

"Oh, Darby!" Clarise yanked her partner in so fast that the permed auburn hair almost whipped off her head. "I have the best news in the entire world. Guess what?"

"What?"

"No, guess!"

"I don't know . . . you won the lottery, you're pregnant, you have a date with Brad Pitt and Markus said you could go? I don't know, but those would be your favorite things to happen."

"You're crazy, girl. All wrong, though very good ideas. But you'll be so excited!" Clarise jumped up and down like she *had* just won the lottery. "Creative Designs Photography is closing down, and Scott offered us first opportunity to buy their clientele list, equipment, and, yes, even their shop!"

"Really? Why are they closing?"

"Scott is retiring, and no one in his family is interested in the shop. He's offering a great deal, told me that since I used to work there, he wanted to give me first shot. This is a perfect opportunity. We'd have the chance to be the top studio north of Sacramento. We'll have to hire more people, of course, but—"

"Slow down. I need some more facts. I need time to consider."

Clarise stopped, and her hands dropped to her side. "Aren't you excited about this?"

"I don't know. I think so, but I need a moment for it to sink in before I invest my life away."

"Darby, it's exactly what we've dreamed of."

Yes, she thought, *but is it what I'm dreaming of now?* "Let's get the details, then let's talk," Darby said.

"I'll do that," Clarise said as she stormed out of the room.

Clarise stayed on the phone most of the day until Darby was sure she couldn't take her partner's screech of excitement one more time. At last she couldn't and escaped to the movies alone, something she'd never done before. But a super-sized

Coke, Reese's peanut butter cup, buttery popcorn, along with a romantic comedy made her feel worse than when she'd arrived. The couple on the screen was gooey and lovey for the second half of the flick. What could be sadder than a single person watching a romantic comedy alone? Darby found out when she ran into someone she knew—her old boyfriend, Derek Hunt, and his gorgeous wife.

"You're back!" Derek called across the lobby while she was trying to sneak off unseen. He ran and hugged her. "Tell me about the trip. I couldn't believe it when I called the studio and Clarise said you were in Europe!"

Darby pulled away and smiled. Derek hadn't changed, except his thick sandy hair might have receded slightly, and his well-defined features appeared more mature. Derek's wife, Rochella, walked up slowly and smiled, but she didn't appear thrilled to see her husband's ex-girlfriend. Long, perfect hair framed her model face, and Darby instantly felt grungy in her jeans, T-shirt, and greasy hands from too much butter.

"I've been back a few weeks," she said, wiping her chin. "You called the studio?"

"Yeah, we wanted more copies of our family portrait for Christmas cards. But tell me everything. Where did you go, what were you doing there? Was it just like you imagined it to be?"

"There's a lot to tell. It's beautiful and amazing—you both should go there someday. Get matching bikes and see the countryside."

"Rochella doesn't ride." Derek glanced at his wife. "But I still want to go someday."

"You should. . . . Well, I better get going." She made a gesture that hopefully looked like she was meeting someone.

"Oh, yeah, of course. Hey, let's meet next week for lunch and catch up. I want to see your photos, which I know you've had developed since the day you got home."

Darby didn't tell him she hadn't taken any pictures. Clarise had been too busy to ask, her mother probably didn't want to see them. Everyone else she'd brushed off with a change of subject.

"See you later," Darby said. "Bye, Rochella." She waved and hurried away, making a detour to the bathroom. Waiting a sufficient time, Darby finally hurried through the parking lot, only to get a honk and wave from Derek and Rochella. They definitely knew she was alone now. Next time she'd watch a video at home—if she could get rid of Julie's weekend friends.

⋄⟫═◯═⟪⋄

Darby was surprised when Derek walked into the studio the next day.

"Rochella asked me to pick up our reprints. And since I'm here, I'm taking you to lunch."

"I'm swamped with last-minute projects. Sorry," she said, glad to have an excuse. Little could be worse than lunch with Rochella and Derek. "Half of Redding had the idea to give old, reconditioned photographs as Christmas presents this year. And it was a last-minute idea too."

"You know, that old photo idea is good, and I still have a few presents to get. Maybe . . ."

"Forget it, Derek. Your parents always like the Hickory Farms packages anyway."

"Very true. Sure you don't want to grab some lunch—just you and me? Come on."

Just then, Darby heard Clarise on the phone down the hall. "Yes, we can even buy the studio," she said with a shriek of excitement for effect.

"I'll go."

⭜⭑

They sat across from each other on red velvet cushions in the dungeon-dark Italian restaurant. Neither spoke for a moment. Darby squirmed while Derek stared her straight in the face and wondered why she'd come. They'd dated from the end of their senior year of high school through three years of college. They'd remained friends afterwards, both saying they'd probably get back together after college. They wanted the last year to play and date and enjoy one more year before entering the "real" world. Then Rochella entered the picture. Derek had been under a spell with the idea that a woman of class and beauty would be attracted to him. He was from a small town; she vacationed in the Caribbean. Darby and Derek's friendship drifted quickly after that, and Darby had realized how much she loved him. It took a long time to release the idea that they were meant to be together again.

At Derek's wedding, she'd met Clarise, who was a friend of a friend of Rochella's. That's where the studio idea began. Clarise's family lived in Redding and since she had the most financial backing, they'd settled the partnership there. A year later, when Derek's job transferred him to Redding, he looked Darby up. But besides their family portrait with what seemed like an added child every year, she rarely saw Derek or Rochella. Now she sat across from him, wondering what to say.

"It's really good to see you," Derek said.

"It's good to see you too."

"So it's Dorothy home from Oz."

Darby's mouth dropped. "I've been thinking that for weeks. How did you remember my love of yellow brick roads?"

"I remember everything."

"And you were the Scarecrow, right?"

"Hey, I was the lions, tigers, and bears. Remember?" He

wiggled one eyebrow and smiled the grin Darby had once thought irresistible.

"I have no recollection." She held up her hands but couldn't help smiling. "Except what about Scarecrow in need of my tutoring help and a few brains?"

"This is getting too nasty for me." His laugh made her feel warm and comfortable while emphasizing her lack of companionship even more. All her close friends were married or pursuing their own careers, and even Grandma Celia with her ever-ready ear had left her. Darby missed having someone to talk to, laugh with, and tease. She'd had that with Derek. They'd put their heads close while discussing ideas, thoughts, and dreams. Even when they were "only" friends, they'd attacked the world with passion—she with her photography and Derek with his dreams of travel and exploration. Now he worked on the ladder of success with some company he didn't have much interest in.

Darby sat back against the cushion. She'd changed since their college days, and so had he. But Darby didn't need that youthful passion now. She only wanted someone to sit close to while watching TV. She longed to play foot wars in fluffy socks and lose herself in warm kisses. At the rate she was going, it would never happen.

Then a picture of Brant Collins flashed into her mind. Did he too wish for companionship and love? What was he doing right now? She glanced at her watch and calculated the time. He'd be either at his office working late or at home, perhaps with some Austrian woman, watching TV or playing foot wars.

"Do you have somewhere to be?" Derek studied her with an expression she'd once loved, his head tilted to the side, one eyebrow up in question. "The food hasn't even come yet."

"No, just checking the time. Clarise will have a heart attack if I'm gone from the office for long."

"Then you better start talking, 'cause I want to hear all about your trip."

Someone really wants to listen? Not because he had his own motive or agenda for my life, but because he really wants to know?

Darby opened her mouth and the words seemed to tumble out—her lonely arrival in Austria, the old man with the rake— everything. Their food arrived, and they ate between discussion and story.

Derek leaned forward in rapt attention as she told about Mauthausen and the interchangeable faces of SS and victims. They discussed what drove one man to hate and another to mercy.

"I never would have thought this before my trip, but I believe every person on earth is capable of incredible hatred or incredible love. We choose what degree we'll live at."

"Are you saying we're all capable of what the Nazis did?"

"I think we are. There were evils beyond Hitler at work, and those evils remain. When we dabble in hatred, selfish pursuits, pride, and contempt for others, our minds can descend without us totally aware, until our actions mirror our mind. I think there were some seriously sick individuals who lusted and relished the evil within them, but I also think there were mostly average people—men and women—who because of many reasons, from fear to self-preservation, were swept into the rush and performed, partook, or turned away from what they normally never would have considered."

"Scary thought, indeed. We are all capable of evil?"

"We are all capable of horrible things; we see it still today. But I think, perhaps, we are also capable of great acts of love. It must be what we put into our lives."

Derek twisted his fork around a last bite of pasta. "So do you think that the things we dabble in or experiment with, be it feelings or thoughts, be it good or bad, will most likely lead to the action and result?"

"Grandma Celia would say you reap what you sow. Are you still on the subject of the demise of man, or are you speaking personally?"

"When you someday get married, Darby, marry your best friend."

"What? Where did that come from?" She laughed, but then noticed the sorrow in his eyes. He touched the tips of her fingers.

"I love Rochella, but I miss my best friend. Rochella's perfect on the outside, a showcase. But we don't laugh like you and I did. We don't jump in the car and go skiing or cycling. We don't do much of anything. When you get married, make sure it's to your best friend. You were mine, and I let you go."

In shock, Darby withdrew her hand. "Derek, you can't be serious."

"I am. I really miss you."

Even a year ago, her heart would have pounded at his touch. "Make Rochella your best friend."

"We have nothing in common."

Darby looked at the face she thought she would always miss and desire. But she knew him as not her own. Perhaps something or someone was out there for her, but Derek wasn't it. Instantly Darby clearly understood that, and she almost smiled with the relief. "Let's see, you have three children in common, marriage vows, and how many years together? This is a marriage slump. Derek, you need to love her, even if your heart isn't fully on fire, or the fire goes out." She paused, thinking of Grandma Celia, her husband Gunther, and Tatianna. "Love is a gift that can be lost when you don't pay attention or keep it alive."

"Is this from experience?" Derek's expression turned grim.

"No, from observing. It's pretty funny coming from me,

the loser at love. But I've seen my grandmother and what she lost. I'm learning to cling tightly to the love we're granted. Whether you have one year or a lifetime, don't forget that love is a gift. A gift to be appreciated and nurtured—for better or worse."

"It's not that easy."

"What if Rochella were taken from you right now? Let's say she was killed or kidnapped or separated from you by a war. How would you feel about her then? You'd fight for her. You'd miss her. You'd remember the million perfect moments you've had together."

Derek was silent. His eyes seemed far away, scanning images and thoughts beyond them.

"You're right." Derek leaned against his hands. "But it doesn't help with today."

"Love her like tomorrow is your last day with her."

Derek slowly smiled. "Here I am, making a pass at you, and you lead me back to my wife. You probably think I'm a jerk."

"No, I thought that long ago." Darby chuckled.

"You can be such a brat." He sighed. "So when are you going back?"

Darby looked at her watch. "I should have been back forty-five minutes ago."

"No, I mean back to Austria."

"Why do you think I'm going back?" she asked, startled.

He gave a boyish grin. "Because I know you. And I know that look in your eyes whenever you talk about it. You seem surprised, as if you don't realize it. I can't believe this. Darby Evans is in love and doesn't even know it."

"What are you talking about?" An image of Brant came to mind. "There is no way I'm in love."

"Don't give me that. I've watched you as you talked about the trip. 'When I was in Austria . . .' or 'This great place in

Austria . . .' You left your heart there. The Alps won you over," he said with half smirk and half accusation.

"You think so?"

"I know so. I don't know whether to be more jealous over you getting to go back or the Alps getting to have you. You really are a good friend, despite my wayward intentions."

"It's not just the Alps. It's Salzburg too. The old city nestled against Mönchsberg with the fortress above. Cobblestone streets with musicians and outdoor cafés and markets teeming with people. You should be jealous," she teased.

"Where are the photos?"

Darby's smile left her.

"You don't have them with you at all times?" Derek said with a laugh.

"Actually, I didn't take any pictures."

"What? You forgot Nikki at home?"

"No."

Derek leaned forward. "What's going on, Darby? You always take Nikki everywhere. You'd drive everyone crazy with all the pictures you'd sneak in. Why wouldn't you take pictures of this place you fell in love with?"

"I don't know. It just didn't seem right for me."

"Do you want to talk about it?"

"There's not much to say. My grandmother talked to me before she died. She said I needed to stop hiding behind my camera and really see the world. Then, when I went to Austria, it didn't feel right for me to shoot it. Maybe I needed some time to simply be me."

"So when are you going back?"

Darby took a long breath. She bit the inside of her cheek. "I am going back, aren't I?"

"I think it'll be soon."

‑‑◦‑‑

The last night before she returned to her mother's house for Christmas, Darby locked the doors to the studio and paused. She peered back through the windows into the front show-room. Christmas decorations wrapped around displays of their framed work on the walls—weddings, family portraits, and children with full smiles and bright eyes. She remembered painting those walls and hanging the portraits. Their grand opening had been one of the best moments of her life—at that point. Could she leave it all behind? Her eyes trailed upward into the night sky. Beckoning stars told her to keep looking up; she'd find the right way.

CHAPTER TWENTY-ONE

As Darby entered the driveway, she noticed the lack of Christmas lights on the eaves of the yellow-and-white house and a Nativity scene on the green lawn. Grandma Celia had loved the Christmas season and lived for tradition with baking, decorating, hot cocoa instead of morning coffee, and fresh pine boughs to bring the mountain feel into the home. It worried Darby that it was only two days before Christmas and the little yellow house wasn't decorated.

"I'm home," she called, setting down her luggage in the entry.

"Darby!" Her mother hurried down the hall with outstretched arms.

"Is everything all right, Mom?"

"Oh yes. I just filled my life too full of activity, especially at the church. I've avoided a bit of this decorating, but I did start going through Grandma's room." Her mother did look better than Darby had seen her in months. "I'm going to get all the food Grandma stored in her room and give it to the church missionary cupboard."

"Food she kept stored?" Darby glanced down the hall. "In her room?"

"Oh, yes. Grandma's kept food and supplies stored in the garage and in her room for years. 'Just in case,' she'd always say."

"I knew she hid money, but not food too."

"I also found letters, newspaper clippings, old birthday and Christmas cards from years and years ago. In fact, I thought you might want to take the letters . . . if you go back. They're written in German."

Darby stared in disbelief at her mother. "If I go back?"

"I've been doing some heavy praying. If God wants you to return, then I'll support you."

"I don't know what God wants. I don't even know what I want anymore."

"You know what God wants." Carole put her hand on Darby's arm. "He wants you, Darby."

Darby felt uncomfortable beneath her mother's gentle gaze. "You *are* too busy at church, Mom," she said, trying to lighten the mood as she walked down the hall and into Grandma Celia's room. Looking around the room, she finally spotted the cross-stitched picture. It hung near the door where someone sitting in bed could read it easily, but anyone entering or standing would hardly notice. Darby stopped suddenly, reading the words.

> Greater love hath no man than this, that a man lay down his life for his friends.
>
> —John 15:13

Her mother stood in the entry. "What's wrong?"

"Grandma thought I knew before I went to Austria."

"Knew what?"

"Grandma wanted me to read that verse before the trip. I've speculated that Grandma Celia escaped from Austria to America using Tatianna's papers. And I believe Tatianna died impersonating Grandma Celia. She died instead of Grandma Celia. It has to be the truth."

Her mother turned to stare at the picture on the wall. "Wait here a minute."

Darby had wondered why Grandma had left so many vague trails for her instead of simply revealing more truths. But Grandma had expected her to know that Tatianna did die at Mauthausen under the name of Celia Müller because of this verse. The speculation gone, Darby could have concentrated earlier on finding the facts.

"I was going to give this to you for Christmas," her mother said as she returned to the room. "I think I should give it to you now."

Darby looked away from the words in the picture to see her mother holding out a wrapped package. "What is it?"

"Open it."

Darby sat on the edge of her grandmother's bed and carefully unwrapped the green-and-gold paper to find a thin box. From inside the box she lifted out a worn leather-bound Bible. It had been white leather at one time, but the years and use had worn the gold leaf from the edges and made the cover a dull gray. She ran her hand over the top and lifted it to her nose to breathe in the scent of the past. "Grandma's old Bible. I forgot about this."

"While I was cleaning in here, I found it in her bedside table." Carole sat beside her. "Grandma had several Bibles, but I remember looking at the words all in German as a child, wondering what they said. But look inside."

"Oh, Mom," Darby whispered. In faded lettering was written *Celia Rachel Lange Müller*. Below it read *Tatianna Elise Hoffman*.

"Yes. It was given to Celia by Tatianna," her mother said. "Tatianna gave Celia even more than her life. I think she may have given her faith as well."

Darby couldn't take her eyes from the Bible. All those years, Tatianna was in their lives, unknown to everyone but Grandma Celia. And had her grandmother's great faith been born from a young girl's sacrifice?

"You need to go back, don't you?" Her mother put her hand over Darby's. "When you do, know that I will support you as best I can. This is bigger than us, Darby. It's God's work still in progress after all these years."

Darby felt as if she were slowly awakening from a very long sleep. Her eyes were barely glimpsing images and distinguishing light from shadow, but still there was a lot of sleep in her eyes, drawing her back into darkness. But she was ready to awaken, finally willing to see and face what she'd long hidden from.

That night Darby talked for hours with her mother as they decorated the house "to make Grandma proud," drank hot cocoa, and watched their annual *The Grinch Who Stole Christmas* movie. She couldn't remember enjoying her mother more. And she was finally able to share all her thoughts with someone. But another part of her, the awakening part, still waited—as if she stood on a precipice, waiting for the perfect time to jump.

⋆⇒◐⇐⋆

Brant drove through the darkness on freshly plowed roads north of Salzburg into the town of Oberndorf. He was not alone in his Christmas Eve journey, though he didn't know any of the fellow pilgrims who crowded the streets and searched for parking places. Their license plates were from many European nations, and he was sure he'd find many more nationalities walking the icy roadways. He got out of his car and knew he was in for a long haul on the frosty night—but that's what he wanted. Time to think, time to breathe the frozen air, time to believe in Christmas again.

Brant parked on the outskirts of town and walked back toward the river. The night was hushed above the crunching of his boots on the packed snow. He crossed the bridge over the Salzach and stopped to look into the familiar waters. Maybe next time he'd drop a wooden boat from the bridge at Salzburg before driving downstream to Oberndorf. That would be a fun activity to do with Frau Halder's grandchildren instead of the soccer practice that left his shins bruised.

He crossed the river and heard a whistle blow at the train station as a bright red locomotive chugged to a stop. The cars would undoubtedly be teeming with more people who, like Brant, searched for one thing—a silent night.

Brant had never visited the birthplace of the world's most-loved Christmas carol. He'd heard "Silent Night" first at home in America. His mother would sing it every evening during the month of December as she tucked him into bed at home in Portland. First she'd sing in German, then in English. Every night he remembered asking her to tell the story behind the song.

On this Christmas Eve, he was in the place where it began. The lullaby with its message of heavenly peace would be sung in all corners of the world tonight in more than two hundred languages. The song would be heard by carolers in America, through cathedral organs in Europe, inside thatched huts in South America, and at candlelight concerts in Australia. Brant followed the growing groups of people until he arrived in front of the Silent Night Memorial Chapel, where the original church of St. Nicholas once stood. Groups of people milled quietly, almost in expectation. If they stood very still, they might find teacher Franz Xaver Grüber and priest Josef Mohr discussing what to do with a broken church organ with Christmas Eve approaching. They might then hear the strum of a guitar that commenced a chorus of "Silent Night" as on that first night in 1818.

Brant watched the people. Some closed their eyes and tilted their heads upward to the clear, dark sky. The small, white chapel could hold only a fraction of the crowd outside. On a higher section of town, the church that housed the original altars and pulpit would re-create the moment when the song was first performed along with a midnight mass. But Brant wanted to be in the place where it began.

He, too, found his eyes moving from the simple chapel into the sky of diamonds on black velvet. He imagined a heavenly host just beyond the sight of his human eyes.

God, you know I'm not good at praying. So I'm just going to talk and hope you understand. His eyes found constellations and the long spill of the Milky Way. God was there and here, he felt, and whispered from his heart. *I want to thank you for a million things, but mainly for showing me how to live the life you've given me. Thank you for Gunther being part of my life—I don't know what I'd have done without him. And thank you for second chances, and thirds and fourths. Right now, you know what Richter is doing, why he comes to Salzburg regularly now and asks to stay with me. You know his motives. So help me know what to do.*

I also keep thinking of Darby Evans. I don't know where she is right now or what's happening in her life, but I hope she is well and that she can find you as I'm finding you.

And also I must remember all those who have lived through hell on earth—give them your peace tonight.

I don't know if that's how I should pray, but amen.

From one side of the street, Brant heard a soft chorus. A gentle wave of voices joined around him, singing in more than one language the hymn that bound them all together.

Brant's voice joined the chorus, first in German, then in English.

"Silent night, holy night. All is calm, all is bright."

⊷≈◐═⊷

In a flurry of hugs and noise, Maureen, John, and the five-year-old twins arrived. Any minutes of sorrow could not hold for long with the twins ready to keep everyone busy. It seemed as if a year had passed since Darby had seen them, though it had only been a few months since Grandma's funeral.

"Auntie Darby, I hope I have a Baby Alive under the tree," Kallie said as they carried presents from the car to the house. "Do you think I do?"

"Well, I don't know."

"I hope, I hope, Auntie Darby." Kallie stopped to look at the presents overflowing the tree skirt. "I weally, weally want a Baby Alive that will wet her diaper."

"Kallie," Maureen scolded as she carried a load of presents from the car. "Don't pester your aunt, and come help Daddy bring in your suitcases."

Darby grabbed the girls as they walked by and whispered, "Maybe you can open one present after the candlelight service tonight."

Two sets of eyes grew as large as silver coins. They giggled and whispered to each other out to the car.

⊷≈◐═⊷

The lights were turned low in the auditorium as they entered in silence. Darby suddenly longed for Grandma Celia's hand that always reached for hers sometime during the service. The candles were lit one by one to the soft song, "What Child Is This?" Mary walked down the center aisle and the Christ child was placed in the little manger on stage.

Who were you really, little child? Darby wondered. *Who are you now?*

Instantly, it was as if Tatianna had sent a message directly through the years. It was simply the act of an old Bible that now rested in Darby's hands. Tatianna dies for her friend. Tatianna gives the legacy of life and a faith to pass down. Tatianna was pointing the way to another one who died, not for one person or family—but for all mankind.

Music rose through the sanctuary as angels entered the stage, some lowered from above, others surging from offstage. Their glittery robes sparkled in the darkness as voices raised a chorus. "O come, all ye faithful. . . ." The wise men brought their gifts and laid them at the foot of the manger. Then other people moved forward. A businessman with briefcase in hand, a woman dressed like a housewife, a young child, and a college-aged girl dressed in tight pants with several earrings in one ear. More people came of different ages, races, and professions. All walked forward and knelt before the child.

At that moment, Darby knew she didn't want to miss what God had to offer. She wanted to be part of it all, the intricate design created with the same care as life, land, wind, and rain.

Her eyes watched the infant asleep in the manger. God as man. God on earth by humble means. God dying a humiliating death. Like Tatianna's gift.

As the pastor prayed, Darby whispered her own wish. *I want the Creator of what my eyes find in the mountains. And I will give you my life. Forgive me and my wandering ways. I don't really know what this means for tomorrow, but I'm trying to believe. I think I do believe.*

The service closed with the gentle "Silent Night."

CHAPTER TWENTY-TWO

When she checked the computer files, Darby hoped to find more answers. All she found was the trail of Grandma Celia's search for the Lange inheritance. Her letters were to Holocaust organizations, Austrian officials. Darby even found the letter to Brant Collins saved on the hard drive. One surprise was the discovery that Grandma Celia had organized putting up the Lange memorial plaque at Mauthausen Concentration Camp. Darby had wondered why it was written in English. The letter to the camp said she wanted something her grandchildren and great-grandchildren could read to remember their heritage.

Grandma Celia would have called it a leap of faith. Darby returned to Redding after the holiday and confronted Clarise with her idea to either sell off her half of the photo lab or become an uninvolved partner. Clarise actually looked relieved.

"Two people from Creative Designs wanted to join in the partnership, and I didn't know how it would work with all of us."

"Really? Then it will work out perfectly," Darby said, feeling a weight lift. Several days of worry had been for nothing. "Let's get something worked up on paper."

While Darby knew she was taking the right step in selling off her old dream, she wondered what her future in photography would be. Derek had mentioned Darby should call their college friend Tracey Rivens. Tracey had worked her way up to an editorial position in *Travel Today*, a competitive travel destination magazine. She looked in an old issue for their company's number.

Tracey was her same friendly self, but the business was straightforward. "Read back issues, know our photos, then send me some samples."

Darby spent two days carefully studying and making notes on the back issues of the *Travel Today* magazines she'd stored in a cupboard at the studio. She noted angles and lighting, landscapes versus action, until she was ready to search her own files. The hiking and mountaineering shots comprised most of what she boxed up and FedEx-ed to Tracey.

⋅⊹═◐◑═⊹⋅

On New Year's Eve, as Darby watched the ball drop over Times Square in New York, she leaned close to the TV screen to see what the area looked like. This had been the designated meeting place for her grandmother and grandfather—only her grandfather had never arrived. The square currently was covered with people cheering and dancing, but once, a long time ago, a young woman had searched the crowd with hopes of finding the man she loved. And later, another young woman, her mother, had searched for the father she wanted to know.

Darby welcomed in the new year, wondering what the next twelve months held. A year earlier, she had written her usual resolutions—exercise consistently, organize the back closets at the studio, do more advertising, get a pet. This year she was selling her half of the partnership with Clarise, and Hanrey and Evans was about to be no more. The world stretched out, with no way to predict what would happen.

She flipped off the cheering crowds on the television and sat in darkness. On a long gold chain around her neck, she wore Grandma's ring. Her fingers felt along the edges as she considered the near future. Once in Austria again, she hoped to prove Tatianna, not Celia Müller, died in Mauthausen. She hoped to start a new career. She hoped to find out what had happened to her family inheritance. But for once, Darby knew her life wasn't in her hands. It was both exciting and frightening at the same time.

⋯⋙◉⋘⋯

For better or worse, by late February, Darby was finally checking in her luggage at San Francisco International Airport and hugging her mother good-bye, for the second time in a year. Her belongings were in a storage unit in Sebastopol, her dream of a photography studio sold off. Darby found her plane on the Departures screen and breathed a sigh. "I hope I'm doing the right thing," she said aloud.

At 11:30 P.M. her old time, Darby's plane bounced and touched down at 9:30 A.M. in München—Munich, Germany. Soon she'd catch the connecting flight to Salzburg, Austria. She couldn't keep her eyes from the green fields of Germany as the plane slowed. She made a vow to herself: *Whatever I do or don't discover, I hope to tell my children and someday their children about this journey. You were right, Grandma. This is my story now.*

CHAPTER TWENTY-THREE

The gray sky spit wet snow against the window
of the taxi. The cold wrapped around Darby's legs as she paid
the driver and tugged her luggage toward the Hotel Zur Goldenen Ente on Goldgasse in the heart of the Old City. After she
settled in, Darby picked up her umbrella before the urge to
plop onto the bed outweighed her new travel smarts.

Snow began a soft descent, but mittens, a hat, and scarf
kept her warm. She stood in the center of Domplatz and
watched the long fall of snowflakes down to the cobblestone
streets. Her breath froze in the air as she breathed in the
good and familiar scent of aged stone. The church bells
began to boom, roaring and echoing off the walls of the
enclosed courtyards and streets. Darby stood transfixed by
the sound, closing her eyes and then opening them again to
see if it was truly real.

I'm here. I'm really here again.

Salzburg was like returning to a friend.

The Mr. Bubble Darby's mother had sent along awaited her in a hot bath that evening. With skin turned pink and fingers pruned, she bundled up in her robe and dialed the Voss home. Somehow the three months had slipped away from her, and she had not called or e-mailed the professor or Katrine even once.

"Professor Voss, this is Darby Evans."

"Hello! How are you?"

Darby smiled at the enthusiasm in his voice. "I'm very good, especially since I'm in Salzburg."

"Right now? You are back?"

"Yes." Darby felt the joy throughout her entire being. Yes, she was back.

"How wonderful that you return! With the mysteries from yesterday, you could not stay away?"

"No, I couldn't." She wrapped the robe more tightly and stretched across the bed. "I believe I'll find part of myself in some of these mysteries, if we're able to solve them."

"You are correct. We always find more of ourselves when we look to the past, especially our family past. And Darby, you come with great timing. I am attending a conference this weekend at the university. You can come with me, if you like."

"What kind of conference, and is there an English version?" Darby asked a bit wearily. "Or will you be translating for me the entire day?" she teased.

"Possibly translating, though there are some workshops in English. The seminar is called 'Holocaust Awareness in the New Millennium.' "

"It sounds great, and I'm honored to be invited. Tell me when and where, and I'll be there. And if you have time, I have more letters for you or Katrine to translate."

"With pleasure. Then, after the conference, we must meet

and see what information to seek. Do you have anything new?"

"Actually, yes. Do you remember Bruno Weiler—I mentioned him in our last conversation before you left for Dublin?"

"*Ja,* the SS guard. I wanted to contact you." Professor Voss's voice sounded excited. "I intended many times to call or e-mail because I found some information about a Bruno Weiler."

"You did?" Darby reached beside the bed into the brown leather satchel she'd bought for her return to Europe. She extracted the file labeled *B. Weiler.* "While I was at home, I found information about a trial and some prison time after the war."

"That is important news. That was after the war? I found enrollment records of a Bruno Weiler in Vienna in the late 1950s. He was attending university there. I wonder if it was the same person."

"My information said he was released in 1957. If it is the same as your Bruno Weiler, we have his next location. Was there any other information? Did he graduate?"

"He was taking graduate courses but dropped out midterm. That is all I could find from the admissions office there. But this is good work. We have become like Sherlock Holmes and his sidekick—what was his name?"

Darby laughed. "I have no idea. I was a Nancy Drew and Hardy Boys fan myself."

"Now it will bother me all night until I remember." Darby heard him sigh as she finished writing Professor Voss's information in her file. "Sherlock Holmes and . . . it has left my mind."

"I'll bring the letters when we meet for the conference. Please tell Katrine hello for me."

"Yes, and Katrine will be very pleased you returned. Before you leave, I am sure she will want some time with you. 'Girls' night out'—is that correct? How long are you staying?"

"Actually, I can stay as long as I want. I'm a free woman."

"Wonderful. Perhaps Austria is your future?"

"Perhaps."

"Watson, that is it!" he shouted.

"Excuse me?" Darby held the phone away from her ear.

"Elementary, my dear Watson. Sherlock Holmes and Dr. Watson. That was his name." Professor Voss chuckled as if he were embarrassed by his outburst. "I am really living up to an 'absent-minded professor' image, am I not?"

"I didn't know how much I'd missed you until now, Peter. I'll see you Saturday at the university, right?"

Professor Voss laughed heartily. "9:00 A.M."

※

The auditorium was crowded with conference attendees. As Darby searched for a seat, she recognized several languages in conversations surrounding her—French, German, and possibly Yiddish.

"Darby Evans!" a voice called from behind. Before she could turn, she felt a hearty pat on the back. People looked their way as Darby and Professor Voss had their reunion in the aisle.

"It is so good to see you again." His hazel eyes sparkled.

"And you also, Dr. Watson," Darby said with a smile.

"Excuse me, but I am Sherlock and you are my sidekick."

"Really?" They laughed together like people who'd known each other for years.

"I have a little something from America for you." Darby handed him a small, wrapped box.

"For me?" He acted like a child as he ripped open the paper. "A new Slinky! And just in time. My old one is a tangle of bent wire beyond further restoration."

"I expect a lot of help now that you have new inspiration."

"You will have it! Did you know the Slinky was invented by a man named Richard James in 1945? In fact, his wife conceived the name. Since that time it has sold over 250 million." Professor Voss opened the box and held the Slinky in his hands, passing it back and forth. "It takes over eighty feet of wire to make it."

"Very interesting. Only you would know the history of the Slinky."

"Come now, I have seats up closer. Remember, I may need to translate everything into your ear, except for the workshops in English."

"I remember. So I am the sidekick after all."

They found the seats reserved by Professor Voss's coat and beaten briefcase. They had just sat down when the conference commenced. An older professor took the stage, speaking solely in German. People laughed several times at what Darby expected to be the usual speaker jokes while Professor Voss tried to give her an overall translation of what would take place in the one-day conference. Darby decided she definitely needed some German classes, and soon. Each workshop teacher stood and gave an overview of his class. Then it was Brant Collins who rose from the front row to stand before the podium.

Brant had been in her thoughts almost daily since she'd returned to Salzburg. On one of her walks through Salzburg, she'd looked up his office, only eight blocks from her hotel. But what could she say to the man until she had some hard evidence to prove who her grandmother really was? Now here he was, standing before her.

He spoke first in German, then in English. Suddenly his eyes turned and met hers. He stumbled over his wording for a moment, then continued without glancing her way again. Brant announced that he was leading the English-speaking workshops.

Darby addressed the professor, who acted suspiciously preoccupied. "Peter, did you know Brant Collins would be here and that he'd be leading the English-speaking classes?"

"Of course I did," he said back with an innocent smile.

"Why are you smiling?"

"Me? Well, it would hurt nothing for the two of you to talk."

Darby's eyebrows lowered. "You aren't doing what I think you're doing?" She couldn't believe it, but his sly smile revealed his matchmaking intentions. "Remember that we have some major issues keeping us from being even acquaintances. Have you spoken with him at all while I've been gone?"

"No, but I think if you could tell him everything you have told me . . ."

"Is this why you invited me to the conference?" Darby whispered loudly as the room applauded the next workshop leader.

"Of course not. It just worked out that Brant was teaching all the English workshops. I thought you would find it very interesting and helpful in your quest into your past."

"My quest into my past. You make me sound so fascinating, like Jacques Cousteau searching the ocean for lost treasure."

"If you do discover the Lange inheritance, it will be as amazing as the Frenchman's discoveries."

"We have a long way to go before that happens."

Applause rippled again, and people began to rise from their seats.

"We now break into our workshops until the afternoon speaker. He is a survivor of Bergen-Belsen," Professor Voss said, standing. He winked and patted her shoulder. "I hope you enjoy your workshop."

⋯⊙⊂⋯

Darby sat near the back of the classroom. The room filled quickly with mostly foreign attendees who would know the common language of English. Darby picked up a neat outline of Brant's workshop, "A Survivor's Continued Nightmare."

Brant entered the room, talking to a young man who took the last seat in the front row. Darby squirmed in her chair, wishing she could slide beneath it. Brant hooked a micro-phone to his shirt and turned the tape machine on before beginning his lecture. His face was tan with a very slight line along his temple toward the dark hair by his ears. Darby would get a similar sunglasses tan when she went snow-skiing often. Something in the way he moved sent a nervous jitter through her entire body.

Before he spoke, his deep brown eyes met Darby's. He nodded a greeting, then began to talk. The talk focused first on the lasting effects the Holocaust had on individual lives. He discussed the intense guilt many survivors felt over living while so many had died.

Brant's words made Darby recognize small signs she'd never noticed in Grandma Celia. Though her grandmother had not survived a concentration camp, she escaped Austria while many of her friends and family had not. Darby remembered Grandma's minor swings of depression over the years, espe-cially during milestones such as the date of her wedding anni-versary. Darby had known of these times, especially recalling occasional words that were out of place for the woman of strength and faith. "Have I done anything of importance with my life?" "I've never endured anything."

Hearing Brant talk about the constant, often hidden, strug-gles of many survivors made her wonder how much her grand-mother had held inside. She wished she'd known sooner, that Grandma Celia wouldn't have had to bear her struggles alone.

As Brant moved to the next part of his talk, Darby fought against the stirring she felt inside every time he looked her way. He was more attractive than she remembered. He didn't seem as uptight, but more at ease with himself and the crowd. Darby found herself watching his hands holding the edge of the podium, or his eyes that looked above the people in the classroom to his own memories of survivor stories.

His workshop moved to the survivor today. He stressed the

importance of recording testimonies and of helping survivors and their families. Darby remembered the lists of people still seeking family and friends on the Internet site "Desperately Seeking."

"A large number of survivors have spent years in silence, unwilling to share their experiences with even their closest friends and family. Now, in their final years, many seek closure or want to record the truth of what happened. History is often twisted to fit modern times. My organization wishes to preserve the facts and lives of the Holocaust victims and survivors so future generations cannot change the truth of what happened."

A few people applauded. Brant paused awkwardly, then nodded.

"In my conclusion, I want to explain what I've only recently discovered. The Holocaust, or *Shoah*, was a horror unlike any humankind has seen. We must ensure that it does not happen again. We must uplift life by protecting those who cannot protect themselves, by rescuing and educating and loving both potential predator and victim. But since most of you here are educators, writers, journalists, politicians, or students aspiring to be one of these, I want to remind you of something I have missed until lately. Be sure to take the time to live your own life. The survivors have gone on with theirs to become statesmen, poets, diplomats, soldiers, film producers, and leaders in their communities. They have continued with life, marrying and having children."

Brant looked down for a long moment, as if he were sharing a deep secret he was unsure how to tell. He looked specifically at Darby, then at the entire class of listeners.

"Steven Spielberg, the renowned American filmmaker, received an Oscar at the Hollywood Academy Awards for best director of *Saving Private Ryan*. As Mr. Spielberg received the award, he said this: 'There is honor in looking back and respecting the past.' That is a statement to be remembered.

There is honor in looking back. We should respect the past. And yet, I must remind you, from personal experience, do not keep your eyes turned back so much that you miss your own today, and your own tomorrow. For we are each granted one life. Learn from yesterday. Heal the wounds of those around you—the pain is everywhere, in everyone. But also, live. . . . Thank you."

The room was deathly quiet until an elderly woman stood and began to clap. Others followed until every chair was empty. Brant was unhooking the microphone when people moved forward to shake his hand and ask questions. His eyes met Darby's, before the crowd blocked the way. She wanted to talk to him. His workshop had been powerful. Yet she could not deny her attraction toward this man who believed her grandmother a fraud. He had spoken with sincerity and depth in his voice. He had given the facts, but she could see how much he cared through his deep, brown eyes. He sought the crowd for understanding. *Do you understand what these people have endured?* his eyes seemed to ask. *Don't return to your life and forget this.*

The line was long to speak with Brant, and Darby was unsure what to say. But it was clear he wasn't the coldhearted man she'd first believed him to be. However, that fact didn't change what he thought of her grandmother; and as yet, there was still no proof to change his mind. Darby didn't even know what he thought of *her.* She left the classroom, pausing in the hallway to collect her thoughts before moving toward the luncheon where she'd planned to meet Professor Voss.

⋆⟞◎⟝⋆

The afternoon passed rapidly with two more workshops. Darby had told Professor Voss about her interest in freelance photography for newspapers and magazines with some possible writing in the future, and he encouraged her to attend two workshops, "Holocaust in the Modern Press" and "Preserving the Images of Yesterday," both taught by an international media giant. Darby found the classes provided headphones that translated the German into English, so Professor Voss didn't have to translate the workshops for her. The information was invaluable, giving her a renewed passion for the work she'd almost given up on. She might make a living yet, and she might love that work in a way she never had before.

As Darby left her last workshop and headed toward the main auditorium for the closing speaker, she rounded a corner and almost bumped into Brant.

"Excuse me," she said, awkward in his presence.

"How are you?" he asked.

"Good, and you?"

"Good."

"I really enjoyed your workshop this morning."

"Thank you."

"Well—," they said at the same time, then stopped. They stood in the hall with people moving by and suddenly both smiled at once.

"Do you realize how much you surprised me when I was introducing my workshop?" Brant asked, shaking his head. "I nearly lost my entire train of thought. I thought you were in the States, and there you are, sitting next to Peter."

"I was just as shocked to see *you* walk up there." Darby couldn't stop a giggle as she remembered his expression. "Now we're even, since you made me cry and nearly burst with anger on the first day we met."

"I don't always bring out the worst in people."

"No, just me." Darby tucked a strand of hair behind her ear, aware of how close they stood.

"I really did feel bad about the crying thing."

"You should have. I don't cry easily."

When Brant smiled, Darby noticed his smooth-shaved jaw and soft-looking lips.

"So you couldn't stay away from Austria?"

"Somehow it lured me back," she said.

"And . . ." Brant hesitated, as if contemplating whether to ask. "Have you found anything?"

"Herr Collins?" A young woman with a handful of papers nudged him from behind.

Brant turned to gather the papers from the petite girl. Darby was surprised she spoke in English.

"Can I do anything else to help you?" the girl asked, biting her lip.

"No, this is great. Thank you, Melissa."

"Any time." Melissa glanced back twice coyly as she walked down the hall, but only Darby noticed.

"They just surround you," Darby said.

"What?" Brant looked confused.

"Still as gullible as ever."

Brant appeared lost, then the light bulb turned on. "Not that again. She's a student from the States."

"I'm surprised you haven't been snatched up by one of these Austrian ladies," Darby said, then realized her joking had struck home, on a very personal note.

"I lose whatever charm I possess with my life revolving around work. Like I said today, I only recently learned the value of living. And look who's talking. Why, Darby Evans, are you still unmarried?"

She gulped. Their joking had turned serious, and she didn't like it aimed her way. "I suppose, much the same reason. All work and no play—you know." Darby consulted her watch. "But look at the time." He grinned as she diverted their conversation.

"Time for the general session, just in time." Brant shook his head. "I'll see you later, Darby."

⋆⇥≡◉═⟨⋆

"Remember me?" Richter said into the cell phone. He walked away from the bright sidewalk down a darkened pathway near the river. A group of tourists passed, chattering in the cold as they turned to cross the river into the Old City.

"What do you want?" the voice replied. "I thought you were never calling us again, never coming back. We've adjusted quite nicely."

Richter clenched his fist. He needed to stay calm. He needed to get this right. "I just wanted to see how you and Mom are doing."

"That's a good one. I know you need money for your debts. But since you asked, your mom and I have never been better in the last two years. So don't try coming back into our lives. It's not going to happen."

"I've cleaned up my life, Dad," Richter said.

"I don't care, Richter. Long ago I quit having a son, so don't call again."

"When did you ever have a son?" Richter slammed the phone against the railing again and again. He cursed and hurled the phone toward the dark waters, hearing a splash a second later.

Now what would he do? His father was his last chance. Yet when had his father ever shown him any love? Richter had been sent to boarding school all year and in the summer to Gunther and Ingrid's. He was an only child, the one neither of his parents ever wanted. They had their life with rich friends and rich vacations, and a kid didn't fit into what they wanted out of life.

He cursed again and pounded his fist against the railing.

"Having problems again, Richter?" a voice said from behind.

Richter turned slowly to face a large, older man rising from a bench behind him. He looked straight at the man whose unwavering stare brought a fearful churning in Richter's stomach. His contact was not supposed to be this early, and it certainly wasn't supposed to be this man. Richter had seen him once, but only in passing. Why would he take the risk to meet Richter in person? It wasn't a good sign.

"Everything is great," Richter said, forcing a smile.

"You were given your loan in good faith. Now I suppose you're going to tell me you need more time—again."

"I told Thom about the old Lange inheritance," Richter brought up quickly. "Did he tell you?"

"It's your ticket to wealth, I suppose."

"I know it is. You don't understand the worth of the brooch alone. And the coins—there may not be another set of this kind in the world. I'll pay you back and have enough to loan you money."

The man didn't join in the joke.

"Anyway, the woman who could be my opportunity just came back to the city."

"So what are you going to do?"

"I have some plans, and you don't have to worry, I make good on my debts. I always have before."

"I'm more interested in the Lange inheritance. I'd also like to hear everything you know about this woman, Darby Evans."

Richter frowned. How did the contact know her name? "Will some of this come off my tab?"

"Just keep me informed. Not through Thom, but straight to me. I'll take care of everything else."

CHAPTER TWENTY-FOUR

Frank Beck looked like any older man Darby would see at an early-bird breakfast at Denny's or walking a miniature dog in the park. He lived in Florida, golfed with his friends, attended synagogue, and drove a motor home in the summer months to destinations with cooler weather—his favorite trip had been a six-week drive to Alaska. His wife of fifty-one years liked to knit booties for their new grandbabies and great-grandbabies and to play cards with her friends. The couple especially loved morning coffee with cream-cheese danishes on the balcony of their condo. But, too often, Frank Beck returned to his previous life, sometimes during the night or when driving past an industrial smokestack or when hearing the sound of a train rumbling on its tracks. Then Frank would find himself hungry, cold, and completely terrified even as he clenched the wheel of his silver Cadillac or sweated on his Serta Perfect Sleeper mattress.

Frank spoke in English, for like Grandma Celia, he vowed never to speak German again. Coming to a German-speaking country for this conference was most difficult.

Darby watched Frank as he spoke to the captive audience. He first told of his life today, then descended into the darkness of a history that lived with every beat of his heart. "It was my job to burn bodies in the ovens. I did my job—or I'd become like them. Very quickly you are numbed to the reality, the smell, and the faces you choose not to see. But one day, right before me, I recognized a face. It was my father. We'd been separated months earlier, and I had tried to find where he was taken. Then I found him right there. I could not think of it. I put my father into the oven to burn." His words faltered.

"Some people do not understand why many survivors continue to seek compensation or the return of properties, heirlooms, and money. Yet the companies that profited from our labor continue to thrive. The banks and insurance companies that would not return monies have earned much interest and wealth from us. Imagine the insurance policy your father purchases and faithfully pays is then used to fund the Nazi regime that destroys your family and life. Then when you attempt to claim your father's insurance after the war, you are rejected, though you hold the policy in your hand." Frank held his fist in the air. "The policy the insurance company gave your father is in your hand after hiding beneath the floor of your barn for six years. There is the proof, but still you are rejected. Why? Because the Nazis didn't issue death certificates when they murdered. Insurance policies require proof of death, not just an eyewitness who saw his father's face before burning it."

He shook his head and his voice lowered. "Yet people say it is long since past. 'Frank, you have rebuilt your life. Leave it behind you.' For my wife, myself, and many others, it cannot be left behind. It is forever part of us. We had every bit of humanity stolen from us. Yes, we survived, but there are pieces that can never be reclaimed."

He paused, looking down at the podium. "And yet, I did not

come here this weekend to emphasize such things. Instead, I want to be a reminder to those who will listen and take the message outward. Again and again, we say do not forget. Simon Weisenthal writes this in his book *Justice Not Vengeance:* 'Hatred can be nurtured anywhere, idealism can be perverted into sadism anywhere. If hatred and sadism combine with modern technology, the inferno could erupt anew anywhere.' I say to each one of you, tell the stories and remember us."

With those simple words, Frank Beck left the stage. The auditorium echoed in serious applause, not a roar of jubilation, but with hands together in honor and respect. Darby could not clap, only watch the man descend the stairs.

The conference closed, and she walked slowly through the crowd toward the exit. She thought to tell Professor Voss good-bye, but he was in the midst of a crowd of colleagues. A blast of cold hit her face as she pushed open the university doors. The clouds churned in the late-afternoon sky, as if deciding whether to create a storm or move on.

She halted on the landing with her hands on the railing. A thousand sentences, words, and feelings from the seminar coursed through her mind, but what could she do with it all? One thing was clear: she'd never be the same. Her eyes had opened a little more. There was so much more to know and learn and understand, and suddenly she wanted to know so much and to pass it along to others. Perhaps her photographs would do that for others someday.

Addressing the gray-and-white clouds wrestling above the tops of the buildings, she vowed, *I'm going to share stories. Like my grandmother before me, I will be a storyteller like I was designed to be. Whether through photographs or words, I want to share with people who are like me—seeking light through the darkness.*

And as Brant had said, she wanted to live her life with all

the fullness she could find. *God, I've lived my life without you for a long time and even now forget you all the time. But I know I need your help. I need you every day.*

The door opened behind her, and several people left the building. Darby adjusted the strap on her satchel, waiting for them to pass. Then she headed back toward the city center. She had some photographs that needed to be taken.

"Darby! Wait!"

She turned to see Brant Collins jogging down the street from the university entrance. "Professor Voss asked me to walk you back to your hotel. He regrets he could not be here himself."

"I think I can manage without help." Darby knew what Professor Voss was up to, and she didn't like it.

"I go this way, anyway," he said, falling into step beside her. He pointed toward the sheer mountain cliff above the cathedral domes. "I live on the other side of Mönchsberg, through the tunnel."

Darby looked toward the mountain. She'd never gone through the tunnel to the other side. The Old City had become like home, but the rest of Salzburg was still a mystery. "As long as I'm on the way."

As they continued on, Darby remembered the first time they'd met and walked these same streets.

"What did you think of the conference?" Brant asked.

"Excellent, very moving. The last speaker was incredible."

"It's amazing to discover what man will do to man," Brant said quietly.

"I can't understand it." Darby glanced at Brant. She wondered what those eyes had seen and ears had heard. No wonder he became lost in his work, forgetting how to live. "I don't think I could hear those things all the time."

"I think you could. You'd do it because it's important to help them. It's important to record their lives and try to understand, if even in the smallest sense. They deserve at least understanding. It's amazing what takes us so long to see."

"What do you mean?" Darby asked.

"Here I am in my thirties and finally starting to see what life is supposed to be about. Not just work or myself, but well, the big picture."

Darby weighed her next words. "You mean the big, big picture. As in, God?"

She saw him hesitate, then plow forward.

"I guess I am. Here we walk with the religion of Christianity influencing most everything in this city. But to get past religion and history and look at it for yourself, the real meaning of God, Christ even, and then accept it for yourself . . . Well, I guess you didn't need to hear this."

Darby almost didn't want to admit that she understood what he meant. "Actually, I know exactly what you mean. Kind of scary, isn't it?"

Brant stopped. "You too?"

Darby could only nod. She was just discovering God on her own and couldn't quite explain without referring to the influences of Tatianna and Celia in her life. She and Brant would start talking about God and end up arguing about who her grandmother was or wasn't. But Darby did wonder, as they continued a thoughtful pace, how two people who had such obstacles between them also had reached the same place in their lives, and they seemed to be moving in the same direction.

They passed through Mozartplatz with its tall statue of Wolfgang Amadeus Mozart, then turned toward the river.

"I'm this way," she said, motioning straight ahead.

"No Cozy Hotel?"

Darby caught the raised eyebrow and small grin. "I'm at the Zur Goldenen Ente on Goldgasse."

Brant smiled. "Staying a bit more Austrian, I see."

"I try not to be too gullible," she said, lifting her head a bit.

He laughed softly as they stepped toward Residenzplatz beside a string of shops and restaurants. The streets were busier with window-shoppers and strollers crowding the sidewalks. They walked until the block of buildings opened to Goldgasse, with its gold sign fluttering above. The breeze was calm in the street that seemed more like a mysterious passageway. A single car could squeeze down the first third of the street, then it narrowed more tightly and only pedestrians could fit all the way through.

"Here I am," Darby announced when they reached the yellow Hotel Zur Goldenen Ente. A wreath of decorations lined the doorway and windows. Tables were folded against one side of the building since it was too cold even for the outdoors-loving Austrians to eat on the street.

"So here you are." Brant shuffled his feet, as if he wanted to say something. He glanced at the five-story hotel connected as one with the other buildings on the block. "I was wondering. . . . I thought I'd ask though it's kind of late notice."

Surprised to see that calm, cool, collected Brant Collins was acting nervous, Darby queried, "You thought you'd ask what?"

"An elderly couple in my last workshop gave me tickets to a dinner concert." His eyes roamed the ground, the opposite building, her shoulder, but didn't look directly at her. Suddenly, she thought she knew. Could Brant Collins be asking her for a *date*?

"I guess the couple bought the tickets but have to leave the city tonight. It's at the St. Peter Stiftkeller, a nice restaurant. You might find it interesting if you like Mozart. It's very Austrian."

"I like Mozart," she said, confused about his intentions again. "Are you giving me the tickets, or are you . . ."

"Well, yes, I could give you the tickets," he said, stumbling over his words. "They're here in my pocket." He fumbled in his black coat, pulled out the two tickets, and handed them to her.

"Or were you asking me to go with you?" she interrupted.

Brant shrugged. "It doesn't matter. You take them and enjoy."

Darby smiled. Seeing him squirm for once was quite nice. "Why don't you take one, and we'll both go? I can meet you in front, or we don't even have to sit together, unless it's reserved seating."

Brant seemed to relax. "No, it's not. But since it's easier for me to go on foot than try to find parking, I could come by and walk with you. . . . If you want me to."

"Sure," she said, trying to sound casual and unaffected by the thought of an evening together.

"I'll be by at seven-fifteen. It starts at eight, but I'd like to get there early."

"I'll see you then." Darby's mind ran in a million directions— what should she wear, what was she doing?

Brant left so quickly that she wondered if he had similar misgivings, similar butterflies. She hurried upstairs after checking her watch. What would they talk about? How could they possibly go somewhere together without bringing up the obstacle that kept them apart?

⋯⇒◌⇐⋯

Darby heard the elevator doors open but waited the appropriate five seconds before opening the door to Brant's knock.

"Hello," she said, uncomfortable with her clothes and hair and shoes and everything she'd tried on and tossed and done in the last two hours. She wondered why she'd chosen the long, black skirt. Would she be able to walk in her black dress shoes? The black shirt with burgundy-and-black scarf suddenly seemed tight, and her face felt hot. She'd curled her straight hair with hot rollers and sprayed them till they barely moved. Did it look too fluffy and unlike her?

"Ready?" she said, hoping he didn't notice her blush.

"You look really great," Brant said with a smile.

That's when she noticed how good he looked, also dressed in black with turtleneck, jacket, and slacks. Her grandmother would say, "Dashing!"

"You do too—look great, I mean." Darby hurried to get her key and purse before he noticed the pile of clothing stuffed on the other side of the bed.

Salzburg was cold and the sky dark as they walked, but as usual, the city had yet to fall asleep. Beacons of light shone on the fortress above and on cathedral towers, around fountains, and from street lamps. Patches of snow glowed on Mönchsberg, but she'd been told that the city hadn't had snow in weeks. Through archways and plazas, they arrived at St. Peter Stiftkeller, nestled against Mönchsberg's sheer rock. As they entered an open-air courtyard in the center, Darby noticed the netting above that hopefully stopped any loose rocks from hitting the building. High above and beyond view, Hohensalzburg kept a watchful eye over the Old City. Dried vines hung from the sides of the netting, probably lush and beautiful in the spring and a wonderful place to eat with the open sky above for those seeking love. Darby liked the dark, wooded restaurant, but it wasn't what she'd anticipated for a Mozart Dinner Concert. She followed Brant's lead up a stairway and down a long hall. They put their coats in a small room, then entered a beautiful hall. Darby paused in the doorway. This was more than she'd hoped for. The baroque décor, chandeliers, wood floors, and tables laden with flowers and china gave the effect of stepping back into the eighteenth century. The waiters wore red jackets with white ruffled shirts, and waitresses moved around tables in full skirts and aprons.

Brant stood beside her in the doorway. "The St. Peter Stiftkeller was first mentioned by Alkuin, a court scribe, during a visit by Emperor Charlemagne in the first century. It's considered the oldest restaurant in Central Europe." He extended his arm. "Shall we, my lady?"

Darby put her arm through his. "Yes, we shall."

The tables were already filling, and they found two seats at a round table near the front of a small stage. Darby sat and scooted herself up just as she noticed that Brant had tried to push her in.

"I've obviously not dated in a while, especially someone with manners," Darby said apologetically, then laughed.

"You speak English—you sound American?" a young woman beside her asked.

"Yes, and you're an American too?"

"We're all Americans on this side of the table." Three other women about Darby's age said hello. "We also have a couple from Brazil." The man and woman nodded. The American woman continued, "Our other couple is from Hungary, but they don't speak English very well. So what about your guy?"

"He's not really my guy, I mean, not my guy at all—," Darby said, stuttering.

"I'm Austrian *and* American," Brant replied. He smiled at Darby, seeming to enjoy her very red face. "Are you ladies here together?"

"Oh, yes. We are four married women on the loose."

"That sounds dangerous. So how did you pick Salzburg?" Brant asked.

"Well, Lucee and I have always dreamed of coming to Europe." She nudged a brunette beside her who was looking at a mural on the ceiling. "Oh, my name is Cate," she said, extending her hand to them both. "Anyway, Lorna loves classical music and plays the violin—and of course, this is Mozartland. Bailey didn't care where we went; she'll travel anywhere. After a bit of research, pulling places out of a hat, finding babysitters for the mass of kids we have between us, and getting the guys to agree—well, here we are."

Lorna, the musician, joined the conversation. "We decided that if you get the chance, sometimes you just have to go for it."

"I agree," Brant said, eyeing Darby. "Why else would I invite you here tonight?"

"Really?" Darby returned wryly. "You didn't exactly invite me—at least not very well."

"We're here, aren't we?" Brant put in with a grin.

Darby shook her head at him in mock chagrin and turned back toward Cate. The woman with pale skin and green eyes studied Brant, then Darby, evidently trying to figure out their relationship.

"So this is the trip of a lifetime?" Darby asked quickly.

"Or the first of many over our lifetime," Cate said, then leaned closer. "My friends are a bit strange at times, but I'm glad to be stuck with them."

"We heard that," Bailey said from a few seats over. She pointed a long, manicured finger toward Cate. "You're stuck with us, so get used to it."

Lorna added playfully, "We need Cate for our journeys. This girl can strike up a conversation with anyone, whether they speak English or not."

At that the four women laughed as only close friends can, as if behind a simple glance were jokes and memories no one but each other could understand. This evening felt right— with a man at one side and other women who understood friendship surrounding Darby. And all this in the magical setting of Mozart's day.

A waiter arrived to take drink orders and Bailey announced, "Champagne for our entire table. This is a night to remember."

"This is the best butter I've ever had," Lucee said, taking a bite of her roll.

"And the bread and cheese," Lorna added with a bright smile. "Except Bailey and I would pay fifty dollars for a Coke with ice."

"I've been loving the ham—oh, the ham in Austria," Cate said with a sigh.

Darby bent close. "Breakfasts here are the best. I love those rolls they serve at every hotel and bakery. And the jams."

All five women noticed Brant's humored expression, and they burst into laughter.

The champagne arrived and everyone toasted together. Suddenly, as if the clink of glasses was the cue, the doors in back burst open and the musicians entered the hall. All eyes were on their entrance as they carried their instruments to the small stage in front—several violins, a cello, and a bass. They sat, adjusted music in front of them and then, like a long-awaited exhale, the first violin began to play. A second later, the other strings joined, dipping and swaying in their individual steps that combined into a perfectly choreographed dance. From the entrance, a rich voice bellowed.

In dashed a dark-haired man in a red Mozart coat, wearing a black hat with white plumage. He moved toward the front of the stage with posture straight, arms out wide, and a slight smile upon his lips. His voice boomed above the strings in an Italian song.

The American women *oohed* and *aahed* enough for all of them, though Darby too felt the exuberance of such a night. The program continued with music and opera between dinner courses: cream of lemon soup with chicken slices, braised fillet of pork on applewine-horseradish sauce served with potatoes, and dessert, *Wespenneste,* a sweet surprise with a cocoa profile of Mozart's face. Darby took in the stained-glass windows and the mural on the carved, coffered ceiling. The sophisticated ambiance was like nothing she'd experienced previously. Brant smiled at her when she looked his way. With their chairs turned during the music, Darby sometimes felt too strongly Brant's presence so near her one side. Once, when he dropped his program, his warm breath brushed the side of her neck as he bent beside her. For one night she wanted to forget their differences. It seemed they both knew without speaking a word that they disagreed greatly, but were willing to put it aside for one evening together.

The musicians returned after the last course and were joined by a couple who pranced and sang around the tables. The man would reach for the woman, and she would teasingly run away. Around and around the tables they sang and chased until at last he captured the woman, drawing her into an irresistible embrace. The room roared with applause as the song ended. The couple skipped to the front and bowed, then turned and motioned toward the musicians, who stood and bowed. The applause thundered through the room. Darby's hands hurt from clapping, but she continued to applaud as the entire entourage exited the hall.

Darby's face felt flushed as they entered the night's chill. She said good-bye to the American foursome, who laughed and chattered as they strolled away. Suddenly she was alone with Brant after one of the most remarkable evenings of her life. She who loved the song of the mountains had found love in Mozart's strings. Better yet, she could tell that Brant understood how awed she was by this night.

"Do you go to these events often?" she asked as he slid her coat around her.

"I've lived in Salzburg for years, but that's the first time I've gone there." They made their way across the small square where taxis picked up patrons.

Darby stopped after they stepped through an archway. "Thank you for taking me. I feel like a child on her first trip to Disneyland."

"You're welcome," he said, looking down at her. Brant glanced behind them and pulled her away from the street and close to him.

"A bike was coming," was all he said before the familiar

jingle of chain and metal passed by. Darby drank in his close-ness, getting a quick scent of aftershave. Just as she was about to move away after the bike passed, Brant's fingers encircled hers.

They walked the cobblestoned street without speaking a word. Their hands spoke in turns, tracing palms and fingers. Their fingers folded together, then slid apart, and together again. Darby's breath was stolen, and her eyes closed at her pounding insides.

Then he stopped and drew her toward him. Darby's back touched the stucco wall, her hands fell to her side. Brant took a step toward her, their eyes locked together in the darkened corner. He lifted a hand and touched her hair, then ran a finger along her cheek and onto her lips.

He opened his mouth as if to speak, then instead bent to kiss her. He hesitated a moment before their lips gently touched. His hands rested on the wall beside her face, his body came closer until every inch of her felt his closeness and wanted him even closer. Brant kissed her softly, then longer and deeper. She felt herself melting away. Then a nagging voice spoke inside her head.

"Wait," she whispered. "Wait. Or I-I don't know what will happen to me."

Brant took a shaky breath and stepped back. He gazed at Darby tenderly, then turned away, running a hand through his hair. Neither spoke as he took her hand, and they began to walk again.

This time Darby stopped. She took both his hands.

"If you could only believe?" Darby pleaded with her eyes. He had to have some faith in her or she could not do this, or allow herself to feel this.

"I do believe—I believe you." His eyes became sad.

"But you don't believe my grandmother." Darby shook her head as he looked away.

"It's not as simple as you think," he said. "Next week I testify in a trial because I trusted without being sure. And I'm already sure about your grandmother. I don't know why you can't face the truth."

"Truth? I know the truth. Professor Voss and Katrine believe it also, so why don't you talk to them? I don't understand why you aren't willing to try—to be open to the possibility. Otherwise, everything I seek is fighting against you."

"There's so much I want to tell you, but—"

"Brant, thank you for giving me the best night of my life," she said, then fled, leaving him standing in the shadows.

⋅⊸⩵◒⩵⊷⋅

Brant counted the floors and saw a light turn on in Darby's room. She was right up there so close, yet so far from his reach. He stood in a darkened shop entrance across from her hotel and sagged against the doorway. He cared for Darby Evans, could even fall in love with her. But he ached for he knew she was the one person he could not have—at least, not now. Perhaps not ever.

She wanted him to believe in something he could never believe. Was he doomed to the fate of Gunther—to never have love that would last?

Brant saw a shadow pass the window. He wasn't giving up without a fight. He'd find out who Darby's grandmother really was. Once she accepted the fact, perhaps they'd have a chance. Or would she resent the truth coming from him? First he'd get the answers. She was too close to let go of now.

CHAPTER TWENTY-FIVE

Darby knew her motives weren't completely clear, but her determination was renewed after a night of very little sleep. The time had come to pull out the stops and begin digging. She needed proof of her grandmother's identity, and Darby hoped Bruno Weiler would be that proof. She had met other dead ends and the SS guard might be another, but Darby was ready to find out. If it went badly, she'd try something new.

A taxi took her to the train station, where Darby purchased a ticket for Hallstatt. As she rode the white ferry across the dark waters of Hallstattersee, the memory returned that her grandfather had driven the ferry—perhaps this very one. She gazed at the driver and tried to imagine what her grandfather had looked like. She'd never seen a photograph of him.

Darby rang the bell on the desk of Gasthaus Gerringer and heard footsteps upstairs. Sophie exclaimed as she saw Darby and rushed to hug her tightly.

"I so happy to see you again," Sophie said. "You still in Austria, I see."

"I went back to California but had to return," Darby said happily, as if they were old friends.

"I believe your same room available today." Sophie reached for a book under the counter.

"I don't need a room," Darby said, wondering what response she was about to receive. "I came to talk to your grandmother again."

"I think she will see you." Sophie's eyes sparkled, much to Darby's relief. "She is much changed since you last came. My mother and I think it because she got her past in open and she know we still love her. Please, give me moment and I will be back."

A few minutes later, Darby stood before the old woman. She looked the same as last time, except there was no *hmmp* greeting. Instead the old woman nodded at Darby's "*Grüß Gott.*"

Darby sat in the chair across from Frau Gerringer. "Bruno Weiler," Darby said, watching for any changed expression. "You gave me his name, and I thank you. I've found that Herr Weiler was at Mauthausen as an SS guard, like you said. I'm asking if you will tell me everything you know about him."

Sophie spoke to her grandmother, then back to Darby. "What have you found, she asks?"

"I haven't found a lot of facts." Darby sighed and looked straightforwardly into the old woman's eyes. "I haven't found the facts I need. But I'm learning a lot about my grandmother and about myself. When I was here before, I came because my grandmother asked me to. I did not tell you that the records say my grandmother was not Celia Müller. They say Celia Müller died at Mauthausen. But I know that Tatianna Hoffman died under Celia's name, instead of her. Now I am here for myself. I want to prove what happened so I can change the memorials and give Tatianna the honor she deserves. If possible, I also want to find what happened to my family inheritance."

The old woman didn't speak for a few moments. Then Sophie translated for her. "She say you are learning many things, as even this old woman is. But your family inheritance. Many people seek such things today, but they are only objects, not lives."

"Yes. And if they are not recovered, it is God's will. But Tatianna gave up her life, and I'm alive because of it. I must at least try to do my part. If I fail, I'll know that at least I've tried."

"She will tell you what she know about Bruno Weiler."

Darby felt she'd just passed some kind of test. She relaxed against the back of her chair and thanked the old woman.

Sophie listened to her grandmother. "She say they all were in school together. Bruno was younger. He was a funny boy, always joking and laughing. But father very stern. Bruno not like to go home when father not working. He ate dinner at her family's house many times. He and younger brother were friends, also good friends with your grandmother's brother. My grandmother married young, but she still live in village and see this." Sophie paused and listened again. "Very near same time of marriage, Bruno leave for Vienna to stay with aunt. He keep in contact with her brother and visit sometime—he cut off communication with Celia's brother; Warner was his name. I'm sure because he was part Jewish. One winter, Bruno comes with Nazi youth information. He try to get village boys to join and go to Vienna, but her father not let brother."

The back-and-forth dialogue continued as Darby took quick notes. "They hear nothing for long time. Then brother get letter about Bruno's position at Mauthausen. Later, her brother join war and was killed first week in battle. They not hear from Bruno again. Then after the war, she read he was charged with crimes and sent to prison. Nothing else after that."

Darby glanced up from her paper. "I found out he went to university in Vienna after he was released from prison in 1957."

"She say his mother moved to Vienna after his father die.

She live with her sister there. Mother name was Dorthe
Schumacher Weiler and her sister was Heike Schumacher.
Heike was not married."

"When was the last time she heard anything about them?"
Darby asked.

The old woman shrugged and scratched her chin before
speaking again.

"She say it had to be around 1950 or 1955. Long time ago."

"Can you remember anything else?" Darby wrote down the
information as the old woman shook her head.

"She say that is all she know of family and of Bruno." Frau
Gerringer put a hand on Darby's arm. "She say she hope you
discover all that you seek."

Darby nodded and clasped the old woman's hand, placing
her other hand on top. "*Danke.* I hope so too."

A distant roll of thunder echoed through the mountains to
the village.

"Oh, I hear that storm coming tonight," Sophie said. She
opened the curtain, and Darby could see the rain already
beginning to fall.

"Perhaps I'll stay tonight after all," Darby said. She had
brought a duffel bag with extra clothes just in case she found
some lead to follow.

"I'll give you your room, then," Sophie said with a bright
smile. "And you will eat dinner with our family."

⊹⇒◎⇐⊹

The mountain storm crashed in quickly, and Darby was glad
she'd decided to stay. She loved the fearful sound of thunder in
the mountains as it rolled down peaks and ridges, echoing
through crevasse and saddleback. Sophie gave her the key to
her second-story lakeside room without showing it to her,
since Darby wasn't a customer but a guest now. She came down

for dinner with the Gerringer family of three women that reminded her of her own family. Later she carried up an electric heater to use until the water radiator that was warmed by a woodstove downstairs grew hot enough to heat the rooms above. Darby fell asleep bundled within the thick feather comforter while winter howled and beat its fist against the windows.

But late in the night, something woke her. Silence. Darby wrapped a blanket around her shoulders and stepped onto the balcony. Her bare feet touched cold snow. She slipped her feet into her boots without tying the laces and returned outside. The moon through the puffy after-storm clouds had turned the lake and air and snow and trees into a deep winter blue.

Darby had never cared much for winter. The season came and stripped the land of life. It disguised itself in purest white, but destroyed all it touched.

"I'm sorry I'm a traitor," Darby whispered to the broken, limp sticks that last fall had probably held bright flowers. "But I can't hate winter tonight."

As she looked into the blue world so still and full of magic, she wondered about the winter that stole life from the land. But perhaps winter was not the end, but actually the beginning. The harsh conditions stripped away all that was hidden in the summer months. It beat and seemed nearly to destroy until the essence of all things was made visible. Both good and bad could not hide from the cutting winds and tempest storms. And only through a winter passing could life be brought to its knees in surrender and prepared for rebirth.

Darby stared into the deep winter sky.

This is your winter, she could hear Grandma say. *We all pass through times of winter. But winter will pass. And as you heal, you find yourself stronger, richer, more alive than ever before.* Darby imagined the gentle hand, pushing a strand of hair behind her ear. The sky called to her, and Grandma's voice disappeared. Instead she heard a voice from deeper within her soul, a voice she'd only begun to know: *This is your winter, Darby. Embrace it as I bring life in you again.*

CHAPTER TWENTY-SIX

Wе have half the letters translated," Professor Voss said as Darby's white breath was cut in two when she closed the door to the phone booth. The cold morning shone with the covering of new snow on trees and walkways, a crystal blanket of white.

"Do they offer any information?" she asked, warming her mittened hand by rubbing it against the side of the phone.

"Not really. They are all letters your grandmother wrote to your grandfather over the past sixty years. They tell what is happening in her life, how much she misses him, the life events of her daughter, and later, grandchildren."

"Why do you think they were written in German? My grandmother never spoke one word of German that I ever heard—until on her deathbed."

"I am no psychologist, but perhaps, because of her vow to never speak German, it helped to write the letters. Or maybe she held a bit of hope that she would someday find Gunther and be able to give them to him."

"It's pretty sad," Darby said.

"*Ja,* but also very inspiring. They had great love. So you are returning to Salzburg?"

"I'm going to Vienna," she said and began to shiver.

"What is happening?"

"I found out for certain that Bruno Weiler knew both my grandmother and Tatianna. His aunt and mother lived in Vienna after the war. Perhaps I'll find one of them in the city or another Weiler. Since I'm partway there, I decided I might as well see your capital before returning to Salzburg."

"You will probably find nothing, but a trip to Vienna is essential for all travelers at one time or another. There are also many places with archives in Vienna, but in German, of course. I wish I could be there to help, but I have classes all week."

"I'll make a quick trip and see what I can find." Darby's teeth chattered. "I have so many trails to follow. There is the search for the brooch and coins. This morning I asked at the museum if any Celtic coins had been discovered in Hallstatt, but they said no. Then there's finding proof about Tatianna, and I'd like to gain more information about my family, especially my grandfather."

"It seems Bruno Weiler is the key to many things now."

"Yes." Her entire body was shivering, and Darby wished for more of the warm fruit tea she'd had at breakfast. "But I'm freezing out here, so I'll call you from Vienna."

"Katrine is here and says to go to Demel's Bakery. It is the best in Vienna."

"I'll do it."

"And Darby." Professor Voss's usually cheerful voice sounded serious. "Be careful."

⋅⇒●⇐⋅

Brant had accomplished little of his workload in the last two days with two companies pressuring him to finish his end of the work. He received notice that he would not be called as a witness after all in the Aldrich case—the duo had opted for a plea bargain. Part of him was relieved; another part longed to face the man and woman and give his testimony. But beyond the Aldrich case, much more was bothering him. He had to decide what to do about Darby. Should he simply tell her everything and see what happened? Suddenly, Brant knew. Professor Peter Voss. Darby said the professor believed her. Once Brant told him the facts, that could change, and Peter would know what to do next.

Brant consulted his desktop Rolodex and punched in the phone number.

"Peter, this is Brant. I need to talk to you."

"Well, all I must say is, it is about time."

Brant shook his head. "Then you really do believe all of this."

"Definitely. Why do you not?"

"Because it can't be true."

"Why not?"

Gunther. Gunther could not have been wrong all these years. "We need to talk. I'll be right there."

⋆⇒◎⇐⋆

Darby had ridden a train only once, and that was an antique locomotive in Mount Shasta, California, which included a staged train robbery. The trains of Europe were like moving from a Model T Ford to a modern sports car. They were a reliable way of transportation here—running on schedule, efficient and comfortable. She climbed aboard a non-smoking car and found a vacant section where the seating was divided into separate rooms. As she stored her luggage overhead, the train *whooshed* from the Hallstatt station. The Eurail pass she'd purchased in Salzburg allowed a week of travel over a four-month period. If Vienna didn't work out, Darby could board a train and go nearly anywhere in Europe. By morning she could be in Paris or Rome or Amsterdam—the thought was tempting.

Snow flurries turned to raindrops as the train journeyed from the northern mountains to the open rolling hills of Upper Austria into the Danube region. After a while near the Danube, Darby looked up from her Austrian Tours map toward the direction of Mauthausen. She was back, riding past what would forever rest on the hillside with its ghosts and ash pile.

The rolling hills and fields succumbed to dense forest—the Vienna Woods that led into the heart of the city itself. Darby grabbed her bag and waited for the doors to slide open. She quickly walked through the smoky train station toward the exit, then halted, gazing up at the buildings and bustle and feeling like Mary Tyler Moore. She breathed the city—ah, Vienna! Home for centuries to artists, musicians, culture, and coffeehouses. The imperial city was a bridge between the East and West, a mixture of cultures and ethnic groups from Viennese to Slavic heritages. These streets had seen empires rise and fall, had been the toast of the classical world and the host for Cold War conferences where surely spies met their contacts with plots of espionage.

Darby had read about the city in her guidebook like every good tourist should, but added her own notes from her grandmother's stories. For Vienna had also welcomed a newly wed couple for their honeymoon. Darby remembered her grandmother saying, "Salzburg is quaint with charm—your darling welcoming with outstretched arms. Vienna is like an enchanter who draws you with his sophistication, though you fear his power."

Darby felt small in the midst of the enchanter. The afternoon sky sprinkled snow flurries as she hurried toward a line of taxis parked along the street. Though she hadn't made hotel reservations, there was no doubt where she'd stay, despite the cost.

"Hotel Sacher, please, *bitte*," Darby said as the driver of a white Mercedes took her lone duffel bag.

"Ah," the man said with a smile. "Very good choice."

The Mercedes zipped forward, darting in and out of traffic. Darby wanted to look at the map and out the window toward the sights, but she kept her eyes on the road ahead. This was carsick travel. As a delivery truck whirled past them and then they zipped around two cars, Darby knew she'd made the right decision not to rent a car with these crazy streets and crazier drivers. They zoomed past a long park and again Darby wished she could read her guidebook and map. Unlike Salzburg, with the old city and sights in the same area, Vienna stretched out with its palaces, parliament buildings, opera houses, parks, and historical sites scattered around the huge "inner stadt" or city center. The famous Ringstraße hemmed it all into a labyrinth of connected one-way streets, with the Danube River making a flowing barrier on one end.

Darby was completely turned around, believing they should be leaving the city, when she saw the massive State Opera House. The taxi stopped on the opposite side of the street. She stepped out of the cab and looked up to a towering hotel with red banners and flags fluttering in the late afternoon breeze. Hotel Sacher.

The driver tipped his hat before speeding away. Darby stood at the red carpet entrance, staring up at the luxurious hotel. Her faded jeans, brown boots in need of polish, and brown, hip-length leather jacket didn't quite fit with the opulence of the hotel, but she eagerly walked inside anyway.

The receptionist smiled and found a single room for over two hundred and fifty United States dollars. Darby signed the paper with a twinge of guilt for spending so much. But it didn't take long to feel it was well worth the cost. She found a hall of photographs of VIP guests: Ernest Hemingway, Princess Caroline of Monaco, John F. Kennedy, Queen Elizabeth II of England, the Dalai Lama, and Thomas Mann, to name a few. She smiled at the portrait of the Bee Gees, then spotted Arnold Schwarzenegger, Austria's golden boy. All were guests of the famous Hotel Sacher, where she arrived alone with her duffel bag. The Sacher had been built in the 1870s on the site of the Kärntner Tor Theatre where Beethoven premiered his *Ninth Symphony*.

Darby took the elevator up and entered her room, feeling like a princess arriving at her royal chamber. The room was fit for royalty with chandeliers, mint green carpet, and matching bedspread and curtains. A white ornate desk and chair sat near a window, and beautiful oil paintings adorned the walls. Somewhere in this same hotel, her grandparents had spent their first nights of love together. The thought made her single bed look very lonely. Darby tugged on the gold chain and studied the ring on the end of it. She ran her finger around the edge. "You've been here before, haven't you? This time you're alone without your other half. A lot like I am."

Darby took off the necklace and settled for a luscious bubble bath before plopping on the bed and perusing the room-service menu. She called in and chose the *Wiener schnitzel* with *Sachertorte* for dessert.

The history of the hotel's famous dessert was created before the hotel was even built, a brochure read. In 1832, Franz Sacher was an apprentice chef when Prince Metternich requested a special dessert for his elite guests. The problem—the head chef was ill and sixteen-year-old Franz was assigned the task. Now the Sacher annually used one million eggs, 70 tons of sugar, 60 tons of chocolate, 35 tons of apricot marmalade, 25 tons of butter, and 30 tons of flour to create its famous tortes, which were shipped around the world.

Slipping gratefully beneath the cool sheets of her bed, Darby

propped herself up and ate her food. The last bite of rich chocolate with the layer of apricot marmalade below the icing
topped off her full stomach. She leaned against her pillow and
flipped through channels, watching CNN and the BBC until
she could move again. The quiet of the room brought thoughts
of Brant. One part wished he could be with her at that very
moment; another part believed it could never work. If Brant
cared for her at all, why did he so easily let her go? Why did
he hold so strongly to his facts on paper when she was in front
of him, asking him to take a chance on her? And she didn't
think they had anything in common, except their tendency
toward being workaholics. When Darby did know the truth
and proved it to Brant, would they be able to put it all behind
them? She didn't think so. The ache inside was not as great as
her anger. How could she ever care for a man who would not
give her the benefit of the doubt, and over the most important
thing in her life?

But before she could address that future, she needed to have
the proof. Not only for Brant, but for her original purpose of
returning Tatianna's name.

Darby eased from the bed and found a phone book in the
desk. She spread out her papers on Bruno Weiler and searched
the directory. She'd never know what the future held or didn't
hold for her until she found the facts. The Ws produced no
Weiler at all. Next she skimmed for the aunt under Heike
Schumacher. There were many Schumacher names. Suddenly
Darby sat up and stared at the name, comparing it to her
notes. There it was: *Heike F. Schumacher.*

Darby checked her watch. It was already nine o'clock at
night, but she dialed the numbers on the telephone anyway.
Some things couldn't wait. Immediately, a young voice
answered.

"Hello," Darby said. "*Sprechen Sie Englisch?*"

"*Ja.* I do," the woman's voice said.

"Good. My name is Darby Evans. I'm looking for a woman named Heike Schumacher who had a sister named Dorthe Schumacher Weiler. The woman would be quite old. Have I reached the correct residence?"

"I do not know about sister of Frau Schumacher, but she is very old—one hundred years next month. She is asleep at this time."

"Are you her daughter?" Darby asked.

"No, I care for Frau Schumacher."

Darby hesitated. Should she ask now or wait until she could speak directly to the older woman? She took the chance. "I'm actually looking for the nephew of Heike Schumacher. His name is Bruno Weiler. Do you know anything about him?"

The woman hesitated. "I think you should instead speak to Frau Schumacher about such things. I give her your name and telephone and she call you back perhaps?"

"Could you please have her call me? It is very important." Darby gave the information and the woman said good-bye so quickly Darby wasn't sure her name and phone number were actually written down.

Darby listened to the dial tone and put the phone down. She may have just ruined her best chance to find Bruno Weiler.

CHAPTER TWENTY-SEVEN

Brant arrived at the home of Peter and Katrine Voss ready to tell them everything. His friend needed to know why Darby's grandmother could not be Celia Müller and why he had kept the story of what he knew about the Lange inheritance to himself. But as Katrine welcomed him inside, he was first faced with the letters of Darby's grandmother.

"I am in the middle of translating a new set Darby brought from her grandmother's house," Professor Voss said. He handed Brant a pile of papers. As Brant sat at the table and examined them slowly, his entire body turned cold. He gasped when he found one paper with a copy of a ring on it.

"What is this?" he asked, his voice straining to speak.

"It is a diagram of Darby's ring—or actually the engagement half of her grandmother's wedding set."

Brant stared at the photograph. "Peter, we need to find Darby. *Now*."

＊═◎═＊

Darby woke early to take a shower. She then waited, paced, and stared at the telephone, willing it to ring. Breakfast was room service again. Outside, the day was sunny and almost warm looking. Darby read about the Vienna sights in her *Lonely Planet Guide*, and finally at noon, dialed the number of Heike Schumacher again. No one answered.

By afternoon, she decided she must go out or go crazy. She slid on her jeans and a wool sweater, gathering her hair into a ponytail. She had packed light for what was supposed to be a quick day trip to Hallstatt, and today was her last change of clean socks and underwear. She buttoned her leather jacket and met a cold afternoon despite the sunshine.

Darby found that the Hapsburg Dynasty reign of six hundred years was evident throughout the capital. The beauty of the city displayed what it had once been—a cultural and political giant of an era gone by. Darby wanted to see everything and had enough mapped and planned for a week of sightseeing. But she barely made it through the courtyard of Hofburg, the Imperial palace, after taking a dozen photographs when the nagging wonder of a missed phone call made her decide to return to the Sacher. The wealth of shopping and the magnificence of the sights would have to wait for another day.

She waited for a bus to pass and noticed a gray sedan parked across the street. It seemed like she'd seen that car before, maybe even several times. But there were cars zipping around everywhere, and dozens of gray sedans with tinted windows. Darby continued down the street and glanced back at the license plate. It was an Austrian plate, nothing unusual.

She walked a few more blocks, down tree-lined streets to the turn of the Ringstraße. A gray sedan drove slowly by, the same license plate. When she came upon the car parked a few blocks up, on impulse, she pulled out her camera and began to click the shutter. The car sped away.

Darby suddenly realized that no one knew where she was. She'd told Professor Voss she'd call, but she hadn't yet. No one knew what hotel she was at, or that she'd made contact with the home of Heike Schumacher. Darby decided to go straight to the hotel.

She let out a sigh when she saw the bright flags waving her to safety a block away. Then a woman with bleached white hair stepped from a doorway in front of her.

"Excuse me," Darby said, stepping around.

"You seek information, do you not?" the woman said in English.

Darby turned around. The woman leaned against the building with a cigarette held loosely between two long fingers.

"Were you speaking to me?"

Darby checked to see if the woman could be talking to someone else. But few pedestrians moved along the street. The woman barely gazed at her as she took a long drag from the cigarette.

"If you want to know the answers you seek, come with me." The woman walked around her and up the street. Darby didn't know what to do. Who was she? Where did she come from?

"Darby Evans, are you coming or not?" She waited impatiently.

Darby tried not to look shocked. "How did you know my name?"

The woman smiled, but there was no warmth in the expression. "Trust me."

Darby edged several steps closer. "What do you want?"

"I want nothing—is it not you who seek answers?" The woman pointed down the alley. The gray sedan sat with the back door open. The engine was running. Through the tinted windshield, she could see a man in the driver's seat.

Darby took a step back, expecting anything. The woman dropped her cigarette and ground it into the sidewalk.

"Are you going to get in? We won't force you. But if you want answers, it will take a little cloak-and-dagger, as they say . . . but you will have your answers."

"How do you know me? Why have you been following me around the city?"

The woman shrugged. "We are only messengers sent to take you where you can find answers. Does the name *Tatianna* mean anything to you?"

"What do you know about Tatianna?"

"I know nothing. But I know who does. But you must choose to come."

Darby paused to consider the choice, her mind turning a million images. Her grandmother in her coffin, Professor Voss, Brant's face the night of the Mozart concert, her mother as Darby promised to be careful. But her need to know what had happened overthrew any mental warnings. Darby quickly stepped to the side of the car where the open door invited her into the dark interior. The woman opened the passenger door and sat in the front seat.

Darby leaned inside. "I need to tell someone where I am going."

"Get in or go your own way," the woman said, barely looking over her shoulder. The man didn't turn at all. "You have but one opportunity."

Darby sat on the leather seat. As soon as she closed the door, the sedan sped forward down Kärtnerstraße. She had been one block from her hotel. As they passed the waving flags of Hotel Sacher, Darby knew she'd made a terrible mistake.

CHAPTER TWENTY-EIGHT

Peter, have you heard from her?" Brant asked, pacing the room with telephone in hand.

"No, she was supposed to call. We have not heard a word."

"It's been all day. I really think we should try to find her." Brant had heard the worry in Peter's voice too. "She could be anywhere, but why don't we start calling hotels?"

"I think you are right. We need to find her. She does not have a car so would probably stay near the Ring."

"Okay, hotels along the Ring. You take three stars, I'll go four. We'll just move up till we find her. I know she was looking for authentic Austrian places, so no more Cozy Hotels."

Professor Voss chuckled, then sounded serious. "She is quite a lady, Brant."

"I know. I'll call you in an hour."

Brant hung up the phone and searched for his Vienna hotel guide, hoping he wouldn't have to run to the information office before starting to call. But he found the brochure soon enough and started circling hotels. He'd been ready to fly to

Vienna last night to find her. Even with the facts firmly in his mind, Brant could hardly believe the truth. If he'd seen Gunther's ring earlier, he'd have known.

Brant picked up the phone. He must find her. But he also dreaded it. What would she think when she discovered her grandparents could have finally found each other, if only for a little while, if only Brant hadn't stood in the way? Would she ever forgive him? Could he ever forgive himself?

◦⇒◦◐◦

No one spoke as they moved from the city. Mile after mile, Darby's panic grew. They drove south, passing signs for Graz and Klagenfurt. She knew in hours they could be in Slovenia, Italy, or Switzerland. These people could do anything to her, and she'd disappear without a trace. No amount of information was worth this. What had she been thinking? Darby decided that if they slowed, she'd try to get out. The doors were unlocked, the door handle beside her. Hours seemed to pass, though the road signs said far less.

"Where are we going?" Darby's voice sounded loud in her ears as it broke the quiet.

"Where we need to go," the woman responded without a backward glance.

"I want to go back. I don't want to know anything, I only want to go back."

The man and woman glanced at each other, but neither spoke. Darby didn't know what to do. The sun dropped low behind them as the man flipped the headlights on. Darby knew the shadows would soon consume the day.

After another half hour, the woman turned in her seat. "Time to lie down."

"You want me to lie down?"

"That's what I said."

"Why?"

"You ask so many questions. Get down." Her voice was stern. Darby did as she was told with her head toward the door and hand on the handle. The car slowed down an off-ramp, but not enough. They continued for more miles, more hours, it seemed.

The engine wound down. This could be her chance. But where was she? From her view, she hadn't seen buildings, only dense trees for a while. If she jumped now . . .

Darby paused too long. The car moved without completely stopping and steadied faster again. Dusk turned to darkness. The car turned in switchbacks, ascending higher and deeper into the woods. She was a fool. She knew her curiosity may cost her life.

"You can sit up." Finally the car ground to a halt. The headlights illuminated a tall, iron gate connecting solid block walls. The gate opened, allowing the car through. Not only did Darby not know her whereabouts, now iron gates locked her within massive walls. Gravel crunched beneath the tires as they curved through the woods. The dense trees would provide many hiding places, but the snow on the ground wasn't inviting. Around a bend, the trees opened, and a large, lit house stood in a clearing.

She could still run. But would she survive the night in this cold? Darby had no idea what direction she'd go. What if she got lost in the Alps? Or perhaps they weren't even in Austria. Darby knew she'd have to take her chances with whatever she was about to face.

The man drove the car around a circular driveway with a small fountain in the center. A walkway led to imposing double doors at the entrance to the house. The flat-fronted, two-story house was not typical Austrian with flowered windowsills. It stood straight and tall, probably intended for elegance. But against the night sky, the windows were the eyes of a creature staring at her, the doors a giant mouth ready to consume her. Darby didn't get out of the car until the driver opened her door. He propped himself against the car and lit a cigarette. Darby followed the woman toward the house.

No one greeted their arrival. The woman closed the heavy door and made her way across the hardwood-floored entry. Down the hall, their footsteps echoed through the house and up a wide, curving stairway. At a doorway, the woman motioned Darby inside, then turned and left without a word. Footsteps on hardwood floors echoed away.

Darby entered the room expecting someone or something. Only a fire crackled with long burnt logs and new wood piled crisscross above. The study had one dim lamp in the corner, and one wall was lined with books. Light danced on the volumes, a reflection from the rock fireplace on the opposite side of the room. Darby wondered where she should stand, or if she should sit in the chair in the corner or the one behind the large, wood desk. The fire beckoned, and she realized how cold she felt, from inside out.

Soon footsteps returned. Darby waited, her back to the fire, near an iron poker. A young woman who looked a lot like the woman from the car entered with a silver tray—her sister perhaps? The girl glanced at Darby curiously and set a tray with teapot, two cups and saucers, and dainty pastries onto the desk.

"Why am I here?" Darby asked the girl.

The dark-haired, dark-eyed girl only smiled at Darby, then hurried out. Her footsteps drifted away.

Darby peered suspiciously at the tray of food and drink. *If they're going to hurt me, I guess they want me comfortable first.*

A painting on the wall caught her eye. She recognized it from a book of Impressionist paintings at home. She moved closer and knew it was an original Edgar Degas painting. Whose home had she been delivered to?

Heavy footsteps would be her answer. She moved to her position by the fire, near the only weapon she could find.

He filled the doorway—large in height and weight with a presence that matched his size. Surely at least in his seventies, an old man in theory; still Darby knew instant fear. She had never seen him in her life, but she knew him to be a man of power. And her life rested in his hands.

"I knew you would come." He headed toward the tray. "Miss Darby Evans, in her persistence, could not resist." He poured two cups of tea without looking at her. "Despite the danger, you would get into a car with strangers, with no one knowing where you are or where you are going. Tonight you could disappear, and no one would ever find you. Not your mother in California. Not Brant Collins in Salzburg. Have some tea."

Shocked by the man's knowledge, Darby sputtered, "What do you want from me?"

"I have few wants from you. It is *you* who sought me." He turned toward her. "First tell me, who am I?"

The light from the fire lit his features: black eyes, thick face and lips. Darby knew. "You are Bruno Weiler."

"At one time, yes, that was my name. Good. Perhaps you should have been a detective instead of a photographer." He moved behind the desk with his cup and sat in the wide leather chair.

"How do you know so much about me?" Darby asked, not moving from her position by the fire. She glanced at the door and knew she could be out of the room before he could move from behind the desk. But what then? Who waited down the hall or outside? What would she do, and where would she go?

"I make it my business to know people who are putting my previous name on the Internet and making contact with my aunt. It can be dangerous to resurrect names that were supposed to have disappeared." He leaned forward with his elbows on the desk and motioned her to sit. "After all your seeking, tell me. Who killed the woman you seek?"

Darby slowly seated herself in a chair, feeling the eyes of this man who had once been a Nazi camp guard, who had gone to prison for his crimes. She tried to stay calm and figure out what to do next. She stared into cold eyes and cleared her throat. "Who killed Tatianna?"

"Yes. This is what I want from you. I want you to tell me who killed Tatianna Hoffman."

"I don't . . . the Nazis."

"The Nazis? Your skills are not as sharp as I expected."

"The Nazis at Mauthausen." Darby hoped that was the right answer.

"But who killed her? Tell me. Who killed Tatianna Hoffman? Who killed her at Mauthausen Concentration Camp? Who lifted the gun? Who watched her look upward, already gone, before a trigger was pulled? Who pulled the trigger? Who killed Tatianna Hoffman while Celia Müller escaped to America?"

Bruno Weiler stared hard into her eyes. Darby's mouth went dry; her hands shook. Tears built on the edges of her eyes.

"You did," she whispered.

"Yes, I did."

Bruno focused on the fire as a log bent and dropped into the flaming coals. "Yes, I killed Tatianna Hoffman. And you have entered the home of her killer."

⋯⊳═◯═⊲⋯

Brant dialed Darby's hotel and asked for her room for the third time. Again, no one answered. It had taken forty-five minutes of calling to find out she was staying at the Hotel Sacher. But she wasn't in her room. He imagined her splurging on the luxurious room, shopping in the city, walking around all alone, searching for an old Nazi. She had traveled the world, but somehow Brant could hardly handle the thought of her alone in Vienna. He wanted to be there with her.

He let it ring over ten times, then slammed the phone down. Where could she be?

Brant dialed the number again.

"Yes, you have a guest there, Darby Evans. Will you leave another message for her? It's urgent that I talk to her as soon as she returns. No matter what time it is."

Bruno's jaw clenched as he looked at Darby. His dark eyes beneath hooded lids told her nothing. "Now that you know, we will talk."

Her hands clung tightly to the edge of the desk as she kept her eyes on the living link she'd sought so long. Bruno Weiler was the last person to see Tatianna alive. He was also Tatianna's killer. How should she feel or think as she sat in the chair facing him? She needed to stop shaking and figure out something to do or say.

"You have questions for me. I see them in your eyes. Let me speak first. I will tell you what no one else knows. Not my children, not my ex-wives, not my colleagues. The few who ever knew are now gone."

Darby shuddered. "I don't need to know."

"But you do. You have most likely spent your whole life wondering, probably running from those questions. But somewhere inside you wanted to know. Didn't you?"

"Perhaps. But more than answers, I desire to leave this house tonight."

Bruno folded his hands and rested his chin on them. He stared at her for a long time. "I already have enough blood on my hands."

Did that mean he wouldn't hurt her, she wondered? Maybe she didn't want to know this man's secrets. He could easily change his mind or order someone else to keep her from revealing them. "Why will you tell me what no else knows? When you can't tell your own family? I'm a stranger."

He raised up heavily and walked to a glass cube on the bookshelf. He picked it up and set it on the desk next to Darby. Inside she could see a gold medal. "I received this for valor and courage. Yet I am a coward. I fear what my children will think of me. I fear their rejection."

"Then why me?"

"I have become an old man. Something about age brings the past forward. I am haunted now more than ever. I see everything with more memory than during the events. I find myself knowing more than I knew then. And you are the one living link to my past. You are the only one I can tell."

Bruno walked to the entrance of the room and closed the heavy door. It shut with a final click. He returned to his chair and again faced Darby. She felt glued to the seat, hypnotized by the truth she was about to hear.

"Few people know me as Bruno Weiler. My mother kept her name after the war, but she died many years ago. My aunt is the only contact to me. You called her home. She is ill and aged, but she knows if someone seeks information about Bruno Weiler, trouble usually lurks close behind. You left your name and hotel, but we already had been tracking you. You almost discovered that the first day you arrived in Salzburg."

"The man in my room?"

Bruno nodded.

"Why have you been tracking me? I'm only trying to prove who my grandmother really was."

"Are you? There is also the matter of your family inheritance."

"Yes, but that is not my main concern. Of course, I'd like to find out what happened to them, but lost riches are not my main goal."

"Many others would have it another way. I've known about you since you were a child. No one knows that I kept track of your grandmother over the many years, and your mother. Once, while on business in San Francisco, I drove by your home in Sebastopol. You and your sister had a tent in the front yard with dolls on a blanket. That was many years ago."

"Why? Why would you do that?"

"I wanted to see what happened with the gift of Tatianna's sacrifice."

"Then Tatianna did take my grandmother's place. I had no proof."

"Oh yes, Tatianna died as Celia Müller. She gave her life for your grandmother's and your mother's and yours. I knew this the day I saw Tatianna die."

The questions on her lips could be dangerous to ask. Darby looked at the man for the cruelty of a murderer, but instead saw weariness, and perhaps, vulnerability.

"Before you ask more," Bruno said, sensing her struggle, "I will tell you. I will tell you everything, if you are ready to hear."

She rested her hands on the table. "I'm ready."

Bruno leaned back in his chair and began his story.

"I knew your grandmother from the time we were children in Hallstatt. Her family was not rich, but well known in our village, especially with the legend of the brooch and coins. Your great-grandfather was the archaeologist who had family ties to Emperor Franz Joseph. My family was poor, my father an embarrassment to me. Today, we call it a dysfunctional family and alcohol abuse. Then, it was simply my life.

"I remember Tatianna came to our village when we were young—the girls were inseparable. Celia's younger brother and I were always good friends. We loved to bother the older girls, and especially, I remember one time: Celia's brother and I must have been around eight. The girls were around eleven. We had tried and tried to find their secret hideout."

Darby saw childhood revelry in the old man's eyes as he drifted into the past. She scooted forward, expectantly, clinging to the words that told the story of her grandmother before Darby knew her.

"After weeks of following their footprints and trying to follow the girls, we discovered their hideout deep in the woods inside the hollow of a gigantic, fallen tree. I can hear Warner saying excitedly how good it was we found it at that time, for the girls planned a secret initiation.

" 'I think it's some secret ritual or something,' Warner said. 'A girl thing for certain.'

" 'Maybe they will become blood sisters,' I said as we sneaked through their hideout filled with dolls, a tea set, and dried-flower bouquets.

" 'No way. Celia would faint if she saw her own blood. Tatianna would do it, I bet, but not my sister. I can tell it will be a big event, though. We better find a good place to hide if we're going to watch.'

" 'In those branches up there,' I suggested. 'They'll never see us from below, and then we can hear and watch them.'

"We had to go outside and around the bottom of the trunk to get into the twists of branches that overhung the girls' hideout. After settling in there, we waited for what seemed forever. Finally they came. I remember thinking how they reminded me of forest fairies with their long, white dresses and flowers in their hair. But young boys aren't supposed to think such thoughts. 'Girls, yuck,' I mouthed with a gagging motion that made Warner start to laugh. We were sure we were caught, but they didn't hear us. Instead, they ducked into their hideout and settled around a small log table. We had the perfect view.

" 'Today is one of the most important days for us,' Tatianna said.

" 'I still can't do the blood sisters thing, Tati. I'll faint.' Celia bit her bottom lip.

" 'Oh, I know. That's why I thought of something better. First, I want to ask you this, but you have to be sure of your answer.'

" 'Okay,' Celia said.

" 'Do you want to be my friend forever and ever?' Tatianna's eyes were large.

" 'Oh yes, I want to be your best friend forever and ever,' Celia said with a large smile.

" 'I just wanted to be sure. Now let's lock our baby fingers together.'

"Across the table, small hands reached. In the center they met with pinky fingers hooked as one.

" 'Celia Rachel Lange, I promise to be your best friend for my whole life. No matter what happens, how old we get, or even if one of us moves far away, I still promise this forever.'

" 'And I, Celia Rachel Lange, tell you, Tatianna Elise Hoffman, that you are my best friend and will always be. No matter what happens or how old we get. And I promise to be your friend forever.'

" 'And ever.'

" 'And ever,' they said in unison.

" 'I wish we could get matching rings or lockets, but this will have to do.' Tatianna lifted a box onto the table. She opened it and reverently took out two long, prickly stemmed roses—yellow roses. 'This will be our forever friendship flower. Whenever we see a yellow flower, especially a yellow rose, we'll remember our vow to be best friends always.'

" 'What a good idea, Tati. I love roses, and yellow is my favorite color. I'll remember today always.'

" 'Forever and . . .'

" 'Ever,' they said again.

"Warner and I stayed in our places while the girls drank pretend tea and giggled about girl things. When finally we left, we put on masks of disgust, though I think we both were a little jealous of a friendship so pure. And the image of their vow with fingers locked together came back to me so vividly when I saw Tatianna at Mauthausen."

Bruno stiffened as if the mention of that place jarred him from gentle memories.

"I want to tell you, I did not change from that boy into a killer in just a moment. It takes time. Almost so slowly you don't see that you're disappearing. I left Hallstatt as a young man to find my life in the city. I came to Linz and Vienna, ready to make my mark upon the world and break free from my family line of failures. I was full of awe and curiosity for the modern world and hoped for a new, more powerful Austria. I wanted to be part of that Austria and joined the Nazi party with its rebellion toward the old ways and passive government. The Party sought power and strength and a greater future for our weakened country. When joined with Germany, Austrians would leave a mark upon the entire world. If some individuals were trampled in the process, it was a sad product of forward movement. Many of us believed these things."

Bruno focused intently on Darby. "I believed these things." Then he turned away, toward the fire, and into yesterday once again. "I did not advance the way I expected. I did not at first recognize that greed, corruption, and even that old class ladder existed larger than idealism. I became SS in hopes of greater advancement and was sent as a guard to Mauthausen Concentration Camp. It insulted me. I wanted a more noble position than guard to felons, political prisoners, and Jews. I was promised my time there was a mere stepping-stone—all future officers did some dirty work. Prove yourself there, and you will advance. So I went to prove I could be the best, the smartest, the bravest. I convinced myself that the creatures in the camp deserved their punishment, and already I was a very angry man. I saw those people as criminals, animals who fed on our future, leeches on our social system—some probably innocents, but such was the cruelty of bettering mankind. It was the pathway to a future mankind and survival of the fittest. They were not like me. They did not feel or think as I did. Behaviors of greed between prisoners were only further proof—a father who killed his son for food, an instance of cannibalism, the constant undermining of authority. I didn't look at the good in them. I could not allow myself to see acts of love and chivalry.

"Many of the other guards were sadistic monsters who lusted after blood and torment. But what could I do about that? I had my advancement and own step-up to be concerned with. Though I was no innocent in it all."

Bruno again glanced at Darby's white face, then back at the fire.

"One day in early summer, I heard of a pretty girl in the jail-house. I heard her name—Celia Müller. I did not recognize the name, for I'd left Hallstatt before her marriage. Some officers were discussing her, how they hoped she would be assigned to the brothel—even though she was a Jewess. She did not look Jewish. She wasn't emaciated, for she had not come from other camps as most others had. She had been for months in prisons and under interrogation, and now she was there and looked better than the others. If only she would speak and disclose the hiding place of the Lange family inheritance, they said, perhaps she would be released to the brothel. I knew immediately—Celia Müller must be the girl from my village, Celia Lange."

Bruno's speech faltered. Darby watched him carefully as he stared, almost entranced, at the crackling fire. Somewhere a long way off, she heard the mournful sound of a train.

"There was no way for me to see her, and I did not want to. At times, a woman's cries could be heard from the prison. It became routine when a certain officer arrived at the camp that the woman would be interrogated. He visited often and was frustrated that she would not reveal it. He had thought time and interrogation would make her give them the hiding place of the inheritance—a wealth for the finder or a huge advancement in rank. A comrade assigned to the jail gave me details as he heard information. He said even Hitler knew of the Lange family inheritance—some Celtic coins, perhaps the oldest ones of our region, and a brooch from Empress Sissi. Celia's father had already died at Mauthausen before I was assigned there. I didn't even allow sorrow for Warner, though he had been my childhood friend. The SS officer had been so thoroughly angered about their death without giving any information about the inheritance that he'd sent the interrogators to the gas chambers. Then they caught Celia."

"At the Swiss border," Darby said.

"Ah, yes, that is correct. Almost got away, they said. They believed she would give them the answers."

"But she couldn't, because she didn't know."

"Correct." Bruno sighed. "I did not see her until the day I was called to execute her. And then I knew. It wasn't Celia, but Tatianna who stood before me."

He spoke with unseen layers of time and regret falling from his face. His strong expression turned vulnerable, guilty, and sympathetic at the same time.

"Some guards enjoyed adding suffering to their victims. They would wound them and then walk close to see the pain before finishing them off. I aimed straight for Tatianna's heart. She watched the sky as if waiting to leave. I pulled the trigger."

A log fell into the flames, and sparks popped in the quiet room. Darby saw the scene in Bruno's faraway gaze. She had seen one tiny passport photo of Tatianna but could picture the woman perfectly. A bullet freeing her from her torment, freeing her spirit toward life.

"So I, not anyone else, killed Tatianna Hoffman. And as I took her life, she gave me mine."

Startled, Darby asked, "What do you mean?"

"I pulled that trigger and instantly understood. I knew Tatianna had somehow given her life for her friend. Already I had begun to question my beliefs in the darkest hours of night. I performed my duties, but I felt haunted by feelings that I couldn't and wouldn't face in the daylight. Tatianna changed that. I knew so clearly, as if a veil had been taken from my eyes. I saw it all. I looked at myself and detested what I saw. It triggered my redemption from the Nazis, though always my name would be associated with them, and always my hands are stained with blood—no matter what I have tried to do."

Bruno cleared his throat. "Now you know. Now I have spoken it to someone. Not even my children know."

"What did you become? Did you stay in the camp?"

"Only a week later, I received the promotion I so desired. I took it and went to Germany. Once it was my greatest desire, but then, my greatest opportunity. I became a betrayer to the Party I had given my oath. They never knew it was me. I was even imprisoned as a Nazi war criminal, even though I spied for the other side."

"Why didn't you reveal that at your trial?"

"The Nazis hadn't disappeared. Their power was greatly injured, but not destroyed. And if I revealed my truth, it would endanger others. I fulfilled my duties as the good Nazi, and then Bruno Weiler disappeared. I moved to America for ten years, then later returned to Austria. I was given financial help from some friends I helped during the war. I received some physical alteration, then began a new life as a new man. As you can see, I have done well . . . on the outside."

Darby nodded, glancing at the Degas painting. "Yes."

Bruno looked at it also and smiled wryly. "People would call me a powerful man, but inside, all men are only men. And for me, my life will always return to Tatianna. She had a power in death I have never found. It was in her face. I heard about it once at a church service in America. There was a man who was stoned to death; Stephen was his name, if I remember correctly. They say his face shone like an angel. Tatianna's face was like that—like she was really free. I have never found what she had. The blood of others will always be with me."

Darby could see the struggle within Bruno. She wondered what she should feel for him—anger, hatred, fear? But she could find none of those for this killer of Tatianna and of others. "My grandmother would say that the blood of Jesus purchases the blood on our hands and all of our sins. His life for ours, like Tatianna, but also to save all mankind. If only we ask."

"Celia Lange said those words? Tell me, do you believe these words?"

"Me?" Darby felt her face flush as she was suddenly on the spot. It was one thing to quote her grandmother, another to state her own belief. "Well, I would have said 'no' not long ago, probably six weeks ago. But now? Yes, I do believe it. I believe God forgives us when we ask. I believe Jesus died to provide that forgiveness. His life for ours. In a very strange way, Tatianna showed me that."

"How can you, or I, know for certain?"

"I'm wondering myself. I guess that is faith."

"Would you grant me forgiveness?"

"What? You are asking me to forgive you?"

"I cannot say it to Tatianna or Celia or the others. But will you give it?"

"It is not mine to give. I would, if I could. I think that is a matter for you and God."

Bruno nodded slowly. "You don't make it easy for me."

"I will give you the forgiveness I can give. But I think that only God's will make you feel complete."

"Perhaps I will seek him and see."

Darby glanced at the fire, reduced to embers. The tea in her cup had long grown cold. She could see a swirl of what had to be snowflakes in the window behind Bruno. She put her hands in her coat pockets, and Bruno moved to the fire. He added several logs, then took the poker and stirred the embers into a tiny flame.

"Now you know." He stood by the fire, close to her. "Warm yourself, and I will get some tea." Bruno replaced the poker. "It is late, but I apologize I cannot allow you to stay tonight. The less you know about who I have become, the better."

"It must be difficult, living a new life," Darby said as she rose from her chair. Her back ached and her muscles longed for the soft bed at the Sacher. But that was a long way off. Then, with a start, she remembered that only hours ago, she wondered if she'd ever see the Hotel Sacher again, or her mother, her friends, or Brant Collins.

"It is the world I live in. Everyone has secrets. Money, power, position—they all link the good and the bad. A man must be careful, especially a man of position with my kind of tainted past. And you, my dear. Do not make the same mistakes. Remember, the family inheritance remains an interest for dangerous people. Many have been killed for much less money than the inheritance is worth."

"I'll be more cautious, I promise."

Bruno left for hot water and returned with more food and tea. She hadn't realized her hunger until she began eating. Outside, a car engine rumbled to life. On her way out, Bruno pointed the way to a bathroom down a hall. Photographs lined the wall, and Darby was shocked to see one portrayed a younger Bruno shaking hands with President Reagan. She didn't linger long.

"Time to go," Bruno said, extending both hands. As her hands were gathered into a tight embrace, they looked deeply at one another. Tears brimmed in Darby's eyes. She knew they could never meet again.

"I will have a letter delivered to you from a certain ex-Nazi, Bruno Weiler. It will tell that Tatianna Hoffman died at Mauthausen Concentration Camp, not Celia Lange Müller. It will be your proof, I will make sure of that. Then, if you do find the Lange inheritance, it will be yours. But still, be careful, Darby Evans. Remember my words, for I insist that you hear me clearly. I know of others who desire what should be yours. I cannot be there for you."

"Thank you. Know that you and your secret are safe with me."

"I do not doubt it."

Darby walked alone to the front door and glanced back toward Bruno as she stepped outside. He nodded as she closed the door. The same driver was in the car as she again sat in the back. The woman was not there. The driver only spoke when it was time for her to lay her head down and then again when she could rise. A touch of dawn lit the east as they arrived in front of Hotel Sacher. Weary in every inch of her body, Darby plodded toward the entrance. When she looked back, the gray sedan was already gone.

CHAPTER TWENTY-NINE

A desk clerk handed Darby messages from Brant, who had called throughout the night. *What could that be about*, she wondered, but was too tired to care. Plus, it was too early to call him. Darby entered her room and dropped onto the bed without taking off her clothing. She closed her eyes.

Far away an insistent sound disturbed her. She awoke to the phone ringing and ringing beside her head. The hour hand on her watch had moved only a few times.

"Hello?" she said with her eyes still closed.

"Darby, where have you been? I've been worried sick about you. Didn't you get my messages? Why didn't you call?"

"It was too early."

"Are you okay?"

"I was a few minutes ago and having a great dream—Brant, is that you?" she said, awakening a bit more.

"Where were you?"

She sat up in bed and noticed the light shining around the edges of the window shade. "I had some information to follow up."

"And it took all night?"

"Brant, is there a reason I have to tell you where I've been?"

"No, no, I've just been worried. But if you don't want to give me an explanation, that's fine."

"Why have you been worried? And wait a minute, how did you find me?"

"It's a long story. Are you sure you're all right?"

"Yes, Brant."

"Well, you aren't an experienced traveler, you could have made a naïve mistake . . . I had all sorts of images going through my head."

"Me naïve, inexperienced?" *If he only knew.* "I'm learning rapidly."

"Okay, okay. Now that I know you're safe, you must get back here right away. Or I can come get you?"

"What is so desperate it can't wait?"

"I need to speak to you in person—today. I went to . . . just get back to Salzburg."

"All right. I'm sure there's a morning train to Salzburg. I'll be on it."

"I'll be waiting."

Darby flopped against the pillow. What could be so important it couldn't wait? She imagined Brant worried and pacing in his apartment. The image made her smile. Suddenly Darby sat back up. Maybe he'd been with Professor Voss. Did that mean he believed her story?

⋆⇒◎⇐⋆

Darby wondered about it all the way back to Salzburg. She found humor in Brant's early-morning call. Mr. Serious worried about her? She could imagine his eyebrows pinched, jaw clenched, fingers anxiously punching telephone buttons. For some reason, Darby found that funny. Perhaps he had some new information? But she knew the story now, and soon she'd have proof in her hands. Darby didn't know how she would explain her source, but if Brant pushed too far she'd tell the truth—"If I tell you, I'll have to kill you." She laughed out loud, imagining Brant's expression.

One mystery remained—the inheritance. But Darby was too tired to think of that—at last, her purpose was accomplished.

Darby leaned against the headrest as the train gently rocked back and forth. She hoped to catch some sleep as the Austrian countryside whirled by and she was delivered to Brant. Whatever he felt desperate to tell her would be no surprise to her. She was about to prove the facts to him.

⋆≡◉═⋆

Richter could not believe what he was hearing. "Could you say that again?" he said into the phone as he took a drag from his cigarette.

"You are freed from your debts," the voice said. "And I want you to leave Darby Evans alone."

"I don't understand. Why would you simply cancel it all?" Richter didn't know whether to be elated or suspicious. Suspicion rose higher because he knew no one simply canceled debts, especially this man.

"Just do what I said."

The phone clicked, and Richter heard the dial tone. His debt, his fear for the last six months was canceled. It didn't make sense. And why was he told to leave Darby Evans alone? Suddenly he knew. The inheritance. He tossed the phone on the couch. *She must be close. And I won't be cheated now.*

⋆≡◉═⋆

The trains were punctual, but never early. Still Brant came to the Bahnhof an hour before Darby's arrival. He waited in the terminal and watched the schedule of incoming trains. Then his cell phone rang. He considered turning off the power, but wondered if it could be Peter.

"Hey, Brant! It's Richter. Where you at?"

"I'm at the train station. Is there something you need?"

"I'm just in town and thought we'd get together."

"I have plans. Next time, probably."

"Hey, I've been trying to contact that American woman."

"Why?"

"Since you weren't moving on her, I thought I'd take a shot. Where's she staying?"

Brant froze. "How did you know she was back in Austria?"

"You told me, remember?" Richter laughed. "You're too young to lose your memory."

Brant could not remember telling Richter, but perhaps he had. "I'm at the train station getting ready to pick her up. She's returning from Vienna."

"Really? Well, I can tell by your voice, I've jumped in a little too late. The two of you are finally connecting? I must be rubbing off on you."

"I need to go, Richter." A train arrived at the station, but not Darby's.

"Okay, I'll get ahold of you another time."

Brant clicked his phone off and stuffed it into his jacket. Richter was looking for Darby? Why? No matter what, Richter had better stay away from her.

❖══◍══❖

"Salzburg!" The conductor called over the speaker. Darby already waited in the narrow doorway with her bag. The train's rocking slowed and the brakes screeched as the train pulled into the Bahnhof. She pushed the door lever before it opened automatically. Brant knew something, and finally she was going to discover what it was.

Darby saw him walking the length of train, searching the doorways. Their eyes met, and she felt a rush of emotion. If he opened his arms, she was sure she'd fall into them forever. Fatigue and the fear from the previous night had left her open, ready for Brant. But his hands were stuck hard into his coat. He reached only for her duffel bag, and his face held no joyous greeting.

"We need to talk." Brant's eyes spoke desperate words. "Alone."

She was tired of mysterious games. All she wanted was a few more hours of sleep. She followed Brant from the train station in pants she'd worn twice and slept in once, a shirt that had been wrinkled at the bottom of her duffel, and a jacket that smelled slightly of smoke from her adventures in train stations and car rides. Brant stopped in front of a dark-blue sports car and dumped her bag into the trunk. He hadn't said a word since they'd left the station. He unlocked her door and closed it behind her.

"Brant, I'm tired, delirious, and I've had way too much coffee on the train. See, my hands are shaking." Darby held up a hand. Brant gripped the steering wheel and didn't look her way.

"Why are you so serious? What's going on?" Then she saw that his eyebrows were creased into one, exactly as she'd imagined. She laughed. "Let me guess . . . in one day, you've decided that you can't live without me—you're crazy about me." She leaned toward him, laughing more until she noticed his expression—still looking ahead, jaw set, hands on the wheel. "You were supposed to laugh."

Brant started the car and zipped into traffic.

"Where are we going?" she asked in a whine, trying to relax against the headrest with eyes closed. After more silence from Brant, she opened her eyes and insisted, "Stop the car or talk to me or take me to my hotel. This is ridiculous."

Brant made a sharp turn and maneuvered into a parking place. He shut off the engine and faced her. "I've been trying to figure out how to say this. Where would be the perfect place? Maybe we should go to my apartment or to your hotel."

"This looks good to me. Now talk."

His eyes studied her, as if memorizing every detail. Darby felt uncomfortable under his gaze, wondering what she looked like after a night of little sleep and the early train trip.

"I believe her, Darby. I believe Celia."

His eyes watched her response, but Darby was uncertain. This was the news she'd hoped for on her return to Salzburg that morning. And did he really mean it? "You believe my grandmother really was Celia Müller?"

"Yes."

"Why? Did you read the letters? What makes you believe now?"

"Where is your grandmother's ring?"

"I'm wearing it." Darby removed the gold chain from beneath her shirt and coat.

"Can I see it?"

"Sure." She unclasped the back and handed it to Brant. What was he doing? she wondered as he slid the ring off and handed her the gold chain. This was not what she expected of him.

"Darby, I don't know where to start. I've looked at it over and over again." He ran his hand through his hair. "I didn't believe her. I mean, how could I? But now—"

"Brant. I know."

He lifted a finger to her chin, then touched her lips. Darby knew she should back away; there was too much to work out. But she couldn't move. His hand lingered against her cheek, then suddenly pulled away. Brant turned and gripped his fist on the steering wheel. What was he tormented by? Darby wondered. He straightened up as if in decision and took something from a box inside his coat pocket. It was a ring. The two slid together, and the curved settings snapped into place.

Darby froze inside. She took the rings, now one. "Where did you get the other half?"

"I told you about the mentor who changed my life? That man was Gunther Müller."

"Gunther Müller. My grandfather? My grandfather was alive after the war?"

"Darby, your grandfather is alive *now*."

CHAPTER THIRTY

My grandfather is alive. You're certain?"

"Yes. He's been very sick, has had a stroke, and wasn't supposed to survive. When I was going through his things, I found the ring."

Darby shook her head, drew her feet onto the seat, and wrapped her arms around them. Her eyes stared out at the noon traffic and shoppers as her mind fought to comprehend Brant's words. "Where is he?"

"Here, in Salzburg."

"Here!" She put her hand over her mouth.

"His stroke was last fall, and he's been at a rehab clinic in Munich for months. Then, right after Christmas, his wife moved him to a nursing home in Salzburg. He's been here ever since. I visit several times a week, but only in the last month has he made real progress with his speech."

"His wife? He remarried?"

"Darby, I take all the blame for this. If I had better investigated when your grandmother wrote me—but I had no idea.

They could have been together—your grandparents. But I sent that letter back. I didn't tell Gunther—didn't want to put him through something like that."

"No, Brant," Darby said slowly. "This isn't your fault, it's his. He never came for her. She mourned her whole life. He remarried and got on with his life while my grandmother was writing him letters every year."

"Gunther only married to help a friend of theirs. I promise you, he never got over Celia. But he truly thought she was dead. He was at the Hungarian border when he got word Celia had been caught. He stayed for months, and then the notice of death came from Mauthausen. Of course, he believed them. He paid all the money he had to try to get her body. All he received was this half of the ring, which was a miracle in itself. With that ring, he had no doubts that his wife and child were dead."

Darby's body shook, and tears fell in streams down her cheeks. Of course, it made sense. But the horror pulsed through her. The two of them could have been together—all of them could have been together. It would have changed everything, their entire lives. Her mother would have had the daddy she so longed for. Suddenly Darby was struck by the realization: her mother did have the father she sought. Gunther Müller was alive.

The questions, accusations, truths, and lies pounded in her head. "I have to see him."

"We'll go right now."

Brant immediately started the car and took off.

"Wait," Darby said. "Take me to my hotel first. I'm meeting my grandfather for the first time. I need to clean up." She turned to him. "Does he know—about me, my mom, and sister?"

"No. I haven't seen him since I saw the copy of the ring. I wanted to tell you first. Perhaps I should have prepared him. He's weak, not well. I don't know what to do."

"I don't either. We'll decide when we get there. I just need to see him." She laid her head against the side window and watched the world zip past. Somewhere in that city her grandfather lived and breathed. The missing link in the family, the missing link in her life.

⁂

Brant sat on the edge of the bed as Darby showered. He looked at a shoe she'd left on the floor and picked it up. It was the black dress shoe with the chunky heel she'd worn the night they'd gone to the dinner concert. The side of the bed closest to the window was rumpled. So that was the side she slept on. The same one he liked. He closed his eyes and listened to the sound of the shower.

Brant shook himself. He needed to think of other things and not get himself too caught up with Darby Evans. She was in shock. But how would she feel after that shock wore off? Would she be angry at him?

And what of Gunther? He knew the old man would understand. He'd know Brant had been protecting him. But would meeting Darby be too much?

He wished Darby would hurry so they could go see his old friend.

⁂

Darby grabbed Brant's arm. "Wait," she whispered before he opened the large oak door to the care facility. She pivoted, taking in a breath as she gazed down the cement walkway lined with landscaped trees and grass and then toward Brant's car in the parking lot.

Brant put his hand on hers. "Ready?"

She exhaled with her entire body. "I think so."

Brant opened the door and Darby entered. The white floors

looked cold and clean. Their footsteps echoed down the long hallway. She heard groans and laughter in different rooms as they walked. After a turn down a long hallway, Brant stopped at a closed door. "This is it."

"You go first."

Brant opened the door, and Darby peered over his shoulder. The bed was covered with a blue bedspread, but no one was in it. Brant entered first and checked the small bathroom.

"What does that mean?" Darby asked, her pulse pounding. "Is he all right?"

"He was starting to get around last time I was here." Brant checked his watch. "It's too early for dinner. I'm sure he's fine, or I'd have heard something."

They heard footsteps from the room next door. A cleaning woman entered, and Brant spoke to her in German.

"She said he's in the chapel."

The woman glanced at the wall clock and spoke again.

"I guess chapel is over. He's probably in the game area."

"I thought you said he wasn't well."

"He's been improving. And Gunther's a fighter, that's for sure."

Darby was about to leave the room when something caught her eye. A miniature rosebush on a small table in the corner of the room. It blossomed with yellow roses. She touched a petal the size of her fingernail.

"Yes, this must be my grandfather's room," she said quietly.

"I wanted you to find the memorial your grandfather made for Celia in Hallstatt. I hadn't seen it in years and forgot that the nameplate is covered. You have to open it to see her name. But there is a rosebush growing at the base. It blossoms yellow roses."

"My grandmother's favorite flower."

"At least once a year, under the cover of night, Gunther would take his own yellow roses from his garden to her grave. He never missed a year."

"And all the while, my grandmother was living and missing him on the other side of the world, tending her yellow roses."

Brant turned Darby toward him and drew her into his arms. "It's going to be okay. Somehow, it's going to be okay."

Darby rested against his chest for a minute, then slowly pulled away. "Let's find him."

They left the room and headed back down the hall, turning right. Above the sound of their footsteps, Darby heard a deep, steady voice speaking as they reached the doorway.

"That's Gunther," Brant said, sounding surprised as they stopped. "He sounds much better than just a week ago." Darby's eyes moved to a table with chess figures and two men sitting on opposite ends. The man speaking had his back to them.

"Wait." Darby grabbed Brant's arm. She looked at the thick, peppered-gray hair, a little in need of a comb in the back where a fuzzy piece stood up. Her eyes caressed a wool sweater over his wide back. Her grandfather. His voice was only slightly slurred, but she caught a hint of laughter within. "What is he saying?"

Brant whispered close to her ear. "He's teasing the other guy, and, as typical for Gunther, is giving the man a Bible lesson. He said that when we take communion and say we partake of Jesus' body and blood, we accept that we may face the sufferings and trials that Jesus faced. But God has conquered all things, and so we have nothing to fear. He just asked the man, 'Have you partaken? Perhaps that is why you are losing?' I can't believe he's talking so well."

"So what do we do?" Darby asked softly. "Perhaps we should have a doctor tell him. What if we set him back? What—what if . . . what if he doesn't want a granddaughter after all these years?"

"He wants you, Darby. Don't be afraid of that. I don't know what we'll tell him or not tell him. Let's meet him and go from there." Brant slid his hand around hers reassuringly. "Are you ready?"

"Yes."

"I'm with you, every step." He led her forward. "Gunther?"

"Bra-nt."

Gunther turned slowly. A smile beamed from his face and Darby noticed light blue eyes that might resemble her mother's, but there was no immediate recognition of other features. Gunther smiled at her, even raised an eyebrow at their hands, but nothing would have told them who they were to one another. She could have bumped into him anywhere and never known this man had some of her same blood.

The two men spoke German, so Darby was only able to understand a word or two that indicated Brant's surprise over Gunther's health. Then Gunther turned his attention back to her, saying something and extending a hand.

"American," Darby heard from Brant in another round of German.

"Ah, an A-merican?" Gunther said, interested. "Bend down here."

He reached for her hands, and she wondered if he'd notice her trembling within his own unsteady fingers. Darby bent down and looked up at him, extending her hands.

"You w-atch for this man. He very disturbed at times." He winked and grinned up at Brant. Darby's tears began to flow.

"Is there something wrong, my child?"

The words *my child* brought a surge of emotion. Darby saw her grandmother's dreamy eyes as she spoke of this man. She remembered the letters of love, so deep and youthful and full of tomorrow. She saw her mother, waiting and searching the Times Square crowd, hoping, hoping that he'd appear. And the ghost who haunted their family was right in front of her—alive and breathing.

A sob broke in her chest as she looked down at the floor. She heard Gunther's chess partner wheel away in his chair, and she tried to force herself to stop crying, but the tears only flowed harder. The hand holding hers tightened, and she felt a gentle pat on her back. He spoke to Brant in German and waited for an answer.

"Gunther," Brant said tenderly, "This is Darby Evans. She is your granddaughter."

The hands pulled away, and Darby heard his gasp. Her tears stopped, but she could not look up.

"Her grandmother's name was Celia Müller."

Gunther spoke hoarsely in German. Brant began an explanation in Gunther's native tongue. Brant knelt beside her, speaking upwardly, with his arm around her. Darby remained before him, unable to look up from the floor, like a child waiting for either stark rejection or arms of love. She heard Gunther exhale, long and deep like the final breath had left his lungs.

A hand touched her hair as Brant stopped speaking. The shaking fingers lifted her chin. Their eyes met, both with tears.

"My grandchild. I never had a child, never thought. . . ."

Gunther's fingers touched her cheek, a strand of hair, her forehead.

"When did she die?"

"Four months ago."

Gunther's mouth dropped, and his light eyes looked away. He put his hand upon his head and shook it slowly as if not able to believe his ears. He exhaled another long, deathly breath, and Darby could feel him shiver from deep within.

"Gunther?" Brant asked. "Are you all right?"

"No. This is worst, and best, of days." His hands shook violently, and he clasped them together.

"I think we should take you to your room."

Brant pushed the wheelchair. Gunther held Darby's hand the entire way and glanced up often, as if to be sure she was still there.

They entered behind a nurse who spoke to Gunther and

examined him closely. Gunther disagreed with the woman. Darby wished she could understand them.

"Are you sure?" Brant asked. "If you need rest, we can come back in a few hours. I don't want you having a setback."

"I don't want y-ou to go. I want you here. I want her, Darby, here. My grand-daughter. I w-aited my entire life to see her."

Brant helped Gunther into the bed and carefully removed the older man's shoes. He pushed a button to elevate the bed to a sitting position, then covered Gunther's legs with the blue bedspread. Gunther reached a hand toward her, and Darby moved a chair close.

"I still cannot understand. How?"

"Tatianna Hoffman died at Mauthausen. Somehow she took Grandma's place. My grandmother was told you were dead, and when you never came to your meeting place, she believed it."

"I believed she was dead," Gunther said, shaking his head. Suddenly, he sat up straighter. "Oh, dear Lord. She didn't. She could not have!"

"What is it?" Brant asked.

"Ingrid. Ingrid was with them."

"Who is Ingrid?" Darby asked.

"My wife. Ingrid went with Ta-tianna and Celia to Swiss border. She was with them the night the Nazis met them. Ingrid knew everything."

Brant sat in the chair beside Darby. "Ingrid knew Celia escaped and Tatianna was taken by the Nazis? And she never told you?"

"Never. She told me Ce-lia was taken."

"What did she say happened to Tatianna?" Darby asked.

"She say Tatianna was so close to border a-nd after Nazis took Celia she decided to leave Austria."

"When did she tell you all of this?"

"The night she beg me to marry her. The war had just ended, the c-ountry was mess, divided by A-mericans, British,

CINDY McCORMICK MARTINUSEN

Soviets. Ingrid's ch-ildren were Nazi babies, and she need pro-tection. I had been in re-sistance, injured for the cause—a perfect co-ver for her. I a-asked everything about night of Celia's capture. She could have said truth. I would have g-gone to America and found Celia."

"But she needed you for her own safety." Brant stood up swiftly in anger.

"You know what?" Darby sat forward. "Grandma's letters. One was from a woman with 'I' initials. The letter was from 1942, three years before the war ended. She told Grandma Celia about Tatianna's death and also that you had died. The woman told Celia to quit writing and get on with her life in America. The woman also said she had a Nazi friend she might marry."

Brant and Gunther eyed one another. "Ingrid," Brant said.

Gunther began to shake again. "I have tried my whole life to do good. How can this happen? How?" Tears burst from his eyes. He moaned and curled onto his side. Darby jumped up and leaned over him, wishing to protect him from all he must feel. All she could do was wait.

His wide back continued to shake with years of lost sobs. Darby looked at Brant and saw the fear in his eyes.

"It's all right, Gunther," Brant said, cradling the old man in his arms. He spoke softly in German. Darby couldn't stop her own scattered tears and saw Brant wipe his face from time to time as he rocked his old mentor. Finally, Gunther's sobs slowed, and she believed he was asleep until he reached for her hand. His thick hand held hers and stroked it gently.

Brant opened a drawer on the nightstand and handed Gun-ther a handkerchief. The old man wiped his face and blew his nose like a trumpet sounding. He chuckled as he turned and sat up. "I m-eet my granddaughter for the fir-irst time and act like a blubbering fool. I a-apologize, my dear."

Darby sniffed. "Oh, don't be sorry. You've lost her all over again. And you've been betrayed."

"Yes. And I could have gone to my grave without ever meeting you. See, I should be thankful." His smile was weak but sincere. "Please. Will you tell me about her?"

Darby smiled at the stranger she instantly loved. "She was absolutely amazing. Learned the computer before anyone in our household. She became an American citizen before I was born and never spoke German again."

"She h-ad to leave this all behind, perhaps," Gunther said.

"On the outside, I know she did, except I grew up with tales of the Austrian Alps. So in a way, she contradicted herself. She did not speak of the difficult times to me. My mother had a long struggle, wanting her father—wanting you—so they quit speaking of you before I was born. Yet I know she didn't leave you behind. She was a brave, independent woman who loved with a full heart."

"That sounds like Cel-ia. Though I ne-ever considered her brave or inde-pendent."

"Oh, she was. She jogged in a senior citizen marathon and volunteered two days a week at the public-school kindergarten. Perhaps she had to become strong once she lost you. She also had a strong faith in God."

"Then it is God who saved us both—made us to be strong without each other."

"Yes," Darby whispered. Her eyes found Brant's dark, compassionate eyes. She could barely tear her gaze away from him as she continued to tell about her grandmother. Memories from childhood, Grandma Celia's favorite American movies and books, her to-die-for New York cheesecake. Gunther took it in like a starving man tasting food once again. Darby talked, with Gunther asking questions, until night fell around them. "Grandma has a rose garden in our backyard. Her favorite flower bush in the center of the garden—"

"Yellow roses," Gunther finished. He looked far away and infinitely sad. "I've been placing those flowers on her memorial for sixty years—and all that time she lived and breathed."

"A few nights before she died, Grandma told me how much she loved you. She said you were her Prince Charming, and she never loved a man again. She wrote you letters, one every year. I have them with me."

Darby found her long, black purse and took out the packet they'd picked up from Peter Voss before arriving at the nursing home. "We were trying to find information in them. But the last one has not been opened. It was written September 15 of last year. She died October 3."

Gunther reached for the letter and held it against his chest. "October 3. Wh-at was I doing that day? Why did I not feel her, her spirit leave? Why did I not know she lived all these years?" Gunther caressed the neat cursive words on the envelope. "I would kn-know that writing any-where."

The door to Gunther's room opened, and the nurse appeared surprised to see them still there. Brant talked to her, with Gunther adding a few words before Brant and the nurse exited the room.

"They think I'm old and need some rest," Gunther said with a smile. "I don't want you to leave yet."

"Brant will take care of it. But you could use some rest. And perhaps some time alone?" Darby motioned to the letters on the edge of the bed.

Brant returned. "They gave permission for us to stay awhile longer, maybe even the night, but only if Gunther is able to rest. They want to prepare him for bed and to eat his dinner." Gunther frowned, and long creases furrowed his forehead. "I promise to bring her back. We'll be in the cafeteria."

Darby glanced back at Gunther before she walked out. He was already opening the letter from his bride.

CHAPTER THIRTY-ONE

They made small talk as they picked up trays in the cafeteria. Both chose a meat stew with dumplings. Darby could tell something was bothering Brant. They carried their trays to a quiet, indoor garden room.

Brant stirred his food and hardly ate. Darby gobbled hers down and ate both their breads. She asked him three times if he was feeling all right. After they had cleared their trays away, they walked to the end of the glass room. The stars twinkled above in the dark, cloudless sky.

"I need to ask you, Darby," Brant said, his eyes troubled, "can you ever forgive me?"

"You have to know it wasn't your fault. You didn't lie to them. You were protecting Gunther. I'd have done the same thing."

"I've spent my career trying to help people subjected to the evils of others. And my one chance to help the person I love most . . . They could have had her last months together."

"They have eternity together."

Brant turned his head toward her. "Yes, they do. Thank you."

"No," Darby whispered. "Thank you, for giving me my grandfather."

Darby stood on her tiptoes and kissed him on the cheek. He gathered her in to his arms and she rested her face against his chest, hearing the steady beat of his heart.

"Darby, I think I'm beginning to need you in my life."

"You do need me."

He pulled away slightly and saw her smile. "Oh, really?"

"Yes. Because I think I'm beginning to need you too."

"You already need me. You need me terribly."

"Oh, really?" Inside, every part of her agreed with him. "One thing about this forgiveness . . . can I take it back the next time you infuriate me?"

"You think you'll keep seeing me in the future?"

"Well, since we love the same man, I'm sure our paths will cross."

She laughed as he drew her close again.

Someone cleared a throat, and Brant quickly dropped his arms from around Darby. A nurse stood, looking embarrassed, at the entrance to the indoor garden. Brant took Darby's hand and led her toward the older woman. They discussed Gunther, and then the woman hurried away.

"He's ready for us. But we have strict instructions."

"As long as we can stay with him."

Gunther waited in the room lit with only a small lamp. His arms were folded over a sharp line of white sheet and blanket. Suddenly Darby wanted to take him away, far away—all the way back to Grandma's home in California. He needed rest, and it showed in his eyes, though his smile was joyful at their return. But she hoped it would happen, that he could be in the house his wife had made into a home.

"We can't talk anymore, or they'll kick me out," Darby said

as she grasped outstretched hands. "You must sleep, and I'll be here when you awaken."

"I st-still find it hard to believe. My granddaughter."

"Yes, I almost fear I'll wake up to find it untrue. But you must get strong. You have a daughter—what a wonderful surprise you will be to her. She waited and hoped until it destroyed a place within her. She needs you to be strong for her. And you have another granddaughter and some energetic twin great-granddaughters."

"The family I believed to be dead. I will rest and get strong for th-them."

"Yes, so sleep. Sleep."

"Will you?" Gunther patted the bed beside him and moved over. "I've never had my child so near."

Darby glanced at Brant, who was sitting in a chair in the corner. She felt her lip twitch and nose burn. "And I've never had my grandfather so near."

The bed groaned as she moved the metal railing down. Darby remembered only months before she had rested with her grandmother. Carefully she sat on the bed and stretched out. Her arms were awkward, looking for their place. She rested her head on the pillow, moved and squirmed until it felt right. Not long ago, Darby had circled Grandma's body. Now her grandfather cradled her tightly, her head beneath his chin, his arms on hers. She breathed medicine, age, and a hint of deep spice. He touched her hair and spoke soft words in German that needed no interpretation. Wet drops, not her own, fell upon the pillow. Warm breath rustled her hair. She couldn't move, afraid it wouldn't be true. There were no memories of a father's arms, no bear hugs or loving pats. That longing had never entered her consciousness until now. Darby moved closer yet until she heard the patter of her grandfather's heart. It wrapped around her, beating and beating like a rocking chair with gentle pats upon her back. She could stay here forever.

⋅→⟨◉⟩←⋅

"Darby, wake up." Someone touched her hair and cheek. Her mouth felt dry, her eyes sticky, her arms tenderly held and tangled. She turned toward the voice—Brant's.

"Darby, it's morning."

The arms were her grandfather's, and his breath continued to lull and call her back into rest. It hadn't been a dream. She had a grandfather. She couldn't wait to call her mother and sister. They'd fly there in a day or two, and their lives would be changed forever.

"I have to leave, Darby," Brant whispered.

"Why? What's wrong?" She gently untangled herself, and Brant helped her from the bed.

"My secretary called. I'm not sure how they tracked me down since I turned off my phone, but a nurse woke me and said it was important. I'll be gone until late afternoon. Unless you want to come with me now."

"No, I'll stay."

"That's what I thought." Brant took a step closer and touched her hair. "Take care of him."

"I will."

⋅→⟨◉⟩←⋅

Darby spent an hour dozing in Brant's chair, against the pillow he'd used. Finally Gunther stirred and woke. A morning of activity began. They ate breakfast and later lunch, played several hands of cards, and Darby pushed him in his wheelchair around the hospital and through the indoor garden. They never stopped talking until Darby worried she was letting him do too much. Brant hadn't returned by afternoon, and Darby felt a terrible need for a shower. The nurse gave strict instructions for Gunther to have an afternoon nap.

"I need to leave, but I'll be back tonight or early in the

morning," Darby said. She'd only met him the day before, but felt she'd known him a lifetime. "I need a shower, or you won't want me back."

"I will ta-ake you, even if you smell badly." He chuckled and pinched his nose. "I do-o this whe-en you come close."

Darby laughed, loving his smile and hearty chuckle. "We both have work to do. You must get better. I must give the best news to my family and make arrangements for them to come."

"Yes. Y-es." Gunther beamed. "Bring my family. But fi-irst, I must tell you one, one thing. I hid it. I hid your in-heritance. I mu-st tell you where it is."

Chapter Thirty-Two

Darby stared out the window as the taxi zipped through traffic. It seemed the world should be a different color or perhaps lost its gravitational pull overnight with all the changes she'd experienced in the last days. But people continued to walk with their feet on the same sidewalks as they had yesterday, and wisps of clouds still drifted in a blue sky.

She leaned her head against the cool window and closed her eyes. Her newfound joy mingled with gentle sorrow like oil mixed with water. One emotion would rise to the surface, then the other would bubble through. Her grandfather was alive! Her mother had a father. Her nieces a great-grandfather. Yet Grandma Celia, who had yearned a lifetime for her lost love, had missed him by only months. The smile and stories of Grandma's life had sheltered the sorrow she'd never been freed from. And her joy lived only a plane ride away. What if it had happened to Darby and her love—to her and Brant?

The taxi proceeded down tiny Goldgasse, and Darby was

struck with a wave of exhaustion. For some reason, behind closed eyelids she thought of Maureen. Her sister was tucked away asleep at home, and her life was about to be changed along with all of theirs. Darby missed her sister as she hadn't since childhood. They'd been closer then, and Darby didn't know why she'd allowed them to drift so deeply into their own lives. She vowed to turn that around. She'd also call Tristie in Montana—perhaps fly up for a visit. Her woman friendships were essential to life. She knew that not just from Tatianna and Grandma Celia, but it rang true within her. She'd missed a lot in the last years, but no more.

Darby's head remained against the window, hair cascading across her face. Her feet felt too heavy to move when the car stopped, though her mind continued its race around the discoveries of the last two days. She moved away from the window as the cab driver prepared to open the door, but he was looking somewhere else. Across the car, through the other back window, she could see a man's slacks, belt, and tucked-in shirt. It had to be Brant. She'd be able to see on his face the completion of decades of trials. She'd fall into his arms and find spring after a long winter. The heaviness upon her shoulders would lighten, even leave. Brant. The man she knew she loved, as Grandma Celia had loved Gunther Müller.

The opposite door opened.

"Darby Evans." The face was not Brant's. "Remember me? Richter Hauer. We met in a restaurant when you were with Brant." It took a second for her mind to match this man with bloodshot eyes and a few days' stubble to the arrogant man she'd met months before.

"Ah, I think so. Yes. I remember." Why was this man closing the door and the taxi driver returning to the front seat? "I'm getting out here."

"Brant called me and asked that I escort you to his office. He had a meeting he couldn't get away from." The cab driver hadn't moved. "Go ahead."

"Wait." Darby reached for the door handle. "I have some calls to make and need a shower, some rest."

"Brant said it was urgent. I tried to catch you with Gunther, but you'd left. Gunther told me you were coming here. On my word, what a shock to discover we are related in a way, right? My step-grandfather is your grandfather." He smiled at her with an incredulous look. "Miracles do still happen."

Darby hesitated. This man must have talked to Brant and Gunther to know these details.

"Go ahead!" Richter called again. The driver glanced questioningly at her in the rearview mirror, then the car moved forward down the dark street. Darby didn't speak as her thoughts tried to slog through a molasses of tiredness, facts, and suspicions. Brant didn't like Richter, she remembered. So why . . .

Darby eyed Richter as he peered anxiously behind them. His hands were grasped together strangely. Suddenly, she realized she shouldn't be with him. He looked at her quickly, and she saw danger in his eyes.

Richter grabbed her hand. "I need you to come with me. Everything will be all right. Just do as I ask." When Darby's mouth opened to cry out, he squeezed her hand in warning. "My grandmother, Ingrid, kept her lover's Lüger collection after the war. She passed them down to me." Richter forced her hand against his jacket. She could feel something . . . a gun?

Richter glanced behind them again, leaned forward to instruct the driver, then sat back. The car stopped, waiting for traffic. Darby looked back toward her hotel, where she'd been going a moment before. A moment before she had been safe, ready to call her mother and sister and then rest and see Brant and Gunther, and now. . . .

"I'm in a difficult position, Darby." His face hovered too close to hers. "I must have something that I have long sought. Only you can help me. I have no doubt that Gunther told you where he hid the Lange inheritance."

Darby's mouth opened, but she could not speak.

"Please, Darby. I have little time."

The cab turned onto Residenzplatz. Life seemed so normal. People strolled, carriages waited to give rides, artists hawked their paintings on the street. "What do you want?"

But she knew. Richter raised one eyebrow, knowing she understood. Was this why Ingrid had deceived her grandmother so long ago? Had the greed for the Lange inheritance not only cost many lives, but also enticed deception long after the Nazis had been destroyed?

The taxi halted, and Richter tossed a bill forward. Darby realized they'd only gone a few blocks from her hotel when Richter grabbed her hand and yanked her outside. Panic raced wildly through Darby. Should she scream? Run into one of the shops? Then Richter pinned her close to him.

Richter had parked his car near the restaurant where she'd first met him, the day she'd first met Brant. The more she sought an escape the more trapped she realized she was—like a butterfly in a jar.

"Just show me where it is, and nothing will happen to you. I promise." He walked her beside a white BMW and almost dropped his keys as he unlocked the door.

"No." She planted her feet, remembering too well her foolish impulse to jump in the car that took her to Bruno Weiler's house. And this was different. All the television shows said to never, ever be forced into a car. "I'm not going anywhere."

"You are. Get in." He pushed her toward the open door. She tried to get away, but Richter grabbed her with a fierce hold. "I have a gun, right here in my pocket. Come with me, and you'll be safe. But I can't let you walk away."

She hesitated a minute too long so Richter pushed her inside. "Move across. You're driving. Take the keys."

"Where am I going?"

"You tell me." Richter shut his door firmly.

Darby searched the tourists and carriages and shopkeepers for anyone to help. *This can't be happening!*

"So tell me where we're going," he insisted.

Darby didn't say anything. He pulled out the gun and rested it on his lap.

It really was an antique Lüger. It appeared almost ridiculous pointing toward her instead of resting inside a museum case.

"I'll tell you where it is, and you'll let me get out."

"You tell me where it is, I'll get it, then I'll let you go." He stared at her as she carefully moved through traffic. She could see him from the corner of her eye.

"It's in Hallstatt."

"Hallstatt?" Richter thought for a moment. "You mean the grave?"

Darby nodded.

He looked surprised. "Why didn't I think of that before?"

When Richter glanced at her, Darby knew they thought the same thing. "I wish you had," she said.

-◦=◦=◦-

Brant had just convinced himself that he had not seen Darby with Richter in a taxi, leaving Goldgasse together. Then Richter's car had pulled from a side street down the one-way exit. Darby was driving. Brant was on his way to see her, to watch her sleep, to share her phone calls. His important meeting had been nothing—another frustrating interruption. Frau Halder didn't know who the urgent message had come from, but she'd taken it seriously. Brant sometimes had mysterious clients meet with him secretly, but this time, no one showed up at his office.

He had parked beneath a tree on one of the streets surrounding the plaza, then begun walking when he saw Darby inside the taxi from across the street. He wondered why she was leaving Goldgasse. Then he saw Richter beside her.

Shocks of denial pounded through him as his mind tried to decipher what he'd seen. He should have followed them when they passed in Richter's car, but he sat too long. It couldn't be.

Brant suddenly remembered the "coincidental" meeting the first day he'd met Darby. Richter had come to the restaurant by chance. Then something had happened in Vienna two days before, or someone. Darby hadn't explained why she disappeared for the night. Was everything a lie? His mind brought up all sorts of ideas. Perhaps she wasn't even an American, but someone Richter and Ingrid had recruited to finally get the Lange inheritance while Gunther was recovering.

And this morning. He had been called away from the hospital. Did it give opportunity for Darby to ask Gunther where he'd hidden it? Only Brant knew Gunther had hidden the heirlooms at all. Gunther had only withheld the location.

Brant looked back toward his car and wondered what to do, and how this could be true. But it seemed the truth was before his eyes. He'd been betrayed once again.

CHAPTER THIRTY-THREE

Daylight faded in the valley as Darby and Richter drove the north edge of Hallstatt Lake. Night would come soon. Darby noticed the last reflection of pink on the water as she drove. This man promised her safety once she revealed the hidden treasure. Could she really believe him? He'd already told her several lies. Could this be, perhaps, her final glimpse of sunlight? She checked the rearview mirror again. No one had followed them from the city. Surely Brant would wonder where she was, be searching for her maybe. But he was too far behind.

God, you can't want this to happen. Not after everything. Not after this journey you've led me on.

Had Tatianna thought those same words? What doubts and fears did she have during those last steps before death? Darby wanted to be strong, setting her jaw and holding her head high. But inside she felt weak and shaky and feared she might crumble at any moment. She prayed for strength over and over again.

Richter had been quiet the last few miles. She imagined him hatching his plan to retrieve the inheritance, and then what? Darby needed her own plan and could only think of the Gerringer home in Hallstatt. If she could somehow get to them, perhaps she'd make it.

"Take a right at the next curve," Richter said.

"That's not the way to Hallstatt," Darby said, her voice rising. This was not in her plan.

"There's something I must do first."

⋅⊷⟭◌⟬⊶⋅

Brant had tried roads and places in Salzburg but couldn't find Richter's car anywhere. He'd stopped by Darby's hotel, called a dozen times, driven to Richter's favorite places, and started once toward Munich and Ingrid's house. Instead, he phoned again on his return to Salzburg, but no one answered. He'd gone to Gunther's, only to leave without talking to him. For how could he break this news to the old man now? But could the old man be in danger? The police would believe none of this—it was all speculation.

Late afternoon faded quickly into night. He drove into a parking lot and hit the brakes hard. *Think, think,* he told himself. If only he'd tailed Richter and Darby immediately. Brant picked up his car phone and tried Richter's cellular but received only a recording that indicated the power was off. He called Darby's hotel again, feeling like he was repeating her trip to Vienna. Could that have only been days ago? Again, there was no answer in her room. The front desk said they hadn't seen her. Next he dialed Ingrid in Munich. The line picked up.

"Frau Müller is in Gosau today," the housekeeper said. "She's finishing work there before closing the house."

Brant hung up before saying good-bye. Gosau was over an hour away. And what if Darby wasn't there?

He squeezed the steering wheel. There were only two options he could think of. Either Darby had betrayed them and was involved with Richter and Ingrid, or Darby was in trouble. His eyes said she'd tricked them. His heart told him differently. Yet his feelings had certainly failed him before.

Brant battled back and forth. Darby had appeared in Salzburg at the same time he began to suspect Richter and Ingrid were involved in something. She'd disappeared in Vienna for an entire night and never given an explanation as to where she'd gone. Richter was looking for her when Brant picked her up at the train station. And the ring—the one piece that had convinced him. Ingrid most likely had seen it on Celia's finger years ago. She could have made a duplicate and given it to Darby. The evidence and seeing Darby drive off in Richter's car all pointed one way.

But then he remembered other things. Darby so childlike and afraid after her room was broken into. Could that have been part of the act? Was she capable of faking their night at the dinner concert and her interest at the Holocaust conference? Were her laughter and kisses only for dramatic effect? And if Darby was partnered with Ingrid and Richter, why hadn't she gone straight to Gunther for the information they sought?

Then the image of Darby asleep next to Gunther made him ignore the facts and believe in her. He'd watched them sleep so deep and safe and secure. Though they'd just met, they were not strangers, but grandfather and grandchild brought together at last.

"If she's not involved, then she's in danger," he said aloud.

Brant turned the car out of the parking lot while hitting the buttons on his phone. He didn't want to worry his old friend, but he needed to know one thing: where was the inheritance hidden?

⊷═◉═⊶

The sign said *Gosau*. Darby turned the car to the right. "Are we going to Ingrid and Gunther's house?"

"Just follow my instructions." His voice revealed his own conflicting thoughts. "I need a few supplies. We can't dig with our hands, now can we?"

Darby remained silent as they drove miles of twisting mountain road through dense forest and along a silver stream that caught the last lights in the sky. The car was warm and comfortable with the scent of men's aftershave, but Darby felt sick. The road rose from the forest into a long mountain valley and into tiny Gosau. Richter directed her up myriad streets to a hillside house—Gunther and Ingrid's, she assumed. The smaller house next door must have been where Brant had spent his childhood summers. She imagined him as a boy exploring forest grottos and visiting Gunther on the porch of the larger house.

A black car was parked in the driveway of the larger house.

"What will my grandmother think of you, I wonder?" Richter smiled slightly as he slid the gun back into the jacket pocket. Darby hesitated, glancing around as she got out of the car. Richter watched her every move until they were inside the house. No one greeted them. The house was empty except for a few belongings and some furniture covered with sheets. Darby heard a steady *swish* from somewhere, and Richter motioned her toward the stairway. He followed close behind.

Inside a room at the end of a hallway, a woman stood with her back toward them, sweeping the hardwood floor. Bookcases lined the walls, and a small couch sat covered with a sheet like a punished child left in the corner. French doors opened toward the second-story porch, where the lights from the village below glittered like beacons through the glass.

The woman turned quickly as they entered. With one hand

over her heart and the other on the broom handle, she scolded Richter in rapid German. Age had changed Ingrid's beauty, but not robbed it. She stood with straight posture, holding herself with something of grace or pride. Her hair was pinned up for work, but her clothing was stylish beige slacks and a clean white-and-tan shirt. For an elderly woman, Ingrid would be considered beautiful, and Darby felt a jealous sting that this had been Gunther's wife for the last fifty-five years. But the lines in Ingrid's face weren't from laughter; she seemed unable to smile or to sing.

"Grandma, speak the English you insisted I learn. I have brought my American friend to meet you."

Darby and Ingrid evaluated one another in silence. Then Ingrid spoke to Richter in a hushed tone in German.

"Her name is Darby. Darby Evans."

Ingrid put her hand over her mouth and dropped the broom with a loud clatter.

"Darby, meet Ingrid," Richter said quietly. "Your step-grandmother."

Ingrid stalked toward Richter, speaking angrily.

"English, remember?" Richter shook his head, then grew annoyed and defensive at Ingrid's words. "There was nothing else I could do. We were about to lose it all. Darby told me where it is. Gunther told her."

"You talk with Gunther?" she asked Darby, her voice sounding strained. "Why you bring her here, Richter?"

"I needed supplies on the way to Hallstatt."

"Hallstatt?" Ingrid said, turning away.

"Yes. Right there, all these years. And we thought it was a simple pilgrimage to his dead wife."

"It was," she said bitterly. "Why you come here? Why bring her?"

"Everything will be fine. Darby is coming with me to get the coins and brooch, then we'll do something. . . ."

"What?" Ingrid asked. "Did you think? What will we do with her?"

"I don't know."

Both pairs of eyes glanced her way. They started firing words back and forth in German. Darby searched the lights of the village for a way out.

"I'll be in the basement, getting supplies," Richter said.

"*Nein*. Take her with you."

"You may want to say some things to her." Richter stared for a long time at his grandmother, then at Darby. All at once Darby realized she wanted to ask Ingrid a thousand questions and accuse her of even more. "I'll be downstairs, not far away."

"Be quick about it, Richter," Ingrid said, standing tall as if trying to compose herself.

The women listened to Richter's exit, down the stairs, through a door. Darby walked toward the French doors. She peered at the railing and beyond it, wondering if she could jump the ten or twelve feet to escape. But wouldn't Ingrid immediately call for Richter? She could easily overpower Ingrid, but what would she do—hit an old woman? No other house was nearby except for Brant's old, deserted cottage.

Darby opened the doors and stepped onto the wood balcony. She glanced back to see what Ingrid did. The older woman sat on the edge of the couch, her head down in thought. The deck was high, too high, it seemed. She'd get hurt and never be able to run unless she could hide in the darkness somewhere. It may be her only chance.

Ingrid stood in the doorway and flipped on the porch light. The illumination over the older woman's head brought deep shadows below her eyes. "What did Gunther say?"

Darby leaned back against the railing and faced the woman who'd destroyed her grandmother's and grandfather's lives. "I had the letter you wrote Celia telling her that both he and Tatianna were dead."

Ingrid raised her chin and glared coldly at Darby. "I did what I had to do at that time. Your grandmother was my friend, a long time ago."

"Your friend?"

"I knew someday this would come. I don't know how, but I knew. And you could never understand."

"You're right, I could never understand." Darby wanted to tell Ingrid what the lies had done to her grandmother, her mother, and even her own life. But where would she begin? And would it matter?

"It wasn't my fault. It was the war. You can accuse me, but your grandmother would not have lived without me. She was a mess. I saved her as much as Tatianna did. We all did things we did not expect—war does that. Even Celia. She betrayed Tatianna."

"What?"

"You know so little but accuse me still."

"How did Celia betray Tatianna?" Darby's heart pounded. She'd always had one thought that she feared to consider— that her grandmother escaped by using Tatianna, betraying her. Sure, she knew her grandmother would never do that, but what about in such a treacherous time? Darby paced into a dark corner of the porch. "My grandmother was not a betrayer."

"She admitted it to me."

"Tell me."

"Tatianna and Celia made some pact or vow of friendship as young girls. When Celia's father was captured by Nazis, Celia was given information that Tatianna was the person who revealed his hiding place. Celia believed it. I believed it too. I became friends with all of them in Salzburg. Tatianna was always reading her Bible and talking about how she served a loving God. She wanted to be a missionary and use music to bring beauty into the lives of the poor. I didn't believe it—

until later. The two girls loved each other, as much as Celia and Gunther loved. Then everything began to fall apart. Her father taken, we knew Celia had to hide. The news that Tatianna was the one who told shocked Celia. Celia accused her and left with Gunther. Tatianna was devastated. But later Gunther sent for Tatianna. I volunteered to drive Celia out and Gunther arranged for Hallstatt. When I arrived, it was Celia and Tatianna who were there."

Darby sat down in the armrest of a wooden chair and glanced up into a diamond sky. At least her grandmother hadn't actually betrayed Tatianna, but instead their vow of belief.

"Then what?" Darby said it like a challenge, while listening for Richter's footsteps below. "How did it happen that Tatianna gave her life for my grandmother, and you stole what was left?"

"You make judgment so easily when you not there. I not intend what happened. Your grandmother escaped because I take her. I made difficult choices, and after war, I was in great danger—my children also. Gunther gave safety for me, and I believed he was dead when I wrote Celia that letter. I told myself that Celia rebuilt her life in America. I was sorry to find that she die last autumn."

"How did you know?"

"She contacted me last year while searching for inheritance."

"My grandmother called you? Last year?"

"Yes." Ingrid's face was shadowed as she looked away from the light.

"Why didn't you tell her the truth then, when they still had time?"

"After that many years? It was too late. I always thought Gunther knew where the inheritance was but also wondered if somehow Celia got it out of Austria. When she call, I knew for sure that Gunther must know. Celia say she sick, and I sorry for that. I call once, and your mother give me news of her death."

"And you never told her about Gunther." They had been so close. Celia and Gunther could have at least had a few months together. But again, the greed over the Lange inheritance took lives away. Darby felt an almost uncontrollable urge to slap Ingrid. She was shaking, overwhelmed that she could harbor such anger toward another person.

"I need to protect my own," Ingrid said. "And Celia dying— why then tell her about Gunther, after all the years? I have to do hard things. You not know the choices you make until in the danger. You do not understand."

"Then make me understand," Darby said firmly. She may never know if Ingrid didn't speak now. "What happened the night my grandmother escaped?"

Ingrid breathed into her hands, then wrapped her arms together. "Chaos. The world was in chaos. The plan was to take Celia out, and Gunther would be a decoy at a house in Upper Austria. He would follow later. We pretend it was great adventure—Celia's escape to America. I get Tatianna and Celia at Hallstatt. We took several days to go through the Alps—we have to take one road, then switch to another. We try to laugh a lot. But inside I know we all sad and afraid."

Ingrid folded her hands and spoke calmly, but her words took them both back to the last night together. Darby could see the three in their car, speeding toward hope and safety. . . .

> The car switched back and forth down the alpine road. Tatianna hummed a tune of the Glenn Miller Band.
>
> "One more mile," she said with her hand on Celia's. "I will miss you, my friend."
>
> "It won't be forever," Celia said softly. "We'll return after the war, or you will both come to America. Never can we be apart."
>
> "That's right." Tatianna spoke with a confidence Ingrid didn't understand.

The car rounded a bend and slowed. Ingrid knew it to be the last, and then they would be separated from Celia—probably forever. She hated the thought but felt envious all the same. She didn't have the money to leave, so she'd have to find her own way of survival without anyone's help. A sign for the coming Swiss border flashed by them.

"Oh, dear God," Celia said. "Dear God, help us."

"How could they be here?" Tatianna hit the brakes.

The car lurched forward as Ingrid saw a black car blocking the road, directly in front of the Austrian-Swiss border. Suddenly headlights beamed behind them.

"Where did he come from?" Tatianna held the wheel tightly. "Celia, get in the back, and both of you lie down. I'm going to ram straight through."

"No, you'll never make it!" Celia shouted.

"I'll give it my best."

"Stop!" Celia grabbed the steering wheel. "This isn't your fight!"

"Listen to her, Tatianna!" Ingrid said. "We'll all be killed if you try."

"Okay, okay." Tatianna's voice calmed, and she brought the car to a quick halt.

Celia turned in her seat and looked fearfully at Ingrid and Tatianna. The vehicle behind them stopped. Head-lights glared through the window. A man in the front car got out and opened the back door, waiting.

Celia touched her round stomach and closed her eyes for a moment. "I want you both to go home as quickly as possible. I should never have endangered you by allowing you to come—I'm sorry for that."

Tears filled Ingrid's eyes. She knew Celia was only being strong. They all knew Celia would not get away. She'd never see Gunther again, would never hold that baby in her arms. Ingrid felt tied with fear for Celia, but with just as much fear for herself. Would they come after her too?

Celia leaned close to Tatianna. "I have to ask one thing first. I'm so sorry, Tati. I didn't believe in you. After all these years together. I know you so well. I know your heart. But I lost faith anyway. When it counted most, I let you down."

"Stop," Tatianna whispered. "It's all right."

"No, it's not. Please. Will you forgive me?"

The girls stared into years of memories.

"I forgive you, my dear one."

"Thank you." Celia reached for the door handle. She winked at Ingrid and smiled at both of them. "Hey, remember, the heroine always gets away."

"Stay inside," Tatianna ordered, grabbing Celia's hands. "Listen to me. I love you like a sister, no, more than a sister. I'd do anything for you, and this is the only thing I can give. Ingrid, get up here in the driver's seat."

"Tati, you can't go to them. They simply want me. I won't endanger your lives any more than I already have."

"Stay in the car," Tatianna ordered.

Before Celia could speak or move, Tatianna was out of the car. She motioned to Ingrid and slammed the door. Ingrid climbed over the seat as Tatianna walked forward. Her shape was illuminated in their headlights, making a long shadow across the ground.

"What does she think she can say to them?" Celia asked, putting her hand on the door. "I'm going out there."

"Stay inside!" Ingrid hissed. "You have your baby to consider. Perhaps she can do something."

"Like what?"

"I don't know. Just be silent, or they'll take us all."

Celia watched as the man in SS uniform met Tatianna. She took some papers from her coat and handed them to the man. He looked them over and began to move toward the car where Ingrid and Celia waited. Tatianna blocked him, her mouth moving rapidly. Finally, the man in black uniform peered at the car for a long moment, then pointed Tatianna to his vehicle. He slammed the door as she got in.

"What is she doing?" Celia tugged at the papers in her own pocket. "Oh, dear Lord. No! She changed our papers! They think she is me!"

"Celia, don't you dare get out, or they'll kill us all!" Ingrid's terror rose, waiting for guns or men to take them too.

The vehicle behind them moved away. The black car parked before the border crossing pulled backward and slowly passed them. Celia yelled and lunged across the seat as they saw Tatianna. Tatianna waved and motioned for them to go ahead. Then she was gone.

Ingrid looked from her hands in her lap back to Darby's face. "Your grandmother would not stop crying, but I drove her across border and try to tell her not to worry. The Nazis would discover who Tatianna was and let her go, I say. I do not know if she believe me. Celia made me promise to help Tatianna. I promise, but of course, I could do nothing."

"Couldn't, or wouldn't?" Darby asked.

Ingrid was startled from her faraway thoughts. "I help save your grandmother also. She not make it across the border without me. I took her to contact location. I never see her again."

"But you heard from her."

"Yes. During war, she kept making danger for us with her letters. 'What happened to Tatianna? Her family? Of course, Gunther?'"

"So you told her they were all dead."

"I told truth about Tatianna. I heard nothing of Gunther and believed he was dead. Her letters had to stop. You don't get letters from America asking about Jews and political prisoners when you live with SS officer—you would be thought a spy and shot. You cannot understand war. I have only myself—not an escape like Celia. People were starving or murdered for nothing."

"But in the end, we know who was Celia's real friend."

Ingrid turned away and, with a start, Darby wondered where Richter was. She also wondered how much time she had left. This was no game, and she was running out of time. Darby hurried to the edge of the deck again and looked down. There could be rocks; it was hard to see in the darkness. She glanced back, but Ingrid watched in silence. She thought Ingrid's expression said, *Go. It's your one chance.*

She was about to jump when she heard a noise. In the dim light, she spotted someone in a chair below. A red glow from a cigarette illuminated his exhalation. Richter was waiting.

Darby yanked Ingrid back into the room and closed the door. "What's he going to do with me?" Darby implored Ingrid to help her. The door slammed downstairs. Richter was coming.

"No. Richter will not hurt you." But Ingrid's eyes moved away.

Perhaps Darby should run back out to the deck and jump. But as she made a move to do so, Richter walked casually into the room.

"Time to go." Ingrid would not look at him. "Come on, Darby."

"Leave her here with me," Ingrid said suddenly. "After you go to Hallstatt, pick me up. We'll leave her here. It will give us time."

Richter shook his head. "No. She's coming with me."

"Don't make this worse for us," Ingrid said, taking a step toward Darby. Her hand lifted, then dropped back to her side.

"Perhaps we'll come back here in a few hours. But I want

you to be in Munich, waiting for me. I'll take care of everything."

Richter took Darby's arm. She glanced back at Ingrid and saw fear in the older woman's eyes.

CHAPTER THIRTY-FOUR

A glacial moon shone through icy sheets of clouds as they arrived in the small village—the village Darby loved and where her family had once lived. Richter continued to assure her of her safety, but his words were of little comfort. What *could* he do with her after he'd retrieved what he wanted?

"The scenic town of Hallstatt," Richter said. His fingers twisted on the steering wheel. He was close, very close. "Thousands of visitors walking here every year with a fortune beneath their feet." The car crept into the sleeping village. "To your right, famous Hallstattersee, perfect for diving or sailing. To your left, the Celtic museum where you can see relics from the oldest salt mine in the world. And up the hill in the cemetery, the Lange family treasure, lost, but soon found."

Darby's heart sank as they passed Gasthaus Gerringer. One light was on in the entry room, but the rest of the house was dark. They continued through the Marketplatz down to the parking lot below the lower church.

Richter nervously glanced around as he parked. Tall street-lamps lit the asphalt lot and danced in the dark waters of Hallstattersee. But no one else was around. Richter hopped out and walked around to open her door. Cool night air hit Darby's face as she left the warmth of the car. Richter handed her the keys.

"Open the trunk," he ordered.

From within the trunk, Richter grabbed a flashlight and gave Darby a small toolbox and hand shovel. She evaluated the narrow street, knowing she could run to the Gerringers' home in minutes. But would she make it two steps away from Richter?

"Remember what I have," he said, knowing her thoughts.

She nodded and felt the cold fingers of fear reach further inside her. Richter slid his arm around her waist, trying to hide the small shovel between them.

Their footsteps echoed along the dark concrete as they started up the steep road. "Talk to me."

"What do you want me to say, Richter?"

"I don't know." He stopped and turned her toward him. "I guess, I don't know."

From the road, they turned up a stairway onto a steep upward trail. Darby imagined Gunther's annual pilgrimage at this time of night. Over sixty years for nothing.

"This wasn't how I wanted it," Richter said quietly, pausing to look at her. "Don't think I'm enjoying this. I've traveled the world, gambled and played with the wealthiest men, but here I am creeping up a dark mountain, sneaking, forced to drastic means. It's not what I want."

"You chose this, Richter."

"I can't live a life in poverty, can't leave everything I know behind. I've worked hard taking care of my grandmother. My father and uncle used her money."

Darby remembered how Bruno Weiler had changed from a

youth seeking grandeur into an SS killer—all with the best of intentions. Selfish ambition, denial, conceit, and greed led downward until evil was justified as good. Bruno only saw himself by a jolt of humanity in the face of Tatianna. Was there a way to open Richter's eyes?

"I've made mistakes, and it only takes a few to mess yourself up," Richter continued.

"Why should I pay for your sins?"

He turned toward her and thought for a moment. "It's hard, I know. But doesn't someone always pay for another person's sins?"

Darby opened her mouth to speak when she heard a car approaching.

"Wait." He pulled her into a dark alcove. On the road far below them, a police car drove by. Richter cursed. "Why is he here?" They waited as the car continued down the street and out of view. "We're moving too slow. Come on, but be quiet."

They switched back and forth up mountain stairways and passages until the red lit candles behind a wooden gate bid them entrance.

Richter pushed the gate open. "Which one?" His voice was hushed and anxious as his flashlight bounced from one headstone to another.

They walked the gravel rows, though she knew the general location. On the top, near the bone house. Every moment prolonged was a moment more.

The headstones in daylight with tall, narrow roofs were symbols of lives once lived. In the cold night, the roofs were arrowhead fingers pointing from grave to sky. The flowers planted in rich soil in spring were bright and hopeful in daylight with dim, red candles flickering undying love. Night and winter brought the flowers into a matted mass, like spirits caught and tangled, unable to find escape from the ground.

The red candles were one-eyed creatures, staring and promising that soon she'd join them.

"We're wasting time." Richter squeezed her arm till it hurt.

"At the top, in the Protestant section."

They walked carefully between eyes and spirits to the upper graves. Even the few stars that broke in from the clouds peered at her coldly with no twinkle or hint of peace. The shadows no longer hovered and jeered, but waited to consume and make them her own. She saw where houses, not too far away, were swallowed in shadows. Houses that offered safety and life.

Richter dragged her along awkwardly with the shovel in one hand. The gravel ground beneath their feet; she hoped loudly enough to awaken someone. Winter snow was still piled behind the bone house and on several graves. Darby followed Gunther's instruction to the middle grave close to the upper railing. She moved from grave to grave until she stood in front of a wood and wrought-iron headstone. The wooden post had a pruned rosebush twisted around the base and up a wooden cross. Like some of the other headstones, a black plate covered the nameplate. This had to be it.

"Are you sure?" Richter whispered.

Darby knelt on the edge of a short, concrete border and opened the metal door. Inside it read *Celia Rachel Müller*.

"This is it." Richter's voice had changed, and she wished to read his expression. He handed her the shovel and flipped off the flashlight. "Dig."

Darby gathered her hair into a ball and stuck it into the back of her jacket, then she began to push the hand shovel into the cold dirt. She uprooted several bunches of flowering plants and rested them on the ground, leaving the rosebush at the top of the grave alone. With every reach of the shovel, she pushed herself closer to the end of her chances. Her hope was dwindling.

Richter had moved away. He was listening, watching, seeing

if they were followed. He was nervous. She could imagine his thoughts. *What am I going to do with her? Brant will be looking now. Gunther will tell him we've come to Hallstatt. They could come at any moment. Can I let her live? How can I?*

Darby shivered as her hands pushed the shovel into the grave. What would it be like to die, and to die tonight? She pictured her mother far away at home . . . probably having breakfast or taking a stroll with her friends. Gunther would be sleeping safely in his bed. Brant? Where was Brant right now? She wished for tomorrow and a thousand tomorrows to be with him.

Darby brushed her hands off on her pants and continued to dig. This grave devoid of a body—would it take her life? She looked down into the cold, frozen ground her hands reached into. It was the only grave here without a body.

She stopped. A quiet, comforting Voice spoke in her thoughts and she realized, *There's something here that you want me to find. There's something in the dirt of this empty grave that's for me. I'm in the valley of the shadow of death, and you are showing me something. What? That I am to meet you tonight? That the cold ground will not be my home? What?*

Suddenly her fingers touched something. Using the shovel in her right hand, Darby hit a hard object.

"Did you find it?" Richter said from over her shoulder.

"I think maybe."

She could see only his profile as he looked one way, then the other. When he faced her straight on, she saw only a black shadow.

"Hurry up!" Richter loomed over her. "Get it out."

He flipped on the light and kept it shining into the hole. Darby continued to dig and move the dirt away with the shovel and her hands. A rectangular shape was uncovered several feet down. Darby pulled and dug until the earth released it. She set the object on the concrete border.

It was a metal box wrapped in heavy plastic. Richter took out a pocketknife and cut the waterproofing. Then from somewhere surrounding them, Darby heard something. She couldn't get a direction but thought she heard footsteps. Then Richter heard it too. He flipped off the flashlight, grabbed her close to him, and crouched by the grave. His eyes pierced the darkness like a hunter seeking its prey. The noise stopped.

"Come on," Richter insisted. They crept in the night, beside bushes and around to the tall, white cylindrical building of the Bein Haus.

"Stay there." Richter pushed her against the side of the entrance wall. The stone chilled her back. Richter sat a few steps away, listening. She noticed the gun in his hand. And even then she could hardly believe it was real. Richter holding an antique gun in his hand, her on the ground of a bone house. The surreal moment should feel anything but that. It was more real than any moment of her life, for it could be the last.

Richter tried to pull open the heavy doors, then noticed the lock. Her eyes caught the image of a skull on the door as he swung the flashlight around. Above the door, Darby remembered the symbol of Alpha and Omega—the beginning and the end.

Richter found something in the toolbox as he returned the gun to his coat. He bent in front of the door. Darby was on the ground beside him, her eyes closed. She heard the sound of rapid sawing and then Richter removed the lock. The heavy door opened and a stark, musty smell billowed like ghosts loosed from their chains. Richter pulled her up and pushed her inside. She stumbled in and leaned against the corner. Darby knew a thousand empty eyes stared. Open jaws cried eternal screams. Richter again paused and listened. Then he closed the tomb door behind them.

"I need to see what we have here," he said, flipping the flashlight on. "Then we'll go."

Darby crouched in the darkness as he opened the metal box. "At last. I almost didn't believe it, but here they are." Richter held up the three coins, one at a time. He flipped them over and examined them in the light. "Amazing."

Shaking against the cold cement wall, she felt fear again. Thousands of bones circled the room and waited, waited. She wanted to be strong and have faith. *God, I'm so afraid. Why are you letting this happen?*

And then she thought of Tatianna. A woman who gave her life that others could live. Grandma had said once that death was a stepping-stone, like childhood into adulthood. But to Darby, that step terrified her.

She remembered Grandma saying, "Eternity is closer than we realize, Darby. Like a child cannot perceive the workings and thoughts of his parents, so are we children unable to see eternity all around us. For like the apostle Paul said, 'To live is Christ, but to die is gain.' "

But I want to live.

And then she saw it—in a flash of understanding. Brant had said not to forget to live. To live is Christ. To live something meant more than just believing in it. Tatianna knew it. Grandma Celia knew it. No greater love than to give up your life for a friend. And to truly live was to live for what you believed until the gain of eternity. This was what she could only find in the shadow of death. This she found in a grave empty of a body, in a house of bones without souls. Perhaps, at the last moment of her life, she was finally discovering what it was to live.

Richter snapped the lid closed on the metal box. "It's not here. Where is the brooch?"

"Gunther said he never had it."

"Why didn't you tell me!"

"The coins themselves are priceless," she stammered.

"They'll be enough. Celia's father gave the coins to Gunther, but not the brooch. He knows nothing."

"Fine," Richter said, his voice calming. "The coins will have to do."

"What happens now, Richter?"

He stared at her a long time, and she could almost hear his thoughts, searching for what to do. It all seemed to lead back to the easiest escape for him. "My options are limited." He shone the flashlight on his watch. "How did it get so late? I've got to get out of here."

He swept the flashlight around the room, revealing a mass of skulls with dark eye sockets. He ran his hand over his chin, then glanced down to where she sat against the wall. His jaw tensed as he bent and gathered the coins back into the box, then stood with the box under one arm. His eyes on the door, Richter pulled the gun from his pocket.

A sharp knock suddenly sounded.

"Quiet!" Richter hissed and flipped off the flashlight. He crouched, grabbing her tightly against him.

Darby heard shuffling footsteps outside, then another quick knock on the door. She wanted to call for help, but the gun was pushed against her ribs.

⤜≡◯⫘⤏

Hands clenched to the wheel, Brant tackled the miles in what seemed to be slow motion. His car couldn't go faster, but it wouldn't be fast enough. He'd called the police in Salzburg and Hallstatt. But no one helped. They'd keep an eye out, but there was no evidence of a kidnapping. Brant knew he looked like a jilted lover. He dialed numbers on the car phone. It rang and rang. He was about to hang up when she answered.

"Ingrid, have you talked to Richter?"

"I haven't seen him. Why?"

"Ingrid, listen to me. I don't know everything, but I know enough. If Richter has been there with a woman, there is serious danger—I must know the truth."

Ingrid paused long enough for Brant to know she knew something.

"Did he call you? Has he been there? Tell me!"

"I do not know what you mean—"

"Listen to me, Ingrid. Gunther and I know about Celia, that you lied to her and to him. We know all of that. Now if something happens to Darby, I also know that she was last seen with Richter. You have to tell me!"

The line was silent.

"Are they in Hallstatt?" he asked.

"Yes."

"Now I know for sure. I just passed Bad Goisern and will be there in fifteen minutes."

"Brant," Ingrid said, "you'll never make it in time."

CHAPTER THIRTY-FIVE

Don't say a word." Richter held the gun aimed at Darby as he let her go and crept toward the door. He was thinking, trying to decide what to do. "It's probably a priest, but maybe . . . if you call out, I'll have to kill him, and you."

Darby wrapped her arms around her chest. "I won't say a word."

"I'll be back." Richter took off his jacket, put the metal box of coins under his arm, and tucked the gun into his waistband. He shone the flashlight in her face and opened the creaking door. He stepped out and ran as the door closed her in, dooming her to complete darkness. Her heart pounded, and her eyes strained to find even a shred of light. There was none. She put her ear to the door and heard Richter's footsteps but no voices. Her eyes jumped around to see anything, but could only feel the hundreds of eyes looking her way. There was no sound beyond, no sound within. And no escape anywhere.

Sudden noises outside made Darby scurry backwards. She hit the stacks of bones hard. Skulls fell from the shelving, rolling onto the floor. She screamed as one landed in her lap.

Then the door opened, and she saw a lighter darkness from the crack. Her hand found the shovel nearby. She waited in the corner, heart convulsing, eyes frozen on the doorway, waiting. No one entered.

On hands and knees, still clutching the hand shovel, she moved toward the side of the door. Any second she expected Richter to jump inside. She heard more noises—muffled voices that seemed to disappear among the headstones outside. Minutes later, car doors slammed—perhaps a trunk, too. Then tires screeched away.

It crossed her mind that perhaps someone had gotten Richter. The police? Brant? But why hadn't they called out to her? Seconds were hours. At last she pulled the door inward and carefully peered outside. If she could make it to the hillside behind the white tower, she could hide there. She took a few breaths, said a quick prayer, and dashed from the building. No one stopped her. She ran in blindness, red candle eyes staring as her legs scraped against concrete graves. The dark shadows against the mountain would give her safe harbor. Almost there. Then her feet hit something and she sprawled forward. Gravel cut into her hands and chin. She'd tripped over the metal box and scattered the coins. Her hands wildly gathered the coins, picked up the box, and she moved on. She jumped over a stone fence and up the steep incline of forest above. Her feet stumbled. Silent noises and spirits were behind each step. Not until she had buried herself deep into branches and forest did she pause. No one had followed. No one was there.

Through the trees and down below, she saw lights and heard noises. Then footsteps moved toward her. Darby was near the wooden stairway that went up the mountain, and the footsteps were coming up. She crouched against a tree trunk, feeling as if her body must be illuminated in the darkness. Her legs felt too long, her breath too visible, and she wondered which way to bend her head. The footsteps stopped nearby.

Darby held her breath. *God, help me. If you don't want me to die, help me live—truly live!*

Voices shouted below and lights danced around the cemetery. The footsteps sounded again, moving up and past her. Wooden stairs creaked as the figure climbed higher; then the weight transferred to the earthen pathway and disappeared.

"Darby!"

She froze in place in shock, wishing to close the gap between herself and the voice calling her name.

"Darby! Darby! Where are you?"

"Brant," she whispered. "Brant." Her voice wouldn't reach him. "Brant!"

A light sifted the mountainside. She got up and began to push toward its source. The light swiveled toward her.

"Darby!" He jumped the small fence and ran through brush and branches. "Thank you, God!" He drew her into a swift and gentle embrace. The flashlight fell and rolled down the hill as he held her in his arms.

As Brant picked her up, her head fell against his chest. His heartbeat became her lullaby. She was safe.

CHAPTER THIRTY-SIX

Darby didn't need an English translation to know that Brant was growing angry with the Austrian officers. She didn't have any more answers. Richter was not to be found, though the police were sure he wasn't the man Darby had heard run up the mountain. They'd traced Richter's footprints back down the mountain. Even more amazing, he'd left the coins behind.

Darby told the police about the sound of a car and voices. Yet Richter's car was still in the parking lot, and Ingrid had been found still in Gosau—alone. It almost seemed like someone had taken Richter and left the coins behind for Darby—but who, and especially, why?

Darby sat on the cold picnic table, a blanket around her shoulders, as morning began to shine over the tall mountain. Darby could tell the pieces she knew—Richter's plans and motives. But no citizen came forward to tell what had happened. Muddy footprints had been found on the wooden steps, but the trail ended through the woods and back at the parking lot.

"I'm taking you home." Brant touched her forehead tenderly. "The police can talk to you more this afternoon." He gathered the blanket more tightly around her shoulders. "I'll tell them we're leaving."

A single tear slid down Darby's cheek. Brant's finger caught it as he hugged her and pressed his lips against her forehead.

"You're safe now," he said.

Her gaze lifted over Brant's shoulder toward a hunched old man watching the scene. It was the elderly man with the rake. As he turned away and took painful steps back toward his home, Darby saw a generation limping away with the stories and memories departing with them. Grandma Celia had told her much, but left out even more. It would all be lost soon. The pages closed. The book shelved. Darby wanted to keep it alive as much as she could. To tell the story as she knew it, and keep the words of life alive.

Brant kissed her forehead again before crossing the street to a group of officers. Darby's eyes closed in utter exhaustion, though a peace grew in her soul. God wasn't ready for her to leave quite yet. And she was ready to truly live for him.

A vehicle passed, and the police angrily motioned it to continue. She glanced up. The gray sedan moved by, then stopped. Darby stood up. A man emerged from the crowd of curious onlookers and walked to the car. Before opening the passenger door, he stared directly at Darby. He looked familiar somehow. As he ducked inside the car, she noticed mud caked on his shoes. Darby's own feet felt frozen in place. She knew the car was the same one that had taken her to Bruno Weiler. Had the man who took Tatianna's life now saved hers?

Brant walked toward her and stopped when he saw her expression. The tinted glass made it impossible to see in, but as the car started past, the backseat window rolled down.

"Is everything okay, Darby?"

A puff of smoke streamed from the window, and then Darby saw Bruno Weiler.

"What is he doing in Hallstatt?" Brant asked.

"You know who he is?"

"Of course. He's Minister Johansen—one of the most powerful men in Austria."

Darby glanced up at Brant, then back to the car.

Bruno tipped his hat at them, and the gray sedan pulled away.

Darby sat wedged between Aunt Helen and Uncle Marc as the New York cabbie drove through traffic.

"Slow down," Aunt Helen squawked. "You'll kill us all."

Darby smiled as they pulled to the curb. She'd become quite accustomed to crazy taxi drivers. Her mother hesitated in the front seat before getting out. The noise of the city surrounded them as the doors opened. Another cab halted behind them, and the door burst open.

"Auntie Darby," her niece called and hurried toward them. "Kallie's Baby Alive wet Daddy's leg." She covered her mouth as she laughed.

Darby saw her sister's family fuss inside the cab as Kallie slowly got out, and Maureen looked for baby wipes. Darby then noticed her mother. She stood on the sidewalk, oblivious to the cars zipping past or the flashing lights and signs of downtown New York. Waiting like a frightened child, her eyes searched the crowd. Darby walked close with camera bag and tripod in one arm and put the other arm around her mother.

"What if he doesn't show up?" Carole asked.

"He will."

"I've done this before. I've waited here—many times. Right in this noisy place, I've searched the crowd. He never came on the promised date."

"He didn't know. He knows now."

Darby looked at the elongated triangle of Times Square. It was nothing like the quaint European plazas. It bustled with traffic zooming around what she'd have thought to be a large road divider. Tourism had come to Times Square with shops, Disney stores, Good Morning America, and billboard advertisements flashing from tall buildings. It smelled like city streets and some other smell coming from the hot dog vendors—not the scent of a juicy dog, but the stringent smell of a warming element inside the vendor machine. That smell with exhaust fumes was Times Square. Not the place for a romantic meeting as Celia and Gunther had imagined, but Gunther had told his young bride to meet him at the only place in America he had heard of in 1939, except for Ellis Island. So this had been the designated place. Over sixty years later, the reunion would finally take place—on the April 3 wedding anniversary of Gunther and Celia.

Darby had spoken with Brant the night before while he was still in London waiting for his delayed plane to take off. They'd take the red-eye and be here as scheduled. Darby prayed it would be true, especially as she looked again at her mother's face.

Kallie and Kellie ran to Darby and hung on her jacket. "Auntie Darby, Kellie said I'll have to leave Baby Alive at home now because of what happened on Dad's leg."

"Girls, come here and stay close," Maureen called. They scurried to their mother, who bent down and whispered in their ears. John was still wiping at his leg.

"Let's make a deal," Darby said to her mother. "You look at

that giant TV screen, and I'll search the crowd. I told them to meet near the ticket booth. They'll come. But I'll tell you when I see them, and then you can look."

"That might be best. My heart jumps at every young man I see, thinking it could be your Brant."

Maureen now walked up to Darby. "John is taking the twins to get a hot dog, and Aunt Helen and Uncle Marc are joining them. So where are they?" She bit her fingernail.

"They'll be here," Darby said. She gave her sister's hand a reassuring squeeze, though her own anxiety began to rise. What if, what if, what if. Then, across the square, she saw them. In flashes through the crowds, she saw Brant's dark hair. He was pushing Gunther in a wheelchair through the people.

"Mom," Darby said. Gunther searched the crowd, and suddenly their eyes locked. He put up his hand and Brant stopped. Then Gunther struggled to rise from the chair.

Carole gasped, her hands over her mouth. Instant tears streamed down her cheek as she took a few steps forward. Darby and Maureen waited behind.

They moved toward each other as if in slow motion, then stopped a foot away. Darby felt wetness on her own cheeks as Gunther reached out and gathered Carole into his arms. At last, father and daughter were meeting for the first time.

Maureen wiped away tears too. "This is their moment. I'll go find John and the girls and be back in a little while."

"Are you sure?" Darby asked, seeing the emotional struggle in her sister's face.

Maureen nodded and backed away.

Brant helped Gunther onto a park bench, then headed toward Darby.

"You made it," she said softly. In the busyness of plans and her return to America, they'd found little time to be alone in weeks. Now they were closing one chapter of their lives. What would the next one bring?

"We couldn't miss this day." Brant extracted an envelope from his coat. "I brought a letter from the museum in Hallstatt. They wanted to thank your family for donating the coins. I also have the final papers on the memorial for Tatianna at Mauthausen."

"All in German, I suppose?"

"Of course. You know, it's time you start learning your own German."

"I was waiting to see where I lived before I enrolled in classes."

"Professor Voss and Katrine already found a course in Salzburg for you. They are anxious for your return."

Darby smiled. "It's something we'll have to discuss."

"Among other things." Brant reached his fingers around hers.

"So what do you think happened to Empress Sissi's brooch?" Darby asked.

"You're very good at changing the subject," Brant said, shaking his head. "If Gunther never had the brooch, it could be anywhere. Perhaps some Swiss bank or vault in Argentina. Guess that's for another day. Right now, there's only one mystery I'm concerned about."

"And what is that?"

Brant turned her toward him and held both hands. "What happens tomorrow, and the day after that."

Darby's eyes swiveled toward her mother and Gunther. They were in a world alone, unknowing of what occurred around them. They talked with heads close and tears flowing. Darby wiped her own cheek again. Then, through the noise and bustle, Darby sensed a presence like a lost memory recalled.

She couldn't see her face, but instantly knew—Tatianna. The girl waited in a jail cell—one of the ones Darby had seen in Mauthausen. She stared at the morning light growing through her cell window. Then, Tatianna stood as the door opened, and took the long walk between guards across cobble- stone roads, past barracks and fearful eyes. They led her to a line of others. Her eyes saw a man beside her, a man with nail holes through his bare feet. She looked upward and saw a bird conquer the sky with outstretched wings.

Darby turned back to Brant and smiled. "We may even have the day after that."

The trail was steep and the air crisp as I hiked toward the empty wooden bench above Hallstatt, Austria. I'd been there only five months earlier, wondering if I'd ever return. After all, it had taken eighteen years of European dreams to get me there the first time.

I can still see the map on the floor as my cousin and I plotted our someday Europe trip. I was ten; she was fourteen. Later, in French class, my friends and I researched foreign exchange programs that would make our dreams come true. After I got married, I bought a *Europe on $50 a Day*, certain we'd go in a year or two. But it took longer than my plans. And through the waiting I discovered that dreams are never truly fulfilled on your own.

My husband and I at last touched European soil when I was researching *Winter Passing*, my first novel. We flew to Amsterdam, then headed to Austria via train. Every day passed in a flurry of wonder. We walked Vienna streets and palaces at midnight and wore mining clothes during a salt mine tour. Suddenly we were home again, and I wondered if I'd conjured the story during a long sleep.

Austria haunted me as I worked on *Winter Passing*. Just as Darby had to return, I felt I must also. But was that my dream, or God's plan? And then, amazingly, I was in Austria again.

This time three friends from high school—Katie, Jenna, and Shelley—stopped their lives to explore Austria with me. They waited below in a café as I climbed the steps above Hallstatt and found that bench as evening shadows descended. It was Easter Sunday. I'd recalled this view so often in the past months that it felt as familiar as an old friend. I took it in, breathed the memory, and realized clearly how God was working in the smallest details of my life.

On this trip, I glimpsed God's view again . . . in an elderly man raking leaves in Hallstatt, an elderly couple watering flowers in the cemetery, and a woman telling of her Nazi grandfather who saved his best friend's Jewish wife from almost-certain death, going to prison himself instead. I stood with three friends in Salzburg as midnight bells boomed the glory of God. My feet walked Mauthausen and Dachau—where people like me had seen the ashes of their dreams destroyed, along with their lives. I wondered how to live with their stories and sorrow breathing within me as I left those towers behind.

I'm home again, in Northern California. But in my mind's eye, I often look out my window and see green hillsides and sharp peaks. I see cobblestone pathways and hear church bells ring. While I know where my home is, and I get glimpses of trails ahead, I also have an empty wooden bench thousands of miles away that holds special words just for me. For that place in Hallstatt was more than a bench along a trail. It's a place I recall now as I continue my upward climb. I look back and remember what I engraved in memory: *Cindy, you glimpsed God's face today. Don't forget this when you leave it behind.*

And as for you, my stranger-friends who read this book, I wonder who you are. I wonder about your times of winter and your long-held dreams. I prayed for you that day on my bench. My prayer then, and now, is that God will give you a view you've never seen—whether it's from your back porch, a rock by the sea, or perhaps even in Hallstatt, Austria.

Seasons of change, busyness, joy, and fear come as surely as the autumn leaves next October. But we can continue upward when our breath has been stolen by the steepness of the climb. We discover God's strength through a winter and find ourselves more closely linked to him as springtime comes. And along the way God fulfills dreams—some we didn't even know to consider. And as we journey together with him, we find *he* is the true dream, holding the smaller ones in his hand. That's what our benchmarks truly tell us.

I hope we carry our benchmark words together. And we return there often.

Acknowledgments

All I am, have, or do is because of God—Alpha and Omega.

I must thank my uncles (John, Chris, and Andy) for stories, laughter, and dreams.

Grandma and Ron—years of love, postcards that stay with me. Michelle Ower, Alanna Ramsey, Laurie Williams, Kim Shaw, also Sherie Silva, Marian Morgan Hunt, and Christi Harrington for friendships that last. Jon Walker and Tracey Bumpus, writing encouragement and much more. To my Martinusen extended family I send appreciation and love (Mom Martinusen and all), and also to Shawn Harman.

Specifically in helping *Winter Passing* come to life:

David—you give so much and ask so little. Everything (sharing dreams, our babies, first trip to Europe, morning coffee, and every day) has been with you.

Cody, Maddie, and Weston—my gifts from heaven, each so unique, each such joy.

Dad and Mom—for giving more than I'll ever know. I wish I could write what you both mean to me.

Jen—from pine nuts and forts through many seasons together— both blood and heart sisters.

Tricia Goyer—recall our first Mount Hermon Writer's Conference and laugh out loud. Thank you for every call across these one thousand miles, and for honesty in my writing (even when I didn't like it).

Katie Martinusen (from third grade to infinity and beyond), Shelley Chittim, and Jenna Shelby—friendships that go the miles—be it jogging in the rain, all-night chats, or an adventure to Austria!

My One Heart sisters—oh, for prayers, praises, and encouragement when all courage was gone.

Janet Kobobel Grant—your wisdom, love, and friendship—and you're an amazing agent too.

Curtis Lundgren and Ramona Cramer Tucker—editors and friends.

Tyndale staff—you make me feel at home, and what a great group you are (Anne, Ken, Travis, Sue, Lorie, Becky, Ron, Justin with your great cover, and all the rest).

Anne de Graaf—for a good-bye in Hoek van Holland that said so much.

Robin Jones Gunn—you've mentored by example on friendship, motherhood, writing, and more.

Wendy Lee Nentwig—our friendship across such distances.

Marlo Schalesky—honesty and lessons we've learned together.

Joe Evich—writing socks, conference gifts, and dear friendship over the years.

The Wagnleitners' (Reinhold, Elisabeth, and Anna)—Salzburg and Mondsee tours, Maroni, Reinhold's patience despite my many questions, and especially for open Austrian arms. I know we'll meet again.

Chittims (Shawn, Shelley, Mike, and Deb) and Joe Gazzigli for weekends at the Mount Shasta house—I'd still be typing without that time on the mountain.

Thanks to Rudi Haunschmied and Martha Gammer of the Mauthausen/Gusen Web site in Austria.

Cathy Snider—that electric coffee-cup warmer meant so much, really. You kept my eyes open on many late nights and tired afternoons.

AUHS District Office—I missed you all when the book was done. Thanks for letting me drop into your world for a while.

Shelly Gates—for old days of maps and stories that started this all.

To my friends at church, Bible study, and that wonderful writer's group (Maxine Cambra and all) who have encouraged and supported with prayers. I could write another book to thank the many people who have touched and influenced my life. I hope each of you already know how important you are to me. This small work could not have been done without each one of you. I can only say I gave my best for all you've given.

Suggestions for Further Reading

Non-fiction:

Coca-Colonization and the Cold War: The Cultural Mission of the United States in Austria After the Second World War by Reinhold Wagnleitner

The Night Trilogy: Night Dawn the Accident; All Rivers Run to the Sea: Memoirs by Elie Wiesel

The Celts: The People Who Came Out of the Darkness by Gerhard Herm

Schindler's Legacy: True Stories of the List Survivors by Elinor J. Brecher

The Holocaust: A History of the Jews of Europe During the Second World War by Martin Gilbert

Why History Matters: Life and Thought by Gerda Lerner

Fiction:

The Zion Chronicles series; the Zion Covenant series; *Twilight of Courage;* all by Brock and Bodie Thoene

Web sites:

Many Web sites have information about the Holocaust, Austria, and World War II. These sites also provide archives, testimonies, and other links. Here are a few from my research:

Austrian Press and Information, Washington, D.C. — *http://www.austria.org*

Mauthausen/Gusen Information Pages— *http://linz.orf.at/orf/gusen*

Mauthausen Memorial (English version)—
http://www.mauthausen-memorial.gv.at/engl/index.html
Holocaust/Shoah Research Resources—
http://www.igc.org/ddickerson/holocaust.html
United States Holocaust Museum—
http://www.ushmm.org
Austria Tourism—*http://austria-tourism.at/*
City of Salzburg (English version)—
http://www.salzburg.com/engl/

Cindy McCormick Martinusen's life usually revolves around her hometown in Northern California. It includes her husband of eleven years and three amazing children: "Mom, how fast does the fastest rocket travel?" "Mom, watch me dance." "Mommy, you be dinosaur and try eat me." Though she doesn't claim monetary wealth, she says she's rich with great friends and a close-knit family. Cindy enjoys movie and bookstore nights, dates with her husband, her writer's group, Bible studies, playing city league softball, trying to fly fish, snow skiing, and staying up late in front of the fire with a good novel or historical book for research. While all of these compose everyday life for Cindy, she's seeking what Paul truly meant in Philippians when he wrote, "To live is Christ."

Winter Passing is her first novel.

Cindy welcomes letters written to her in care of Tyndale House Author Relations, P.O. Box 80, Wheaton, IL 60189-0080.